BIRDS IN THE NEST

by

Wendy Hart

Contents

Copyright

PO Box 619
NEW FARM QLD 4005

Whart690@gmail.com

IBSN 978-1-7635489-2-3

About this book

Birds in the Nest is based on the life of the author's paternal grandmother. The author documented and verified the raw facts. Except where there is repetition, the names of the protagonist (Minnie) and her family are unchanged. The dates of significant events and names of towns and places are correct. I have knitted the tale together with a lot of fiction. Outside Minnie's family, characters are fictitious.

We all knew that Minnie had survived a tough childhood. I was able to draw on the limited tales Minnie shared with others, as well as family stories and photographs. However, from the research for this book, I learned the word 'tough' does not adequately describe the horrendous early life of Minnie and her sisters. Because of the dogged determination of her stepmother, Minnie and her five sisters found their way to Australian shores. Four of the girls survived. These pages record the untimely death of Adeline. Alice died in Brisbane in 1921 at seventeen. Today, literally hundreds of Australians can identify as descendants of the four surviving little girls who arrived as assisted migrants in 1910.

The story is not a record of history, but I have endeavoured to capture the times. Most importantly, hopefully, I have captured Minnie's indomitable spirit.

Dedication

In loving memory of:
Denis Poulsen
My cousin, friend and childhood hero.

Chapter 1

A flicker of light sent shadows dancing up the wall when Minnie lit the kitchen lamp. The thirty-one-year-old Ulster woman had left her bed and sleeping husband, Albert, at three a.m. Feet whispering over the cold linoleum, she crept through the darkness towards the kitchen. A quietness, punctuated only by the rhythmic breathing of her slumbering children and the whistling wind, blanketed the house.

The sounds of the outside grew louder. A vicious wind slammed against the external weatherboards and invaded the gaps in the roof iron sheets. Minnie blew on her palms and jiggled her knees to keep warm. After donning her gingham apron, she wandered over the bare floorboards and opened the woodstove door. She lit scraps of newspaper and flung them among the embers from the previous night. The paper curled at the edges before giving life to the embers.

Soon, the stove pumped warmth and stinking steam into the room. Then, the patter of a child's feet shattered the stillness. Minnie's second-born child and eldest daughter, eleven-year-old Hazel, entered, her teeth chattering. Hazel helped her mother in the kitchen each morning as part of the regular schedule on the family farm, Oaklands, thirty-five miles north of Brisbane. Hazel began this role when she was just six years old. Minnie shot the child an endearing smile and rubbed her hands through the girl's flowing hair, almost an identical colour to hers. 'My dear Hazel, Mummy can always count on you.'

Once Hazel had tied the waist string of her candy-striped apron, mother and daughter cooked breakfast. The rest of the household dragged their feet as they entered the room. Half asleep and squinting, the family munched fried eggs in silence. Before the sun began climbing up the sky, Albert and five children scurried to herd and milk the cows.

When the rest of the family had left, Minnie and Hazel moved on to bread-making, but Minnie couldn't concentrate. She rushed to the window, leaving Hazel in a puff of yeast and flour.

Minnie drew herself to her full five-foot-nothing and looked at her reflection in the frosted window. Waist-length almond hair braided and coiled into twin buns framed a thin, unblemished face the colour of buttermilk. She'd favoured that hairstyle for almost twenty years, protecting her hair from life's elements and hazards.

Rummaging in the pocket of her washed-out apron, she plucked out a lace-bordered white handkerchief and used it to wipe a clear patch on the window. However, when she squashed her nose against the cleared glass, she saw only blackness and a veil of thick fog—no paddock, trees, fences, or cows. Minnie's heart sank when she realised she couldn't see her three youngest children, Eunice, Bert, and Peggy, who performed their daily task of herding the cattle. She knew her treasured little ones would be freezing and wrestling the bitter gale.

She sensed a soft touch on her shoulder, and when she turned, she glimpsed Hazel leaning on the table. 'Mum, what's wrong?'

Minnie sought her daughter's saucer-shaped, sapphire blue eyes. 'I want to know Eunice, Bert, and Peggy are safe.'

'They'll be fine. They're used to the job.'

'But this wind may topple them. They're like cardboard in this fierce blow.'

When the sun climbed higher, casting slithers of light over the paddock, she spotted the outline of a girl under a strawberry-blonde mane. It was her fourth surviving child, eight-year-old Eunice. She moved behind the herd, followed by her younger siblings, Bert and Peggy. Heading towards the dairy, a weathered building surrounded by a fenced holding yard, the barefooted threesome wore several layers of clothing, including heavy coats and beanies.

Minnie extended her arms to Hazel. When she came to her, she drew the girl close, then released and clasped her hands. 'Oh, my darling, it is a relief to see my tiny ones giggle as they run and skip.'

'Mum, why do you worry so much, always fearing the worst?' Hazel arched one eyebrow and stared inquiringly.

Her daughter's reaction sent a pain spearing through Minnie's heart. 'I don't have it in me to face another loss.'

Because she regretted her statement to Hazel, she gestured with her chin at the hissing stove to distract her daughter. Hazel hurried over to it. 'I'll put the bread dough in the oven and dress for school before the others rush in, pushing and squabbling about who gets the warmest spot.

Minnie had avoided an uncomfortable probing and gave out a breathy sigh. She had told the children the barest sketch of her life's rocky journey, trying to push it into the archives of her head.

Her birthplace was on the opposite side of the globe. Its pristine beauty concealed disease, death, and social upheaval. She had lived a miserable childhood until arriving in Australia as a teenager. Summoning up, the past served no purpose other than to haunt her. However, sometimes, snippets came flooding back uninvited. *She knew she would never purge herself of the memories but saw no point inflicting them on others.*

Then she returned to her window spot, where she feasted on the sight of brilliant colours ranging from flaming red to soft pink spilling from the rising sun. The children neared the dairy, but their movements now took on an athletic form. They jumped and dodged every which way. Her skin tingled when she registered the reason for the changed movements. As they herded the cattle, they played their customary winter game, leapfrogging the icy grass and landing on the smooth patches warmed overnight by sleeping cows.

Little birds, don't forget the aim—herding those red-coated cows and delivering them to the dairy. Be sure you find the lot because we cannot afford any losses, and your father will go berserk.

A mild-mannered man, some things, including the occasional missing cow, plunged Albert into a fury. His voice grew as loud as a bullhorn, his face turned crimson, and his nostrils flared.

Minnie counted as each animal filed through the gate kept open by the feet of her eldest son, twelve-year-old Harold. Her second daughter and third surviving child, nine-year-old

Billie, balanced on the side of the fence. As she sucked in a lung full of air, she said below her breath, 'They have rounded up the lot.'

Chapter 2

Moneyglass, County Antrim, Ulster, Ireland—April 1897

'Not much further, darlings.'

Dressed in a sage flouncy skirt with a yellow fleecy shawl draped over her shoulders, Mary Craig, a woman of Scottish heritage, climbed a gradual incline in the glorious Antrim countryside. Her daughters, four-year-old Jeannie and two-year-old Lizzie, scampered each side, gripping the gathers in her clothes. Like miniature versions of their mother, both girls had sparking blue eyes, fair skin, thick almond hair, and prominent noses. She held a bundle wrapped in a knitted woollen rug.

Mary raised her head towards the azure sky dusted by a few wafer-thin clouds. 'Darlings, please keep moving. We're going to a special spot, Mammy's favourite.' Mary loved country rambles, a lifelong habit. She wanted to introduce her daughters to the majestic beauty of their lush County Antrim home.

'But Mammy, my legs wobble like jelly,' cried Jeannie. She scrunched her nose, and tears welled in her eyes. 'And

Mammy, we should check our baby,' she said.

Mary inhaled deeply and contemplated Jeannie's question. Although they had walked for twenty minutes, they'd made slow progress. Mary wheezed with each step.

She crouched, caught her breath, and peeled the shawl back to satisfy Jeannie, revealing a peaceful newborn. The baby, her namesake but called Minnie, breathed the measured breaths of sleep.

After a brief hike, they reached the top. They feasted on the view of the still waters of Lough Neagh—a landscape of cultivated pastures, rambling meadows and dense foliage. Jeannie and Lizzie, cheeks rosy with exhaustion, jumped up and down and shrieked. Her daughters' reaction warmed Mary. 'See the colourful flowers? They're like a rainbow. Why don't we pick some?'

With Minnie held to her chest, Mary trailed Jeannie and Lizzie through the crisp air, carrying the sweet fragrance of spring blooms. Lizzie wobbled, tripping over her feet, as she scampered through the sea of wildflowers.

Mary turned the other way, gripping Minnie so close she felt the infant's heartbeat. Her throat narrowed as if something had lodged there and prevented her breathing. She fished out the white linen handkerchief tucked into her sleeve, then coughed until she expelled a glob of phlegm. Her recent annoying cough must be a throat tickle relating to her pregnancy and Minnie's birth. Considering it unworthy of further thought, she returned to admiring the splashes of vibrant colour.

This paradise, the haunt of local teenagers, had played a significant part in Mary's life. She'd spent many hours there with chums. They'd chatted about parents, teachers, county festivals, and Catholics. Life in these parts had changed. Because they believed the future lay in industry, friends drifted to the Belfast factories and fabric mills.

She tore herself away from her tangled musings and wandered over to where her girls plucked bluebells and chased butterflies. She extended her arm and gestured to a lower point. 'Darlings—Clonkeen, where our farm is.'

Jeannie and Lizzie's eyes sparkled as they followed their mother's finger to a group of thatched roofs scattered amid a chocolate brown and emerald backdrop. Lizzie clapped as she glued her vision to the smoke pouring from Clonkeen's chimneys. 'Up, up, up. Smoke goes whoosh and up to the shiny sun.'

After about an hour of soaking up the delights, Mary spoke. 'We must hurry home.'

* * *

With Jeannie and Lizzie clambering at each side, Mary hurried towards their farm, taking a more direct route when they reached the outskirts of the village of Moneyglass.

A stench wafted from a potted laneway breaking from the path near the journey's end. The girls released their grip on their mother's skirt and clamped their nostrils between their fingers. 'What's that rotten stink, Mammy?' asked Jeannie.

Mary knew rotting garbage and excrement, mixed with murky, stagnant water, caused the stench but could not think of the right words to explain it to innocent children. When the girls peered at her expectantly, she drew a breath to reply but only exhaled. 'It's a Catholic settlement. They're poor and live in dirty, smelly mud huts.'

Jeannie glanced up at her mother. 'Why?'

'The tricky reasons go back hundreds of years, darling. Ask Da; he knows all about it.'

They strolled through the aromatic smells of maturing crops towards their cottage, a four-room, low-set, whitewashed stone building hidden behind rows of swaying stalks. Generations of Mary's husband's family had farmed this land. An army of workers tended lines of plants. The men wore heavy linen work shirts above thick trousers, and the women ground-hugging skirts and multi-coloured shawls with fraying fringes draped around their shoulders.

When they reached home, Mary opened the ancient wooden door by kicking it with the toe of her shoe. A cocktail of odours—peat, stale tobacco, and boiled cabbage—gushed out.

Jeannie and Lizzie thundered to a play area nestled outside the back entrance—a patch of thick grass in the shade of the rear external wall. Mary settled Minnie into her cot before rushing to the hearth. Utensils hung on hooks above, and a pot oven, a griddle, and a three-legged pot straddled the hearth base. She stirred the ashes and added kindling and peat to the fire before setting a water container on a hook above the flame.

When the water bubbled, Mary flopped into a hearthside chair and sipped a mug of steaming tea. She panted, and a tightness stretched across her chest. Mary mused how a delightful stroll could cause such listlessness.

She tore herself from the luxury of the seat and strolled to the door overlooking the play area. 'Girls, play inside and keep me company while I cook supper.'

She set pots above the hearth and placed a side of mutton in the pot oven. Soon, the aroma of the meat wafted through the cottage, almost stifling the odour of peat. After about half an hour, the daylight filtering through the window began fading, and she plonked cabbage, turnips, and potatoes in the bubbling water.

Her ears pricked at the clonk of heavy boots stirring up gravel as they marched to the entrance. The door flung open, and Mary's husband, George, barrelled in. Moist from labouring in the constant drizzle, he wore suspender-supported thick grey trousers and a weathered cap. 'Butterfly, I'm home.' He always called her that. As Mary crouched over the flame, she scanned his tall, thin, muscular form. She couldn't help but think again about his striking appearance - sandy hair and blue eyes that reflected his thoughts and his forever-engaging smile.

Lizzie and Jeannie shrieked with delight as their father scooped them up in his powerful arms. George played with the lasses, his smile lighting up his entire face. He lowered his daughters to the ground, but they were unsatisfied. Giggling and chanting, they jumped on him and clung to his trouser legs as if trying to scale his body.

As he pretended difficulty, George freed himself from the girls' grip, scoured the mud from his boots, and lobbed them and his cap on the pile of protective clothing in the entry. When he'd finished, he grasped Jeannie under the armpits and tossed her. Next came Lizzie's turn, and he tickled her until she collapsed to the floor, writhing uncontrollably.

'I'm worn out,' said George as he stepped towards the fire-place. He sank into the worn tartan armchair, acknowledged by the family as his exclusive domain, where he lit his pipe and sent spirals of tobacco smoke to the rafters.

Mary spooned servings of mutton onto metal plates. 'The

food is ready.'

George ran his tongue around his lips. 'Smells delicious. I've worked all day without a break and am famished.'

They finished the evening meal after eight p.m., and Jeannie and Lizzie scampered to bed, leaving George and Mary chatting before the fire. Mary hacked repeatedly and felt a sting in her throat. Although she willed it to stop, the coughing went on and on. George rested his calloused hand on his wife's soft palm. 'Are you well? That cough sounds throaty.'

'Oh, it's nothing, not even a cold. It'll pass.'

The colour drained from George's features as he tugged at his earlobe.

'I took advantage of the lovely sunny weather to take the girls on an outing,' said Mary. 'We climbed the road overlooking Lough Neagh. It brought back memories of our frolics there as teenagers. So many of our school friends live in Belfast now.'

'I ran into Michael Boyd a few days ago. He and his wife shifted to Belfast and had four wee ones after the move. Michael ended up working long hours in a shipyard. From his description of their home, it sounds like a filthy, overcrowded slum,' said George.

Mary inclined her head. 'I appreciate what attracts them to the city, but I would rather we raised our children here.'

George's face crumpled, and he frowned in disgust. 'As always, you are too kind. Promises of high wages lure these stupid people. When they arrive, the hot and filthy factories shock them, and their employers expect them to work in those conditions. They find out that the city only offers them rat-infested, crumbling slums to live in.'

Mary choked back a knot she sensed constricting her throat.

'It's not our concern.' George, face red and angry, stared into Mary's eyes. 'You're talking rubbish. It does concern us. The thinned rural workforce increases the workload on farming families.'

Mary wanted to scream. Her husband's views were far from the mainstream. He made them known to anyone prepared to listen, especially his favourite—the evils of the local divisions between Catholics and Protestants. She spoke more sharply than she'd intended. 'I know you've got unbending opinions on every topic imaginable, but there's no need to try to force them down my throat.'

The sound of a baby's cry filled the room. Mary vaulted from her chair and hurried towards the girls' bedroom. When she returned, she found a shamefaced George. He didn't apologise, but Mary saw sorrow swimming in his eyes. She pretended the argument had never occurred. 'Minnie refused the feed and is now sound asleep. Our voices must've disturbed her.'

'Before I collapse in bed, let's check our lasses,' said a yawning George. Lantern in one hand, he extended his other arm to his Butterfly and guided her to their daughters' bedroom. On entering, they set the lantern on the table. Arms entwined, they tiptoed to the double bed and watched Jeannie and Lizzie sleep, eyelids fluttering in dreams.

The couple took a few paces and watched Minnie slumber in her crib. 'A sweet, peaceful baby,' said Mary. 'I'll rouse her for that feed if she doesn't wake.'

George squeezed his wife's hand. 'All bonnie and just the start of our family.'

'The next will be a wee lad,' said Mary.

* * *

Despite a menacing cough that worsened daily, Mary soldiered through the rest of 1897 and 1898 with household tasks, caring for the family, and helping in the fields during busy times. She sensed her lungs gurgling and took shallow breaths because of the pain of drawing breath. Forever tired, even while rising, Mary had shed pounds.

It occasionally crossed her mind that she may be suffering from consumption. Still, she chased the thought away, knowing the condition usually signalled death. She hoped the enforced break before Christmas 1898, when the icy weather kept them inside, might enable her to recover strength.

As a racing blizzard whistled and raindrops lashed the windowpanes, Mary and her family, dressed in multiple layers of woolly clothing, gathered around the mountainous fire. Inhaling the overpowering smell of peat, they peered at the icicles that clung to the eaves of outbuildings, bare tree branches, and stone walls. Between cries of 'I'm bored' and 'my toes freeze', Mary grimaced as her daughters, pigtails bouncing, chased each other, whinged, and screamed. She shook her head and then recited the homily, 'Little birds in the nest must agree.' As usual, it did its magic, and the deafening din stopped.

Peace restored, Mary lounged in a hearth-side armchair, gazing into the fire and cradling a mug of warm tea. A stream of breath, ripe with tobacco, made her break out in goosebumps. George's familiar stubbly chin rubbed over her cheek. 'Is something the matter?' He stroked her hand. 'You seem out of spirits.'

'I'm not sure what ails me. I am forever drained and listless.'

She glanced up at a beaming George, who arched his eyebrows and offered an optimistic wink. 'Perhaps another baby and maybe a boy?'

'Perhaps.' Hope burned within, but her heart whispered that a baby wasn't coming. What then caused the fatigue?

She burst out in a coughing fit, and although she willed it to stop, the hacking continued. George rose to a rigid upright position as he sniffled and wiped at his nose. She wondered if his actions reflected worry, compassion, concern, or all three compounded.

Chapter 3

Clonkeen, County Antrim, Ulster,
Ireland—December 1898

By February 1898, George's thoughts as he spread fertiliser during the day and slumped before the hearth at night never left his wife's health. Her coughing worsened. She looked gaunt, and her bones protruded from her body.

George hunched in his tartan throne as he read an article about consumption in the local newspaper, *The Ballymena Observer*. He twitched. Consumption had ravaged the area forever. Held in fear, locals referred to the condition by the horrible names *graveyard cough*, *white plague*, and *robber of youth*. The symptoms described in the article were like Mary's.

The written words sent a stabbing sensation through his chest and forced him to face the cruel reality of his dilemma. He may lose his Butterfly, the love of his life. With his full-time job managing a farm, he now faced the responsibility of nursing a sick wife, running a house, and caring for three toddlers. He couldn't climb this mountain alone.

He bolted upright. Only one brave, headstrong person could offer advice and comfort. He grabbed his coat and hat and set off into the chilly, pitch-blackness with *The Ballymena Observer* wedged under his arm.

Guided by the moonlight, he staggered through the frigid air across the meadow to the neighbouring farmhouse, where his sister Sarah lived with her daughters, Frances and Katherine. A pioneer of women's rights, Sarah operated the farm herself. The short, slightly built woman put in a twelve-hour day, doing tasks usually reserved for male farmhands.

He rapped, and Sarah opened the door a sliver, revealing hair of a similar colour to his, tied back in a loose ponytail. The fire's warmth poured out. 'Whatever are you doing out on this dark, wild night?' Sarah said in a stunned voice. George went to speak, but her work-roughened hands whisked him towards the fire before he could say anything. 'You'll catch your death of cold. Come in and let the fire warm your bones.'

Sarah's voice drifted through the sparks as he warmed over the raging fire. 'George, please tell me what your problem is. I can see the torment in your eyes.'

He sensed his skin tighten, and no words came out of his mouth when he opened it.

'Why *The Ballymena Observer*?' Sarah asked as she scrunched her nose and stared at her brother penetratingly.

'Please stop asking your usual never-ending questions, Sarah. I come to discuss a problem, but first, I must take a deep breath,' said George in a distressed tone.

She shot a weak smile that begged for forgiveness. 'Sorry, I didn't mean to rush you. Would a cup of tea calm your nerves?'

'No, but I would love some water.'

When Sarah brought the water, he spluttered on the first sip. His heart hammered. 'The paper contains a depressing article about consumption. Plenty of research, but no cure.'

His intestines twisted, and he stopped talking and sucked in some fulsome gasps of peat-tinged air. He looked straight at Sarah. 'I fear the greedy *graveyard cough* has my Butterfly in its sights.'

Sarah's work-worn face softened. 'I've noticed she's lost weight and coughs and wheezes,' said Sarah. 'But don't jump to conclusions.' A glimmer of hope rippled over her brow. 'We need a doctor's opinion because it could be something else.'

Pacing the earthen floor, George knotted his fingers. 'I am sure it's the *graveyard cough*, an illness we've seen far too many times. I lie beside her and feel the sizzling heat radiating from her.'

Sarah smiled reassuringly and squeezed George's hand. 'You must be ready for whatever lies ahead. And you must talk to Mary. You can count on support from Frances, Katherine, and me. Mary will need loads of rest.'

Gratitude flooded him. He flung his arms around his sister and gripped her for what seemed to him to be forever. 'I've always been able to rely on you for help.'

* * *

The next evening, as the lamp's glow cast shadows on the wall, George and Mary chatted. 'I'm concerned about your health, Butterfly,' George said as panic attacked his insides. 'You cough all day and wrestle a raging fever at night.' He dragged on his pipe, filling the room with a tobacco aroma. 'Would you consider seeing the Toome doctor?'

Mary responded loud and fast, 'I won't consult a doctor. It's a chest ailment, treatable by herbal remedies.'

As icy dread rushed through his veins, George scoured

every region of his brain, searching for the kindest approach. 'Butterfly, have you considered this may be consumption?'

Terror coloured her voice. 'No, no, no! My precious children need me.' She persisted in protesting about visiting a doctor. 'If it's the *white plague*, we'd waste money as there's no cure.'

'But darling, someone might know something because scientists are busy searching.'

'No new treatment can stop the killer disease.' She sobbed as if tortured. 'The possibility of the *white plague* has consumed my thoughts for months. But dread made me deny it, and I am relieved to share the worry.'

George rushed to Mary, threaded his arms around her, and she buried her head in the crook of his neck. He sensed moisture seep through his shirt. 'We must tell our lassies. They need to know,' said George.

That night, Mary grappled with the sheets as heat poured off her. George lay awake tossing and turning as he pondered the unenviable task of explaining to such young girls that they would grow up motherless. The youngest, Minnie, turned two in a few months.

The next evening, George gathered their daughters at the hearthstone. Before the discussion started when Lizzie asked, 'Why have you got big, black, puffy patches under your eyes and red wiggly lines inside them?'

When Lizzie said those words, George's hands shook, and his stomach churned. So he spat out the awful news less eloquently than he'd planned.

The announcement was met with stunned silence, except for the fire crackling. Then, a chorus of tortured wailing shattered the silence. George imagined his insides fell.

He braced himself. 'Be brave for Mammy's sake, and don't

discuss this with anyone outside the family. Because no cure exists, the condition makes others fearful.'

Mary limped in and struggled to her chair. Jeannie and Lizzie fell into her arms and released a deluge of tears. Minnie toddled over, supported herself on the chair's edge, and raised her arms. George boosted her onto her mother's lap, and she joined the grief-stricken huddle. Mary made soothing statements. 'Darlings, it's all right. I'll fight hard. I aim to live to bake your birthday cakes, enjoy fairs and Orange Day parades with you, and see your marriages.'

Stomach knotted, George stared at this heart-wrenching scene. He no longer tried to hold the pent-up tears but allowed them to fall.

* * *

Spring awoke the world. George led the party, spreading seeds for the year's crop. Jeannie worked close beside him. She peered up at him through eyes reflecting sadness. 'Da, I'm not working fast because I miss Mammy working with us. My tummy twists thinking about how sick she is.'

George's heart thumped against his ribcage. He was concerned for his lasses. Just how, he wasn't sure, but Mary's sickness would profoundly affect their lives.

When the gruelling day's work ended, Jeannie sprinting several paces before him, he traipsed to the cottage. Inside, Mary, draped in clothes hanging off her skinny body, stared out the narrow window. Jeannie clung to her from behind. He stopped and observed this touching mother-and-daughter moment, thinking the child clung to Mary like she would never let her go.

Mary twisted towards Jeannie, a single tear sliding down her gaunt face. 'Darling, you sneaked up on me. I watched the clear blue spring sky and listened to the merry chatter of workers as they flung fans of seeds to the soft breeze. The air flowing through the window carried the scents of ploughed soil and fresh growth at planting time.'

'Did you see foxes and ferrets?' asked Jeannie.

'No, but Mammy's proud; her big girl notices. During winter, the creatures hide and return in spring.'

'I'm strong, and I'll drag a chair outside in the sun where you can see everything.'

'It's a lovely thought, but Mammy's weak.'

Jeannie pouted. 'You promised to fight.'

'You lasses are my world, and I will fight. As Da explained, we must keep my illness secret,' said Mary. 'It's best the neighbours don't see me skinny and coughing.'

George swallowed a lump in his throat as he gazed in awe at what he sensed was a precious moment.

Chapter 4

Days later, Mary lost the strength to rise.

Sensing that her brother felt overwhelmed, Sarah chatted with George at the hearthside and suggested ways of sharing the burden. 'You manage my farm, and I'll nurse Mary and take care of your family. Our families will eat together, and I'll ask for help from Mary's mother, Frances, and Katherine. George pulled Sarah in and gave her a crushing hug. 'Thank you. No words can describe how grateful I am. I felt weighed down by the burden of everything that fell on me—nursing a sick wife, caring for young lasses, cooking, and washing.'

Each day, George sauntered to the fields where, with well-practised hands, he sliced the air with a scythe and led ungainly draft horses. His thoughts, however, were with his Butterfly, whom he knew writhed on a bed of pain, chest gurgling, and brow smothered with beads of sweat.

Waves of anticipation pumped through him as he toiled. After each day's work, he sprinted to the cottage and made a beeline to the bedside. Sometimes, as she fitfully slept, he gently held Mary's once lovely hands, now reduced to bone covered by paper-thin skin. Other times, he swallowed the lump in his throat as she cried out in agony.

He could see a flicker of lingering determination whenever

he gazed into her eyes. When fully awake and alert, she mustered a feeble smile and whispered her request to see the girls.

Overwhelmed by profound gratitude and admiration, George observed in awe as Sarah prepared the room for the girls' visit. He felt a tremor in his hands as she replaced the stained sheets with crisp, clean ones and propped Mary on a mountain of plush pillows.

* * *

As the days of Mary's bed confinement dragged on, her condition deteriorated. The hollows under her eyes deepened, and her lips grew thin and pressed tightly together. She resembled a fragile bird, stripped of its feathers, aged, and worn. Gradually, the fire in her eyes faded.

Early in July 1899, in a raspy, parched voice, she delivered heartbreaking news to George. 'Darling, the end draws near. I fear it's only a matter of days.' George's insides writhed, and his entire body erupted in a glistening layer of sweat. 'I vomit blood incessantly, my chest rumbles with discomfort, and each breath is like torture.'

George wiped away tears using the back of his trembling hand. Mary strained to speak further, 'Please, allow me a few moments to compose myself. Then, bring our lasses to my side. It will be difficult for them, and they deserve to hear it from their Mammy.'

A few minutes later, George reappeared with Jeannie and Lizzie at his sides and Minnie in his arms. He boosted the girls onto the bed, cringed as he flopped, and braced himself for the gloomy scene about to unfold. Mary's lips quivered as she pulled her three babies to her. 'Soon, Mammy will go to sleep forever, darlings. Although Mammy won't be at birthdays, parades, and festivals, she'll watch down on you always.'

The sound of Mary's desperate sobs filled the air, accompanied by the wailing cries of Jeannie and Lizzie, their voices echoing with heartbreaking sadness. Minnie, only two years old, cried too, and a pang of sorrow struck in George's heart, knowing that Minnie would soon forget her gentle Mammy. The older Jeannie and Lizzie would at least have memories to treasure. Eventually, Sarah, Frances, and Katherine carried the sisters to their beds.

As George trundled from the fields on 6 July, an eerie feeling attacked him. He found Mary lying in a bed of excruciating pain, drifting in and out of consciousness. He dragged a chair to the bedside and caressed her hand. Outside, a thick blanket of ominous clouds veiled the moon and stars, casting a shadowy gloom.

Mary struggled to part her lips, attempting to speak despite the agony it would cause. Sensing her determination, George gently kneaded her shoulders, urging her to rest and think of nothing. Finally, Mary rasped out her words, her voice frail and weathered, 'Look after our lasses. It would be best if you considered remarrying. I trust you to choose the right woman to raise the girls into strong women.'

Mary slipped away as the first rays of light broke free from the grey clouds. Although not an unexpected event, the stark reality of it, Mary's lifeless body, sent George staggering backwards. As he unleashed a torrent of tears, he repeatedly muttered, 'My Butterfly was only twenty-seven years old.'

The events of that dismal period seemed blurred. George shared the heartbreaking news and comforted his distraught daughters.

The next day, under the sun's warm glow, they bid farewell to Mary and laid her to rest. Uneasy in his seldom-worn best attire, George leaned on Sarah's shoulder for support as they gathered with loved ones in the graveyard. A gentle breeze carried the fragrant scent of heather, enveloping the sombre atmosphere. Led by the townland's clergyman, those assembled offered prayers for Mary's soul.

* * *

George's heavy heart weighed him down, but his determination to provide for his family pulled him back to the fields three days after Mary's death. The ripe crop, the best for years, promised handsome returns.

Each day, he toiled in the fields from the break of day until the setting sun painted the sky gold. As he laboured amongst the rhythmic swishing of scythes and accompanied by the earthy scent of crushed stalks, his mind constantly wandered to the unbearable loss of his beloved Butterfly. As dusk descended, George tramped to the cottage and collapsed into his armchair, his presence merely a ghost amid his family's bustling activities. He confessed in response to Sarah's prodding, his voice quivering with emotion, 'Throughout the day, a dull ache for Mary throbs in my chest.'

Sarah responded with a gentle smile, her eyes filled with understanding. 'Brother, Mary's absence has created a void in many lives, especially those of the wee lasses. With my unwavering support, you must strive to fill that space.'

Her words paved the way for George to share another haunting worry. Trembling, he spoke of his burning anxiety about the future. 'What will become of us? Minnie is just a baby. I have no skills in cooking, cleaning, or caring for infants. Farming is the only skill I know.'

Sarah's expression turned serious as she reassured him, 'Do not fret. We'll continue to live as we are, with you working both farms. With the assistance of my girls, I'll care for both families. This temporary arrangement will ensure that every stalk of this abundant crop reaches the market. After the harvest, I'll teach you the art of cooking and cleaning.'

George tilted his head and chuckled, a rare moment of lightness amidst the darkness. 'You must be a patient teacher, for your pupil possesses no talent in such matters.'

* * *

For the rest of July, George was exhausted after working outside in the sun and rain all day. As soon as he got home, he went straight to his armchair and spent the evening reclined in it. He couldn't stop thinking about Mary as he stared into the fire, smoked his pipe, and drank countless glasses of whisky.

Despite his daughters doing things to attract him, he ignored them. They tugged on his clothing, and Lizzie even balanced on the armrest of his chair, showing off her skills. When that didn't work, she made loud noises by banging metal cutlery against pots and pans, but nothing stole his attention from his pipe and the whisky bottle.

A whirlpool of gloom consumed George, and he felt he couldn't escape it. His grief overwhelmed him. He knew the loss of their mother must distress his daughters and that they needed him to comfort them. Even though he would never admit it to anyone else, the sight of his daughters reminded him of Mary and plunged him deeper into all-consuming self-pity.

Sarah scolded him. 'You weren't a drinker before, but now you drink buckets full every evening.' He felt the urge to defend himself and protested, saying, 'Give me a break, Sarah. The whisky helps me relax. This harvest is tiring, and I miss Mary.'

* * *

As she cleaned the breakfast dishes at the end of July, Sarah declared, 'Let the lessons begin. The only remaining plants are the barley, and the crop won't ripen until October.'

George pondered, I don't fancy learning women's work, but I must. Sarah can't do everything for us forever. He appreciated her support but didn't want to exploit her kindness. So, he put on a forced smile, pretending to be enthusiastic.

George admired Sarah's dedication to teaching him, patiently explaining every step of washing, cleaning, and cooking. However, he didn't approach the tasks eagerly. His mind often wandered to memories of country walks with a young and joyful Mary.

As George's disinterest persisted, he absentmindedly waved a wooden spoon, causing pork broth to bubble over a steel pot. Sarah frowned and raised her eyebrows in frustration. During a laundry lesson, George became lost in thoughts of the past and accidentally dropped a piece of clothing, sending it floating downstream. Frustrated with the lack of progress, Sarah placed her hands on her hips and said, 'This isn't working. I give up.' She then stomped back towards the cottage.

With the lessons abandoned, things returned to their previous routine. George resumed his old habits after a less strenuous day in the fields. He reclined in the tartan armchair, surrounded by peat, tobacco, and whisky aromas. He ignored everything and everyone around him as he stared into the fire. However, a voice within him urged him to give up his drinking and become more involved in family life.

As Jeannie, accompanied by Lizzie and Minnie, left the room amidst an icy silence and headed towards the bedroom, she turned and spoke to her father. 'We miss Mammy. It's like you're gone too. You don't kiss or cuddle us anymore or even say hello. Don't you love us now that Mammy is in heaven?' The words from his young daughter speared George's chest, leaving him stunned and motionless.

He turned to Sarah, her body pressed against the wooden dresser. She stood there in silence, her arms tightly wrapped around herself as if seeking solace from her embrace. 'Jeannie is right,' she said, her voice filled with a mix of anger and sorrow. The words escaped her lips in a low, almost growling tone, starkly contrasting to her usual soft and melodic speech. 'You need to consider your children,' she continued her words hanging heavy in the air. 'They have lost their mother and are crying out for their father. When you're consumed by self-pity, they go to great lengths to seek your attention.'

'Sarah, you're right,' George replied, his expression grave. The weight of his actions pressed down like a heavy burden on his shoulders. 'I've been using alcohol to drown my grief instead of comforting my girls. 'I promise to try harder. But bringing up girls requires a woman's touch,' George continued, his voice filled with uncertainty. 'I'm unsure how to contribute.'

Sarah's gaze softened, her eyes reflecting compassion. 'Try talking and reading to them as you used to,' she said. 'But don't push your crazy opinions or use language beyond their understanding.'

The room fell silent, the weight of their conversation lingering. George nodded, a sense of determination settling in his heart. He knew he must step up for his daughters and be the father they needed.

* * *

The following evening, George grabbed Jeannie the second he stepped through the door and lifted her so high that her feet floated above the ground. She squealed and laughed heartily, and his stomach fluttered at his daughter's delight.

After supper, the family lounged around the fire. George nervously blurted out the statement he had rehearsed all day as he laboured under a cloudy sky. 'I can't care for you as Mammy did. A mother knows what her daughters need, but I can challenge your brains and stir your quest for knowledge. I want you to be freethinkers.'

George paused to rein in his emotions before speaking again. 'I have let you down since Mammy died,' he said, sorrow rising in his voice and forehead furrowed. 'Instead of comforting you, I have buried myself in my grief.'

Jeannie and Lizzie stared blank-faced, and Minnie sucked her thumb as if she was alone. George drew a huge breath as he realised the girls didn't understand what he said. He tried again. 'Each evening, we will gather at the hearth, read aloud, and talk about the day and troubling events.'

Sarah's voice floated with cooking odours from the kitchen.

'Lassies, he's prone to go into lecture mode about his passionate views. Tell him to cut out the big words if you can't understand.'

Faces smothered with smiles of delight, the girls raced over and jockeyed for space in the tartan chair, where they cuddled into him, rubbed his limbs, and stroked his hair.

'Welcome back, Da,' Jeannie said. 'We missed you.'

George tingled, and his heart warmed. Mary had gone forever. Fortunately, he had these three sweet lasses as a reminder of his Butterfly.

The tradition of evening fireside chats began. George constantly weaved his mantra into their talks—be *faithful to the religion you were born into and respect all others.*

Chapter 5

In December 1900, Da went away. Jeannie said he'd return with a new wife. As the oldest, Aunty Sarah trusted Jeannie with information.

Minnie's tummy fluttered with hope seasoned with questions and doubts because mammies were a mystery to her. A whisper told her not to ask, so most of her questions stayed inside. She overheard a conversation between her sisters.

'What do we know about her?' Lizzie asked as they brushed and braided their hair.

'She comes from Derry, forty-five miles away, and she's called Charlotte,' Jeannie said.

'Has she two heads and green hair?' Lizzie said through giggles.

Jeannie frowned. 'This is no joke. She may be cruel. She wants to replace our sweet Mammy.'

Jeannie's words made Minnie tremble. Their new mother would undoubtedly be kind. 'Will Da still love us?' she asked.

Jeannie sniffed. 'Who knows? Maybe she'll steal his heart.'

Minnie's tummy ached. Da meant everything to her, and the thought of this stranger stealing his affection made her queasy.

The sisters lingered in their bedroom on the day of Da's

scheduled return. Lizzie, the last to rise, stretched and shed the mountainous bedclothes. 'How do we impress this woman?' Outside, the rain bucketed, and the howling gale swept branches and anything not tied down.

Jeannie, admiring her profile in the looking glass, called to Lizzie. 'We wear our best clothes. Perhaps we could have a welcoming party?'

Minnie curled up on the bed, chin resting in her upturned hands, listening but adding nothing.

The door inched open, and Aunty Sarah crept in. 'Am I interrupting?'

'We want to welcome Da and wondered if you would permit us to bake a cake,' said Jeannie.

'It's a kind idea, but we don't know when he'll arrive because of the weather. You girls can stage some entertainment on Christmas Day, just over a month away.'

Da had yet to appear by nine, and Aunty Sarah waved towards the bedroom. 'Time to toddle off.'

Lizzie pouted. 'Don't shoo us to bed because we want to greet our stepmother.'

'Lizzie, you'll have plenty of chances to meet her later,' said Aunty Sarah.

Minnie drifted in and out of disturbed sleep. When awake, she listened to the never-ending beat of raindrops on the roof and water racing across the ground. Then she heard horses' hooves and rotating wheels headed towards the barn. Next, footsteps sloshed and stumbled.

The bedroom door creaked, and the familiar ring of Da's deep voice echoed. Her father tiptoed into the room, followed by lighter steps and a powerful scent Minnie recognised as the mauve wildflowers she had heard called lilacs.

'There lie my sleeping wee angels,' Da said. 'They're a tight bunch but so different.'

'They're so cute,' a sharp female voice replied. Minnie's body tensed.

'The tallest lass, the one in the middle, is Jeannie. She fusses over her sisters and considers herself their mother.'

'I'll step in as a mother, and she can become a daughter again,' said the female voice. 'I'll teach them good temperate Protestant habits so they'll not be work-shy and will disdain drunkenness.'

'On the left, curled on her side, is Lizzie, the second lass. She doesn't mince words; she says it as she sees it. To the left is Minnie, the youngest, forever full of questions.'

'Jeannie plays mother well,' said the unfamiliar voice. 'The baby's wee fingers curl around her arm.'

Da must have seen Minnie wriggle, so he bent over. 'Darling, I'm sorry to wake you. We tried to creep.'

When they'd gone, Minnie lay awake. She'd sketched a picture in her mind of what mammies were like. The voice, sharp enough to cut glass, didn't match the image.

* * *

Before daybreak, the sisters stirred. Lizzie sprung from the bed. 'Are they here?' she asked, racing to the window.

'I heard them come in the dark,' Minnie said.

Jeannie frowned and opened their door. 'Let's see what's in store.'

They found Da with a woman. The couple, dressed in sweaters, mittens, and multiple pairs of socks, snuggled under rugs next to the glow of the fire. 'Good morning, darlings.

Please join us,' Da said.

Once they'd claimed places around the fire, Da shot a besotted grin as he gestured to the woman. 'This is your stepmother, and you should call her Ma; Mammy lives in heaven.' He moved his focus to Charlotte. 'Now you get to see my wee lassies, Jeannie, Lizzie, and Minnie, in the daylight—all so pretty and smart.'

Minnie smiled as wide as she could, even as fear gripped her heart as she reflected on how her father stared at this lady. Lizzie gave a cheeky grin. Jeannie smiled, but Minnie could tell she forced her smile.

The corners of Charlotte's mouth briefly curled upwards. 'I'm sure we'll get along.'

Minnie studied Charlotte. Neither fat nor thin, tall or short, she leaned towards sturdiness and arranged her wavy brown hair in a bun. She smelled of that flowery stuff like last night.

The inviting aroma of porridge wafted from the griddle. Charlotte rose, ladled the creamy mixture into metal bowls, and laid them before the girls, with thick toast spread with a generous layer of home-churned butter.

Minnie nibbled, trying not to let the spoon tremble as she glanced at Ma. Jeannie stared intently at their replacement mother while Lizzie tucked into her food. 'Yum, I'm starving.'

Charlotte cleared her throat. 'We say grace before eating and do not talk with full mouths.'

Lizzie dropped her spoon at once, shamefaced. Da peeped over *The Ballymena Observer*, grinned, and rolled his eyes.

Charlotte turned to him. 'George, neither do we read until all have finished eating.'

Once Charlotte had said grace, the girls ate speedily and silently before scurrying away.

Later, the sisters muttered as they gathered in a semi-circle on the frigid bedroom floor. 'She's a strange one', said Lizzie. 'Mammy never made us say grace. And speaking to Da like that!'

Minnie sucked her thumb and stared distantly at Jeannie, who turned her nose up. 'She hasn't two heads or green hair, but I think we can expect things to change,' said Jeannie.

* * *

Days later, the family lounged around the hissing fire after supper, listening to the wind roar and raindrops lash on the windowpanes. Wrapped in a handwoven rug, Minnie kneeled at the foot of her father's armchair. She looked up at Da. 'Why do folk stop me and ask about Ma?'

He pinched the bridge of his nose. 'Because it's unusual for an outsider to settle here. They itch with curiosity, and what I overheard in the pub today confirmed this.'

A curt voice sliced the peat-tinged air. 'The pub? I thought you didn't visit.'

'My visits are rare, and because I lingered in a booth, the gossip mongers expressed plenty before noticing me.' He leaned towards Charlotte. 'Talk of you, my dear, filled the bar room.'

Charlotte rubbed her hands together.

'Locals follow your every move,' said Da, a hint of sarcasm in his speech. 'They've nicknamed you Derry Lass; the latest craze is Derry Lass watching.'

'Ha, ha. I bet they criticised plenty!' said Charlotte, eyes fiery.

'They acknowledged you work tirelessly, saying you swing

34

an axe as powerfully as any man.'

'Stop side-stepping. There must've been grouches,' said Charlotte, face pinched. 'Did they talk about the poachers?'

George scratched his temples. 'No, what's that about?'

'Last week, I caught a couple of lads eyeing our chicken pen, so I chased the scoundrels with a hoe. I never saw them again, so it worked.'

'True, I saw it,' said Minnie.

George tilted his head and burst into explosive laughter. 'Bet those young fellows never admitted to their chums that a woman armed with a hoe frightened them.'

Charlotte rolled her eyes.

'I'm proud of your bravery,' said Da.

'Thank you for the compliment, George. But I wish these people wouldn't pry. I wonder if they'll ever accept me.'

* * *

The once green meadow turned grey, and a vicious, icy gale flattened anything in its path. Within a month of Charlotte's arrival, the family spent a week sheltering inside, savouring the warmth of the blazing fire. Sweet fragrances wafted from the kitchen area as Charlotte made treats for the Christmas celebrations.

Sarah and her daughters joined them on Christmas Day, bringing the outside chill and gifts.

Minnie's stomach spun with rapture when she opened her gift. 'She is beautiful.' She gazed at the rag doll, her body fashioned from cream canvas, with a mouth of red embroidery. Then she stroked her limp form, fiddling with the strands of wavy wool stitched into the top, and rubbed the sturdy stitches in the embroidered lips.

'Katherine and Frances made that doll, fussing over every seam, stitching, restitching, and putting all their love for Minnie into it,' said Aunty Sarah as she gazed at her girls proudly.

Minnie ran to Aunty Sarah, Katherine, and Frances and spread her arms as if to hug the entire world. 'You are the best aunty and cousins. I love you so much!'

A beaming expression swamped Frances's fair features as her saucer-sized crystal blue eyes feasted on her young cousin's outpouring of glee. 'What are you going to call dolly?'

Minnie stared at the wall opposite as she rubbed the back of her neck before turning towards Frances. 'I'm not sure,'

'What about Bella,' said Frances as she flicked back her unruly curls. She glanced at her sister, Katherine, seeking approval.

Minnie mulled it over. Bella is a lovely name, made for this sweet doll. She flashed a bashful smile before nodding her head.

They feasted on stuffed turkey and plum pudding around a table alive with laughter and merry chatter.

Afterwards, they acted out a play based on the Christmas story. They'd rehearsed endless times under Frances's direction. Dressed in costumes pieced together by Frances and Katherine, Jeannie played Mary, Lizzie took the part of Joseph, and Minnie played baby Jesus. They finished with well-practised bows. Da, Charlotte, Aunty Sarah, Frances, and Katherine cheered and clapped.

Aunty Sarah turned to Charlotte. 'I hope you enjoyed the show. It's the girls' special welcome.' She shifted her focus to Da. 'My girls, especially Frances, want to help your wee lasses prepare and perform live plays. They suggested *Sleeping Beauty* and *Jack and the Beanstalk*.'

'Sounds grand. Can I order my ticket?' said Da, a smile claiming his face.

After the performance, they gorged on the delicious candies, toffees, and cakes, the products of the sweet odours swirling from the griddle in the past days. As the day passed, Minnie struggled to keep her eyes open. She couldn't miss anything, and the hope that every day would mirror today smothered her.

Aunty Sarah rose and called to Frances and Katherine, 'Girls, time to go. The weak sun fades fast, and it's icy cold outside.'

With the visitors gone, Minnie collapsed on the floor and succumbed to sleep.

Chapter 6

Toome, Antrim 1901

The icy weather transitioned into warmer days, and they adjusted their schedules accordingly. Saturday visits to the Toome market were the weekly highlight. The cornerstone of community life, the market offered the chance to meet and chat with townland folk while sourcing provisions.

In May 1901, Jeannie, Lizzie, and Minnie skipped through the narrow, cobblestoned Toome Streets towards the town square while Da and Charlotte walked more sedately behind. Structures of scraps of iron and fabric and more substantial shelters of timber and canvas lined the route. These, and the barrows crammed in the smallest of gaps, sold everything—pots, pans, lengths of cloth, sides of meat, and vegetables.

Crowds of shoppers jostled through the air thick with chatter and a buzz of merriment. Vendors, clutching rolls of banknotes secured by string, yelled praise of their goods through cupped hands.

They paused at stalls where Charlotte examined the wares, squeezing and pummelling the fruit and vegetables. Charlotte lifted a pumpkin at one outlet, ran her fingers over its skin, and then raised it to her nose. She gave the vendor a piercing stare. 'How much?'

'Tis fourpence, madam.'

'Ridiculous,' said Charlotte. 'I'll pay two, and that's too much.'

The bartering continued until they settled on three pence. Charlotte and the vendor shook hands to seal the deal. 'Congratulations, madam,' he said, 'You have polished negotiating skills. You missed your calling; you should be a market trader.'

Charlotte pursed her lips. 'You should have been a crook, sir. You have the right makings.'

The family wandered further, weaving around barrows through swirling smells of livestock and ripe fruit and the more pleasant aromas of baked goods and scented soap. A slippery paste of animal dung and vegetable leaves covered the ground, leading Da to ask the girls to step carefully. Minnie raised her arms and peered up at him through pleading wide eyes, and predictably, he hoisted her onto his broad shoulders. She secured herself by grabbing two clumps of his thick locks. 'Ouch, Minnie, don't yank. Pat my hair and softly press your feet against my chest.'

George weaved his way through the jostling crowd. Minnie savoured her expansive view. She peered down at Jeannie and Lizzie, who called out warnings. 'Crushed herbs ahead,' said Jeannie.

'Pew, horse poo. Do not step on it, or your shoes will pong,' said Lizzie.

They took a brief break when they reached the town square, where a sea of locals gathered. Da knelt, and Minnie alighted from his back. They soaked up the carnival-like atmosphere, and Da chatted in Ulster Scots, laughed, and shook hands with acquaintances.

Minnie fidgeted with the wrinkles in her blouse and the ribbons in her hair. She saw activities different from those on other market days when she spun. Folk scurried as they decorated the streets with red, white, and blue bunting. Others hung orange sashes to lamp posts.

She leaned towards Jeannie. 'Why are they making the town pretty?' Is there going to be a party?'

'Sort of. Orange Day is coming,' said Jeannie.

Minnie scratched her head and sent Jeannie a questioning look. 'What is Orange Day?'

Jeannie opened her mouth to answer, but Charlotte's voice boomed from behind before any words emerged. 'Orange Day is an important day in the Ulster calendar,' said Charlotte, her voice coloured with enthusiasm. 'We celebrate our victory over the Catholics with a march led by a band with drums and trumpets.'

As Minnie listened to Charlotte, she glimpsed her father out of the corner of her eye. He propped himself against a wall, shoulders hunched and hands in his pockets. He rolled his eyes. She took some timid steps towards him and, when she got closer, noticed a frown creasing his features. Mute, he stared into the distance.

Accustomed to him always being the centre of attention, his shrinking stance perplexed Minnie. *His posture and expression signalled an opposing view of Charlotte regarding the Orange Day festivities. She wondered why.*

* * *

12 July 1901

With record speed, the girls completed their chores of milking the cows and goats before retreating to their bedroom. It was Orange Day. The first rays of light filtered through the window as they wiggled into their brand-new, starched linen outfits of powder pink decorated with lace of darker pink. They arranged their hair more carefully than usual before pulling on their shoes and fixing ribbons around each other's braids.

They raced each other to the hearthstone where, chanting and jumping, they waited for what seemed ages. Finally, Charlotte appeared. 'Well, well, three anxious wee lasses await. Da has the cart ready. Let's get going.'

As they clip-clopped to Toome, Minnie's chest tightened at the conversation floating from the jockey seat of the cart. 'I'll drop you and the lasses at the march and return to collect you.'

'Whatever are you suggesting?' asked Charlotte.

'Attendance at this event is against my principles. We cannot achieve peace while celebrating the Catholic defeat in the four-century-old Battle of the Boyne. This event stirs the pot and creates needless trouble.'

'George, forget your silly views. As a matter of principle, Ulstermen should honour Orange Day.'

Minnie heard annoyance rise in Charlotte's voice. She couldn't see the faces of the jockey seat passengers but knew her stepmother would be furious, her face bright red and eyes fiery.

Several long minutes elapsed with no sound escaping from the front seat. Minnie, confident that more words would come, sensed her blood freeze.

Charlotte shredded the silence. 'If you're serious, we all go home. The entire district will be there, and tongues will wag if I appear alone with the lasses. If we turn around, your lasses won't be able to attend an event they've been looking forward to.'

Minnie's heart hammered. They wouldn't see the march and gobble those yummy sweets or get to show off their frilly dresses. Enveloped by raucous sniffles and wailing, she twisted to face her sisters. Hunched on the bench seat behind her, they both grimaced.

What next drifted to her ears struck up a tune in Minnie's heart. 'The girls are too young to understand the significance. So they're not deprived of a fun outing; I'll stay in the background until the march ends,' said Da, a note of resignation in his speech.

Toome buzzed with a carnival atmosphere. The sisters trailed Charlotte, who found a plum viewing position. Da disappeared into the shadows.

Participants stepped out to cheers and shouts of loyalty to the United Kingdom. First, musicians blowing trumpets and beating drums clad in kilts and tartan trousers appeared. Behind them, waves of grim-faced lodge members marched in rows. They wore dark suits adorned with marigold sashes. Drawn by the colours, music, and rumbling cheering, Minnie clapped and tapped her feet in time to the stirring tunes.

The event changed to carnival mode, and Da reappeared. Minnie sensed warmth radiating through her body, glad that Charlotte had won the argument and that they were at this fairy tale celebration. The sisters skipped behind their father as he shouldered through the crowd. Tempted by the delicious smells drifting from various stalls, they stopped to devour buns and sweets.

When evening fell, someone lit a bonfire. It burned like a furnace and grew larger than the nearby houses. Da beckoned to his daughters, squatted, and explained, 'It's a long-standing tradition to ignite a bonfire on Orange Day.'

As soon as he had finished his explanation, a booming voice rumbled from the depths of the crowd. 'Now the fire is lit, add a few Catholics. Their burning fat will make the flame spit and sizzle.'

Dread spiked Minnie's insides. She grasped Jeannie's clothes in a vice-like grip. The outburst instilled an understanding of Da's comments about the event making trouble. The Catholics would retaliate, and brutal images played out in the theatre of her mind.

* * *

When they left, Jeannie pointed ahead. 'Oh, no.'

Two groups of dishevelled youths stood ten yards ahead on opposite street sides. Minnie heard them shout at each other but couldn't decipher any words. However, airborne stones whirled above the family's heads. Minnie felt the urge to flee. 'Isn't there another way?'

'I'm sorry, darling. We must follow this route to collect our cart and horse,' said Da. 'You lassies hold hands and walk close to Da and Charlotte. Walk quickly and keep your heads low.'

They forged forward. As splintered glass landed at their feet, they passed a lad who yelled over his shoulder, 'Aim for windows displaying orange banners or Union Jacks.'

The two gangs scowled and made threatening gestures

to each other. One youth shook his fist at the opposing group. 'You Catholics will pay. We'll break the skulls and gouge the noses of those stupid statutes in your churches and graveyards.'

'Orange heads, deserters of the true faith, you'll end up in hell!'

One lad stepped from his ranks and onto the thoroughfare when they neared the gangs. 'Protestant bastards, come out and fight like real men.'

Pushed by his mates, one of the Protestants fell out of line and faced his tormentors.

Arm spread sideways, Da squatted. 'We must hide.'

Screeching and thumping echoed as the lads laid into each other. Onlookers, cheering and booing, gathered and closed around the wrestling pair, and others joined the fighting.

The lines of worry furrowing Da's face widened by the minute. 'We'll shelter in that recessed shop entrance.' Motioning with his chin to the right, he whispered to Minnie. 'Pass the message to your sisters. We should race and not attract attention.' Minnie repeated Da's directions to a white-faced Lizzie in a barely audible mutter.

Like scurrying mice, a crooked line with Da at the head hurried towards the shop entrance, twenty yards away.

Seconds before arriving, one ruffian knocked his opponent to the ground with a bang. As the family collapsed into the recess, blood-curdling groans reached them. Terror bled through Minnie's body before a dizzy sensation sent her crashing downwards. Before she landed, Da rescued her by wrapping his muscular arms around her.

The victor dragged the fallen man to the roadway's edge and kicked him repeatedly. Then he lifted the fellow's head by a tuft of hair and banged it forcefully until the sound of bones cracking rocketed through the nippy night air.

More onlookers gathered, and chunks of paving stones, loose rocks, and wood planks joined the air assault. The crowd stormed forward, yelling and screeching before inflicting more injuries on the youth lying on the road with blood streaming from his skull, nose, and mouth. Punches flew everywhere until a tangle of bloodied bodies littered the cobblestones, and the odour of blood overtook all smells.

Trembling, Minnie pressed into her father's chest and heard his heart bang. Her sisters sniffled and cried, and Lizzie's voice floated above the background noise, 'I'm scared. We'll die.'

Policemen wearing olive green uniforms came into view. At first, the crowd thinned slowly, but when the officers waved wooden batons, the group fled.

The family took the opportunity and raced to their cart. A dry-mouthed Minnie felt waves of gratitude that they made it out safely, snaking through her. She glanced at her sisters, who stared ahead without flinching. Lizzie shot a terrified pout at her father. 'Why do they fight?' she asked.

Before George had a chance to answer, a curt female voice replied. 'They are drunken Catholic troublemakers ruining this lovely day.'

When they reached the safety of their cart, the air exploded out of Minnie's mouth in a massive sigh of relief.

* * *

As they munched their porridge in October, Da told the sisters he planned a train trip to Belfast on Saturday.

They rose from the breakfast table, and Lizzie flung herself into her father's waiting arms. Jeannie beamed and clapped when Lizzie landed. The air bubbled with excitement, and Minnie bounced on one foot. 'Oh, you're the best Da in the world,' she said as she rained endless sloppy kisses on her father.

Da's eyes sparkled as he laughed teasingly. 'I see you think the trip will be fun,' he said.

The trio squealed with delight. 'I've never been on a choo-choo train,' said Lizzie.

'I bag a window seat. Da and Charlotte can peer over me,' said Jeannie.

'Charlotte won't be coming,' said Da in a monotone voice.

Lizzie and Jeannie shot Da puzzled looks.

'Ma needs to rest. Let's make the trip before the cold weather sets in.'

'I want Saturday to come quickly,' said Minnie, lips drawn into a circle. 'It'll be more fun than Christmas.'

* * *

On Saturday, they boarded the first train to Belfast at Toome. After what seemed like ages, the iron wheels halted at a crowded, dusty platform.

They gathered outside the station on the wet, shiny footpath. With a soil-engraved thumb, Da pointed to the south. 'We will go towards the high street, three blocks that way.'

Father and daughters linked hands and stumbled through the thick haze of steam billowing from factory stacks. Their route took them over a bridge, unveiling a view of outlets bleeding murky, grey-coloured fluid. 'That stuff stinks.

Yucky,' Minnie complained.

When they reached the High Street, a noisy scene confronted them. The roadways, covered with a paste of raindrops, slushy mud, and animal dung, looked like a battleground. Horse-drawn double-decker trams plied the streets and competed with carts loaded with boxes and barrels. A crowd of people clogged the road's verge.

The unaccustomed perpetual motion and deafening noise made Minnie shiver, and her heart banged wildly. She turned her back on the mayhem, hung her head, and remained in that pose until she sensed Da's rough hands touch her shoulder. He twisted her towards the jostling traffic. Minnie couldn't fathom why her father had rotated her with such force.

'Life will present many hurdles. Don't shy from the unaccustomed,' Da explained. 'Face challenges head-on. You may not understand this now, but you will one day.'

Minnie glanced over at Jeannie and Lizzie, who, with gaping mouths, stared at the jostling traffic. She followed their eyes to a double-decked tram and imagined her eyes had popped out of their socket at the novel sight. The sisters gazed up at their towering father, tugged at his shirt, and begged him to take them riding on one. 'Please, Da, please. We want to sit on the top.'

A laughing George arched his lips upwards. 'Let's go, and yes, it would be nice to peer down from the balcony level.'

He guided them, hands resting on the backs of the younger two, to the tram stop. Soon, a tram came to a screeching halt, and the girls tittered as they climbed the spiral stairs to the balcony. They claimed a wooden seat at the rear.

A dazzled Minnie gazed at the sights and sounds, absorbing every detail as she and her sisters squealed in delight.

'Oh, Da, we can see everything from here,' said Jeannie.

The tram stopped outside a dingy grey stone building surrounded by an unkempt garden. The sisters gawked at the skeletal, shallow-eyed wretches shuffling in threadbare clothes.

'That place scares me,' Jeannie grimaced.

'Haunted, do you think?' Lizzie replied.

Da interrupted with one of his detailed, almost sermon-like commentaries. 'The building is a workhouse. It is for homeless individuals and the inmates toil for a place to sleep and food to fill their bellies.'

The family alighted from the tram at the next stop. George took the children to wander among Belfast's premier parts, home to wealthy Protestants.

They briefly inspected the handsome buildings with mani-cured gardens in tree-lined avenues. A pungent stench wafted from the nearby backstreets. 'What an awful stink,' said Lizzie. 'Let's find where it comes from.'

The sisters galloped off, although Da shouted after them to wait. Minnie knew from the crunch of his boots that he followed them.

Not far into their race, the trio saw rows of shacks flanking gloomy alleyways. Crows flew over stagnant puddles riddled with floating garbage. Rodents skittled over the alleys, and raw sewerage clogged open drains.

Stomach tumbling, a sour sting attacked Minnie's throat. Jeannie and Lizzie stood frozen, both with arms wrapped around their chests.

Minnie averted her gaze towards the heavens and cupped her head in her hands. She glimpsed Da, sprinting towards her. When he almost reached her, she cried. 'Da, I feel like vomiting.' Da bent down to her height and lifted her chin. He shook his finger at her. 'Never run away. It's not safe.' Uncharacteristic anger shrouded Da's face. She threw her arms around him, and the tenderness of his touch told her his anger had dissolved. Comforted by his warmth, she let out a final sob as she nestled into him and promised herself never again to stray.

Jeannie gazed at Da through widened eyes. 'People cannot live here. There's nowhere for kids to play.'

'Folk live here because they have no choice.' Da explained that the rapid growth and never-ending arrivals meant a housing shortage.

As they exited the stinking maze, Minnie asked, 'Why are the kids sad, Da?'

'Children as young as six work long shifts in fabric mills and factories.'

The shock delivered by her father's words sent Minnie's head spinning. 'But they're only our age.'

'We must leave for the train,' said Da. 'After seeing these youngsters, don't complain about doing chores.'

The three responded in unison. 'No, Da.'

Chapter 7

Winter arrived, bringing black clouds, freezing wind, and lashing rain. The family sheltered inside. 'Girls! Stop and be quiet!' yelled Charlotte.

Minnie, Jeannie, and Lizzie ignored her. With her sisters pursuing her, Minnie rounded the table. They wrenched the tablecloth, sending a pot and several metal mugs crashing to the floor.

Charlotte fixed her eyes on the items strewn across the floor. 'Look what you've done!' Jeannie held Charlotte's angry gaze. 'Sorry, Ma, it was an accident, truly.'

Charlotte turned every shade of red and purple. 'Do not answer back, lass. I won't have it.'

Anger simmered inside Minnie. 'You're a fat cow,' she muttered under her breath. Charlotte had fattened over the last few months and became fatter by the day.

Given Charlotte's fury, the girls fell silent and sat upright for the rest of the day. Only the splutter of the fire and the howling gale disturbed the silence.

When they entered their bedroom, the girls burst into hearty giggles. 'It is a treat to escape Ma and be alone,' said Lizzie.

'Ma's anger frightens me,' said Minnie.

'Puffs of smoke came out of her ears, I swear,' said Lizzie.

Minnie writhed over the bed. Lizzie passed her freezing fingers across the squealing Minnie's cheeks, provoking further laughter. Jeannie attempted in vain to quieten the pair. 'The raging weather and sleet could keep us inside for days. We mustn't make Ma cross.'

The next day, they woke later than usual to a watery sun struggling to break through heavy fog. They wiped the sleep from their eyes, then sprung from their bed to the sting of the freezing air.

They found Charlotte before the hearth, one hand planted on her back, the other rubbing her belly. 'Where is Da?' asked Lizzie.

Lips drawn tight in disapproval, Charlotte shuffled across the room. 'Because you girls slept so late, he braved the cold and beating rain alone to tend the animals. Respectful daughters would be out of bed early, eager to assist. I forever tell your father he spoils you lasses.'

By the following day, Charlotte's mood had dramatically changed. As if nothing had happened, Charlotte smiled softly at the girls and was uncharacteristically quiet. With a dumbfounded look swamping her face, Jeannie jabbed Minnie, 'You and Lizzie must behave perfectly. Who knows when her temper will erupt again?'

The girls spent the rest of the lockdown period cuddling their father at the hearthside as he read aloud. Charlotte remained mute, and when Minnie surveyed the room, Charlotte quietly hummed as she knitted booties. Minnie wondered why.

* * *

When 1902 arrived, the wind lost some of its fury, and a weak sun appeared daily, but the nights remained chilly, and torrential rain fell.

On a freezing night in mid-February, thick clouds hid the moon, blanketing all beyond the window in liquorice black. A glimmer of light radiated from the hearth fire, and the flickering lamp light spilled through the open bedroom door.

A blistering gale lashed at the walls and breached cracks in the mortar. It whistled between the rafters and down the chimney. The sisters, limbs tangled around each other, cuddled beneath their quilt. They listened to the raging wind that flung items through the air, then thumped them to the ground and snapped tree branches. Minnie's teeth chattered. Lizzie spoke from beyond Jeannie's prone form. 'It's cold, my bones freeze, and my feet are like ice blocks.'

Charlotte screeched so explosively it made the cottage shake. The back door slammed. Heavy footsteps sloshed a path to the barn. Minnie heard George's voice, but the drenching rain muffled the words. When the girls charged to the window, they saw a dim speck of light flicker.

'Da's carrying a lamp, and the rain's sploshes all around,' said Jeannie.

The clop of horse hooves and the rattle of cartwheels sounded. The horse's hooves trotted towards the gate and escalated to a canter in a flash.

Questions crammed Minnie's mind. Why had their step-mother cried out? Where had Da gone?

Charlotte screeched again. And again, and again. The shrieks grew in agony until they reached a noisy climax. 'The loud noise will break the house, filling the rooms until the walls go bang or the pressure and roof pop,' wailed Lizzie.

Minnie sensed blood rush to her face, and her hands trembled.

Jeannie flashed a determined look. 'Let's find out what's happening. I'll lead.'

Hands entwined, the shivering sisters heard horses' hooves and revolving wheels, then tightening leather. Shoes struck and squished on the boggy ground. The door opened and boomed as it blew shut. Their father spoke in what Minnie recognised as Ulster Scots to a woman, who responded in a distinctive Ulster accent.

Minnie listened to her father's calls to Charlotte. 'I'm sorry to leave you alone for so long. This storm is wild and delayed my trip there. Then, on the way home, there were tree trunks, barrels, wayward fence posts, you name it.'

Charlotte's voice came from the bedroom. 'George, for once, please spare me your long-winded explanations. Please, someone, help me get this baby out.'

The woman who accompanied Da, a tall, redheaded lady clad in layers of clothing and carrying a coal-black leather bag, set a pot of water over the flame and barked orders to Charlotte. She cringed at the sight of Minnie and her sisters and ordered them to bed. The trio obeyed the stranger and scampered off but lay awake.

* * *

When they woke, the weather had calmed.

The redheaded lady accompanied them to the low-roofed bedroom shared by Da and Charlotte, which was filled with an unusual, sweet, milky smell. Da stood, framed by the window filtering insipid light into the space. Gazing at the bed's occupants, George beckoned, 'Meet your new sister,

Carrie.'

Minnie's stomach fluttered. She didn't know Charlotte expected a baby or how babies came. Lizzie whispered to Jeannie, 'Explains the booties.' She added, 'As it is.'—a ditty Lizzie learned in the schoolyard that became her signature phrase used whenever she could find no other words.

Straining on tiptoes, Minnie peered at the extraordinary sight. Charlotte, propped up against fluffy pillows, gazed tenderly at the infant. As Jeannie and Lizzie scaled the bed-clothes, Minnie raised her arms and gestured to the mattress. Da boosted her onto the bed.

Minnie perched atop the mattress. Lizzie clambered closer and loosened the wrap, revealing a delicate newborn with puckered skin and rosy lips. Minnie propelled herself on her bottom and planted a slobbery peck on the infant's plump cheek. She giggled when Carrie squeezed her finger. The incredible sight sent her mind into freefall. 'She's pretty like Bella, but this bubby moves, gurgles, and smiles. I think the waves in my tummy tell me I love this baby.'

However, she didn't understand how last night's terror had led to this perfect soul. It must be a miracle. Da appeared captivated by the newborn. He couldn't take his eyes off her. *Will Da love us now that he has a baby with Charlotte?* The question left her with a hammering chest.

Within days, statements made by Charlotte quelled Minnie's fears. 'Nothing changes with this addition. As always, we must share the load. I'll need to reallocate chores. Jeannie and Lizzie, with my help, will take on some baby care jobs.' She then announced that the three sisters could feed the fowls, collect the eggs, and milk the cows and goats. A melody sounded in Minnie's ears at the words that next emerged from

Charlotte's lips. 'Oh, and your father and I have agreed that there will be no divisions between us and that we will function as a single family. Carrie is your sister, your father, and all four children and I belong together.'

The words were melodic to Minnie's ears. *Da still loved her, unchanged by her miracle sister.*

* * *

'Hello, Da. Jeannie and Lizzie have left me alone and raced off to school, so I'll spend today here,' called Minnie from under her red hood within days of Carrie's birth. She stood between the cottage and a trench that carried water from the cropping fields.

Da sauntered over to her. 'A swift wind blows, and heavy black clouds roll in. You would be better off sheltering in the cosy house with Charlotte and Carrie.'

Minnie choked back the lump in her throat. 'My cloak's warm like a blazing fire, and I'm as strong as a bull.' With Bella tucked under her arm, she sidled up to her father and brushed against his leg. 'I need to know you're close. Bella and I'll stay outside the border ditch.' She pointed towards the drainage trench that carried excess water from the cropping area.

'Wait for spring, when the sun shines and the wind calms.'

Her father's response made her feel like her heart sank, but she persisted. She was determined to convince Da to allow her to do so because she found the cropping activity thrilling compared with confinement in the cottage. Most importantly, she wanted to be close to her father. 'Please, Da, the whistling wind doesn't scare me. I'm tough, and Bella will protect me,'

Minnie said as she fluttered her eyelashes.

'I can see you are keen, so you may stick around,' Da said as he muffled a chuckle. 'But, I need you to promise to stay outside the field. On these blowy pre-spring days, Da prepares the soil for this year's crop by ploughing, spreading, and raking fertiliser. Workers and tools, including that heavy plough and those clumsy, giant draught horses, weave every which way.'

Minnie drew Bella to her lips and kissed the ruby-stitched mouth. 'Like the best friends we are, we can sit together and see everything. Such fun!'

Minnie spent her preschool days crouched at the edge of the cropping fields. Engulfed by the acrid odour of soil, she and Bella watched as workers broke the earth with spades and hoes while others put in the day bent over, removing weeds.

Sometimes, Da left his work and shepherded Minnie among the tilled chocolate fields. He recited rambling details of the art of farming—types of plants, times to sow seeds, fertilisers, and the differences between weeds and plants.

Minnie kept the promise to stay clear of the work area. However, busting to get close to Da, she grasped any opportunity to catch him unaware. She approached from behind and slipped her hand into his coarse, barnacled hands.

'You frightened me,' he said, 'but what lovely wee hands.' With a slick movement, he winched Minnie onto his shoulders where she lapped the tickling sensation of the wind whizzing past her dangling plaits.

'You are so strong, Da. Giddy-up!' She pressed her feet against his ribs. A chuckling, Da obliged, bursting into a canter.

* * *

As the farming year closed, Minnie and Bella were crouched in their usual position when the unmistakable crunch of Da's boots headed towards them. Minnie doggedly peered into her father's eyes. 'I've watched the weather, the crops ripen, and the workers' jobs all year. I want to know everything about farming.'

'Minnie, why learn to farm? Farming is hard work. It would be best if you absorbed everything at school.'

'School will be fun, but I can help you, too.'

'Well, at least having both gives you choices that avoid the harsh life of the hovels and factories,' said Da. 'Keep looking and try doing what you see. Scythes and ploughs remain out of bounds so we do not find your foot cut off.'

Minnie hung on to her father's every word and soaked up each step of every task before copying them. If she found a job difficult, Da lent a hand. It gave her the closeness to Da, her hero who understood her the best, that she craved.

Chapter 8

June 1903

Minnie bolted upright in bed, her sleep disturbed by droning talk. Although she couldn't decipher the words, the voices were familiar.

Careful not to disturb her sleeping sisters, she slid from the bed. Her feet whispered across the darkened room to the wall. She slumped against it and wriggled down onto her haunches. The wall's jagged stones scratched her legs, but she didn't cry out for fear of attracting attention.

She craned her neck and peeked. Her heart gave several juddering beats when she saw the outlines of Da, Ma, and Aunty Sarah by the yellowish glow of the lamp outside. She couldn't follow the speech but sensed gloom shrouding the room.

Aunty Sarah said, 'Consumption's a scourge that attacks and murders young people. *Robber of youth* is the correct name.'

'You're upset, but name-calling won't help,' Da said. 'Someday, there'll be a cure. Scientists worldwide are studying causes and potential treatments.'

'Enough of your research talk,' barked a wailing Aunty

Sarah. 'Nothing will come in time for Frances.'

Panic enveloped Minnie, and her thoughts got fuzzier. She must discover what the despair concerned.

* * *

Minnie confided the dreadful talk she'd overheard to Lizzie and Jeannie. The pair stared stone-faced until Jeannie spoke. 'Consumption is that awful disease Mammy died from. Kids in the playground say horrible things that cannot be true. I don't listen because I think about the dreadful time when Mammy died,' said Jeannie. 'We should ask Da. He'll set us straight.'

Grief bathed Da's contorted birch-white face, and it took him four long pipe puffs to answer. 'Cousin Frances is sick.'

Lizzie crunched her nose. 'Did Frances catch a cold, or is it a sore tummy?'

'I wish it were that simple.'

'Will she be better for our next play?' asked Jeannie.

The skin at the corners of his lips folded into the briefest half smile, and then Da said, 'I'm afraid not. Frances can't get out of bed because she is too weak.'

'What makes her so sick?' asked Jeannie.

After that question, the room fell silent. Da cleared his throat before dragging on his pipe twice more, sending smoke rings ripe with the smell of tobacco spiralling towards the rafters. 'Poor Frances has a feared illness for which there's no cure.'

Minnie thought the blood froze in her veins. 'Da, does Frances have that sickness all those scary words are about?'

'Consumption has stalked this area for many years, terror-ising the locals.'

Jeannie flushed and peered up at Da. 'Are you telling us our sweet cousin is going to die?'

'Eventually, yes.'

Minnie ran to George and clung to him until she realised her fingernails dug into his upper arm, leaving red marks.

'My lassies, please don't tell anyone Frances is ill with consumption,' Da said.

Lizzie's face crumpled. 'Frances has the same wicked sickness that stole our Mammy, right?'

'Yes. People are frightened of the disease and will avoid our family because of its incurable nature.

'It's not Frances's fault, and it wasn't Mammy's,' said Minnie. 'Meanness to sick people is horrible. They shouldn't be awful to the already sad families?'

'Dread brings out the worst in folk,' said Da, sorrow shadowing his forehead.

* * *

September 1903

A film of grief floated over the cottage. However, nothing detracted from Minnie's first school day.

The day dawned awash with sunlight, a rarity for Ulster autumn. Minnie stood between Jeannie and Lizzie, her insides vibrating with anticipation. She clung to Bella so tightly that her knuckles turned white.

Lizzie's mouth twisted into a teasing smile as she tried to wrench Bella's limp body from her sister's grasp. 'You cannot take a rag doll to school, Minnie. The teacher will take her, and the kids will laugh, calling you a baby.'

Jeannie's eyes darted between Minnie and Da, who stood with arms threaded around Charlotte's enlarged waist. 'Give Bella to me, and I will ask Da to keep her safe until after school,' Jeannie pleaded.

Minnie pouted as she reluctantly parted with Bella, handing the ragged body to Jeannie. As she said farewell, George drew her close. 'You have been an enormous help. You have taken on more than I thought a wee one capable. I hope you'll help after school.'

The compliment whisked Minnie's breath away. Wow, he thinks I am a big, helpful girl.

Twin plaits dangling, she joined the older pair on the hike to Ballydunmaul National School. They journeyed along a narrow lane encased by overgrown hedges, hardened by years of use by mules, carts, and carriages. Calls of lowing cattle, clucking poultry, and acrid and gamy odours wafted from farms.

As the breeze made the tree branches tremble, Minnie strutted ahead of her sisters on a carpet of fallen leaves.

When she reached the schoolyard, a rush of joy flooded her. She entered the single classroom in the grey stone school building. A slither of light filtered through the four high windows, and an open fire crackled.

The schoolmaster, Mr Underwood, a tall, thin, grey-eyed man with thinning dark hair, directed her to a wooden seat behind a worn and scratched desk. A girl with a ponytail of coppery hair sat next to her leant towards over. 'My name's Leena.'

In a voice no louder than a whisper, she replied, 'Hello, Leena, I'm Minnie.' I've made a friend, and it wasn't hard,

Minnie thought. Other than fleeting meetings at fairs and the market, she'd never made friends outside her family.

Breathing in the odour of chalk, damp paper, and ink, Minnie surveyed the dim room, taking in one thing at a time. The blackboard caught her attention first. Soon, she would understand the writing scrawled on it. She moved on to the colourful maps on display.

At lunchtime, Minnie played with her new friend, Leena. After lunch, Mr Underwood outlined some rules and said, 'You must speak standard English, not Ulster Scots dialect, in class.' Da didn't allow Ulster-Scots at home, but Minnie understood many words because of their everyday use in Clonkeen. 'People use the dialect only within Ulster and is of no benefit in other places life may take you,' explained Mr Underwood.

Now, Minnie appreciated Da's stance.

A sniggering male voice drifted from behind. 'Nae, bother.' A burst of giggles followed. Expressionless, Mr Underwood, peering over his silver-rimmed spectacles, stared in the speaker's direction and said, 'Don't tark that tark at schul, you tark at hame.'

* * *

When the bell sounded at the end of lessons, Minnie perched on the low, whitewashed wall facing the schoolyard, waiting for her sisters. The shared wall marked the frontage of their school and a Catholic school adorned with crosses and statutes.

Minnie cocked her head and saw two clusters of boys. One group stood before her, and another about ten feet away outside the Catholic school. Lads, with hands fisted, the oldest, about fourteen, glared at each other through fiery eyes.

'Protestant, Protestant, ring the bell, Catholic, Catholic, go to hell,' said the boys from her school.

'Catholic, Catholic, ring the bell, Protestant, Protestant, go to hell,' roared back the Catholic boys.

A hard lump formed in Minnie's belly, and the strength drained from her limbs. She spotted Lizzie and Jeannie running towards her. She vaulted from the wall, rushed to them, and sobbed as she folded her arms around Jeannie.

Jeannie peeled her sister from her chest. 'What is wrong? Didn't you enjoy your first day?'

'I loved it, but what's this?'

'Nothing, really. It happens every afternoon. The boys from our National school torment the Catholic lads. You'll get used to it.'

As they headed home, Minnie heard taunts of 'Carrot top land thieves' and 'Catholic idiots' from behind, followed by screeching and thumping. She twisted around and froze at the sight of lads throwing punches.

It mimicked the skirmish on Orange Day. Why do kids copy big people? 'This is horrible. I want to go home.' She shook and felt she was about to vomit.

As the threesome sprinted, leaving the crashes and the unmistakable smell of blood behind, Minnie's mind flooded with questions. Why did they fight? She knew it concerned religion, yet it made no sense. Because he knew everything, she'd ask Da.

* * *

That night, Minnie balanced on the broad arms of the tartan chair, her arms wrapped around her father's neck as they basked before the fire. Between pipe sucks, Da asked questions about her first school day. She described details in a bubbly voice tinged with enthusiasm.

Then, a note of pessimism worked its way into her voice. 'An awful thing happened after school.'

Da peered deep into Minnie's eyes and flashed the kindest smile as Minnie recounted the incident. 'Kids from our school and the Catholic school yelled nasty words, threw stones, and bashed each other like the fight after Orange Day.' She rubbed her temples. 'I've thought about it and reckon both sides are silly.'

George grinned. 'Clever lass, you've figured it out.'

'But it makes no sense. Isn't it two different flavours of religion?'

'Yes, darling, well described,' said George as his chest ballooned and he flashed an encouraging smile.

The scent of lilac drifted towards them. With a face hard as stone and a voice coloured with sourness, Charlotte hissed with a rasp at the end of each syllable, 'You lecture this poor six-year-old about subjects beyond her, grabbing the chance to pedal a one-sided view.'

A flush swept across George's brow. 'But Charlotte, my lass, understands and has developed ideas herself.'

'As a parent, you must tell her the truth. We trounced the Catholics centuries ago, and they should accept their rightful place,' Charlotte said. 'Frances's illness demands our attention. These idealistic talks must wait.'

Minnie mused on Charlotte's words. They planted a determination never to be discouraged from discussing issues with

Da.

Chapter 9

The redheaded lady bustled into the cottage six weeks into the school year. During Charlotte's labour, the girls waited outside in a gentle draft perfumed by felled oat plants. They chattered, shawls fluttering as the sun and clouds vied for domination in the autumn sky. Everyone predicted a boy.

'It seems likely, as there've been four girls,' said Jeannie.

'Daughters are better, but 'tis fair Da has a companion,' said Lizzie, sporting her characteristic cheeky grin.

After several hours, the wail of a newborn spilled out, and the midwife appeared, saying, 'It's a healthy girl called Alice.'

'Another girl,' said Jeannie as they moved inside.

'Da's lucky to have five brainy daughters and Charlotte to wait on him. Soon, Alice will learn to draw his tea,' chortled Lizzie.

Minnie experienced the same awe as when Carrie had arrived. Da kissed Charlotte, patted the baby, and then looked down on mother and child with hands folded across his chest. He smiled, but Minnie thought the smile appeared hollow.

Later that evening, Minnie smelled tea and tobacco smoke. Da reclined in the tartan armchair, staring at the ceiling. She crept behind him, threaded her arms around his neck, and placed her warm palms over his eyes.

'That is my number three daughter, Minnie.'

'How did you guess?'

'Easy, I could recognise those soft wee hands anywhere.'

'Are you disappointed that our little one isn't a boy?'

'What matters is a healthy child, not the gender.' He drew his lips into a smile, but the smile didn't reach his eyes. 'There may be another baby, a laddie.'

Da's protests about his lack of disappointment didn't convince Minnie.

Minnie reflected on the contradictions of the last few weeks. Having started school, she was on the way to learning to read, and today, she had gained a sweet baby sister. Meanwhile, her dear cousin Frances wallowed on her deathbed. Da had warned them that Frances's end was approaching.

* * *

In February 1904, they gathered in a windblown churchyard covered by a thin smattering of snow. Squashed amongst a cluster of weeping, quivering women, Minnie peered into the freshly dug grave. She sensed something warm behind her. When she pivoted, she saw Da's protective arms encompassing as many women as he could reach—Aunty Sarah, Katherine, Charlotte, Jeannie, Lizzie, and Carrie. Vestments billowing, the preacher offered prayers. To Minnie, the words lacked meaning, so she allowed her mind to wander. Why a lively, youthful person? Despite her father's explanations, this disease must be a curse.

Minnie cringed as a coffin containing Frances's frail remains descended into a cavity surrounded by headstones and simple wooden crosses. Aunty Sarah's body shook as she wailed, 'My baby has gone, and I won't see her smile again.'

Minnie crept into the tartan chair next to Da on the night of the burial. He put his arm around her shoulder and pulled her into his chest. She felt comforted by the warmth that seemed to radiate through the rough texture of his jacket onto her cheeks. She raised her head. 'I'm sorry about Frances. I miss her stories and plays, but most of all, I long for my darling cousin. It is like I cry inside.' She sniffled, and her vision blurred.

Da tapped the stem of his pipe on his skull. 'Sweet lassie, none of us knows how long we have, so we should grasp every opportunity. Prepare to return to school and learn all you can.'

'I can hardly wait for school to start because I love the lessons, but my favourite is reading. Like you, Mr Underwood knows everything,' Minnie said, 'When I grow up, I want to be a schoolteacher as clever as Mr Underwood.'

'That's an excellent goal,' said Da. 'Never lose sight of it.'

Their discussion drifted to Irish emigration. Seeing this as a rare chance to chat out of Charlotte's hearing and block out the sadness, Minnie soaked up everything as she relaxed in those protective arms.

Chapter 10

In early December 1904, the redheaded lady appeared again. Protected from the freezing, rainy weather, Da and his five daughters waited by the crackling fire. Later, the midwife emerged and announced, 'Great news. It's a boy!'

George rushed to the bed and waved for the girls to follow. The sisters gaped at the newborn tucked in a carved wooden cradle. George slipped his shaking hand into Charlotte's. A bubble of hush, disturbed only by the steady echo of the infant inhaling and expelling air, hung over the space.

George joined his daughters at the crib. He shifted his weight between his legs and turned to the girls. 'This weeny baby is your brother, Samuel. What a treasure.' Unabashed, he drooled at his newborn son as the sweet fragrance of freshly washed new skin floated in the atmosphere. After feasting on the sight, he grabbed each daughter and twirled her. 'Lassies, this day's precious. I wish it could last forever.'

The infant woke, shattering the stillness with a cry that soon became a roar. George lifted the bawling bundle and handed him to Charlotte, shooing the girls from the room.

'We haven't finished looking at Sam yet,' said Lizzie.

'Sam is tiny and needs to feed, then rest.'

'We want to cuddle and play with him,' Minnie protested.

George shook with laughter. 'Minnie, there'll be plenty of time to cuddle, but now he's hungry.'

George didn't work the next day. A battery of neighbours and friends flowed in to offer congratulations and bring gifts. A gust of icy wind blasted in whenever they opened the door for a well-wisher. The guests shed protective outer layers and added them to the piles of boots, shawls, and coats at the entry. Jeannie and Lizzie made cups of tea for the callers, but many brought stronger refreshments.

As they entered, visitors congratulated Da, but some crucial people were missing. Minnie knew it must be a bittersweet occasion for Aunty Sarah and Katherine, as they still struggled with the grief of losing Frances. Minnie had often seen them staring blankly into space, with hair strands blowing across their faces. Unsure of what to say, she changed her direction to avoid them.

Elation gurgled through Minnie's veins when Katherine and Aunty Sarah appeared. She jumped up and down and embraced them. 'I'm so glad you came,' she said.

'I am here to welcome my nephew,' said Aunty as she gave an antiseptic smile.

The air became more charged with each passing minute. It peaked when those assembled with toddlers balanced on hips sang and danced. Laughter and chatter echoed.

Minnie attempted to speak but could not project her voice above the thunderous noise. She reasoned no one noticed her, so she wandered off. Out of sight, she squatted, facing the yellowing pocked wall, and released an ocean of tears onto the frigid floor.

Eventually, George sought his daughter out and knelt beside her. 'Why does my weeny princess hide and cry on this happy day?'

'Da, watching your shining smile makes me want to cry.'

'Why?' asked a confused-looking George after wiping stray wisps of hair from his forehead.

'Because you have a boy, you may not love me still.'

Da stroked Minnie's shoulders. 'Rubbish. I'm delighted to add a lad to my collection of lassies, but I love you all. In my heart, there's space aplenty for each of my children.'

The statement was music to Minnie's ears. She vaulted up and squeezed her father with all her might.

'I plan for you to practice teaching by passing your farming skills on to Sam,' said Da.

What a responsibility. Da trusts me that much! Her stomach fluttered, and Minnie stared at her father without flinching. 'I won't let you down, Da. Not only will I teach Sam, but I'll watch out for him forever.'

* * *

Minnie sprinted home with the speed of a racehorse, ignoring the sharp pain tearing through her side.

Lenna's whimpering voice carried in the breeze, 'Why don't you skip a bit after school or play with me as we stroll home?'

'I must get to my baby brother,' Minnie called over her shoulder.

Today's speedy retreat mirrored her departure each day since Sam arrived three months before. Usually an attentive student, Minnie's brain had become crammed with thoughts of the sweet boy since Sam's arrival.

When she reached her destination, she hurried into the cottage with her hand planted over the ache in her side.

Charlotte crouched over the grill, adding carrots and onions to a pot, gushing the delicious smell of stew. Minnie tugged her stepmother's apron. 'Ma, please lift Sam from his crib.'

Charlotte placed Sam in her waiting arms, and he jerked his little arms and legs. 'Bubby, Minnie's home and will play with you until the sun goes to sleep,' said Minnie. After a long session of roaring like a lion, holding Sam in bear hugs, and mooing like a cow, she jiggled him until he slept, snuggled in the crook of her neck.

When spring chased the cold and wind away, Minnie asked Charlotte if she could take Sam outside. Charlotte agreed.

Minnie sensed her insides vibrate as she prepared Sam for his first outing. To protect him from the breeze and drizzle, she smothered the boy in layers of clothing, pulled a knitted green-blue beanie down his forehead, and stretched it over his ears for the final touch. Now, she could show off her dear little brother to the field workers!

But Sam was bigger now. 'You're too heavy for sis to lump,' said Minnie. 'Sis has it figured out. There's an old peat cart in the barn, and I reckon I can use it to push you.'

The next day, Minnie walked in a fast-paced strut, pulling the cart behind her with Sam tucked inside, surrounded by a few toys. She wheeled him along between the rows of plants. Skin shining in the constant drizzle, Sam's eyes followed the workers as they hoed and raked. They cooed at the toddler. He rewarded them with a gummy grin and released a ribbon of dribble onto his chin.

Before the busy harvest, Minnie used the slack time to ramble. She wheeled Sam over the bumpy surface to the gurgling brook, where they splashed and played in the white-crested ripples of the shallows.

He was such a delightful boy. Thankfulness simmered within Minnie as she pondered her luck in having such a happy little brother.

* * *

August 1906

Minnie sprawled on the boulders that fringed the bubbling watercourse. With her skirt pulled up to her knees, she dipped her bare toes in the shallow depths. Balanced between her legs, Sam gurgled and tittered as he splashed and kicked his piggy-pink feet in the white-capped flow.

As Minnie savoured the coolness of the flowing water, she thought of the approaching autumn. It would halt these visits to the brook. Her mind flitted to Sam. Tradition mapped out his life. Like generations of Da's family, he would raise crops on this land.

Silhouettes, at first specks on the horizon, moved towards her. As they drew closer, Minnie recognised her sisters. Jeannie called when they were almost upon her, 'The redhead is here. Charlotte has had a baby boy, George Junior.'

'Sam will be jealous,' quipped Lizzie, smiling mischievously. Lizzie's words describing the event left Minnie speechless. Silence hung in the air for several long seconds, broken only by rushing water.

Jeannie must have sensed Minnie's astonishment. 'He's no longer the spoiled youngest,' she said in a voice tinged with a hint of amusement.

Lizzie chuckled, her laughter echoing over the meadow. 'Ha,

ha, you can't wait on Sam anymore because that would mean ignoring George Junior,' she teased.

Minnie scrunched her face. Deep in thought, she imagined the joy that two brothers would bring. The idea eluded Lizzie, who couldn't grasp the concept.

'That isn't right,' Minnie told Lizzie, her voice filled with conviction. 'Caring for and loving two brothers means getting twice as many kisses and cuddles.' She gently ran her fingers through Sam's mass of blonde curls, relishing their softness. 'You must use your legs so I can carry George Junior.

Turning towards Jeannie, Minnie said eagerly, 'My tummy flutters. May I take Sam to meet our new brother?'

'Not now,' Jeannie said. Charlotte and the baby sleep.'

As Jeannie and Lizzie retreated, Minnie withdrew her feet from the brook and sprawled on the turf while Sam played nearby. Twilight approached, and the last rays of the sun shone into her eyes. A breeze danced through the tree branches, making the leaves whisper to each other as she closed her eyelids and rested her splayed hands over her face.

She pondered on Lizzie's sarcastic remarks. Was her sister resentful or even jealous of her closeness with Sam? No, as always, Lizzie teased her. Her mind drifted to other events.

Her life started badly with the loss of her mother and then Frances's death, but things improved. Samuel brought happiness with him, and now another brother joined them. I hope this boy is like Sam.

Chapter 11

On a morning about halfway through the 1907 harvest, Charlotte scowled at Da. 'You can't feel rested because you tossed all night and sweated until the sheets were wet.'

Charlotte's words made Minnie's body ache with fear. It troubled her that Da seemed to find this harvest so taxing.

Minnie had first noticed Da's severe cough when working beside him. A coughing fit from deep within made his body shake and sent his scythe tumbling. Then, breathless, he'd hunched over and gasped.

She studied Da's appearance. His skin looked like soft chalk and hung off his limbs. He appeared much older because deep lines bracketed his lips, and his forehead resembled a maze of ditches.

Each evening, Da ate a smidgeon of food, then shook his head as he heaved himself out of his chair. 'I must collapse after working hard.' After he headed to bed, the family gathered at the hearth. Minnie missed the rich aroma of Da's pipe, forever a sign of his presence in the room. Questions raced around her mind, but no one discussed Da's condition.

Da's cough resembled the coughs spluttered by Frances before she'd died. No, no, no. Not that. The hacking would go away if she didn't consider it. Wouldn't it?

When the workload eased at the end of the harvest, Da's condition didn't improve. His cough worsened until it took on a rasping ring. He avoided the harvest celebrations. 'Too tiring,' he protested.

Sprawled on the bed, Minnie and her older sisters chatted about school, the weather, and Sam's recent antics. The conversation shifted to their father's weight loss, the spluttering that trailed him like a pet dog, and his never-ending exhaustion.

'Da has the *white plague* but hasn't told us,' Lizzie said in her usual forthright manner.

Minnie's stomach churned with disbelief. 'I can't believe it. It just can't be true!' She covered her ears with her hands and rushed outside.

Inhaling the bracing twilight air, infused with the scent of fallen plants, she leaned against a pile of rugged rocks for support. It felt like her entire being had turned to ice, her heart and blood frozen. Rainwater trickled down her neck, causing her collar to chafe against her neck.

Maybe it wasn't the *white plague* after all. It was just a chest infection, like Leena's grandparents had. Such a deadly disease couldn't possibly afflict her father, her hero and mentor. It had already taken so much from her, and she couldn't bear to lose more.

Memories of Frances's last days flashed through her mind—the skeletal figure, the rasping chest, and the horrifying bursts of blood. *She refused to accept that Da carried this dreaded illness and would meet the same gruesome fate.*

* * *

All the signs point to consumption, thought George, as he curled in his tartan fireside chair. He followed news of tuberculous research, a habit formed when Mary had fallen ill.

Winter had arrived, bringing stinging winds, beating rain, and skies stacked with grey clouds. The family, as usual, confined themselves indoors for the worst of the cold weather. They warmed themselves before the fire as the violent wind and raindrops hammered on the window panes.

George's eyes panned the room. He paused for a long minute to study each of his children. He gazed at Jeannie, thinking how quickly his eldest daughter approached womanhood. His eyes stopped at George Junior, who slumbered tucked under quilts. The lad wouldn't remember his Da if the *white plague* took him. George wondered if Sam would recall him. They were such a wonderful family, but how would they manage without him?

The patter of tiny feet sounded. He looked up and saw Carrie, her face smothered with a concerned smile. 'We know how hard it has been with you working with that naughty cough,' she said, a solemn tone rising in her infantile voice. 'Minnie, Lizzie, Jeannie, and I have been talking. We're going to spoil you during winter and make you well. Lizzie has pushed rags in cracks so the angry wind cannot sneak in.'

'Thank you, darling. I'm lucky to have a team of pretty nurses.'

Chapter 12

Christmas 1907 was a quiet affair. Something inside George whispered that this would be the last festive lunch. Deep within, he knew the truth, but for the sake of his family, he wanted to stay positive and fight.

An impressive array of tasty food—glazed ham, roast potato and carrots, soda bread, and creamy butter—graced the table. It looked and smelled delicious. Although his stomach rumbled at the sight of the spread and its rich and tempting aroma, George could only summon the will to eat the tiniest portion.

George was unhappy when Jeannie carved the poultry, something he did every year. He growled, 'Am I reduced to uselessness?' Jeannie stuttered, and a visible lump appeared in her throat. 'I didn't mean to hurt you, Da. I just wanted to help.' She hung her head low and turned her back towards George.

Feeling ashamed of his behaviour, George pushed his seat back from the table and took a few steps towards Jeannie so they could talk. 'I'm sorry for the hurtful remark, my darling Jeannie. My illness has been getting to me, and it's no excuse. I guess it's self-pity,' he said.

Charlotte, watching the scene unfold, had given up hope,

and the lines bracketing her mouth showed it.

* * *

Spring 1908 approached. Thin gossamer clouds replaced the bleak winter ones. When seeding began, George groaned as he hauled himself from the bed.

On arrival at the fields, heavy with the earthy odour of tilled soil, he burst out in a furious coughing fit. 'Must be age, rattling like an old-timer.' He wanted to conceal his symptoms because of the fear of consumption that swamped the community.

The workers exchanged glances and rolled their eyes in disbelief. Later, he overheard a whispered conversation between two co-workers. 'George has the cough and all the signs of *the dreaded*,' said one worker.

A reply tinged with certainty came. 'The monster revisits.'

After a violent coughing fit a few days later, George spewed out a wad of blood-tinged phlegm, something he knew to be an advanced symptom of the unmentionable. He consulted the doctor in Toome, who made the expected diagnosis. George sensed his facial muscles tighten but accepted the inevitable, vowing to do all he could to ease the family's load.

When he arrived home, George told Charlotte. In a resigned tone, he said, 'I saw the doctor today, and he told me I suffer from consumption and won't have long to go.' Charlotte embraced him, holding her husband in a vice-like grip. When she released him, her lips arched into a slight smile. 'We've had our trials but respected each other's views.'

The conversation moved to the future. George sensed moisture pool in his eyes, and his throat tightened with emotion. 'What lies ahead for those unfortunate youngsters makes my heart hammer,' said George, his voice quivering. He wiped his clammy hands against his trousers as he considered the plight of his three elder daughters, who would become orphans on his death. 'I want to ask you something,' he stammered, his voice barely audible. But he couldn't find the words to complete the sentence. However, he and Charlotte held each other's gazes as wordless communication passed between them. For several long moments, the only sound in the room was the soft crackling of the fire.

'I'll continue caring for Jeannie, Lizzie, and Minnie,' said Charlotte.

George exhaled, feeling a weight lift off his shoulders. His heart swelled with admiration for Charlotte's courage in confronting problems. He looked into her eyes, the flickering light from the fireplace dancing in their depths. 'Thank you so much. No words to describe the comfort your promise brings. I fret about all the children, especially the older three girls.'

'You can leave this world without concerns about your lasses.'

Exhausted, breathless, and sizzling hot, George limped to bed. His body tensed at the thought of never seeing his children again. They faced a grim future, and he dreaded breaking the traumatic news. But this he must do.

* * *

Battling a raging fever and a shooting pain stabbing his chest, George spent the night thinking of the daunting task that lay before him. The very thought sent bolts of apprehension through his limbs.

As he fought with the sheets, he planned the kindest way to break the unwelcome news. Finding words that relayed the truth without inflicting too much despair posed a challenge. His head swam. Coughing and spluttering, George shuffled around the house all day, rehearsing his lines. He sensed tears well in his eyes, aware he would never get the words perfect.

The family ate champ, a local specialty potato pancake, and boiled vegetables that evening. When they finished, Charlotte carried George Junior as she led Alice and Samuel to bed.

As George limped to his chair, a voice within him screamed, *I cannot do this. It is too hard!* As if to underscore his tortured mood, he gazed at a starless sky. The only noises were the fire crackling and the splatter of raindrops outside.

He saw four pairs of wide blue eyes stare at him. Soon, he would never see these precious lasses again. He choked back the lump clogging his throat as the foursome followed him to the hearth. Carrie bounded onto his lap and buried her face in his shoulder while the other three crouched at the chair's base.

He opened his mouth several times, but his vocal cords wouldn't function. On the third attempt, stuttered speech found a path from his lips. 'I have dreadful news. I suffer the *white plague* and will last only a few months.'

As the dreadful truth emerged, an uncanny silence closed in. Carrie shattered the silence with an agonised wail. Carrie's reaction made George feel his insides were being torn out, piece by piece. He looked down at the other three girls, faces streaked with tears. Jeannie, looking terrified, sprung up and planted herself on the chair's wide padded arms. 'Oh Da, we feared this but hoped you didn't suffer the *white plague.*'

Lizzie squeezed into the space beside Jeannie and wrapped

her arms around her sister's waist. She gazed at her father. Between sobs, she stuttered, 'Yes, we saw you were skinny and coughed. We crossed our fingers and hoped for a chest infection.'

George wrung his hands as his gaze moved between Jeannie and Lizzie's red, swollen eyes. 'You wonderful lasses didn't deserve this after growing up motherless. I have endeavoured to be both mother and father to you. It's been a pleasure being your Da and imparting values of perseverance, hard work, and tolerance. Please promise to live by those values.'

They answered by peering into their father's eyes and gulping.

Charlotte tiptoed into the room. She loosened Carrie's grip on her father, lifted her from his lap, and carried the weeping child to bed.

George's pulse quickened, and a mass formed in his stomach when he noticed that Minnie, jaw dropped and face colourless, remained crouched on the floor. He beckoned to her and gestured to his lap. She hurled herself onto it, bursting into heart-wrenching sobs, and burrowed into his chest. He ran his rough hand down her hair, wondering if this lass were brave enough for the uphill battle the future would bring.

She lifted her face from her father's chest and slapped her hands over her ears. 'I don't believe it. Please, please, Da, tell me it is not true.' She searched her father's eyes. 'Would it be different if I'm extra good, Da?'

George's blood froze. 'I'm sorry, but even that can't save me.' Although his voice failed initially, more words eventually came as a breathy sigh. 'Stay brave despite the odds. Memorise these words and never forget them.'

After making this pronouncement, George went to bed and

never left it again.

Chapter 13

The weak morning sun filtered through the half-drawn curtains, casting a pale glow into the dimly lit room where George's lifeless body lay. Sarah gently shook the five girls awake, their white linen nightdresses clinging to their bodies as they stirred from their slumber. Tangles of uncombed hair cascaded down their shoulders, framing their tear-streaked cheeks.

As the girls joined hands, forming a solemn ring around the bed, Minnie's gaze moved from one sister to the next. Their ashen faces and bloodshot eyes mirrored her grief. A soft voice drifted from behind, cutting through the heavy silence. It was Charlotte, standing alongside Aunty Sarah, a few steps away. Tears trickled down their cheeks as they spoke.

'Aunty Sarah has tirelessly supported us through these dark days,' Charlotte said, choked with emotion. Minnie turned, her eyes meeting her stepmother's tortured gaze. 'She has taken turns with me to watch over your father when he was too weak even to lift his head or speak.'

Minnie struggled to focus on Charlotte's words; her mind clouded with anger towards the merciless disease that had stolen so much from her. It had now claimed her dearest treasure, her father. A gut-wrenching howl escaped her lips, reverberating in the room. 'Da, Da, please wake up,' she cried, her voice filled with desperation. 'I don't deserve this punishment! I need you; I can't bear to live without you.'

Her pulse pounded in her ears, the rapid thudding drowning out the sounds of her sobs. Clinging tightly to her father's lifeless body, her clammy hands refused to let go until Aunty Sarah pulled her away. 'Minnie, we must accept what has happened,' she said softly, her voice coloured with sorrow.

'But Aunty Sarah,' Minnie pleaded, her voice choked with grief. 'I want him back. I can't imagine living without him.' Grief hung heavy in the air as the weight of their loss enveloped them all.

'Sobbing will not restore him to life. I'm sorry, darling.'

'This greedy sickness steals the people I love,' said Minnie as harrowing thoughts about the void this loss left circled her head. A giddy feeling overtook her.

A gloomy shadow rippled across Sarah's forehead. 'The disease runs rife. It has touched us all with its fury.'

'Why, my Da? Now, no one will cuddle me before the fire and answer my questions.'

'Darling, accept that your father has gone, but remember, you were a source of pride to him,' said Aunty Sarah. Arms encircling Minnie, she knelt and rocked her niece from side to side. 'He'll look down on you, so keep up your helpful behaviour.'

Panic chased Minnie as she wriggled from Aunty Sarah's arms musing about her future, as well as Jeannie and Lizzie's. Charlotte owes us nothing. Dread prickled Minnie's skin. What will we do if she casts us out? Where will we go, an orphanage? Shivers ran down her spine as she envisaged no longer romping with and playing mammy for Sam and George

Junior. She sighed, relieved that the boys slept and were not part of this sad scene.

Minnie spent the day roaming the cottage, stroking and inhaling the residual smells of Da's belongings—pipe, well-worn boots, tea mug, cap, and braces. She ate nothing and noticed Charlotte didn't touch a morsel of the supper she'd prepared.

* * *

Minnie squatted with Sam and George Junior a few days later, building a tower of yellow wooden blocks. The dimming light signalled that the rest of the family would soon return from the fields. She turned her gaze to the boys. George Junior had fallen asleep on the hard floor, thumb in mouth and legs splayed wide. She looked at Sam and pointed. 'We've made a tall gold castle.'

The tall tower shook at the top and threatened to tumble. Face smothered with a cheeky grin, Sam reached the pinnacle and doubled over in laughter as he sent the tower crashing. He and Minnie got to work rebuilding their creation.

Both were deep in concentration when Minnie saw Charlotte and Aunty Sarah wander in, shed their capes, and settle down to enjoy tea together. The women didn't notice Minnie, the slumbering George Junior, or the playful Sam.

The two hunched over their cups of tea and conversed. Eyes pinched closed, Minnie took shallow breaths and soaked up every word Charlotte and Aunty Sarah said.

'I'm not afraid of fieldwork; the older lasses will help, and Minnie gained cropping experience from years of shadowing George. As a team, we're capable of an impressive day's work.

Still, I lack knowledge of farm management—the seasons, protecting maturing crops from frost, and the most favourable time to harvest,' said Charlotte. 'I hate to imagine what I would do with a scythe, probably cut someone's finger off. And the horses would trot off, dragging me with the plough.'

Aunty Sarah let out a booming chortle. 'My daughter and I can give you lessons.'

'Thank you, Sarah. Your generosity through this crisis leaves me wordless. And you wrestle with your demons.'

Charlotte's words were music to Minnie. She, Jeannie, and Lizzie featured in the plans. Minnie's body relaxed as if poison had drained from her veins, and she was eager to share this welcome news with Jeannie and Lizzie.

Regret filled those same veins over her past thoughts about her stepmother. *Hidden beneath Charlotte's steel mask lived generosity and softness.*

* * *

Following a dour graveside service, they buried Da's remains a week after his death.

Nature staged a gloomy day. Although it was summer, dark clouds inhabited the sky. They unburdened themselves of more drizzle than usual. A rapid wind swept the countryside, flattening the long grass and reeds.

The gathering recited prayers in solemn tones in what seemed to Minnie to be slow motion. She recognised the blessings from Frances's burial but gained no comfort from the words. The oration of 'ashes to ashes and dust to dust' sounded like a perplexing riddle. *What does it mean? How can it tell anyone about what Da meant to us?*

Jeannie, Lizzie, and Minnie stood at the grave's edge, grasping each other. Alice and Carrie squatted in front. Charlotte sheltered under an umbrella at the rear. Neighbours and friends lined the opposite side, raindrops soaking their best clothes. However, they kept their distance from George's family. Faces turned down, they fastened their gaze on the ground, their fingernails or ill-fitting shoes—anything except Minnie's family.

Minnie wished she would wake from this nightmare, safe in her father's arms, but she could not escape the truth. The coffin containing the father she loved above all else descended into a cavity surrounded by mounds of moist earth.

Minnie's legs turned limp as rags, but she willed herself to remain upright. She felt her blood rush and the air suspended in her choked lungs. As mourners scattered soil, Minnie let out a soft yelp of pain.

At eleven, her childhood had ended.

Chapter 14

After the finality of Da's burial, Minnie couldn't sleep, eat, or function. It took Charlotte a lot of scolding and cajoling to get her moving. 'Although your father is not with us, we must plant, fertilise, and harvest the crops.'

Each dawn, Minnie joined Jeannie and Lizzie as they followed Charlotte through the morning mist to the crops. All four wore a uniform of an ankle-length red hooded cape with hair tucked into the collar. Minnie laced her arms around her chest because her billowing cape and the clothing beneath failed to block the chill of the blistering breeze.

The four worked hard until the sun went down, tending to the soil, removing weeds, and cutting mature plants. They harvested flax using the traditional method of pulling the plants by the roots. The girls had a hard time pulling out the plants, and the ground made a gurgling sound. Foul-smelling mud covered the roots, and some worms came out.

Throughout the day, Minnie's sisters questioned her, 'Is this a sprout, a new plant, or a weed?' and 'How can I prevent this slimy worm from eating this plant?' Minnie felt proud when she could answer these questions. She had learned much from her father, and if she didn't know the answer, she looked up at the sky and asked him. 'It annoyed me how Minnie followed Da like a puppy,' Minnie caught Lizzie murmur to Jeannie. 'Now it's handy that she picked up so much.

A laughing Jeannie turned towards Minnie and Lizzie. 'We're pretending to be men, doing the work of male farmhands.'

Charlotte straightened from her hunched position. Lines bracketed her mouth, and she cackled with a hint of cynicism. 'Maybe we don't need men. Women can do anything.'

* * *

Winter entered with a vengeance, the temperature daily dropping to below zero. The whistling wind, sharp with frost, nipped Minnie's nose and ears until they were red. Although protected by wool and leather, her hands and feet froze.

At the onset of the cold weather, they needed to buy horse manure and allow it to decompose for fertiliser. A few days before it became too chilly to work outside, they heard creaks and clunks as a cart drawn by a draught horse and stinking of manure trundled towards them. The local driver, Pat Donnelly, tightened the reins and groaned as he struggled from the jockey seat.

'Tis cold. Would freeze that scarecrow,' Pat said, his knobbed finger pointing to the sole occupant of the empty fields. 'The fast wind isn't good for my arthritis; it freezes the weary bones. Never known such a chill. Other old-timers have never seen winter this nippy.' He unloaded his foul-smelling cargo before climbing into the cart and flicking the reins.

I'm right. It is freezing! Minnie thought.

The next day, it snowed. Sam and George Junior ran to the window to watch the snowflakes falling and forming a thick, white carpet on the ground.

It had been four months since their father had passed away. We made it through the season, Minnie thought. Can we keep going?

* * *

In the frigid January air, Minnie eased open the ancient, creaking door in response to a persistent rap.

As the door swung open, she recoiled. Aunty Sarah stood on the doorstep, her trembling knees knocking together and her teeth chattering. Snowflakes freckled her dishevelled garments and clung to strands of damp hair that hung limply over her shoulders. Her haunted eyes brimmed with tears, and a pink hue from the cold rimmed her nostrils. She attempted to speak, but her sniffling only muffled her stuttered words.

Jeannie and Lizzie, motionless as statues, flanked Minnie, their expressions frozen with wariness. Charlotte rushed forward, extending a steadying hand to her distraught sister-in-law. She guided her towards the nearby table. With a comforting touch, Charlotte slid a chair under Sarah, taking a seat beside her and stroked her trembling hand. 'What's wrong?' she implored, her voice filled with concern.

Sarah, unable to control her emotions, released tortured sobs, her cries echoing through the room. 'Allow me to make you a hot cup of tea; it will help soothe your nerves, and then we can talk,' Charlotte offered. Sarah declined the tea and buried her head in her upturned hands, creating a cocoon from which her agonised wailing emerged. Charlotte paced back and forth, her agitation palpable. 'Please, Sarah,' she pleaded, her voice tinged with urgency, 'Take a deep breath and confide in me. I cannot assist you if you don't share the cause of this uncontrollable bawling and trembling.'

Sarah remained bent over the table, but some stuttered sounds were audible above the crying. 'My child is ill. My baby, the only one I have left.'

Charlotte's voice lost its hard edge, and gentleness flirted with her words. 'Please tell me what's wrong with her? I love that lass.'

Sarah raised her head but focused on her hands, clenching and unclenching them. 'Katherine's wheezing and complaining of tiredness. She has been sick for two months and now has a gurgling chest, boiling fevers, is always tired, and has lost weight.'

Sarah's description triggered a bolt of numbness up Minnie's spine. She, her sisters, and her stepmother exchanged knowing glances.

Charlotte broke the silence but did not mention the name of the dreaded. 'Terrible news, but you're not alone,' she said. 'We'll do all we can for dear Katherine and support you as you've supported us. Have you consulted a doctor?'

Sarah sniffled while trying to stop the fluid from dripping from her nose. With quivering lips, she said, 'I prefer ignorance, so there's still hope. If a doctor diagnoses the *white plague*, then hope is dead.'

As always, Charlotte was practical. She advised, 'This is terrible, but calm down. Let's get medical advice and focus on caring for Katherine.'

Sarah sprang from her seat and walked a few steps to the bristly internal wall. As she leaned on it, she burst into a tirade punctuated by heart-wrenching wails, 'This hideous disease has robbed me of everything I treasure. It murdered my brother, my firstborn, and now it's turned to my other child. Forget George's talk about fancy scientists and bacteria. The *graveyard cough* is a curse that stalks my family, intent on claiming as many as possible. Why, why, why?'

When Sarah left, Minnie contemplated the dreadful news. *This awful disease keeps chasing us and robbing us of dear ones. Will it ever stop? Who will be next?*

* * *

A few days after Sarah's visit, the three sisters gathered around the hearth with Charlotte, making plans for the coming season's crop. The four younger children played on the floor, not straying far from the fire's warmth.

Charlotte blinked while adding peat turf to the blaze. She opened her lips as if to speak, then closed her mouth. After repeating this action several times, in hurried speech, she announced, 'In March, I expect another child conceived before your father's passing.' She fiddled with wisps of her wavy hair that had broken free of her bun. 'Unfortunate timing, but not planned.'

Minnie looked at the floor's flagstones. She took some shallow breaths until Lizzie kept the discussion moving. 'Terrible timing is an understatement. In March, we plant for the season's crop. And because of Katherine's sickness, we may need to sow seeds on Aunty Sarah's farm.'

'My pregnancy isn't a disease,' said Charlotte. 'I'll carry my share of the load except the few days before and after the birth, like my other pregnancies.'

With a flourish of her hand, she dismissed the girls. As they pulled themselves from their chairs, a hunched Sam wandered over. His hands clasped his stomach, and he looked forlorn. 'Ma, my tummy aches'

* * *

Within a week, Sam's face flushed with exhaustion; his forehead creased as he gazed at Minnie, and his eyes reflected pain. 'My belly hurts, Sis. Please help me,' he pleaded, rubbing his abdomen. Minnie gently touched his stomach, which felt as tight as a drum.

In a few days, she noticed that George Junior had the same pale and sickly appearance. Both boys moved around with blank expressions, barely showing signs of life until almost the end of February. 'Let's put them to bed and hope that rest will help these poor little ones,' Charlotte suggested.

They alternated caring for the boys in the cottage, which slowed down the fieldwork as the already insufficient work-force dwindled. When Minnie took her turn in the fields, she returned to find the feverish lads curled up in sweat-soaked bedclothes. Sometimes, they would cry out in agony, while other times, they seemed utterly unresponsive. With trembling hands, Minnie attempted to feed them spoons of soup through their cracked lips. However, as soon as the soup reached their mouths, they vomited.

Despite the attention heaped on them, the boys showed no improvement. Minnie shared her concerns with Jeannie. 'If they don't recover, my heart will break.

Jeannie listened sympathetically but gave a resigned half-smile. She drew Minnie close and embraced her for a long moment. 'We all love our boys, but we must face whatever happens. All we can do is continue the tender care and hope.'

Chapter 15

'Jeannie, fetch the redhead and be quick. This pain rips me apart,' cried Charlotte.

Jeannie cantered, slamming the door with a thundering bang. Minnie and Lizzie wiped the sweat from the gasping Charlotte's forehead.

Thankfulness rushed through Minnie when Jeannie appeared, the midwife in tow. Shaking, she grabbed a ragged shawl and shot outside, leaning against a stone wall to brace herself against the rapid spring breeze. As the sun descended, she thought about the strain of adding the needs of a newborn to their overtaxed workload.

Minnie froze, and she choked back bile when the whimper of a baby echoed. The midwife appeared and called, 'Another little girl.'

Minnie clenched her teeth in a false smile but held back the words orbiting her brain. *Please, please take it away. We don't want a baby. Our sweet brothers are ill, and we have too many to feed.*

As soon as the midwife retreated, Minnie, hand clapped across her mouth, ran to the edge of the field. She fell to her knees and heaved the contents of her stomach onto the ground. When she finished retching, she wiped her face with a handkerchief and plodded inside.

She joined Lizzie and Jeannie at Charlotte's bedside. Sheepishly, Carrie hid behind Jeannie's skirt. Jeannie smiled, but the smile seemed phony. 'We're going to call her Adeline,' Jeannie announced. Blood smeared the floor, its coppery reek clogged the air, and their stepmother looked ashen white.

'Ma must have bedrest for several weeks,' said the redhead.

Carrie shot a pleading glance. 'We need to spread seeds. Our brothers are sick, Ma's unwell, and we have this weenie bub to care for.'

The woman entered the boy's room and re-emerged, brow covered in frown lines, with a handkerchief clamped over her nose. She dug out a bottle and teat from her Gladstone bag, thrust them at the girls, and instructed them to use them to feed the baby goat's milk. 'Slips of lasses cannot manage, so call kin,' she said, her voice raised to a high-pitched boom.

Without clearing the bloody mess, she rushed to the door.

A stunned silence swallowed the cottage, and a nervous anxiety snaked through Minnie. Carrie and Alice broke the muteness by whimpering and shedding enough tears to fill a dam.

Minnie wrung her hands as she drummed her feet. 'We'll die. Three sick, leaving not enough to spread seeds, and we cannot turn to Aunty Sarah with Katherine ill.'

Jeannie said, 'The local people are kind underneath. They'll forget their fear and come to our aid.'

Under her breath, Minnie whispered, 'I hope you're right.'

* * *

The next morning, Minnie went to replenish their turf supplies. She gazed from the turf house across grazing livestock to the neighbouring fields, her shawl billowing in the breeze. A team of workers raked the tilled chocolate moist soil, spread seeds, and dug trenches. Children waved their arms and made cat noises to circling birds who attempted to swoop and snatch a meal for themselves. Minnie thought the lively scene heralded that the entire district was busy planting the season's crop, which was not good news for them.

She remembered the purpose of her trek and, with a pile of peat briquettes secured under each arm, raced towards the cottage. She flung the door open and burst into the warm house. Inside, Lizzie, face folded in concentration, bottle-fed the newborn. Although it took the baby ages, she emptied the contents.

Seated upright at the table, Jeannie beckoned Lizzie and Minnie. 'There have been no offers, so it looks like we are preparing for farming, housework, and nursing,' she said confidently, but her brow showed a web of worry lines.

Minnie raised an eyebrow. 'I told you so. Everyone seemed occupied when I went to the turf house to collect some peat. I don't believe they're about to rush and help.'

'We must prepare to do everything by writing a roster, and if helpers appear, we thank our lucky stars,' said Jeannie. 'Minnie, grab a pencil and paper. Lizzie, please search for a calendar.' Jeannie took the pencil in hand. 'I suggest two do farm work each week and the other housework, including nursing Charlotte, Adeline, and the lads.'

Minnie trembled and sensed goosebumps form on the back of her arms. 'I want Da back. He would guide us through these problems. Lizzie and I should go to school, but we struggle with jobs that adults find difficult. Da wanted me to become a teacher.'

'Da is not returning, but he would expect us to apply his teachings about resilience. Our beloved brothers, who cannot rise from their sickbeds, depend on us,' said Jeannie. 'If we do nothing, we starve to death.'

'I suggest Minnie stays in the house, does the housework, and cares for the three ill ones,' said Lizzie solemnly. 'She's so close to the boys, like their second mother.'

Minnie had never loved Lizzie so much. She had always suspected that despite her teasing remarks, her sister understood her special bond with their brothers. Thankfulness pulsed through her veins.

* * *

The sick ones did not improve, and the local folk kept their distance.

Minnie and Lizzie put aside the classroom for farming, housekeeping, and nursing. Every morning, Minnie farewelled Jeannie and Lizzie as they unlatched the door to a howling wind and shuffled out into the fields. She crammed the rest of the day with cooking, sweeping, doing the laundry, bottle-feeding Adeline, and caring for Charlotte and the lads.

Minnie didn't see Jeannie and Lizzie until dusk when the mud-smothered girls dragged their feet into the cottage. After polishing off a meal of mutton, mashed potatoes, and boiled vegetables, the younger ones scampered to bed while Jeannie, Lizzie, and Minnie warmed themselves next to the fire.

'The wind blew savagely today, ripping through our clothes,' said Jeannie.

Lizzie placed her upturned hands on her lap. 'My poor palms.

Yesterday's blisters burst, but today, more appeared. Gigantic bruises and scratches cover my feet. Want to see?'

'Oh, Lizzie, we could do without a private viewing of your stinking feet,' snapped Jeannie, her eyes heavy with exhaustion. She reached over and rested her hand on Lizzie's knee. 'Better sleep so we can start early and add to the blister collection.'

The hair on the back of Minnie's neck stood on end as she stared at her sisters' overtaxed bodies. It wasn't fair that they'd had this work forced on them. At least Jeannie and Lizzie got an undisturbed sleep compared to her fitful one, broken by Sam and George Junior's cries of suffering and Adeline's clockwork whimpers for her four-hourly feeds. Charlotte still couldn't rise from her bed.

The next day, their trials sank to a new depth. 'The light stings and stabs my eyes. I feel bad. Please help me,' cried Sam. Aided by Jeannie and Lizzie, Minnie strung dark material over the windows of the boys' bedroom.

Their agonised cries dominated the following days as they writhed on the crumpled sheets in the velvet darkness of the cave-like room. Minnie saw nothing but pain when she gazed into her brothers' eyes. Charlotte continued to wallow in her bed.

Hopelessness overtook Minnie. As she knelt, circling a moist cloth on George Junior's forehead, she arranged her hands in a steeple shape and flung her head upwards. 'Please, God, spare my brothers. I love them, and I've been through a lot for a young lass. Both my parents and other loved ones died from that terrible disease. *Please, God, no more!*'

* * *

As the days merged, the girls' load didn't lessen. Minnie found it hard to drag herself from bed each morning, but she knew they would starve if she retreated under the blankets.

Minnie and Jeannie strolled to Moneyglass to buy a replacement teat for Adeline's bottle when a group of barefoot boys wearing shabby clothes and sporting bruises, cuts, and snotty noses pounced from behind a barn. Hands in pockets, they blocked the entire path.

As they neared, Jeannie said politely, 'Excuse us.'

But the lads moved until they were so close that Minnie could smell onions on their breath. A fire of hatred shone from their eyes. 'You are little witches,' one said.

Minnie stared dumbfounded, but the gang continued ridiculing them. 'Your mother, father, and cousin died from the *graveyard cough*. Your clan breeds the monstrous disease, sending it to target the rest of us.'

Minnie poised to lunge, but Jeannie held her back. Minnie freed herself from Jeannie's grip enough to stamp her feet. 'It is not true.'

'Is so. My da says the jinx grows on your farm, and a rotten pong floats out. It could be something your bad-tempered stepmother brought from Derry.'

The boys disappeared as quickly as they'd come. Jeannie threw protective arms around Minnie. 'Take no notice. They're ignorant and only repeating what they hear.'

When they reached Moneyglass, Minnie entered a store as Jeannie rested on the low, crumbling wall outside. The shopkeeper scowled. 'Get out. I don't want your type in my shop. You aim to spread the *white plague*.'

Heat surged to Minnie's neck and face as she fled onto the pavement, where stunned bystanders gawked. She wanted to melt into the cobblestones, run or die, anything, but her feet refused to move. Relief flooded her when she sniffed the distinctive perfume of Jeannie's body and felt her sister's arm resting on her elbow. Jeannie guided her through onlookers to home.

Sam and George Junior didn't improve, but Adeline thrived. She guzzled the goat's milk, which worked wonders. As time passed, Minnie viewed her as a blessing rather than the burden she'd seemed initially.

Minnie fretted about her sick brothers, and she missed school. *Will I ever return?* Every night, I dream Da has returned, but he doesn't. *Can I escape from this hard slog of a life?*

Chapter 16

April 1909

Minnie sniffed lilac. With the gait of a much older woman, Charlotte, skin grey and drawn, limped from her sickbed. Pain etched the deep lines on her gaunt face; she hastened to the boys' bedsides through the ever-present pungent odour of sickness.

Her jaw clenched, and her hands shook as she looked at her sons. Palm pressed to her breast, she reeled, bracing herself against the wall. She regained her balance and pushed herself up.

'They are sick with a fever, constant vomiting and diarrhoea, and light sensitivity. Minnie has taken excellent care of them,' said Jeannie. 'There is no wheezing or coughing. Hopefully, that means we can rule out the *graveyard cough*.'

Charlotte placed her palm on George Junior's forehead, wincing as she removed her hand. 'The poor wee chap sizzles,' she said as she shifted her gaze to Sam. After she studied the limp, sweat-ridden bodies of her sons, she muttered, 'I'm sorry I couldn't care for you, my darlings. Mammy has recovered and will go to Toome to seek help.'

In the morning, a doctor, an older fellow with a shock of silver hair, arrived. As a watch chain swung over his ample tummy, he examined the lads as the girls looked on. Charlotte stayed in the background, speaking only to answer questions, horror in her eyes. The doctor studied the pair through compassionate brown eyes, a frown lining his face.

He turned to Charlotte. 'I believe your sons have tuberculous meningitis.' He explained, 'Infants in contact with consumption victims can contract it. Unlike consumption, which attacks the lungs, this condition affects the spinal fluid, leading to pressure on the brain. Even if they survive, their lives might not be worth living. I'm sorry.'

Minnie took a few steps backward and leaned against the wall. She watched as a shadow of dread moved over Charlotte's drained features, and she said below her breath, 'The monster disease had tried to trick us by changing into something else, and now it wants to gobble my brothers.'

'I wish I had better news, but unfortunately, there's little hope,' said the doctor. He instructed them on how to keep the lads comfortable: 'Growing evidence suggests this condition is contagious, so limit contact and place a cloth over your mouth and nose. You should change the sheets at least once daily and then wash them in boiling water.'

As the door creaked closed, Charlotte burst out, 'It is as if a scythe has cut my heart into a thousand pieces.' She wept into her lap while the crying Jeannie, Lizzie, Minnie, Carrie, and Alice circled her.

Minnie shook her head. 'I cannot live without those lads.'

But Charlotte still held hope. 'We must pray for a miracle.'

* * *

No miracle came. Before slipping into unconsciousness, the boys' heads swelled until they were too large for their frail bodies. Although the doctor warned them to expect this, the sight made Minnie's stomach drop. She could barely recognise her dear brothers.

Charlotte camped beside their beds, watching over their fever-ravaged bodies. Jeannie, Lizzie, and Minnie took turns keeping her company through the long nights, often falling asleep on their chairs.

The sun descended below the mountains on 22 April. Thick clouds covered the moon and stars, creating a funeral black sky. Charlotte signalled to the girls to farewell George Junior. 'Wee George makes gurgling sounds. His chest rattles with what is called the death rattle. Say your goodbyes.'

Later, with the toddler wrapped in a rug, Charlotte held him to her and paced. 'My poor baby, you didn't deserve this.' A waterfall of tears fell, reaching her son's pallid skin.

As the bird calls signalled the start of the day, an eerie quietness shrouded the dwelling, and George Junior's brief journey ended. Charlotte clung to the wrapped bundle. Although Jeannie pointed to the boy's peaceful look, Charlotte refused to part with him.

'He's gone, Ma,' Jeannie whispered. 'He is with God now, in a better place.' She prised the infant from her.

A sour taste rose in Minnie's throat as sorrow spiked in her stomach. One boy she'd nurtured was dead in his mother's arms. With a bear-sized skull, the other lay unconscious, destined to join his brother.

Minnie listened as the distraught Charlotte prayed aloud. 'Dear God, I have suffered more than my fair share of trauma and trials. The terrible illness claimed my husband and son, and now it aims to snatch my other son. Please restore him to health and spare him from death.'

Despite Charlotte's pleas, the inevitable happened six short days later. As little Sam drew his last breath, Charlotte sobbed. The girls joined hands and cried.

* * *

Not long after, they bowed their heads behind another coffin, this time for their cousin, Katherine. A preacher recited prayers, and they sprinkled soil on her casket. Minnie fumed at the all-too-familiar empty words. How can they mean anything? *I can't understand why a loving God would do this to my family.*

Outside, new spring life bloomed. Delicate green shoots broke through moist earth, leaves sprouted from naked branches, and the fragrance of wildflowers danced. Within the cottage walls, tears flowed for the three young lives taken by the *robber of youth.*

Has this string of disasters destroyed my stepmother? If she goes too, will we survive? Who'll be next? These unbearable questions consumed Minnie.

The cruel losses dampened Charlotte's spirits. She didn't venture outside the house for several weeks and played no role in the fields. Instead, she spent her day slumped in an armchair, staring into the fire. Although she ate just a few crumbs, she drank so much tea that the odour flooded the cottage. Sometimes, she wiped moisture from the corner of her eyes but didn't explain.

One evening, Minnie and her older sisters gathered around Charlotte. In a soft voice, Jeannie said gingerly, 'Lizzie,

Minnie, and I are worried about your mood. We need to talk about the future.'

Charlotte's eyes burned with anger. 'I've suffered the most horrid experiences imaginable. That killer disease murdered my husband before robbing me of watching my sons grow. As the boys sizzled on their deathbeds, I lay in a bed of pain because of birth complications, and poor Adeline fought for each breath.'

Minnie and Lizzie stroked their stepmother's trembling hands. 'You hurt, but so do we because we grieve for our brothers. Unless we confront our troubles, more disasters will destroy those left,' said Lizzie in an uncharacteristic solemn voice.

Charlotte gave a taunt smile. 'Such wisdom from a wee one. I'll get back to the fields.'

Admiration for her stepmother flooded Minnie. 'Ma, you're brave; nothing stops you.'

'It's necessary, darling, because we need food and clothes. No harvest means hunger,' said Charlotte with steely resolve.

Jeannie's lips curled upwards. 'We were worried you'd lost your courage, but you haven't.'

Charlotte gave a cynical half-smile. 'The need to eat always wins.'

'Don't hurry. Take a walk daily for a few days before your return. One of us will come with you,' said Jeannie.

Charlotte agreed, and each afternoon, Charlotte wandered with Minnie by her side. Minnie went to lengths to protect her stepmother from the treatment the locals dished out. She crossed roads and changed the route to dodge anyone likely to make hateful remarks. Minnie and Charlotte waved when they spotted the Carson, Hume, and Adair families, but the folk crossed the track. Predictable, Minnie thought.

'People we once considered friends avoid speaking to us, and no one ever visits. Why?' asked Charlotte.

Their gazes locked. They needed no words.

Charlotte returned to the fields and resumed her share of household chores. At nightfall, she slumped into an armchair, staring into nothingness. Minnie had spotted flashes of determination behind her stepmother's indigo eyes, causing her to whisper to Jeannie, 'She's planning something. I wonder what?'

That year's harvest produced lean pickings, and further disaster followed when their oats crop failed because of early frosts. Again, Minnie despaired. *Will we ever be free of this harsh existence?*

Chapter 17

Charlotte sought the girls' attention after supper one evening. 'We've struggled long enough. Earning a living here is taxing, and our neighbours don't want us. Who will fall prey to consumption next? I propose we leave.'

Minnie peered at her sisters. Their mouths hung open, and Jeannie pulled her eyebrows together.

After several minutes of stunned silence, Lizzie spoke, 'Where would we go?'

'Australia,' Charlotte said. 'We qualify for an assisted passage.' Her face beamed, and she flashed the widest smile. 'It's a bright land, brimming with opportunities. The sun shines all day, and we are eligible for a farmland allocation. We can start afresh!' Confused, Minnie's thoughts raced, and she felt her colour rise.

'This is a life-changing decision. We should think about it before committing,' said Jeannie. Peering into Charlotte's eyes, Minnie saw the single-mindedness that told her Jeannie's pleas wouldn't change Charlotte's mind.

Their stepmother's back stiffened, and she squared her shoulders. 'We're going, girls.'

Jeannie, Lizzie, and Minnie retreated to their bedroom. Minnie bit her lip repeatedly until she tasted blood before confiding in her sisters. 'I suspected Charlotte planned something, but not sailing to another country, especially somewhere so far.'

Lizzie rocketed out and returned, a smirk overtaking her face. She was holding an atlas opened at a world map and thrust it at Minnie. 'See the big pink blotch?' she pointed at the bottom. 'That's Australia. It's twelve thousand miles away.'

Minnie sniffled and then howled, but Lizzie swallowed a grin and kept talking, 'They pack passengers on boats, and the sharks gobble everyone if it storms and overturns. Australia is full of savages carrying spears and armed bushrangers. It's baking hot and never rains!'

'Lizzie, you are frightening Minnie,' said Jeannie. 'But Charlotte is right. Leaving is the answer, although I wonder why she's quickly hatched this plan?'

'One upside,' Lizzie said. 'There are loads of men, and we might attract lines of eligible suitors.'

Minnie's head spun. 'It's unfair that all these terrible things are forcing us from our home. I dreamed of escaping, but Da warned us against leaving Ulster and running away.' She wrung her hands. 'By going to Australia, I break my promise to Da.'

'But Da said that fleeing the *white plague* was an exception. And he didn't expect to be buried before he reached forty,' said Jeannie. 'We cannot continue here with everything weighed against us, and Charlotte wants to go to Australia. We know that once she decides something, nothing will change her mind.'

'Charlotte's sister, Annie, a midwife, lives in Brisbane, Australia, and Charlotte may want to join her,' said Lizzie.

Jeannie sighed and stared at Lizzie. 'Much more helpful. Yes, that could be the reason.' She then turned her attention to Minnie. 'A better future lies anywhere but Ulster. You'll go to school, our kin won't die like flies, folk won't consider us untouchable, and we'll get a farm.'

* * *

A few days later, Charlotte said, 'The Queensland Government has accepted our application. We sail on the *Rippingham Grange*, which departs London in February and again in October. Let's start our journey soon and depart before winter for the February voyage.

Jeannie frowned. 'October is preferable as we need to organise and pack.'

Charlotte's body tensed with impatience. 'It is tight, but we'll be ready by Christmas with hard work.'

A week later, Charlotte interrupted the supper conversation. 'Fred Carson asked about buying the farm. We've agreed on an attractive price and will sign the papers in Belfast tomorrow. We can stay until we depart.'

'That gossip vine works fast,' snickered Lizzie.

'Well, it has saved advertising and auction costs,' said Charlotte.

Jeannie's mouth turned down. 'But there's so little time. Besides the farm, we must sell the furniture, ploughs and animals.'

'The boat won't wait,' said Charlotte, face and voice sharp.

Minnie tossed the comments about in her head. *Why the haste?*

* * *

On a Saturday, Charlotte and the girls arranged the farming implements and animals on the turfed area outside the cottage. An ocean of people was present, with the atmosphere rivalling a harvest festival. Minnie recognised townland folk and wondered how they dared show their faces after their recent indifference to her family. People from Toome, Randallstown, and Ballymena attended, many of whom were familiar to Minnie from the Toome market.

Minnie trailed Charlotte all day, watching every encounter. Locals offered their hands to Charlotte, but she did not shake them, instead shooting a curt nod.

Many people made shallow remarks. 'You must miss George,' said Elizabeth Hamill.

As he brushed past, Alex Hume said, 'Sorry about the young lads.'

Tom Lawson shouldered through the crowd to Charlotte and said, 'Hope all goes well in Australia.'

Charlotte, hands on hips, stared vacantly at him.

People strode between the rows, and Jeannie, Lizzie, or Carrie shadowed each one, signalling any show of interest to Charlotte with a wave. Then Charlotte dashed over, Minnie close behind, and the negotiations began.

'How much is that plough?' inquired a prospective buyer, James Adair, a near neighbour.

'It's worth more, but I'll take two pounds.'

He cleared his throat. 'Give me a quid.'

'Way too low. The lowest I'll take is eighteen shillings.'

'Come on, Derry Lass, we've been friends for many years.'

'We were never friends, and I named eighteen shillings as

my lowest price,' said Charlotte in a severe voice.

Minnie swallowed a chuckle.

'Me and my kin have always been kind to you and yours.'

'Is that why you scurried away as we neared you last week?' said Charlotte sarcastically. 'Your small talk is boring me. Say seventeen shillings and call it quits.'

Minnie held back her laughter by gritting her teeth and staring without blinking at her scuffed shoes.

Adair snorted but fished in his pockets.

When the sale ended, few items remained. 'What a success, girls. We did well; my pockets overflow with cash,' said a smiling Charlotte. 'Now, we're ready to head for London.'

* * *

Swept up with the flow, Minnie joined the packing. She pondered the gigantic leap they intended to make as she worked. While she admired Charlotte's conviction, she remained uncertain. Her tummy turned at the thought of leaving her Aunty Sarah behind. With both daughters gone, wouldn't she be lonely without them? Jeannie and Lizzie, exposed to Charlotte's daily glowing descriptions, now accepted that Australia would be their home. But Da's words rang in Minnie's ears. Were they running from something? Did this flight make them exiles?

She sketched pictures of Da, her cousins, and brothers and planted happy childhood memories deep within—the fireside chats, Da's deep voice, Frances's plays, and riding on Da's back. She hoped to forget all the other details of her troubled childhood.

With the major packing done, they spent their last week in

Ulster gathering clothes and personal items.

On the day before their departure, Minnie grabbed Bella. She regretted not taking better care of her precious companion. Her body was grimy, the red stitches in her mouth had loosened, and the button nose hung by a single thread.

The door squealed, and a lilac scent drifted in before stout footsteps. 'What's this filthy thing?' asked Charlotte, trying to wrench the tattered toy.

Minnie's vision clouded as she resisted. She opened her mouth, but her throat clammed up. Then she forced the words, 'Bella is my doll. Frances...'

Charlotte's eyes narrowed as Jeannie entered. 'Let her take her doll. Frances and Katherine stitched it with love, and the dolly kept Minnie company as she watched Da plough and dig.'

'Only to keep Minnie happy. It'll use up valuable luggage space, and the lass is too big for dolls.'

On their last night in their childhood home, Minnie couldn't sleep. She listened to her sisters toss and turn as she stared at the rafters illuminated by moonlight.

At daybreak, a horse-drawn cart stopped outside the cottage. Aided by the driver, the passengers heaved their luggage aboard. They travelled through the mist over wet roads towards the Toome Railway Station.

Minnie's nostrils filled with the scent of icicles, reminding her that her nose and ears would never again numb from the chill.

Minnie didn't glance back.

Chapter 18

The train let out dense puffs of black smoke, and the brakes squealed. Its engine lurched as it jolted to a halt at a railway station signposted in peeling black letters—Gallions, Royal Docks.

The platform, an uneven surface of stone slabs caked with mud, spanned as far as Minnie could see. Business people in dapper suits and bowler hats strode along the platform. Labourers decked out in patched flannel shirts and misshapen tweed caps joined the endless stream as it zig-zagged between porters and luggage carts. Bells rang, signalling arrivals and departures. Dust, hurried by a gusty wind, blanketed everything—seats, benches, engines, carriages, luggage, and commuters' clothing.

Wrapped in tiers of clothes smudged with soot, Minnie and her family fought through the masses. Charlotte led the crooked line. Next came Jeannie, Adeline on her hip, then Minnie, holding Carrie's hand. At the rear came Lizzie, gripping Alice's hand.

Near the exit, the family formed a circle. Nervousness reverberated like an electric current through their intertwined, trembling hands. Alice peered into the mob and slammed her gloved hands over her ears.

'Whatever is the problem?' asked Lizzie.

The child let out a series of high-pitched screams. 'An evil person hides behind the crowd, eyes us, and will jump out.'

Lizzie jammed her hand across her young sister's mouth, but Alice's muffled screams continued.

Charlotte searched for a path from the railway station. 'Stay calm and ignore the pushing, girls.' She gave them a reassuring smile and ushered them to the exit.

When they reached the cobblestone road, the oppressive stink of steam and dust made Minnie lurch a few steps backwards. Charlotte pointed across the street to the gas-lit entrance of their lodgings as a gush of wind sent Carrie crashing to the gravel. They scooped her up and, armed with a handkerchief, wiped the blood from her scraped knees. Next, they fought against the fierce gale and dragged their baggage over the road.

A gust of warm air greeted them when they inched open the door. Minnie's face swelled into a smile at the warmth drifting from the grate. At the front desk, a disinterested-looking clerk shuffled a mountain of paper. He looked up and eyed Charlotte. 'Good evening, Madam. Are these youngsters with you?'

Charlotte nodded.

'Where's your husband?'

Charlotte offered a twisted smile. 'We are a party of seven women who've found our way from the countryside outside Belfast without male assistance.'

Lizzie winked at Minnie, and the pair burst out in muffled giggles, which they attempted to conceal by clamping their palms over their mouths.

A shadow of the brightest crimson crept up the clerk's neck

and face until it reached his hairline. He returned to the pile of papers, plucked one out, and ran his nicotine-stained fingers down it. 'I guess your surname is Craig, assisted immigrants bound for Brisbane, Australia, on the *Rippingham Grange*.' Without further remark, he pointed down the corridor to the female dormitory.

Charlotte opened the door to a large room filled with columns of bunk beds. The dormitory looked over a busy, narrow street. Papery scrolls of green-grey paint dangled from the walls, and spidery cracks laced the ceiling.

Lizzie wrinkled her nose. 'It's cramped, and there's luggage on the floor and smelly shoes everywhere.'

'Did you expect fancy furniture and paintings?' said Charlotte in a sharp voice. 'It'll be sufficient for our brief stay.'

Alice and Carrie raced to claim bunks. 'I bag this top one,' said Alice.

'Because I am bigger, that's mine. Jeannie, Lizzie, and Minnie get these three beside each other,' said Carrie.

Exhausted, they slipped into their chosen beds for a few hours' rest.

When they woke, they wandered to the common room. 'The air's charged with hope,' Minnie heard one man say as he and his wife exited the room.

A host of people gathered—fellow immigrants who would share the voyage. Some sprawled on the brocade-covered couches, and others milled in groups around the fire that sent curls of pine-scented smoke dancing across the room. They all spoke English but with a variety of accents.

A balding, overweight Englishman slumped back in his chair. 'Like my father and grandfather, I have spent my whole life underground. I lived in a coal-mining town on the Mersey

River, where I met and married my Martha.'

A Scottish Highlands accent rose from near the far wall. 'Why leave a stable job?'

'Coal mining is dangerous. An accident might kill ye.'

'At least you received a weekly pay packet. For Highland crofters, making ends meet is almost impossible, and the landlords are rogues. Me and me guidwife decided we would emigrate for the sake of our wee ones.'

An Englishman asked Minnie where she and her family came from.

'Ulster,' Minnie said sheepishly.

'Couldn't pick the accent.'

'Our father is dead. Ma is taking us on the big ship,' Carrie said in a bubbly voice.

A chap with a thick Scots accent and thinning ginger hair approached Charlotte. He introduced himself as Ross McLeod, a dockworker from Glasgow, and gestured to a short, plumpish woman beside him. She had warm brown eyes and an unruly halo of dark curls. The lady turned on a broad, infectious smile that dimpled her rosy cheeks. 'This is my guidwife, Rose. We were admiring your bonnie wee lassies.'

Charlotte gazed at the girls, her face reflecting pride.

'Ye are brave to undertake this lengthy voyage with all these bairns, especially in your condition. Rose and I will help.'

Charlotte gave a taut smile before averting her gaze to the floor rug. Minnie noticed her older sisters exchange looks and raise their eyebrows.

Rowdy voices wafted from a table near the fireplace. Minnie spotted two men, one of whom spoke with an Ulster accent and the other a Scottish brogue. 'We build magnificent ships in Belfast. That's where they built the *Rippingham Grange*.

'Och aye, Glasgow is home to the world's finest shipyards.'

Mr McLeod wandered towards the shipping enthusiasts, lowering himself onto a vacant chair. 'My friend is correct; the Glasgow shipyards build the finest ships.'

Mrs McLeod peered over her shoulder at her husband. 'He's found kindred spirits. He doesn't leave his obsession with ships at the dockyard. At home, he forever builds model boats or buries his nose in books about ships.'

Charlotte heaved herself out of her seat and headed towards the door. The girls fell in behind her.

As Minnie lay awake that night, she felt like she floated on a cloud. These people showed a genuine interest in her sisters and her. Mr and Mrs McLeod offered Charlotte help. It was a treat after being shunned and called hateful names.

* * *

Lizzie, Minnie, and Jeannie woke the following day at daybreak while Charlotte, the younger girls, and the other dormitory occupants slept on. Although it was early, the stink of rotting garbage, open drains, and the rumble of traffic filtered through the windows. They squatted on the icy stone floor, using the bunk legs as headrests.

Minnie shot a barrage of questions at her sisters. 'Why did you behave strangely when Mr McLeod said, 'Your condition, 'to Charlotte?

Jeannie pressed her index finger over her pursed lips. 'Charlotte is pregnant.'

Minnie shook her head vigorously as she scrambled her brain for an explanation. 'No, it can't be.'

Jeannie placed a reassuring hand on her knee. 'Lizzie and I

suspected this.'

'How'd you know? Did Charlotte tell you?'

'No, she didn't, but we noticed a growing lump under that long black cape she drapes herself in.'

Minnie refused to believe it. *Her sisters were under a delusion.* The pitch of her voice raised, and she said, 'Not true. You're making this up.'

'It's the truth,' Jeannie said. 'Yesterday, when Charlotte explained the medical checks today, she instructed us to say that Da died just a few months ago. And she mumbled something about people minding their own business.'

'That means she wants to pretend Da is the father,' said Lizzie.

Minnie felt a tight ball of sadness, disgust, and anger form in her stomach. She answered Adeline's cry, welcoming the chance to escape. As she changed Adeline's nappy, she digested this bombshell news: If Da wasn't the baby's father, she, Jeannie, and Lizzie wouldn't share any blood ties with the baby Charlotte carried.

She averted her gaze upwards. 'Da, you were right that present-day emigrants are fleeing exiles. Charlotte has a reason to run and tricked us into making this Australian trip.'

* * *

London—26 February 1910

Minnie turned in her bunk to face the window. She saw nothing but murky grey. Today, they'd turn their backs on the familiar and sail towards a new beginning.

She swung her legs out of bed and joined the rest of her family, who packed as they giggled and bantered. Weighed down by baggage and braving the bitterly cold deserted streets, they followed Charlotte as they headed towards the shipping terminal. The watery sun struggled to break through the lifting fog.

Voices spilled out of the austere red brick building. With the girls bunched behind her, Charlotte joined the winding queue. A lean, sandy-haired bureaucrat peered over his spectacles when they reached the desk. 'I need to ask the male party leader some questions.'

'I'm the closest thing to the man in this family,' Charlotte said, flashing a wide but empty smile.

His Adam's apple bobbed as he said rapidly to Charlotte, 'Name? Place of residence? Your Queensland Government papers, please.' He lowered his glasses before motioning with a pencil towards a waiting zone.

When the flow of people had ceased, crew members stood at attention. They wore starched white uniforms with shiny brass buttons and shoulders adorned with navy blue stripes. A tall, bearded man with a shock of black hair, who announced himself as the purser, stepped forward and spoke through cupped hands, outlining the details of the passage and ports of call. 'We carry three hundred and thirty-three passengers, mainly government-assisted migrants and a full cargo hold. Captain Lay expects to dock at Thursday Island six weeks out of London.'

As the purser droned, Minnie studied the *Rippingham Grange*, which was docked feet away. The masts and funnel challenged the sky.

Eventually, the crew slammed the hold closed. Passengers

hauling baggage and children scurrying around them stormed the gangway. Folk screamed, and some tripped over their feet. Toddlers whined.

After elbowing through the frenzied pack, a wave of confusion rippled through Minnie's veins as she surveyed the luggage-strewn corridors branching off the decks.

'Girls, we must search for our cabin—number ten, in the middle of the upper deck,' said Charlotte.

'I've found it,' said Lizzie.

Charlotte unlatched the door. The girls playfully pushed each other from the narrow opening to glimpse inside. Carrie pulled her head back into the corridor. 'It's small,' she said.

Minnie entered and pinched her nose between thumb and forefinger to stem the musty odour. 'How can seven of us live in this cramped cabin for two months?'

Carrie looked up and, mouth hanging open, studied the six thin berths—three bunks taking up the entire length of opposite walls. She pointed upwards. 'I want to sleep on a top one.'

'Darling, that bed isn't for wee ones. It's a steep climb and two feet from the ceiling,' said Charlotte.

Carrie pouted. 'Please, Ma.'

'Carrie, I said no, and I mean no. And all of you, this cabin will be comfortable if kept tidy. We'll keep items in the two-foot-high space under the bottom bunks. I asked a sailor about the luggage storage, and he offered stowage in the hold.'

Alice pointed to the porthole. 'See the waves?'

'There's no air. Let's go on deck,' said Lizzie.

A bubble of jubilation swamped the deck. Crowds lined the pier, and singing wafted up, joined by airborne streamers and confetti. Intermingled with the joy were pockets of sadness.

Nearby, two girls sobbed on the shoulders of the man between them.

A brown-eyed, gangly, freckled-faced boy about Minnie's age popped out from behind one weeping woman. The boy gave Minnie a mischievous, toothy grin. *What a rascal.* But what caused his family's distress? Minnie wondered if she would see him again. He may share his story.

$$* * *$$

The boat departed at dusk, and Charlotte headed to the cabin once the engines started. With a frayed shawl draped over her shoulders, Minnie clasped the deck railing, her sisters beside her. London's lights reflected across the ripples as she breathed in the cold, fishy air until the city dwindled to a distant speck. Her shawl flapped like a sail as the wind speed increased.

The vessel crept out of the river towards the English Channel, and the sea became choppy. Six-foot waves lurched against the keel before drenching the deck. Her sisters scampered away to the safety of their cabin.

The howling gusts, the sharp seawater splash, and the salt flavour were all strange to Minnie. Yet, a voice whispered to her, *soak up this unique experience.* She pressed her feet against the decking and grasped the railing so hard her knuckles turned white.

One by one, the passengers sharing the experience succumbed to seasickness and disappeared below. Eventually, Minnie did too. She plodded across the soaked deck and cautiously climbed the slippery steps to the upper deck. Below deck, she stumbled along the unlit corridor and pressed her palms against the wall at every lurch until she found their cabin.

When Minnie pushed open the door, a wave of unpleasant sights, sounds, and smells assaulted her senses. The putrid stench caused Minnie to pinch her nose between her thumb and forefinger. Scattered near the bunks lay buckets and chamber pots encrusted with dried vomit, adding to the repulsive atmosphere. Alice's voice trembled as she cried, 'My belly's jumping! Everyone, even baby Adeline, has been sick.'

The ship's strained rigging groaned and creaked throughout the night, creating an unsettling bobbing sensation. At dawn, Minnie, groggy from a fitful sleep on the narrow berth, propped herself up on her elbow. Stealthily, she jumped to the floor and tip-toed to the porthole, hoping for a last glimpse of England. However, a thick fog, as dense as applesauce, engulfed the steamship, obscuring any view.

As Minnie peered, she felt warm breath against her skin. Lizzie had silently joined her. Amidst the fog, a constant, thunderous honking sound threatened to rupture their eardrums. 'Must be a horn that warns ships about the fog,' Lizzie remarked.

Minnie and her family spent the day confined to the stifling cabin. The question haunted Minnie, *'Are we sentenced to two months imprisonment on a bouncing boat?'*

Chapter 19

The next day, light flooded into the cabin. Minnie sprang from under the bedcovers and dashed to the porthole. The boat cruised on a calm sea awash with sunlight, past rocky outcrops that rose like towers from the seabed.

Eager to escape the cramped cabin, Minnie roused her family so they could explore. Charlotte refused the invitation, saying she would prefer to remain in the cabin.

Lizzie headed the charge. As they descended the stairs, the vibration of chatter and laughter and the potent smell of salt, timber, and hemp swirled up from the main deck. Lizzie stopped, bringing the procession to a halt. She swivelled around and grinned at her sisters. 'The deck is jam-packed. Everyone from our lodgings is there,' she said.

As the sisters filed onto the deck, a booming chant of 'Ulster lasses' and clapping rose from those assembled.

Minnie sprinted into the outstretched arms of Mr McLeod. The skin at the corners of his mouth crinkled into a smile. 'Bonnie wee lass, Minnie.' He rifled in his pockets, unearthed some boiled sweets, and flicked one to her. 'Don't tell the other sweet bairns.'

Lizzie prodded Minnie and gestured to a girl who had fallen out of a snaking line of giggling youngsters as they whizzed past. 'We're hunting a stowaway. Will you join us?' said the girl.

'Minnie, you take Carrie and Alice. Lizzie and I will stay here and watch Adeline,' Jeannie said.

With Carrie and Alice in tow, Minnie trailed the stowaway hunters as they hurtled along corridors, ignoring the *No Admittance* signs. They searched under tables, inside lifeboats, and beneath piles of canvas.

Minnie stopped to recover her breath. Hands planted on hips, she stared as the leaders of the motley band climbed the ladder-like stairs to the bridge. When a stern-faced sailor shooed them away, they retreated and returned to the main deck, where they gathered in a cluster. The cheeky boy who'd skulked behind the emotional women when the ship set sail screamed through cupped hands, 'Stowaway! We'll keep hunting.'

Most of the kids wandered off. Minnie lingered, and her tummy fluttered with delight when the girl, about her age, who'd invited them to join the chase, sidled up. As golden curls flowed over her shoulders, she flashed a smile that lit up her face. 'I'm Harriet.'

Minnie returned the smile, gazing into Harriet's green eyes. 'Hello, I'm Minnie.'

'Will you be joining Morgan's Midgets?' asked Harriet in a bubbly voice.

'What's that?'

'The grownups have formed a social committee. The ginger Scotsman, Mr McLeod, is chairman. Morgan's Midgets is for kids.'

'I'd love to, but I'm not sure,' said Minnie, a hint of hesitation in her voice. 'It depends on my sisters.'

'Anyone under eighteen may join,' said Harriet. 'I've seen your sisters. They all look under eighteen, and you can bring the tiny one.'

'I'm pretty certain we'll join. I'll tell my sisters.' Minnie skipped away to find them. A stream of delight bubbled through her. *This voyage should be fun.*

* * *

The ship sailed through clear waters until just out from Thursday Island. The girls spent every waking hour among the cheerful chatter and laughter on the deck, playing, talking, and attending Morgan's Midgets.

As the sisters prepared for another carefree day, they gobbled a breakfast of slices of bread, spread liberally with butter and jam to conceal its staleness. 'Eat fast, so we don't miss the fun on deck,' said Carrie.

Alice hopped on one leg as she turned to Charlotte. 'Ma, come and see the fun. The people know our names,' she said.

'Hold your horses because if we eat faster, we'll choke,' snapped Lizzie.

When Jeannie unlatched the cabin door, Carrie and Alice charged to the main deck, which was already a hive of activity. The others followed.

As soon as their feet struck the deck boards, Minnie, Carrie, and Alice joined the snaking line of children. Under the leadership of the freckle-faced Peter, they prepared for their daily stowaway hunt. Lizzie sniggered. 'Spare us. Jeannie and I will stay here, chat with the grownups, and watch Adeline. Minnie, you go with Carrie and Alice.'

At two o'clock, Morgan's Midgets met in the main level

hall for the final rehearsal of *Sleeping Beauty*. Using the skills passed down by Frances and Katherine, Minnie and her older sisters acted as directors. Carrie and Alice were part of the chorus.

That night, the performance outstripped Minnie's hopes. The budding actors received thunderous applause. Embarrassed and thrilled, they bowed as they stared into the audience. Minnie guessed they were searching for their parents, and she looked at Carrie and Alice. As usual, Charlotte had elected to stay in the cabin. She wondered why Charlotte avoided social events.

* * *

26 March 1910

Minnie woke in a nightdress, drenched with sweat. When she squeezed her nose against the condensed porthole glass, the sun, still low in the sky, projected light arrows across the glass-like ocean.

As Minnie's eyes darted around the confined space, she saw the rest of the family was asleep, foreheads shining with sweat.

It was Minnie's thirteenth birthday, but she doubted anyone else would remember.

Carrie squirmed, jumped from her bed, roused the rest of the family, and directed them, including Charlotte, into two lines. Raising herself to her full height, using the wand from the *Sleeping Beauty* production, Carrie conducted the group singing 'Happy Birthday'.

The song sounded like birds chirping, and Minnie could tell from how they sang in parts and the harmony of the words they had rehearsed many times. She couldn't believe her sisters had gone to such trouble. By the song's end, she was trembling uncontrollably.

After gulping breakfast, Minnie kissed Charlotte's cheek and hurried to the main deck behind her sisters. There were more surprises.

Mr and Mrs McLeod leaned against the railing. Mrs McLeod clutched an apple green parcel tied with string, which she handed to Minnie. 'Happy birthday, bonnie lass,' she said as she flashed a fulsome smile,

As Minnie unwrapped the tissue paper, the sound of crinkling filled the air. She untied the intricate knots. Peeling back the layers, she discovered a beautiful cloth-bound version of *Anne of Green Gables*. The scent of fresh ink and paper and glue oozed from its pages. A rush of excitement washed over her, causing her heart to flutter.

Unable to contain her joy, Minnie ran towards Mr McLeod. She leapt into his waiting arms, feeling the warmth of his embrace and the steady rhythm of his heartbeat against her chest. Mrs McLeod laughed. 'I see, you like the gift. We purchased the book, a recent release by an American author, from a London bookshop.'

'Thank you. It's the best present ever,' said Minnie, stroking and caressing the book. A rush of gratitude overcame her, but she scolded herself. Really, Bella was the best present ever, and this book is the second best. Oh well, only a little lie.

As lunchtime arrived, the delicious aroma of freshly baked cake filled the air. The cook presented a two-tiered masterpiece adorned with thirteen flickering candles. Minnie took a deep breath, blowing out the candles one by one, the soft whooshing sound echoing through the room. Passengers gathered around, eagerly awaiting their slice of the sweet, gooey cake. After indulging in the delectable treat, the group ventured outside to play deck games. Laughter filled the air as they enjoyed each other's company.

As night fell, Minnie climbed into bed, cradling her treasured birthday book against her cheek. She tingled all over as she reflected on the day. It was her best birthday ever, filled with joy, love, and the enchanting world of *Anne of Green Gables*.

Chapter 20

Jeannie and Minnie inspected the damage after a brutal storm. About ten hours earlier, a crew member approached the pair to tell them one was brewing and that all those on board should stay below.

Saltwater ponds lay on the deck, but they couldn't see any damage. They took a position beside Mr McLeod, who supported himself on the railing when screeches of 'Land, land' assailed the air. Passengers stampeded to the opposite deck railing.

'Let's see for ourselves!' Jeannie exclaimed excitedly.

The crowd's frenzy engulfed Minnie, Jeannie, and Mr. McLeod, carrying them along. The crowd lining the deck railing cheered and clapped as the land grew closer. Some were so aroused that Minnie thought they would throw themselves overboard. They stayed to watch as sailors moored the steamer. 'It is Thursday Island, part of Australia, a short distance to the north of the mainland,' said Mr McLeod.

A chap in a white uniform jumped from the pier onto the ship and spoke with the captain. 'Tis a pilot with experience of local conditions who acts as a guide for the Queensland coast sector,' said Mr McLeod, sounding knowledgeable.

A mixture of delight and thankfulness revolved inside Minnie. Glancing at Jeannie, she saw a light in her sister's eyes. They grabbed each other's waists and danced a reel.

'We've reached Australia, at last,' said Minnie.

'Wonderful, isn't it?' said Jeannie.

* * *

From Thursday Island, the steamer cruised south along the Queensland coast. It stopped at the fledgling ports of Cairns, Townsville, Rockhampton, and Gladstone to deliver cargo and passengers intending to settle in those parts. At Cairns, Minnie bid Harriet an emotional farewell.

Whenever the boat docked, enthusiastic locals gathered to welcome the ship. The girls explored various ports and enjoyed the peculiar timber buildings perched on stilts under steep tin roofs.

On April 24th, energised passengers lined the deck, embracing each other and chatting loudly about the upcoming arrival in Brisbane. Lizzie and Minnie walked around the deck, their footsteps leaving imprints in the layer of soot blown from the funnel. We left Clonkeen an eternity ago,' said Lizzie as she flashed a devilish smile.

On edge from nerves and anticipation, Minnie and her sisters retired to their cabin, where they fussed over the special outfits they'd kept for this occasion. 'The best view is from the front of the upper deck. How do we beat others and bag the spot?' said Carrie.

'Rise early and take turns guarding the space,' said Charlotte.

* * *

The girls sprang from their beds when the first shaft of sunlight pierced the porthole, then reserved and guarded the prime position. They gathered at their observation point, the younger ones fidgeting with bonnet ribbons. A cool breeze tempered the sun's warmth and stirred up ripples in the water.

'Are we there yet?' Alice asked.

'Darling, the ship needs to leave the ocean, then sail up the river,' said Charlotte, clad in her cloak despite the warm weather. The red scarf covering her head fluttered in the soft breeze.

Then the *Rippingham Grange* halted, its engines churning. A pilot boat came alongside. Minnie watched each vessel's crew members pitch ropes and effortlessly leap between boats.

'They jump far,' said Carrie, rubbing her temples.

'They're monkeys,' said Alice.

The *Rippingham Grange*, under tow, entered the Brisbane River. At the water's edge, mangroves sprouted from bulbous roots in the mud. Smooth, tall trees surrounded by spindly brown grass and a few cottages flanked the never-ending bends.

'It's different from the northern cities,' said Jeannie. 'Much browner, and the grass and trees are spindlier.'

Minnie didn't join the conversation. Instead, she conjured up a picture of their farm nestled under trees like those growing on the riverbank. She could see a quaint cottage amidst the yellowing leaves of a maturing crop dancing in a gentle breeze.

Charlotte's shrill voice jolted her out of her dream world. 'Look.'

A small pleasure craft cruised alongside the ship, and those on board waved fabric of every shape, colour, and union jacks.

Carrie shrieked, 'Look! More!'

A burst of colour came into sight, followed by the thunderous noise of sails, banners, flags flapping, and people chanting. A host of pleasure crafts and fishing boats weaved and dodged in a synchronised dance. The joyful atmosphere was contagious. Cheers and applause filled the air, stirring up a whirlpool of emotions in Minnie. Goosebumps prickled her skin, a sensation that mingled with the cooling droplets of water that clung to her face and clothes.

A larger craft jammed with occupants motored alongside, driving gusts of water against the keel. The family erupted in spontaneous laughter when sprays of water drenched them. Passengers in the welcoming boat displayed pieces of cardboard inscribed with 'Welcome, Rippingham Grange'.

Brisbane came into view. A melodic Irish lilt drifted from the main deck, 'I expected a sleepy fishing village, but it is a miniature model of Dublin. Soon, another voice competed with the sound of water crashing against the hull. 'Och aye, some sandstone buildings like Edinburgh! I imagined a desolate, backward outpost. But it's a busy city.'

A rush of excitement overtook Minnie, her heart beating faster as she scanned the scene before her. The city, with its mixture of flimsy timber and grand stone buildings lining a maze of roadways, now lay in plain sight, no longer just an image in her imagination.

* * *

Monday, 25 April 1910

The tug slowed at a vast green copper dome straddling an impressive sandstone building. It roared and churned up a fountain of foam and murky brown water as it guided the vessel to what crew members called Norman Wharf.

Minnie looked at a hedge edging the pier. As they got closer, she realised it wasn't a hedge but a crowd that spanned the jetty's length and were three or four deep in places. They were excited to see the ship! But surely ships arrived frequently? Perhaps they waited to welcome loved ones?

Once the customs officers finished their checks, the crew attached the gangway. The waiting passengers, dragging luggage and toddlers, clamoured.

'Stand back and let others use the gangplank first,' said Charlotte.

'Yes, or they'll trample us,' Lizzie said, her face clouded with her trademark mischievous grin.

Several minutes had passed before Jeannie said in her usual sensible tone, 'Ma, we can go now? The crush has thinned.'

As she disembarked, Minnie ignored the pushing, shoving, and jabbing of suitcases from behind. Clasping Carrie's clammy hand, apprehension pulsated through her. Antrim was her entire world. She must embrace the unknown and embark on fresh adventures.

A voice echoed. 'Come on, move.' She told herself she had no reason to doubt that a rich life as a thriving community member lay beyond the rotting gangway. The cheers and waving from the flotilla of boats confirmed this and gave her an overwhelming sense of belonging. And the cardboard signs held by the welcomers were not scraps of cardboard but symbols of acceptance and warmth. Head held high, she took a few gulps of the humid air and finished her march to the port.

She stepped onto a wide dock of dust-coated raw timber boards intersected by railway tracks. Crowds dodged ropes and bollards. People clamoured, stevedores unloaded freight, and merchants scrambled to claim goods. Carts filled with crates, barrels, and parcels darted everywhere. Employers, spruiking through cupped hands of the opportunities they offered, wandered among the arrivals. Reporters jotted notes. Photographers snapped pictures.

Minnie looked down at the unusually quiet Carrie. The girl studied each sight before her eyes roamed to the next. Minnie thought her eardrums would burst from the steady noise and hoped the rest of the city would give some relief from this ear-blasting disharmony.

The family became entangled in a surging mass that swept them back towards the bow of the *Rippingham Grange*. Minnie grimaced as the swarm moved in until a sea of arms, legs, and shoulders imprisoned her.

When they reached the boat's bow, men with pencils wedged behind their ears arranged the passengers into four rows according to height. A man strode to the front. 'We are reporters from the local newspaper, the *Brisbane Courier*. We have reported on your journey since the ship left London two months ago. The gentleman hidden under the black cloth draped over his camera will take group photographs for publication in the paper.'

Minnie posed with other immigrants as she wondered how a boatload of what Da would call exiles proved newsworthy.

When the photo shoot ended, the family regrouped. Charlotte smoothed and rearranged her cloak and tucked strands of wind-blown hair under her headscarf before saying, 'The bustle has dwindled enough to search for Annie.'

* * *

With the girls close at heel, Charlotte shouldered her way through the jostling crowd. Minnie spotted a woman break out of the swirling mass and rush towards them. The woman raced up to Charlotte, wrapped her arms around her, and burst into tears.

Charlotte wiped her eyes and turned to the girls. 'My dears, this is your Aunt Annie.'

Annie wore an ankle-length ash blue dress and a large coal grey hat balanced on top of her piled wavy brown hair. The hat cast shadows over that part of her face above the scarlet-painted lips. The shape and colouring of Annie's features, not hidden by the hat's shadow, resembled Charlotte's.

Minnie giggled under her breath at the headpiece. Unable to keep the joke to herself, she nudged Lizzie. 'The hat is too much. There must be yards of netting. And those ghastly feathers.'

'Like a show pony,' said Lizzie, a comical edge to her voice.

Minnie choked back a giggle. 'Are you copping that strong whiff of flowers?'

'Yes. Drowning in perfume must be a family trait. But lilac is not her fragrance. She smells like jasmine.'

Annie rested one arm on Charlotte's shoulder. 'You're brave to bring a group of young girls on such a lengthy, potentially dangerous journey, although you've experienced more than your share of trials.'

Charlotte exhaled. 'I'm relieved it's over and we're here safely, but I'm not brave. You came here alone at sixteen. Now, that is a heroic effort and a tremendous leap of faith. How long ago did that happen?'

'Twenty years, but it seems like yesterday. Brisbane has been home since. Welcome to my adopted hometown.'

'We visited Mammy on the overland journey to London. She has told the whole of Derry that you've done and are rich.'

Annie arched one brow and knotted her forehead. 'I'm not exactly wealthy, but I have worked my fingers to the bone since arriving. The work paid off.' She elaborated, 'Each week, my husband, Bill, and I live in the city where I own and operate a small private hospital. We own a farm at Samsonvale in the Brisbane Valley, where we spend most weekends.'

'You juggle so much. Who tends to the farm during the week?'

'A share farmer.'

As Annie beamed at the girls, she greeted each one by name. 'Your Ma describes you and tells me about your activities in her letters.'

Despite the background bustle, Adeline snoozed on Jeannie's shoulder. Alice hid under her mother's clothing. Lizzie and Carrie tilted their sunburned faces and smiled weakly but didn't speak. Minnie peered up and shyly mumbled, 'Hello.'

The crowd parted, and a tanned, tall, thin fellow dressed in a dapper three-piece suit stepped out. He gazed at the sisters through warm, camel-brown eyes and gave a smile swimming with kindness. He straightened his clothing and raked his fingers through his thinning silver-threaded black hair.

'Girls, this is my husband, your Uncle Bill.'

He stood with his arms laced behind his back, and his smile

twisted into a fun-loving grin. He winked. 'I've heard much about you ladies, but no one told me you were so pretty.'

His voice sounded like a cross between Da and Mr Underwood. Minnie reasoned that anyone who talked like Mr Underwood or Da must possess extensive knowledge, so she asked, 'Why does a ship's arrival attract such excitement?'

'It's isolated here, and we rely on shipping for mail, news, and imports. Some boats bring determined, hard-working settlers like you. Australia is slowly developing an export industry. The train lines in this waterfront area carry coal, Queensland's major export, to waiting ships. You can see and smell coal dust coating the boards.'

They drifted over to a platform where officials made speeches. One speaker welcomed the immigrants, and another outlined the business and employment opportunities. The formalities were tedious to Minnie, and she fidgeted with the pleats on her bodice. But the sound of Mr McLeod's distinctive brogue drew her mind back to the podium. As chairman of the social committee, he praised the crew.

Minnie hankered to explore beyond this port area and smiled with anticipation when Annie said, 'Let's leave this bustle so you can see your new home.'

Chapter 21

Annie led them past warehouses and shipping offices to a graded, compacted earth road opposite the pier, where two black, highly polished horse-drawn taxis waited. The drivers, both wearing top hats, squatted behind the compartments.

Minnie gasped when she saw the fancy rigs. She'd seen these elegant carriages in Belfast and London but had never ridden in one, assuming only the wealthy enjoyed access to such luxury.

Charlotte, Bill, and the youngest three children climbed into a carriage. Annie clambered into the other with Jeannie, Lizzie, and Minnie. The silk-lined interior and the calfskin seats took Minnie's breath away.

When the driver flicked the reins, the grey horses moved forward. Minnie's heart soared as the fancy traps whisked them through the city. They rode the streets of their adopted home in style. When she craned her neck to see her sisters, she saw faces swirling with pleasure.

Minnie stuck her head out the window, and her sisters also peered at the sights. After a muggy breeze sent their hats spiralling around the compartment, the same wind attacked their hair, sending wisps in all directions and making their eyes water and noses run. They examined everything on the route, spotting no natives with spears. The only bush was on distant mountains that towered over the settlement like a city wall, an unlikely hiding place for bushrangers wielding rifles. It was not as vast as Belfast, but the maze of streets brimmed with jostling crowds. Coupled with the warm welcome, joy bubbled inside Minnie at every sight.

The flower boxes of Ulster towns were missing, but clumps of trees gave out an aromatic smell. Curly strips of bark hung from branches and trunks. Minnie stared curiously. They were unlike the dense green canopies that populated the northern ports, and neither were they the familiar trees of Antrim—oak, ash, elm, and birch.

As if she'd read Minnie's mind, Annie said, 'Eucalypts, known as gum trees. You will see them everywhere.'

The carriage wound along the horse-manure-riddled thoroughfares. Beyond the city centre, timber and tin buildings came into view, similar to the ones they'd encountered in Cairns and Townsville. They balanced on thin stumps. Accustomed to buildings of thick stone, the girls speculated that the slightest gust of wind would flatten these matchstick houses. Will our new home be like that? Minnie wondered.

As the passing scenery claimed Minnie's undivided attention, Annie prattled away. 'The past is history. This land rewards hard work. Work diligently, and success will follow. I'll assist, and I've already started. The good news is that you'll begin employment at a sewing factory in a week.' Annie bobbed her head as if in triumph. 'I wanted to ensure a job awaited you to help you get established.'

Minnie's chest felt burdened and heavy. Da had cautioned against the harshness of factories and slums, and she'd seen it for herself in Belfast. She'd worked hard to avoid becoming a factory worker.

However, a voice within her told her to forget her disappointment and concentrate on the surroundings. But she longingly glimpsed at the mountains surrounding Brisbane. What lay beyond them? Farms where they grew crops and raised cows and chickens, she guessed. *She hoped that before long, she'd find her way over those mountains and discover the treasures hidden on the other side.*

* * *

On a busy road, the carriage slowed at a two-storey timber building with *Public Bar* stencilled in faded ink on the lower floor windows—an intricate iron lace railing adorned the upper level. A noisy commotion spilled out. In the shade projected by the upper floor verandah, sunburnt men dressed in sweat-stained shirts and wide-brimmed hats nursed glasses of a frothy golden liquid. Others weaved through those standing outside and lurched off. Minnie stared. In a disgusted voice, Lizzie said, 'They're drunk.'

'That's the Waterloo Hotel,' said Charlotte. Although Brisbane is a young city, it has over one hundred public houses—locals call them pubs.'

Further along the road, the driver tightened the reins, bringing the carriage to a halt outside a weatherboard house in a row of similar dwellings. After gesturing with her gloved hand, Annie said, 'I searched long and hard and secured this delightful cosy home. 'Because it closes at six p.m., the hotel's proximity will present no problem.'

Minnie focused on the dwelling. Nestled beneath a rusty iron roof that protruded over a verandah, it stood behind a wooden fence, which offered protection from the hum of passing traffic. A flower garden—a faded version of Ulster blooms, alive with bees and butterflies—occupied the narrow strip between the fence and the roadway.

As they climbed from the carriages, the driver deposited their luggage on the open verandah. The girls, beckoned by Annie, climbed the wobbly stairs and clambered across the unpainted boards. Annie unlocked the heavy door with an ornate brass key. A stale, dank smell poured out as Annie supported her weight against the door and gestured to the older girls to carry the bags.

'I'll do that,' said Bill. 'You explore the house.'

Carrie and Alice lunged past Annie. Minnie headed towards the door, stepping across the verandah boards that moved beneath her feet like loose teeth. Jeannie, Lizzie, and Charlotte crossed the threshold at a more sedate pace.

They stepped into a small sitting room with sash windows, a sofa, and two threadbare armchairs covered in a rusty-coloured velvety fabric. It joined a dining area with a longish table and eight matching chairs. Beyond, they found three pokey bedrooms, one with a double bed and two narrow iron beds in the others. Each contained a wardrobe and a chest of drawers. The kitchen, towards the rear of the house, included a stove, dresser, rickety wooden chairs, and a sturdy timber table.

Annie followed three steps behind them, calling a commentary as they studied the interior. The group stopped in the kitchen. From there, they saw Carrie and Alice frolicking in the generous yard.

Annie motioned to a creeper-like plant studded with thorns and deep pink flowers growing in perverse tangles. 'The bougainvillea conceals the privy, known locally as the dunny.' She opened a top compartment of the dresser. 'I've left a supply of essentials—flour, sugar, cereal, matches, soap, and biscuits—in this cupboard. You will find bed linen and towels in the bedrooms.'

'Thank you. You seem to have thought of everything,' said Charlotte.

Annie arranged her painted lips in the broadest smile. Minnie postured. It threatened to crack her cheeks. 'Oh, there is one more thing.' She unlatched the dresser's bottom compartment, plucked out a jar of copper and silver coins, and jingled it under Charlotte's nose. 'The coppers are pennies and halfpennies, and the silver ones, depending on size, are three and sixpence and shillings. They are the same as Ulster but worth about half the amount.'

As Annie swivelled towards the dresser, coin jar in hand, thunderous footsteps sounded. Carrie and Alice, both panting, chased each other. A victorious look etched on her forehead, Carrie called over her shoulder to Alice, 'Ha, ha. I win.'

Minnie spied a dark brown winged insect, the size of one halfpenny, scurrying across the floor. Alice saw it, too. Using a chair to boost herself, she stood upright on the table and let out a loud screech. 'A little monster! It will gobble us!'

'Darling, it looks ugly, but it won't eat you,' said Annie. She turned to Jeannie. 'Cockroaches run wild here. The hardy, filthy devils flourish in the humid climate. Take your shoes off and use them to flatten any you find.' As Annie spoke, another fell from the ceiling onto her shoulder and bolted down her body.

Lizzie lobbed a mischievous smirk at Minnie. When their gazes locked, they couldn't control their amusement. Minnie raised her hand to her mouth to hide her giggles.

Annie laughed. 'Don't worry. It's funny.'

As if contagious, laughter rippled through the room. Minnie's feelings towards Charlotte softened. Her laughter showed the painted face masked a fun-loving person.

Minnie stepped into the backyard, where a sweet scent smothered her senses. She traced the perfume to a row of trees with fleshy branches weighed down by smooth-edged leaves and spectacular white flowers with a yellow centre.

Back inside, when Minnie asked, Annie announced the flowers were frangipani. Something else strange. *Will I ever recognise these peculiar names?*

Annie left a trail of jasmine as she headed to the door, saying she would leave them to unpack. But before she reached it, Jeannie called, 'Please wait.'

Annie stopped.

'I didn't notice a cow, goat, or henhouse. What about milk and eggs?'

Both corners of Annie's lips curled upwards, and Minnie caught her swallow as if to choke back laughter. 'Vendors deliver eggs, milk, bread, and vegetables daily. Use the coins in the dresser to pay them.' She pushed the door open and left.

I am tired, but now we need to put this house in order, thought Minnie. The important thing is that we've arrived.

'It's filthy and stinks. Dust and cobwebs cover everything, not to mention strange creatures like that cockroach,' said Lizzie. Nostrils twitching, she surveyed every inch.

'We'll scrub from ceiling to floor. Then we'll unpack and have this place transformed by nightfall,' said Jeannie. Everyone nodded their agreement and worked quickly. If anyone slacked, Jeannie said, 'Move along so we can complete this by sunset.'

Minnie noticed the curtains ruffle next door, but no one came near. *Close-city living will not suit me*, and that action by a faceless person confirms it. Why didn't the neighbour call and meet them?

When darkness fell, Charlotte headed for the bedroom. As she shuffled down the corridor, her stepdaughters traded glances and rolled their eyes.

'Didn't help clean but rushes to hide, like on the ship,' said Lizzie.

'She's tired because of her condition, I'd say,' said Jeannie.

'It's her fault. She shouldn't be pregnant,' said Lizzie, smirking.

'We're exhausted, so we'll call it a day. At least now the house is habitable. We'll finish tomorrow,' said Jeannie.

Minnie and her older sisters collapsed on chairs arranged around the kitchen table and chatted. After discussing the day's events, the conversation drifted back to the pregnant Charlotte.

'I'm unsure what Annie knows, 'said Minnie in hushed tones. 'Should we tell Carrie and Alice something?'

'What, to watch for storks?' asked Lizzie as she rolled her eyes.

'There are months to decide,' said Jeannie.

The patter of feet interrupted their discussion. Yawning, Carrie edged up and buried her head in Jeannie's lap. 'Sleepy.'

Adeline slept in a bundle on the floor, and the others arranged their bedding.

'We must share because there aren't enough beds,' Jeannie said, brow furrowed. Seeking a volunteer, her gaze circled her sisters.

'Not me, Jeannie,' said Carrie.

'Why not, darling?'

'Alice squirms, and Adeline wets the bed.'

This is a manageable problem, and the solution is simple, thought Minnie. 'Problem solved. Alice will share with me, and Adeline will sleep where she lies. We can spread a rug over her.'

Alice jumped into the bed with Bella propped on the pillows—a telling sign it belonged to Minnie. Minnie gave Alice a goodnight kiss and patted Alice's shoulders a few times.

Minnie and Jeannie stayed awake, talking as they perched on the edge of Jeannie's bed. Her sister's face was alight with anticipation. 'Tomorrow, we get to explore beyond this house and yard. How did you enjoy our first day?'

'It's exciting but also scary. Everything we've seen so far seems so different. And I feel … well, hemmed in. It's noisy, and the neighbours are close.'

Minnie thought she would enjoy a peaceful sleep free from the ship's rocking, but that didn't happen. Alice tossed and dug her elbows into Minnie's ribs, and minuscule flying creatures relentlessly whizzed around, delivering stinging bites.

* * *

Minnie awoke to sunlight streaming through the window. Jeannie and Lizzie joined her at the kitchen table, but Charlotte was absent. Jeannie arched her eyebrows.

'I told you she would continue to shun our company like

on the boat. Now, her bedroom will be her private hideaway,' said Lizzie, scrunching her nose. 'Not that I mind, but she ignores baby Adeline and assumes we'll care for her.'

They got to work and finished unpacking.

The door groaned, and a jasmine scent floated into the kitchen. Little feet pattered on the hallway linoleum. Minnie hurried to the door, where Alice and Carrie stood near Annie. As Minnie drew closer, she saw both girls point to welts on their arms. 'Tiny flying monsters whirled around all night. They bit and stung,' said Carrie. 'We're itchy and have ugly red watery marks.'

As if to strengthen her sister's complaints, Alice lifted her skirt and balanced on one leg. She raised the other towards Annie. 'Naughty sores everywhere.' Her face was solemn, and her bottom lip dropped. 'Are we going to die?'

Annie unfastened her hat pins and hung her hat on a hook on the corridor wall. Minnie noticed she hid a grin by jamming her palm over her mouth. 'No, they're a nuisance, but they won't kill you.' She lifted her gaze to Minnie. 'They're usually a mere bother, but some carry disease. I forgot mosquito nets, but I'll leave some tomorrow. Drape them over the beds at night.'

The conversation ended when Jeannie's voice wafted from the kitchen. 'We plan to explore the neighbourhood today. Could you point us to some shops and —'

Minnie spoke before Jeannie finished the sentence. 'Where's the nearest school? We must enrol Carrie and Alice. They could start before the end of the week.'

'Yes, it's six months since we left Clonkeen, so they may have difficulty catching up,' said Jeannie.

Annie beamed. 'There's a school close. Cross the road, turn

left, and you'll see the Fortitude Valley State School.

They didn't waste a second after Annie said goodbye at about ten a.m. 'Let's explore,' said Jeannie.

* * *

The sun seared their fair skin. Minnie mused that the *Rippingham Grange* crew members told them it was autumn; they must have made a mistake. When they reached the road, a wall of noise rumbled at them as motor cars, horse-drawn carts, carriages, and trams vied with hordes on bicycles and foot traffic. Minnie shuddered when a tram clanged its bell at a cart that blocked the thoroughfare. The cart driver yelled expletives at the horse, which refused to move. Metal on metal boomed as the tram stopped with only feet to spare.

They wandered further. Pedestrians averted their gazes as they shouldered their way forward. Patrons stormed the Waterloo Hotel entrance as soon as the doors swung open. It reminded Minnie of the noise and bustle of London and Belfast, but on a smaller scale. The enormity of differences between this place and her home in rural Ulster made Minnie stiffen.

After shopping for the essentials and enrolling Carrie and Alice at school, they strayed from the main road across brittle brown grass to a less-trafficked area. Alice pulled a face. 'The sun is hot. It's burning me. And dust is flying everywhere.'

* * *

Rows of timber and tin dwellings squatted behind white picket fences, their worn paint peeling under the relentless sun.

The sound of laughter and conversation floated through the air as people leisurely strolled along the cracked pavement, their footsteps blending with the distant hum of cars. The sweet scent of blooming flowers wafted from the meticulously tended gardens, mingling with the earthy aroma of freshly turned soil. Minnie stood there, her eyes fixed on the majestic mountains in the distance, their peaks piercing the azure sky. She felt a longing and anticipation, her heart yearning to traverse those mountains and explore the unknown.

A voice similar to Mrs McLeod called from behind a picket fence, 'Are you bonnie lasses recent arrivals in the colony?' Minnie craned her neck to see a woman with greying hair curling out from under a wide-brimmed straw hat bob up. 'I thought angels had dropped from heaven when I saw a group of lasses all dressed in pastels glide by.'

'I am Ethel Knox. Five years ago, I arrived from Edinburgh.' She gestured with a wave as she slid the bolt on the gate. 'Come in, and I'll give you some pointers about life in this city.'

The gate groaned when Jeannie pushed it. Jeannie tripped over a watering can as they entered and landed on her backside on the turf. Minnie's muscles tightened as she watched her sister slide on her bottom across the manicured lawn. The tension drained from Minnie's body when a laughing Jeannie dragged herself to her feet and smoothed her grass-stained clothing.

Jeannie leaned towards Ethel. 'Do you grease this grass?'

'No, but I give it water twice daily and treat the garden lovingly.'

'Oh, that explains why your grass is green and springy, not spindly and brown like the grass in town.'

After helping Jeannie smooth out the wrinkles in her clothes,

Ethel shifted her attention to Adeline, who clung to Lizzie's hand. She tickled Adeline underneath her chin. 'Oh, how delightful! This little one has such rosy cheeks,' Ethel exclaimed. The sound of Adeline's giggles filled the air. Ethel smiled when Adeline's face lit up, her dimples appearing as she proudly displayed her two gleaming, pearly white teeth.

'As it's an English-speaking country, I assumed things would be similar. But no, everything is different—buildings, plants, and insects. All the differences made me homesick for months,' said Ethel. 'I still miss the monuments and cobbled streets of my hometown. Edinburgh's essence will forever be in my heart.

'We come from a farming area outside Belfast. The endless noise and movement of a city are strange, and everywhere we look, something is unfamiliar,' said Jeannie. 'Many flowers in this garden are unknown to us. Some look like trumpets, others like miniature dolls on a stick. And they are all such vibrant, unusual colours.'

'Follow me,' Ethel whispered, her voice barely audible over the rustling leaves. Her eyes twinkled with excitement as she led the way, the sun casting a warm glow on her face. With Jeannie in the lead, the girls followed the soft crunch of her footsteps. The sweet scent of blooming flowers filled the air as the gentle breeze brushed against their cheeks, and their laughter and hushed whispers created a symphony of anticipation. They weaved through the tidy garden where abundant multi-coloured flowers, plants, and vines poured from garden beds onto the lawn. As they moved, Ethel pointed out agapanthus, lily of the valley, poinsettia, and bougainvillea.

Minnie grasped the opportunity to sling Ethel an endless

stream of questions. 'Have you travelled over the mountains behind us? What is there? Are there farms?'

'I haven't, but my husband has. He goes wherever there's work. There are farms, cows, and crops of wheat, corn, vegetables, pineapples, and bananas. It's a stunning area, I'm told.'

'What are pineapples and bananas?

'There are banana trees here. Come with me, and I'll show you. But there are no pineapples.'

Ethel ushered Minnie along the path by the side of the weatherboard house, the air filled with the tangy scent of citrus. Ethel placed her hand on Minnie's shoulder and directed her gaze towards the towering banana trees growing behind some orange and lemon trees. Their lush green fan-shaped leaves swayed in the humid breeze.

'These trees are amazing,' Minnie exclaimed. 'I imagine it would be breathtaking to journey over those mountains and see more growing.' Minnie smiled warmly, her heart filled with hope.

'May you get to explore the land over those hills and the beauty of these magnificent trees firsthand,' said Ethel.

Ethel and Minnie returned to the front yard, where the five girls waited. 'We must get home for Adeline's afternoon nap,' said Jeannie.

'Please stay just a few minutes and chat on the verandah.'

Jeannie accepted the invitation by mounting the few stairs to the verandah overlooking the garden. The others followed; Adeline perched on Lizzie's hip. In the shade offered by the overhanging roof, they lounged in three wicker chairs arranged around a small table. They left the fourth for Ethel, and the younger three sat and crawled on the boards.

Ethel went inside and soon reappeared carrying a jug of yellowish-orange liquid covered with a lace doily. She disappeared again and re-emerged, balancing a tray of glasses. 'May I offer you some refreshments?' The contents looked suspiciously like fruit cordial, a delicious drink Minnie had savoured a few times.

Minnie downed the liquid. It tasted tangy and quelled the thirst she had built up strolling in the blanching heat. Carrie and Alice, from the slurps made, seemed to enjoy the refreshment. Carrie confirmed this when she turned to Alice. 'I'm glad we walked this way.'

They stayed and chatted until Adeline whimpered and buried her head in Lizzie's blouse. 'She is tired and needs her afternoon rest. We must go,' said Jeannie.

'It was lovely to meet you, sweet lassies, but the visit has ended too quickly. My husband is away doing tree-felling work out of Brisbane. He is absent for long periods, and I get lonely. Please drop in any time. You are always welcome,' said Ethel as they departed.

The chance meeting with Ethel highlighted their first days. However, thoughts of the sewing factory job weighed on Minnie. *What will the sewing factory be like? Will it be as awful as the fabric mills of Belfast?*

Chapter 22

On 1 May 1910, a blistering hot Sunday, Minnie retired early. Tomorrow marked a week since they'd arrived and they started work. Before sleeping, Minnie opened the windows, hoping to attract some cool breeze later. Drugged by the humid air, she fell asleep straight away.

A few hours later, the needling whine of a mosquito intent on locating a hole in the newly installed net woke her. She wrenched the sheet over her head, but she found it suffocating, so she re-emerged and told herself if she relaxed, sleep would come. But it didn't.

Thrashing, jumbled thoughts crept into her mind about the past, present, and uncertain future. Minnie reflected on her first week in Australia. Far from all she'd known, everything seemed upside down—the seasons, buildings, plants, and stars. She'd believed this country offered a fresh start free from sickness, death, and religious strife. However, she found herself in a hot, bustling city coated in a film of dust, and the promised farm hadn't materialised. She thought she could settle into urban living, but not the sewing factory. Visions of the Belfast textile plants repeatedly played in her mind—the thought of working in a similar place brought on a cold sweat.

She twisted and turned. Her pulse quickened. Rolling over,

she faced the window and studied the full moon. The cycle of thoughts kept her from sleep, so she threw her legs from the bed and walked to the kitchen on tiptoes so she didn't disturb the slumbering household.

In the kitchen, she planted her face in her arms upturned on the table and wept, careful not to allow the sound of her sobs to escape.

A voice sounded close, startling Minnie. The gentle touch of a hand stroking her hair followed. She peered up and saw Jeannie's face folded with concern. She stood, buried her face in Jeannie's chest, and gripped her with all her might. Jeannie disentangled herself, lowered herself into a chair, and patted the timber seat beside her to signal Minnie to sit.

Jeannie clasped Minnie's hand and met her sister's gaze. 'What's wrong?' she asked. 'Your eyes are red; you shake like a leaf and look terrorised.'

Minnie continued sobbing. 'Da's death destroyed our lives. When he fell sick, we had to help. Lizzie and I didn't go to school much. Then we had to run the farm and care for the boys, and they died anyway. Now, I'll never be a teacher.'

Jeannie rested her hand on Minnie's arm. 'We've all had to grow up quickly, especially you. You were a baby when Mammy passed away. Da gave us carts full of love and advice in the short time we had him. We all miss him, and we'll go on missing him. We were lucky to escape the death and illness of the *white plague.* So many families remain in Antrim to face the horrors the disease dishes up.'

Jeannie's words didn't soothe Minnie. 'Da warned me that people who left Ireland were running from trouble. Charlotte painted Australia as splendid, but she didn't tell us why she wanted to go.'

Jeannie said, 'I didn't want to leave initially but warmed to the idea. We couldn't return to Antrim when we learned of Charlotte's pregnancy in London.' There were wonderful people on the boat. They weren't fleeing; they were seeking opportunities not available at home. Like many immigrants, we intend to work hard and create better lives. Think about the experiences of Annie and Ethel, whose stories we've heard.'

'Charlotte tricked us. She promised land, but we start work in a factory tomorrow.'

Jeannie leaned closer. 'You're harsh on Charlotte. She shouldn't have gotten pregnant but could have come to Australia without us. One day, you'll thank her.'

Jeannie grabbed a handkerchief from the dresser and wiped the tears from Minnie's cheeks. 'Get back to bed. Sleep, so you're fresh in the morning. Please don't stress about the factory job. Annie's first mention of it alarmed you and it has played on your mind since.

* * *

When Minnie woke, the tantalising odour of cooking porridge intermingled with the hum of traffic and bird calls poured into the room. She drew the drapes. Unlike Ulster's steel grey autumn skies, the sun shone in a cloudless blue sky.

Thinking she might be late, she rushed to the kitchen. At the table, Jeannie and Lizzie hoed into breakfast and washed it down with mugs of tea. Jeannie gestured with her chin to a bowl brimming with steamy porridge covered with a generous sprinkling of sugar. Minnie hurriedly shovelled spoons of the creamy mixture into her mouth, but her mind travelled to their destination. She knew it would be terrible.

As they left the table, Jeannie whispered to Minnie, 'Keep your chin up. This job is our lot, but eventually, we'll find something else, maybe the farm you long for. I promise.'

Slowed by the uncontrollable tremble of her hands, it took Minnie an age to dress. Draped in shapeless dresses over dark, back-seamed stockings and stout lace-up black shoes, the three left home to catch a steam tram. Jeannie led. The tram rattled along its tracks towards them before coming to a screeching halt.

The girls entered an interior crammed with jostling commuters and ripe with the stench of unwashed bodies. They weaved through strap-hanging passengers when two youths dressed in work clothes sprung to their feet and lifted their fraying tartan caps. One young man stammered, 'Youse sheilas take this bench.'

After casting demure smiles, they lowered themselves onto the wooden slat seat. 'Those boys are rough around the edges,' Jeannie whispered to Minnie, 'but what perfect manners. They're not like the rowdy bunch outside the hotel.'

A bell tinkled as the tram hurtled forward. Passengers sucked cigarettes, releasing tendrils of smoke into the stale air. A uniformed conductor swayed as he trundled the narrow aisle, coins jingling in his leather shoulder pouch. Jeannie gave him copper pennies, and he tore off tickets from a metal device strapped to his waist.

They alighted the tram. Lizzie and Minnie followed Jeannie, who consulted the street signs as they snaked through the potholed backstreets of Fortitude Valley. They passed a diverse collection of retail outlets, warehouses, and factories. After a few twists and turns, a queue of about fifty people, mainly women, came into view, ending at a padlocked iron gate. The gate formed part of the six-foot perimeter wire fence surrounding a windowless two-storey building of stone blocks set in neglected grounds. Weeds and spindly grass stubbornly clawed up from the sun-baked, cracked surface of the attached yard.

They merged into this crooked line of factory hands. It buzzed with chatter, spoken with cockney accents, and sometimes in the local drawl. Minnie studied the scene, and the remains of breakfast gurgled in her stomach. She turned to Jeannie. 'This place reminds me of the Belfast workhouse, or perhaps it's a converted jail.'

'Keep an open mind, Minnie. We still haven't stepped inside,' Jeannie hissed.

'I've seen enough to know I'll hate it.'

The workers stormed in when the gate swung open, sweeping Minnie and her sisters with them.

When they entered the ground floor, a tallish man with layers of fat rolling over his trousers approached them. 'I'm the foreman.' Minnie gawked at him. He had hooded cork-brown eyes, a deeply furrowed face, a bulbous nose, and a bald head. He ushered the girls up the stone stairs. At the top was a dimly lit area. 'Wait here,' he said. 'I'll return and show you around when the workshop starts.'

He left them standing among bolts of fabric and spools of tape. Twirls of steam and a rotten stench spilled from an ajar door marked 'Workroom'. Overcome with nervousness, Minnie dug her fingernails into her upper arms. *Why was she in this hellish place?*

Lizzie interrupted her thoughts when she burst out, clamping her nostrils with her thumb and forefinger, 'It stinks.'

A woman with a grimy, multi-coloured scarf tied around

her head scrambled past. 'The pong is machinery oil mixed with stale air.'

Minnie watched as the woman moved on through a swoosh of vapour clouds. Minnie angled towards Lizzie. 'I'm flat out seeing for a foot.'

The foreman poked his face around the door and beckoned to them. They trailed his giant form among countless women labouring at rackety sewing machines. Minnie winced at a sharp poke in her side. She looked up enough for Lizzie to whisper sarcastically, 'Gee, these girls are enjoying themselves. They all seem bored to death.'

Some shafts of light splintered the film of steam. Minnie tilted her head to see that the tendrils of light came from small, unopened tall windows and gas lights scattered in the arched rafters.

The foreman shouted over the background roar. 'The factory makes shirts and pyjamas using steam-powered industrial sewing machines, five times faster than domestic models. Shifts are nine hours on weekdays and four on Saturdays. Management requires employees to meet minimum production targets.'

He explained how to operate the machinery at various points. He settled Jeannie and Lizzie behind monstrous sewing machines on the second circuit.

Fear of being separated from her sisters rushed through Minnie. *Where will this man take me?*

A few steps further, the foreman allocated Minnie to a vast, noisy stitching device. He briefly instructed her how to operate the machine and then called to a short woman with an ample bosom and mousey hair peppered with grey. 'Mab, could you watch over this new girl?' Then he yelled into

Minnie's ear, 'Mab is a seasoned hand. She'll show you the ropes.'

Breasts swaying, the woman addressed Minnie. 'My name is Mabel. Yours?' She flashed a fulsome smile, revealing crooked, yellowing teeth. 'Sweetie, it's understandable you're frightened—no place for one so young. I guess you're about twelve or thirteen. I have a daughter that age.'

Fisting her hands, Minnie opened her mouth but found herself speechless, although she decided she liked the motherly Mabel.

'I'll take care of you. I'm here to provide guidance and support like a work mum. Soon, I hope you'll relax a bit,' said Mabel, face shadowed with concern.

Minnie gazed into Mabel's warm eyes, almost black against her dark clothing, and offered a cautious smile.

Mabel explained Minnie should tease out the threads and machine the side seams before handing the garment to another worker. She also told her of the hooter signalling starting, finishing, and meal break times.' Everyone calls the foreman Porky, not a terribly original nickname. He isn't a favourite with the workers, but I reckon he tries to hide a soft centre. He knew I'd look out for you.'

Minnie pulled threads and operated the rowdy machine in the airless, noisy atmosphere blinded by steam. Looking down at her hands, shock spiralled through her veins as she watched them redden and swell by the minute. The web of skin between her thumb and forefinger throbbed.

She stole glimpses at her surrounding co-workers. It was impossible to tell their age. Their faces were grey and drawn, bodies thin, skin lined and wrinkled. Vacantness lurked behind their eyes. *Will I look like that at thirty?*

To look around, she angled away from her machine. A rush of panic overtook her when she found she could move only an inch either way. Something tugged on her hair at first, gently, but it grew stronger. She leaned towards the machine and gasped when she saw one of her plaits caught in the tooth segment.

Her chest burned, and a sour taste crept up her throat. Other workers gathered and screamed as they tried unsuccessfully to release her hair. Convinced, the plait would advance towards the needle and draw her into the machine's cavernous insides, a lump formed in her stomach. Numbness spread through her, and a voice inside yelled, *I'm going to die!*

The workroom fell silent, and the pressure on Minnie's plait slackened. She looked over and saw Mabel, who threw her arms around her. 'Oh, you poor lass, you're safe now. Don't cry. I flicked the switch. Never take your eyes off the machine.'

'Mabel, you saved my life.' Minnie buried her head deep between Mabel's breasts, clung to her, and let out a muffled sob.

Mable stroked her back. 'Poor poppet. This sweatshop is not for young uns.'

At four-thirty p.m., the hooter sounded, and the exhausted Minnie joined Jeannie and Lizzie at the tram station. 'Such an awful day,' she said, 'worse than I thought it would be. My plait got caught in the machine, and I was sure I would die. But I met a lovely lady, Mabel, who rescued me. Mabel was the only bright spot in the day.' Aghast, Jeannie and Lizzie stared with open mouths. Then Jeannie squeezed her tightly. 'I'm glad you came through it.'

When they settled on the tram for the homeward journey, a yawn rolled through Minnie. They climbed down from the tram at their stop and, with Minnie in the middle, dragged their weary feet home. Minnie followed her sisters' eyes when Jeannie and Lizzie smiled with delight towards their front gate. Carrie and Alice stood there, little Adeline sandwiched between them, and the three yelled greetings and waved vigorously.

Exhausted, Minnie flopped on the bed as soon as they entered the house. Before they ate and slept, she, Jeannie, and Lizzie discussed the eventful shift. Minnie retold her tale of the jammed plait and Mabel's heroic rescue. Fearing being labelled a baby, she kept her lips sealed about sobbing on Mabel's chest.

'I was worried all day that one of my plaits would jam in the machinery,' said Lizzie.

'I was nervous about that, too. And my heart pumped whenever I thought of flyaway wisps of hair winding around the needle,' said Jeannie.

'Mabel said to watch the machine,' said Minnie. 'That makes sense, but there must be other ways to stay safe.'

'Why don't we shave our hair off,' said Lizzie.

Minnie pouted. 'Lizzie, please be serious for once. I almost died.'

'I've got it,' Jeannie said. 'We'll wind our braids into coils and fasten them at the back of our heads.'

'Yes, Jeannie, you're clever. You've always worked something out. We start with the new hairdos tomorrow,' said Minnie.

* * *

They reported to the airless, stinking building six days a week.

Each shift was the same as the last. Under Porky's watch, they toiled until the hooter sounded.

Although Mable remained kind, Minnie made no friends among the workers. Instead, she and her sisters became the targets of tearoom sarcasm and taunts.

It started on their second workday. As soon as Minnie entered the tearoom alone, a scrawny, sour-faced girl of about Jeannie's age looked Minnie up and down before staring unblinkingly. 'Is the baby in the wrong place?' she said in a raspy voice. 'The kid would be better off in an orphanage.'

Minnie sensed her cheeks flush. She couldn't believe the cruel statement, as she had done nothing to deserve this outburst. Determined not to say anything in retaliation, she bit the inside of her mouth until she tasted blood.

The question, 'In Ireland, are they born without tongues, or perhaps the wee lass hasn't learned to talk?' rose from a group near the wall.

That night, a blubbering Minnie recounted the incident to Jeannie and Lizzie. Both shook their heads in disbelief. Jeannie's face crumbled, and she spoke more angrily than Minnie considered her capable. 'Oh, my darling, they're cruel and taking advantage of a young girl who they probably think is alone.'

'Stick with us. We won't let them do this to our sister. Safety lies in numbers,' said Lizzie, her face smothered with determination.

Jeannie's expression and voice softened, and she moved closer to Minnie. 'Lizzie is right. Don't go into that tearoom without us.'

The next day, Jeannie and Lizzie held true to their promise of protection. But Lizzie's theory about the power of numbers didn't ring true. Seconds after the threesome entered the room and joined the queue at the urn, workers assaulted them with, 'Today we have three Irish retards.' Overtaken by shock, Minnie spilled some boiling water, scolding her hand.

She swallowed a screech, knowing any reaction would invite unkind remarks from the room's occupants. However, her accident did not stop the insults. 'The Colleens wear dresses that look like potato bags,' reached her ears from a bunch of women sipping tea around the long wooden table.

The events of that day were not the end. Everything about the sisters, their dress, fashion sense, and particularly their Irishness, became the subject of harsh jeering. Phrases of 'bags of bones', 'Irish morons' and 'Irish retards' bounced around the room.

After weeks of torment, Minnie battled to control her fury. A rusty blonde, a leader of the bullies, met them with a statement, 'The Irish retards want a wee drop of tea?' Her heart pounded, causing her to place her trembling fingertips on her chest. Swallowing deeply, she stumbled backwards a few steps, grasping Lizzie's arm.

'I could hit them,' she told Lizzie.

Eyebrows folding inwards and nose crinkling, Lizzie replied in a calculating voice, 'Never pick a fight you can't win. There are too many of them.'

With her jaw clenched and lips pressed straight, Jeannie spoke over them. 'Violence is never the answer,' she said earnestly. 'It solved no problems in Ulster.' She wagged her index finger at Minnie. 'Don't let them know you're angry. It's what they want.'

Minnie snorted. 'The townsfolk in Clonkeen tormented us. Isn't this place supposed to be different?'

Jeannie shrugged. 'The community here doesn't like the Irish. Some Greens have shown themselves as drunkards and thieves.'

Minnie wrung her hands. 'I can't do this. It feels like everything is piling up against us. Charlotte promised us a farm, but we're slaving away here. What next?'

Chapter 23

'Why are people wrapped in coats, caps, and gloves?' Minnie asked as she and her older sisters settled into a bench seat on the morning tram in late May.

'It looks like they expect a snowstorm, and winter doesn't even begin until next month,' said Lizzie, her face twisted into a cynical smirk. 'The tearoom gossips whine about the weather as if the temperature is below zero.'

'Humph', said Minnie. 'They should go to the north of Ireland. They'd get chilblains and freeze.' She peered at the light blue sky and mused on the local version of 'cold'. A nippy breeze blew like on previous days, but warmth chased away any chill by ten a.m. Then, it stayed warm until an early sunset.

After work, they hurtled onto the tram for the return commute. They sat three abreast with Minnie between her sisters. 'Another day in that dreadful place finished,' said Lizzie, taking a massive breath.

When the tram slowed, Lizzie and Minnie took a running leap. They broke out in convulsive giggles when they contacted the roadway. Jeannie got off the tram sedately once it had entirely stopped. Minnie's laughter ended the minute she completed the daring long jump. A shiver worked its way between her shoulder blades at the stark differences from the neighbourhood they left in the morning just ten hours ago. She moved her gaze between her sisters. Both bore perplexed, almost worried looks.

Dark clouds closed in. An uncanny stillness filled the street, with pedestrian and vehicle traffic thinner than usual. The customary chuckling, loud voices, and clinking glasses didn't drift from the hotel, and the footpath drinkers were absent.

Their little sisters weren't waiting at the fence, waving and blowing kisses. Alarm bells rang in Minnie's head as her heart lurched to her throat in panic. She shot a worried look to Jeannie, who returned it.

The temperature dropped, and Minnie's teeth chattered. The three stepped up their pace and pulled their coat collars to their chins. When Jeannie pushed, the gate groaned, and the haunted quietness extended into the garden. Even the bees and butterflies were missing. Then the clouds rolled in, darker and fuller, and raindrops tinkled on the roof.

What would they find inside?

* * *

The door rasped open to dimness and an eerie stillness. Numbness swept over Minnie, and she noticed beads of sweat gathered on Jeannie and Lizzie's upper lips. What had happened? She heard floorboards creak and dismissed it as imaginary. And again.

When her eyesight adjusted to the dim light, she spied a huddle in the corner. Carrie, Alice, and Adeline huddled on the floor, gripping each other. Whimpers escaped from the tangle of arms and legs, and the girls raised their heads, revealing faces caked with dried tears.

The scent of jasmine clogged Minnie's nostrils, and shoes click-clacked as a frowning Annie appeared wearing a blood-splattered apron. Wisps of hair hung out of her coil and sweat caused lipstick to leak into her face powder. She carried a bucket ripe with the coppery odour of blood, and she inclined her head towards Charlotte's bedroom.

The girls nestled together outside the bedroom. Concern shadowed Annie's features, but she seemed lost for words.

'Why doesn't she tell us what has happened?' thought Minnie. Sandwiched between Jeannie and Lizzie, she stood as if paralysed.

Finally, Annie spoke. Charlotte faced challenges giving birth to her baby prematurely.

Minnie sensed the colour drain from her cheeks. 'Is she all right?'

'She is weary and weak, and we must support her.'

'But what about the baby? Is it well?' When no answer came, Minnie wept. 'Annie, did the baby die?'

'For now, she lives. Let's see her and Charlotte.'

They inched towards Charlotte's bedside, where their visibly trembling stepmother held the bedsheet to her chest. A palm-sized baby lay beside her bed, nestled into a dresser drawer cushioned by a pillow. Minnie drew a sharp intake of breath.

Lizzie pulled Minnie close. 'Tis not the Charlotte we know.' Minnie couldn't find words. Silence shrouded the room until Jeannie spoke. 'I can't think what to say except that we're sorry.'

With a face the colour of chalk, Annie hovered silently. 'This terrible blow comes on top of a chain of tragedies.'

Their attention shifted to the child. Charlotte choked out a sob. 'The mite made an early entry an hour ago,' she said.

Tissue paper skin covered the miserable mite, and she gulped to take each breath. Ever since she'd learned of Charlotte's pregnancy, Minnie perceived no connection to this child, but her feelings changed now she gazed at a living soul fighting for her life. This baby needs round-the-clock nursing. We looked after Adeline until she grew into a healthy toddler. Nothing is impossible.

Minnie swivelled when Charlotte groaned as she struggled up the bed. 'God's punishing me.' She wept. 'I tried to escape the endless suffering, but tragedy has trailed us.'

As the springs squeaked beneath her, Annie lowered herself onto the bed's edge. She stroked Charlotte's shoulders. 'There's nothing to be sorry about,' she said.

Minnie prodded Jeannie's hip. 'We should leave.'

Later, Annie joined them at the kitchen table, where Minnie had worked on a schedule. 'Perhaps we can stay home, turnabout, to nurse Charlotte and the baby?'

Annie raised her hand. 'I doubt the unfortunate mite will live long. It's a miracle she took her first breath. It's Charlotte we need to watch. She'll get over the physical aftermath of the birth soon, but her emotional state concerns me. While she has faced many heart-wrenching trials, this may prove too much.'

Jeannie bowed her head. 'Is there anything we can do?'

'No,' said Annie. 'This is likely to plummet your Ma into depression. Help her as much as you can. It'll be tough, but you can count on Bill and me for help.'

The three sisters and Annie watched the poor, sickly child fight for four days. Eventually, she couldn't draw breath any longer and succumbed to death. A rush of gratitude for Annie's role in this tragedy overcame Minnie. If she didn't loathe

the factory work, she'd forgive Annie for placing her in that employment.

The fatherless child who'd circled half the globe in her mother's womb faded into history.

* * *

Annie's prediction about Charlotte entering a depressive state proved correct, surpassing Minnie's expectations. Charlotte withdrew almost wholly, imposing responsibility on Jeannie, Lizzie, and Minnie. The sisters fed and dressed Carrie, Alice, and Adeline each morning and got Carrie and Alice off to school. Before leaving for work, they entered their stepmother's bedroom to leave Adeline in her care for the day. Invariably, they found Charlotte with her hair uncombed, wearing her nightdress.

When they returned home, there was a fleeting exchange when Minnie scooped Adeline from her mother's arms. Charlotte briefly left her room to have dinner. On the rare occasions when they coaxed her to linger after the meal, Charlotte focused on a distant point through glassy eyes.

'We managed the juggling,' Jeannie said, hurrying to the tram a month after the birth.

'You're not wrong,' said Lizzie. 'By the time we do the morning's jobs, we must race. Imagine how Porky would rant if we arrived late.

'Keep going, girls, because this isn't forever. Charlotte will recover,' said Jeannie. 'She rallied after Adeline's birth and Sam and George Junior's deaths.'

'Nothing will change,' said Lizzie. 'Charlotte bounced back after our Ulster troubles because starvation loomed. A month has passed with no progress.'

'Be patient. This is an awful ordeal coming on top of everything else,' Jeannie said, lips pursed in thought.'

'How long, five years?' Lizzie retorted.

Minnie wanted to believe Jeannie but feared Lizzie might be right. She pondered her lot: Would she spend *her whole life concerned with others' needs and dodging the persistent curse?*

Chapter 24

In late August 1910, Minnie started when the permanently ajar front door flung open, allowing a gust of cool night air to enter.

She glanced up and flashed a warm smile at Bill. Her heart swelled with affection, a strong feeling radiating through her entire being. During Charlotte's self-imposed exile, Annie and Bill called often. The girls regarded Annie and Bill as their adopted parents. Although Charlotte had improved, the visits continued. Minnie's opinion of Annie softened, her scepticism giving way to a newfound appreciation. She couldn't help but wonder if Annie had followed the instructions in Charlotte's letters relating to the factory job.

From the overstuffed couch, Minnie watched Bill take long, measured strides and pause to run his hands through the bantering Adeline's curls. He stopped and greeted the other girls but made a beeline for Jeannie, pressing his palms on her shoulder. 'I have a friendly country fellow, Ben, who I think you will like and whom I want you to meet. I have known his family—an honest, hard-working bunch—for years.'

Jeannie didn't speak, but she gave Bill a slight bow of her head.

'Done,' said Bill. 'I'll bring him here next Sunday. Cook him a tasty roast lunch, so he's interested in returning.'

Lizzie stared at Bill. 'You do so much for us, and now you're a matchmaker?'

When Bill left, Lizzie, Minnie, and Carrie giggled. 'This is thrilling, Jeannie,' said Minnie.

'I hope he's handsome,' said Carrie.

Lizzie shook her head. 'Might have a cauliflower nose and beetroot-red eyes.'

Jeannie blushed. 'Sunday will bring answers.'

The next day, a beaming Jeannie, chin held high, returned home carrying a parcel wrapped in brown paper. She untied the string and rolled out a lagoon blue fabric dotted with delicate daisies. As they rubbed it between their fingers, Lizzie and Minnie marvelled over the softness of the material.

Jeannie inclined her head towards Minnie. 'I hoped you and Lizzie would help me make it into an outfit for Ben's visit. The dress could have a dropped waist and those fashionable puffed sleeves. We'll use Charlotte's treadle sewing machine. One handy aspect of our job is that we've learned to sew.'

Late into the night, they sewed under the lamplight, meticulously perfecting every pleat, tuck, and buttonhole until all three expressed satisfaction.

The whole family prepared for the mystery man's visit. Under Jeannie's leadership, they cleaned the house from one end to the other until it reeked of lye soap. 'Come on, scrub everything until it shines,' she said. I don't want him to think I'm dirty or a poor housekeeper.' She turned to Minnie. 'I'm not sure if we've unpacked the best china. Could you find it and wash each piece?'

Minnie contorted her face into a frown. 'I'm not your maid.' She figured Jeannie had already requested that she do more than her fair share.

'Don't be like that. Everything must be perfect,' said Jeannie. 'I've asked Lizzie to polish the silverware.'

Minnie sighed and searched for the china. A newfound light shone in Jeannie's eyes. Jeannie was more hopeful about the introduction than she'd realised, and Minnie hoped her sister would find her soulmate.

* * *

On Sunday, Minnie and Lizzie arranged Jeannie's hair, and then, clad in the blue dress, Jeannie gazed into the mirror for what seemed an age before she nodded her approval. The three of them strutted towards the sitting room.

Charlotte had stopped hiding in her bedroom and wore a new outfit. She sat in an armchair with her ankles crossed. Carrie, Alice, and Adeline crouched at her feet. The mouth-watering aroma of roast beef wafted from the kitchen.

Minnie scanned the room, decorated with vases of dahlias, poppies, and ferns. She pinched Lizzie's upper arm. 'I don't want to give you a bloated head, but you've arranged the flowers perfectly,' she said.

A smile played on Carrie's lips as she leant towards Jeannie. 'You look so pretty.'

'Are you nervous?' asked Minnie.

The conversation stopped when the front door opened with a high-pitched screech. Bill entered ahead of a short, grinning chap. A face of work-leathered skin framed his bright blue eyes. Bill motioned towards each person as he introduced them. 'Ben, this is Jeannie, and the other delightful young ladies are her sisters. The gracious woman is Jeannie's stepmother.'

'Welcome, Ben,' Charlotte said in a charming voice. 'Pleased to meet you.'

Ben offered his cracked hand to her and then to Jeannie. 'G'day, how're ya going?'

Minnie giggled to herself. I don't think this man will find white tablecloths, sparkling glasses, and flower arrangements appealing. He has an uncomplicated air, and I approve of him as a husband for my treasured sister.

'Ben is a dairyman from Kobble Creek, thirty miles away, and is a tireless worker. His farm is close to our farm,' said Bill.

Charlotte took Ben by the elbow and ushered him to a seat next to Jeannie. Everyone except Charlotte and Lizzie claimed seats at the table, with Minnie perched next to Jeannie. She reasoned this position would allow her to eavesdrop on Jeannie and Ben's conversation without making it obvious.

Grin widening, Ben inclined his head towards Jeannie and asked questions about Ireland. 'And what do ya do here?'

'I'm a tailoress.'

Minnie mused. What a fancy way of saying cloth mill roustabout!

Lizzie and Charlotte reappeared, both balancing plates emitting curls of steam. Ben ran an appreciative eye over the serving before him—a plate piled with two generous slices of succulent roast beef, mashed potatoes topped with butter, glistening carrots, and peas. Charlotte disappeared and returned with a small herb-scented gravy boat, setting it in the centre of the table. 'What a feast! Roast beef and all the trimmings,' said Ben, tracing his lips with his tongue.

Alice jumped up and skipped in circles. She raised her face

to Ben and cupped her chin in her hands. 'Afterwards, we have rice pudding with yummy custard made by Jeannie.'

After they'd demolished the meal, Bill, arms crossed against his chest, complained of the cold. 'Ben, walk Jeannie to my house and fetch my coat. It's close. Jeannie knows the way.'

Minnie stared at her shoes. Bill's flimsy pretext had the desired effect, but Minnie's heart went out to Jeannie. Lizzie would torment Jeannie until she extracted all the details of the stroll.

When the visit had ended, Lizzie and Charlotte threw the predictable barrage of questions at Jeannie.

'Do you like him?' asked Lizzie in her direct manner.

'He is earthy and seems open and kind,' said Jeannie, 'but it's hard to understand him. He has a strange way of stringing his words together, dropping the first letter and shortening nearly every word. And he uses words I've never heard—"bonza," "nipper," and "dinkum." It must be a dialect.'

'I liked him because he's friendly and has a cheeky grin,' said Carrie.

'He's short. Doubt he is five foot four,' said Lizzie. 'Does that worry you?'

'No.'

'The rough hands and broad shoulders are signs he is a hard worker,' said Charlotte. 'And a worker diligently pays the bills. Kindness and dependability are the cornerstones of a lasting union.'

Lizzie, face consumed with a scoundrel-like grin, didn't stop her questioning. 'Well, what happened?'

'We talked about the climate here and in Ulster, farming methods in Antrim versus here, and Australian country life.'

'What else? Come on!' demanded Lizzie.

Jeannie blushed. 'I boiled, then froze, and tingles spread everywhere. I broke out in goosebumps.'

'These are classic signs of attraction, darling,' said Charlotte, bobbing her head as if she possessed secret intuition about such matters.

'Don't keep us in suspense,' said Lizzie. 'How did it end?'

'He's taking me to a dance next week.'

* * *

March 1911

Minnie and Lizzie lounged on the sitting room couch. The evening held the day's blistering heat, and although after 10 p.m., the hum of traffic flowed through the open sash windows and door. As the rest of the household slept, they waited for Jeannie to return from an outing with Ben to the local movie theatre.

Lizzie yawned. 'Jeannie is late.'

'We should wait,' Minnie suggested, concerned for Jeannie's safety. 'Anyway, tomorrow is Sunday, and we don't have to work.'

Soon, the clip-clop of shoes sounded on the verandah boards, accompanied by a gentle hum. A vibrant smile consumed Jeannie's face, illuminating the room as she entered.

Before Jeannie sat, Lizzie rose and pounced. Brow furrowed and nose crinkled, she spat out some direct questions. 'You're late, and what makes you so happy?'

Jeannie's cheeks flushed with a rosy hue as she replied in a wavering voice. 'Ben said he wanted to discuss something privately, so we went to Bill and Annie's garden. Minnie sensed the direction of the conversation but let Lizzie do the probing.

'Well, what was it? We need to know; after all, we're your sisters. 'Lizzie leaned in closer. She pulled Jeannie's left hand towards her and examined it, and the lamp's glow caught a glimmer. 'Is that an engagement ring?' she exclaimed, her voice excited. A timid smile danced across Jeannie's lips.

Lizzie clasped her sister's hand. Under the soft flickering of the lamplight, she marvelled at the sparkling adornment. She screamed so loud that the window frames rattled. 'Wow, this was worth waiting up for. What a rock.' She enveloped Jeannie in a long embrace. When Lizzie released her grip, she spoke with genuine happiness. 'I'm so happy for you and sorry about all those annoying questions.'

Jeannie chuckled wryly, her laughter filling the room. 'Lizzie, it wouldn't be you if you weren't curious and a tease,' she said affectionately. 'Now, I'm going to move and sit with Minnie because I'm sure she would love to see the ring, and she's waited so patiently.'

As soon as Jeannie lowered herself into the space next to Minnie, Minnie gently took her hand. The diamond's beauty and the gold's coolness sent a shiver spiralling down her spine, and she drew her mouth into a circle. 'It's dazzling, so beautiful.'

Jeannie's eyes sparkled. 'Yes, it's lovely, and when he presented it, I nearly fell with surprise.'

'You must have suspected?'

'Ben doesn't talk much, so it wasn't until he began stammering that I realised what he struggled to say, and my heart hammered so much I could hardly get my reply.'

Minnie folded her arms around her sister so tightly that she almost crushed her bones as she mused about the changes Jeannie's marriage would bring. 'Where is Ben?'

'Oh, he walked me home and returned to Bill and Annie's house, where he will spend the night. Why?'

'I wanted to congratulate him on his excellent choice,' said Minnie.

Snickering, Lizzie strode across the room and plunged onto the couch next to Minnie. She leaned towards Jeannie. As if she had read Minnie's thoughts, she said, 'The marriage will free you from that dirty, noisy sweatshop and the watchful eye of Porky.'

'Minnie said dreamily. 'Yes, you will live beyond those mountains and breathe fresh country air while we have a diet of second-hand factory steam.'

Lizzie spoke again. 'When is the big day?'

'It'll be towards the end of the year. Ben will speak to Bill about holding a ceremony and reception at their house.'

Minnie sensed a single tear slide down her cheek. She gazed into her sister's eyes. 'I'll miss you terribly,' she said.

'I promise to write weekly and visit as much as possible. The three of us share an unbreakable bond. We've been through a lot,' Jeannie said.

Minnie then brushed a kiss on Jeannie's cheek. 'We've had our spats, but you've always looked out for Lizzie and me.' A lump formed in Minnie's throat as she tilted her body towards her sister. 'I love you.'

Chapter 25

Jeannie and Minnie spoke a few days later as they washed the dinner dishes. 'We have decided on 8 November for the wedding,' said Jeannie, anticipation etched across her brow.

'How exciting.'

'I wondered if you would be my bridesmaid?'

The question whisked Minnie's breath away, and she imagined herself gliding in a glamorous gown.

'I'd be delighted,' said Minnie, trying to stay composed.

The preparations began in earnest. A few days later, while sipping tea with Charlotte at the kitchen table, Annie attracted the attention of Jeannie and Minnie. 'I'll take you to Brisbane's premier fashion house to have your gowns tailored,' she said warmly. 'They carry a range of dazzling imported fabrics, and they'll take care of all the intricate details, from the drawing board to the final fittings.'

A week later, Annie accompanied Jeannie and Minnie to an establishment on Adelaide Street. A uniformed doorman directed them to a room accessed by a sweeping marble staircase. A gentle breeze carried the afternoon light into the room. Exquisite etchings of gowns modelled by glamorous ladies adorned the walls. Bolts of fabric, spools of delicate lace, and display cabinets overflowing with buttons and accessories filled every corner.

A tall, thin woman with greying, wispy hair pulled tightly into a bun gracefully entered. Annie's forehead furrowed with a glimmer of recognition. 'Mrs O'Neill, these delightful lasses are my nieces, Jeannie and Minnie' Mrs O'Neill reciprocated the greeting with a welcoming smile. 'I'm pleased to meet you. Your aunt, who I've dressed for many years, has spoken about you, she exclaimed. 'Now, let's embark on creating startling outfits.'

With an expansive wave, Mrs O'Neill beckoned towards the bolts, spools, and gleaming glass-front display cabinets. The volume of choice made Minnie speechless. She laid her hand several times on her expanding chest as she glanced at Jeannie. Her sister's mouth hung open in what Minnie assumed was wonder as she spun around, taking in the room's contents.

Annie expressed concern, saying, 'You girls look over-whelmed. May I help?' Jeannie smiled appreciatively and nodded, but her eyes darted anxiously to Mrs O'Neill, silently asking for simplicity. Standing beside Jeannie, Minnie sensed her sister's worry and felt relieved when Mrs O'Neill noticed.

Saying, 'I'll start by making some sketches,' Mrs O'Neill sat behind a drawing board. The girls had an obstructed view of the board's face, and Annie peaked over its sides.

As she effortlessly guided the pencil, Mrs O'Neill com-mented, 'These girls are young and shapely. They should flaunt their bodies, which don't need the support of tight corsets.' Annie seemed hesitant, so Mrs O'Neill clarified the designs were in the trendy empire silhouette style. She then showed Annie a drawing on the wall to illustrate her point. Clutching two pieces of paper, Mrs O'Neill slid from behind the drawing board and padded towards Jeannie with her shoulders drawn back. 'I've sketched this preliminary design for the bride and bridesmaid gowns.'

Jeannie studied the designs. 'They are beautiful. Even better than I dreamed.' Minnie glanced at her sister, immediately appreciating her pleasure. Tears gathered in Jeannie's eyes as she balanced on one leg and held one arm to her chest.

Mrs O'Neill rummaged through lengths of silk, satin, taffeta, and georgette, making suggestions and inviting them to touch and feel the texture. Annie's voice echoed from behind. 'These latest designs seem to use many contrasting materials and textures.'

'Indeed. Often, layers of sheer fabric drape a smooth white satin. You must also consider features such as embroidery,' said Mrs O'Neill as she tapped her nose thoughtfully. Some lovely handmade lace imported from Belgium arrived yesterday. We could include some of it as a unique feature.' Mrs O'Neill turned to Annie, 'Please help select; you've got an eye for pairing fabrics.'

Minnie watched as the older women fiddled with combinations of materials and accessories. While Annie may not be up to date with the latest styles and yards of gathered fabrics, she thought, she has a natural talent for combining colours. Finally, in unison, the sisters grinned and oohed at what Annie pronounced was the ideal combination.

Then, they selected the fabric and adornments for the bridesmaid's outfit. 'The trend is towards rich colours. I suggest brown or pink with soft tucks around the neckline,' said Mrs O'Neill. Annie handed Minnie a length of mocha brown satin. Minnie's stomach bubbled with delight as she caressed the material with her palm. She beamed as she peered into Jeannie's starry eyes. 'This material is as soft as the fluffiest cloud. I swear it is a slice of heaven.'

A host of fittings followed. After weeks of parading and standing as rigid as a statute as Mrs O'Neill and Annie pinned, tucked, and fussed, Annie nodded and flashed a satisfied smile. 'Jeannie, the dress is magnificent and fits like a glove. Ben is going to find you irresistible when he sees you.'

'I hope so,' said Jeannie, elation colouring her voice.' Minnie, we'll both look amazing.' Before undressing, she stole a last gaze at her silhouette in the full-length mirror.

The wedding fever didn't end with the selection of the gowns. It formed the sole topic of conversation at family meals, with Charlotte discussing plans hatched between her and Annie. 'Annie has arranged flowers from a farm. We are going to need plenty. There are bouquets, corsages, floral arrangements for the house, and table decorations.'

Jeannie attentively listened to the details, showing her acceptance with an agreeable smile and an enthusiastic nod. From the corner of her eye, Minnie spied a dreamy twinkle in Jeannie's eyes. *She must dream of the days ahead.*

* * *

On the wedding day, Minnie woke as a spark of light glared through the sheer bedroom curtains to find Jeannie perched on the stool before the dressing table. 'You are awake early. I guess you're excited.'

Minnie, a tangle of hair spilling over her shoulders, raced to the window. 'It's going to be boiling. Steam rises from the ground, and the clouds look mischievous. We might be in for a soaking.'

'We were lucky we took our dresses to Bill and Annie's house last night,' said Jeannie. Charlotte tapped on the door and entered.

'Hurry, girls. Get yourselves dressed and out for breakfast. I'll check the other lasses are out of bed. We must hurry to Annie's place to dress and help prepare.'

After breakfast, they all walked to Bill and Annie's home, where they helped by arranging seating, decorating the sitting room, and preparing food. Lizzie used her talent for floral arrangement by producing vases of colourful blooms among ferns.

Jeannie and Minnie retreated to a back bedroom at about eleven a.m. to titivate themselves and don their gowns.

Annie knocked on the door, and before opening it, Minnie cast an approving eye over her sister, who looked like a serene princess in her billowing gown. Minnie's insides tumbled with nervousness, and she guessed her sister's calm appearance masked an inward disquiet.

The pair stepped at a snail's pace towards the flower-scented sitting room before walking between hushed guests. They inched under a silver ribbon affixed to the ceiling and approached a timidly smiling Ben and the best man. After they took their places, the clergyman lifted his bald head and peered over his steel-rimmed spectacles at Ben and Jeannie. He welcomed everyone and performed the ceremony. At one stage, he stumbled over the words, but before long, the couple exchanged vows, and Ben slipped a gold ring onto Jeannie's finger. Minnie spent her time pulling her mind back from her thoughts of Jeannie's fortune in trading factory life for a peaceful country existence beyond those mystery mountains.

With the formalities over, Ben, Jeannie, Minnie, and the best man laughingly mingled among the guests, who nibbled on dainty sandwiches and miniature pies washed down with beer and tea. Minnie and Jeannie enjoyed a sister moment as Minnie helped Jeannie slip into her going-away outfit. Minnie felt emotion rise within as she embraced Jeannie. 'Don't forget me, and please write often.'

'Minnie, loosen your grip; I can hardly breathe,' said Jeannie. I won't be far away, and we'll visit.' Jeannie wiped moisture from the corner of her eyes with the back of her hand.

To cheers and shouts of 'good luck' and 'every happiness', hands joined, the newlyweds wove through the attendees towards the waiting hansom cab. Dodging grains of rice flung by guests, the couple reached the top hat-adorned driver, who guided them into the carriage.

Neighbours lined the street, and as the horses slowly hauled their load along the roadway, they chanted good wishes, lobbed flowers, and hurled more rice. Choked up with emotion, Minnie watched until the hansom cab became a speck on the horizon, wondering what a future without Jeannie would hold.

The guests disappeared. Brooms, scrubbing brushes, tea towels, and rags in hand, the entire family cleaned the remnants of the event.

Adeline, Alice, and Carrie collapsed to the floor one by one, where they soon slumbered soundly. When they had restored normality to the house, Bill, Charlotte, Lizzie, and Minnie plopped into the overstuffed couches. 'I am exhausted,' said Annie, 'but the day's success justified the effort.'

Charlotte leaned towards Annie. 'Thanks for this. You have a talent for making these occasions special,' she said.

Annie let out a booming laugh, 'Perhaps resourcefulness runs in the veins of all our family?'

As if it was infectious, Bill laughed too. 'Yes, my dear, I'm sure Ben and Jeannie had a pleasant day. I could feel glee bubble in the room.'

Charlotte turned to Annie. 'A few months ago, we discussed the investment of two hundred pounds odd from the Ulster farm. You offered to help me search after the wedding.'

'Yes, I suggested a business for its flexibility between work and family responsibilities.'

Minnie, interested in the discussion, slumped more profoundly into the couch. The notion of all this change sent her a shock of apprehension coursing through her. Her blood chilled, and she felt the hairs on the back of her neck stand on end.

'Give it a week for us to get our breath, and we'll start searching.'

Chapter 26

On her return from work for several weeks after the wedding, Minnie found Annie and Charlotte having intense daily discussions. The older women didn't include Minnie in the conversation, but they didn't keep any secrets. They searched for the business they had spoken of.

Annie and Charlotte gave a running commentary of the day's discoveries each night, rejecting endless possibilities for diverse reasons - the property needed too many repairs, the returns could have been better, or it was too far away. Minnie concluded the two had an unbreakable requirement—it must be close to their present dwelling. Oh well, thought Minnie, it wasn't her longed-for farm.

A few nights later, Charlotte said to Lizzie and Minnie, 'We inspected a boarding house nearby, which I want you to see. When she made the announcement, she explained, 'I think it will be perfect. With hard work, I believe I can transform it into the most popular accommodation in Brisbane.'

The notion of a boarding house didn't appeal to Minnie. She imagined her family sharing space with strangers who might speak different languages or be unfriendly. However, she saw the enthusiasm burning in her stepmother's eyes.

On Saturday afternoon, they met Annie on the grounds.

After Annie relieved Charlotte of Adeline and popped the toddler on her hip, she said, 'I've spoken to the owner, who said we're welcome to look around the grounds. We'll need to be speedy and quiet when we pass through the main part of the property. The manager's flat is vacant so that we can move around without disturbance.' Minnie exhaled when she learned her family would live separately from guests.

Minnie twisted to face Annie and Charlotte, who stood behind. 'These huge grounds take my breath away.' A sharp pang attacked her stomach as soon as she finished the sentence. 'Carrie and Alice have disappeared. Have they run away, or are they hiding?'

With a hint of scepticism, Annie chuckled, and Minnie followed her aunt's gaze to a knotted tree that reached for the sky and towered over the neighbouring houses. Calling to each other between giggles, Carrie and Alice swung and twirled from a lower branch with the agility of a pair of possums. Minnie tilted her head back and joined in Annie's laughter. She recognised it as a jacaranda tree from the trees fringing the roads on her commute, which burst into a purple flame every October and then shed a carpet of velvety purple blooms.

Charlotte, Annie, Lizzie, and Minnie formed a semi-circle and spoke while they monitored the young ones. 'The yard is spacious enough to have a vegetable patch and space for children to play. I see it now—bees buzzing and butterflies fluttering through green beans, red radishes, and juicy toma-toes nestled in swaying branches,' said Charlotte. All nodded. Charlotte moved her gaze between Lizzie and Minnie. Chin held high, hands anchored casually on her hips; Charlotte said, 'Well, what do you think? I'm sure you like the place.'

Lizzie rolled her eyes, looked over to Minnie, and winked.

'So far, so good, but I'll wait until we see inside before giving a final answer.'

Playfully clapping Lizzie on the back, Charlotte confidently quipped, 'It won't disappoint.'

Annie turned to Lizzie. 'Ma is correct. I inspected the place with her last week. The manager's flat is quite something!' When Carrie and Alice answered Charlotte's call to join them, Annie gathered the family around and said, 'We will visit the manager's flat, your new home. We get to it through the main house, and because guests need privacy, we must tiptoe.'

Annie opened the door to a surprise that left Minnie breathless. They entered via the sitting room, a meticulously presented space fanned with brightness and fresh air. The polished timber floor reflected Minnie's image. 'Oohs' and 'wows' in the raised voices of Carrie and Alice echoed, creating a sense of spaciousness. There were more thrills to come. Minnie glanced at Lizzie; even her mischievous sister couldn't hide her approval. Her lips curled upwards, and her eyes shone.

Charlotte led them to the bedrooms at the back of the flat. She guided Minnie towards an ajar door and said, 'I plan for you and Adeline to share this room. Taken aback by the sight before her, Minnie's heart skipped a beat. The mellow pink walls enveloped two beds adorned with striking melon-pink bedspreads. Matching curtains fluttered in the wind, sending them billowing into the space.

The family gathered in the pink room. Alice and Adeline held hands and danced a reel, laughing. Charlotte and Carrie perched on one bed while Annie, Lizzie, and Minnie lounged on the quilt opposite. Charlotte shifted her gaze between her two stepdaughters before fixing her narrowed eyes on Lizzie.

Now that you've seen the inside, what is your decision?' she said.

Lizzie squirmed, avoiding her stepmother's gaze before stuttering, 'The business will be fine. As it is.' Minnie and Carrie nodded in agreement.

'Well, it's settled then. I'll sign the papers tomorrow.'

* * *

The family moved into the boarding house in January 1912. Excited about the superior accommodation, especially the pink bedroom, Minnie wondered if she would have pink dreams.

They worked very hard to establish the business. Charlotte scrubbed floors on her hands and knees and dusted walls and ceilings. Minnie helped her stepmother set up a vegetable garden. The unrelenting sun blistered their fair skin, but they enjoyed the earthy smell of the soil. Charlotte smiled dreamily and said that breaking soil alongside Minnie reminded her of Antrim.

A few days after they moved to the boarding house, Charlotte, Minnie, and Lizzie lingered around the kitchen table as the odour of their supper lamb chops floated in the air.

Charlotte, whom Minnie thought appeared pensive, stared silently from the window at a distant point. She redirected her focus to the girls as a faint smile played on her lips and said, 'I think we've reached the end of the dark years.'

Lizzie drummed her fingers on the table. As if making a considered statement, she said, 'But the curse may have dog paddled over the ocean.'

Charlotte grimaced as she shook her head and muttered. 'So

negative, Lizzie.'

Minnie's chest tightened, and a lump constricted her throat as images of those left behind in Antrim's graveyards rotated before her. Da's voice and Sam's bubbly laugh sounded in her mind. She took her time before speaking. When words came, Minnie said shakily, 'We've lost so many loved ones.'

Charlotte furrowed her brow and gazed at her stepdaughters. 'We'll forever carry the scars of the unhappiness and struggle, but I'm confident we've broken the chain after a long haul, and tragedy won't follow us anymore.'

Lizzie shuddered. 'I hope you're right because I couldn't take any more.'

Minnie hoped with all her heart that Charlotte's prediction would come true.

* * *

Their tireless efforts paid off. The boarding house gained a reputation as a clean, well-run establishment where vacancies were rare.

Minnie watched her little sister climb onto her bed each night, plucking Bella from her cosy spot among Minnie's fluffy pillows. After tenderly rocking and kissing the doll, Adeline carefully placed Bella on the floor and surrounded her with her collection of dolls. The scene made Minnie's heart race. Dear Bella, a constant reminder of those she'd loved and lost and had been a friend and comfort to many.

Before settling into her bed, Minnie returned Bella to her rightful place and tidied up the other toys, placing them in Adeline's toy box. With a pink quilt blanketing her, Minnie listened to the soothing rhythm of Adeline's breath as sleep overtook her.

As she lay there, the events since Jeannie's wedding orbited her mind. She longed for her sister's presence and hoped that she was leading a joyous life, even though she knew only the bare minimum. Jeannie wrote to Minnie each week, but her letters were short and contained only a few details about her new life, which didn't surprise her because Jeannie had never been fond of writing long letters.

She pondered Charlotte's predictions about the rosy turn ahead, finding solace because, so far, everything had gone without incident. However, while things appeared harmonious for their all-female family, Minnie couldn't help but feel Charlotte had become consumed by her boarding house business. It took precedence over all other responsibilities.

The monotony of Minnie's factory job overshadowed the novelty of their new home. After almost two years, the repetitious tasks frayed her nerves. She despised it with every fibre of her being. The harsh reality of the impending morning shift reminded Minnie of her need for rest. Before succumbing to sleep, she prayed for Jeannie's safety.

* * *

As Minnie toiled behind the clunky sewing machine, feeling the rough texture of the fabric against her fingertips, she allowed her mind to wander. She envisioned the joyful laughter and playful games with Adeline that awaited her at home, a much-needed relief for her throbbing hands.

When the hooter sounded, signalling the end of the shift, Lizzie and Minnie hurried to the tram station. The creaking of the timber gate, hanging precariously on one rusty hinge, announced Adeline's rush towards them, followed at a distance by Carrie and Alice. Lizzie frowned at the sight. 'Adeline, you know you're not allowed on the road. Who let you out?' Adeline rubbed her tired eyes, pouted, and pointed at Carrie. Carrie hung her head, her face turned crimson with guilt.

Adeline, wearing a vibrant yellow dress, sprinted towards Minnie and hurtled into her sister's waiting arms. 'I missed you, sis,' she whispered. Minnie twirled her around, cherishing the moment, before gesturing to the gate. As they entered the yard, Lizzie ascended the front stairs while Alice and Carrie raced. 'Alice and I are going to play big girls' games on the swings in the tree. Keep Adeline away,' Carrie called out to Minnie.

They skipped and jumped left alone in the wattle-scented grounds, their footsteps creating a rhythmic melody. As the daylight faded, Adeline climbed onto Minnie's back, her giggles filling the air. 'Move, horsey! I feel so high, like in a castle!' Adeline said, unable to contain her excitement. Minnie's mind wandered to her father, remembering how he used to lift her onto his shoulders.

Minnie waved at the fading sun. 'We should go inside now.' Adeline stamped her feet and pouted, resisting the idea. 'Ma will have supper cooking. And after we've eaten, we can do some drawings together.' Adeline ignored her words, prompting Minnie to try another approach. 'If you're a good girl and go inside, I'll let Bella sleep in your bed tonight.' Adeline's eyes widened with anticipation, and she raced towards the stairs, Minnie closely supervising her ascent.

As they ate, Charlotte spoke of the boarding house, the topic consuming their conversation. Minnie and Lizzie exchanged winks and headshakes as their stepmother gave a long-winded description of her rounds of the auction houses.

When the meal finished, Charlotte rose from the table. 'It is bedtime for Carrie, Alice, and Adeline. Clean your teeth before bed. Carrie, help Adeline and tuck her in.'

'Tuck Bella in next to her. I promised,' said Minnie as Carrie, trailed by Alice and Adeline, headed towards the bedrooms. Minnie and Lizzie helped Charlotte clear the kitchen.

'There were some woollen blankets at the auction house today,' said Charlotte. 'I thought they would prove handy, so I'll bid at the auction scheduled for Wednesday. I reckon I should pick them up for less than half the retail price.'

Minnie felt anger coursing through her veins. She confronted Charlotte, saying, 'Do you only talk about this place? It seems more important to you than your daughters and stepdaughters. Why not read to the children you sent to bed without a kiss?'

With an angry face, Charlotte stepped forward, the tea towel hanging over her shoulder. 'Minnie, I can't believe you would make such a hateful statement. You show no gratitude for all I've done for you and your sisters. I feel like choking you, you ungrateful girl.' Back rigid, Charlotte rushed to the door.

Lizzie's face was expressionless, and after a moment, she said, 'As it is.'

* * *

The following day, as Lizzie and Minnie headed for the entrance, the odour of lye soap and disinfectant floated in the air, swallowing the ever-present hint of lilac water. Charlotte busied herself scrubbing floors on her hands and knees.

'Busy morning?' asked Minnie.

'I cooked breakfast at five and will work until nine tonight.'

Minnie took several deep breaths of relief that Charlotte was focused on her daily chores and had forgotten last night's events.

As the clatter of trams grew louder and the ceaseless rumble of traffic filled the air, Minnie's chest tightened with a mix of anxiety and frustration. The noise seemed to amplify her mounting anger towards her mundane life. She pondered, her thoughts spinning like the wheels of passing cars, desperately seeking a way to break free from this suffocating existence.

Minnie confessed to Lizzie. 'I'm always tired. This urban existence isn't for me. After long shifts in that dingey factory, we come home to care for the children while Charlotte obsesses over her boarding house.'

Lizzie's face scrunched up in a scowl, mirroring Minnie's frustration. 'Nothing will change unless we make it happen. We can't keep being unpaid maids and babysitters forever, but we must leave Charlotte behind and forge our futures.'

Minnie's grip tightened on her navy tunic as she contemplated Lizzie's words. She glanced towards the blueish-green mountains that encircled the city, a fleeting dream of escape flickering in her mind. But duty held her back, anchoring her to Brisbane. She couldn't desert her little sisters, especially Adeline, who was just three.

She leant towards Lizzie as she wiped her nose with a handkerchief. 'I regret my words to Charlotte. After all, she brought us here, although she could've abandoned us in Ireland.'

Lizzie's unwavering voice cut through the city's noise: 'We must face the truth, Minnie. Charlotte may have brought us here, but we must find our own paths. We can't let obligations keep us trapped in this dreary existence.'

While Lizzie's words rang true, she knew she couldn't desert her innocent little sisters, not now. With a heavy heart, she resigned herself to enduring this monotonous life for a few more years, hoping eventually she could break free.

Chapter 27

Towards the end of March 1912, Minnie arrived home from work expecting a greeting from a bubbling, grinning Adeline tugging at her sleeve and begging to start their games. Instead, she found Adeline with a runny nose and face crumpled into a frown. Minnie squatted and scooped her up, and the toddler snuggled into her chest.

Adeline gazed into her sister's eyes. 'My throat stings, my head bangs, and I'm freezing,' she said.

Minnie bit her lips as her mind raced, searching for answers. How can Adeline shiver in this relentless heat? She placed her hand on her sister's forehead to find it sizzling.

Minnie tucked Adeline into bed, cleared the perspiration-soaked curls glued to her face, and brushed the sweat from her brow with a flannel. Before leaving the room, Minnie cupped the tiny face, 'I will leave you alone to sleep, darling. Rest so you are better and can run and play tomorrow.'

That night, spearing screeches woke Minnie. She rushed to Adeline's bedside. Heat rivalling a hot spring rose from Adeline's bed. Minnie's legs went to jelly as a wave of helplessness attacked her as she gazed down at the writhing body of her moaning sister. Adeline pitched her head and vomited on the floor and again.

Minnie cleaned the room to rid it of its rancidity. She settled the child and grabbed Bella. 'We've been best friends for a long time, and you've done everything I've asked. Now please cure my sister.' She laid her next to Adeline, who drifted into a fitful sleep.

Minnie spent the night seated at Adeline's bedside, gently wiping a wet cloth over her tiny form.

At dawn, Adeline looked up at her. 'Am I burning?'

The fear in the toddler's eyes matched the terror clawing at Minnie, but she forced a faint smile. 'No, of course not. It's a nasty flu.'

'It feels like a big burny fire.'

Minnie took the child's clammy hand in hers. 'Try to sleep, darling. You get well, and we can play horsies.'

Anguish pulsed through Minnie when the little one gave a pleading look as Minnie released her hand. 'If I go to sleep, please don't leave me.'

'Whenever you wake, you'll see Ma, Lizzie, or me,' said Minnie, 'and Bella snuggles beside you.'

On the starless night of 29 March, sharp pokes to her shoulder startled Minnie, and she woke to see Charlotte hunched over her bed. 'Adeline is having seizures.' In a split second, Minnie sprung from the bed without wiping the sleep dust from her eyes. She sprinted to the opposite bed just as Adeline's head sank into the pillow, and her eyes rolled back in their sockets, revealing the eye's white. Then, her arms and legs violently thrashed.

Minnie felt frozen as she gazed down at her sister's form and rested her palms on her burning brow. 'Stay with me, and don't give in. Please, please. I need you.' She turned to Charlotte, wrung her hands, and said, 'Oh Ma, whatever do we do?'

'There's nothing to be done except monitor her. At first light, we'll find a doctor.'

* * *

Before seven a.m., Charlotte asked Lizzie to search for a doctor. In less than an hour, Lizzie strode in, followed by a panting, tall, thin man who introduced himself as Doctor Marks. He asked Charlotte about the symptoms and examined the fitting, sweating girl. 'The poor child has meningitis. There is no hope. All you can do is keep her comfortable while nature takes its course.'

A torrent of despair that crashed through her like waves overcame Minnie. Alongside her sisters, she had cared for the three-year-old since birth. She perceived the curse had traversed the vast expanse of the ocean, determined to snatch away yet another cherished soul.

Her eyes searched the room, and she spoke to Dr Marks with a forthrightness she didn't know she possessed. 'How can you know immediately? Couldn't it be something else? Whatever it is, why don't you make her better? We've lost many loved ones and sailed thousands of miles to escape illness and death. Please help us. After all we have suffered, we can't lose her.'

The doctor studied Minnie's face and spoke in a voice tinged with sympathy. 'I'm sorry to hear about your sadness, but the child has all the symptoms of meningitis—fever, headaches, and vomiting. There's no known cure.'

Desperation claimed Minnie's insides. 'Isn't there something you could try?'

The doctor looked into Minnie's eyes and shook his head.

'Perhaps I didn't explain properly that there is no cure. Keep up your excellent care, and I'll call daily.'

After the doctor left, Charlotte let out tortured sobs. 'It's a lightning strike. Two days ago, Adeline was full of energy.'

On 1 April, Adeline became unconscious. Charlotte sent Lizzie to find the local clergyman, the Reverend Ross. He arrived and peered at the toddler before saying, 'You realise the end is approaching?'

Everyone cried. Charlotte cleared her throat before mumbling, 'Yes.'

The clergyman leant over Adeline, whispering platitudes. Moments after the minister exited, a moaning Adeline fell into the pillow.

Minnie held the toddler's tiny hand, expecting a fit. No convulsions came, and Minnie touched her little sister's brow. Her skin had grown cold. Minnie knew her angel had gone to sleep forever. Head bent, she thrust her face into Adeline's shoulder and let out a heart-wrenching sob.

After stealing herself from Adeline's bed, Minnie shed more tears, flanked by her weeping stepmother and sisters.

* * *

Minnie and her family gathered at the Toowong cemetery to farewell Adeline a few days after her distressing death. Minnie leaned hard on Lizzie's arm, her sister taking her weight and preventing her from falling to the sun-baked earth.

The family surrounded her, whimpers surging from the women and the men coughing and twitching. A lump in her throat prevented Minnie from drawing full breaths, and she squirmed when she felt sweat trickle down her spine.

A preacher recited the familiar funeral prayers. A few clouds filled the windless glass-blue sky. Unlike Ulster, no powdery snow freckled the ground. Instead, bark-shedding trees grew from brown grass.

Minnie thought about the mounting number of lost loved ones. How could God now take the innocent soul she believed hers forever? Adeline's death left a cavern, and the thought of how she'd fill the hole sent heat raging through her.

When the formalities finished, Minnie cowered as she sensed arms grasp her. She turned and peered up into Bill's brown eyes, swimming with sincerity. 'I'm sorry. You've attended too many funerals for one so young.'

Minnie burrowed into Bill's chest and left a wet patch on his starched shirt. 'I'm glad someone understands. Adeline meant the world to me.'

Next, she twisted when she sensed the touch of a rough hand on her sleeve. She saw Ben, beads of sweat on his brow. Jeannie, face drained of colour, gripped his bent elbow. 'Mate, dunno what to say. I know you loved that kid.'

Later, the gathering moved to the boarding house where Jeannie drew Minnie to her and whispered, 'Before Christmas, you'll be an aunt.'

Minnie tittered through snivels and hiccups and kissed Jeannie. 'What fantastic news.' However, unable to rid her mind of thoughts of the sorrowful loss, Minnie asked no questions.

As no one wanted to eat or speak, the group dissipated until only Charlotte, Lizzie, Minnie, and Mr Muir, a guest from room ten, remained. Staring at the plaster ceiling, the group reclined in the brown leather chairs circling the kitchen table. A sad-faced Charlotte, lips trembling, clutched one of

Adeline's frilly dresses. Minnie's stomach dropped as she looked on.

Minnie twitched in response to a sharp jab in the ribs. She inched closer to Lizzie, who muttered into her ear, 'What's that?' Minnie's gaze followed Lizzie's eyes. Mr Muir's hand rested on Charlotte's shaking hand.

Charlotte, glancing at the clock, jumped to her feet. 'Loss has chased me forever. It shatters my heart that sadness has struck again, but I must keep operating the business.'

At least her obsession with her business will stop Charlotte from lurching into a prolonged depression, Minnie mused.

'Yes, we should sleep to prepare ourselves for an early morning,' said Lizzie, yawning.

* * *

Minnie shivered whenever she glanced at Adeline's empty bed. Without the welcome distraction of thoughts of Adeline, her job became unbearable.

Charlotte returned to her gruelling work schedule. Minnie wondered if the activity helped keep her mind from the devastating events. Her stepmother spent more time in Mr Muir's company, and Bill and Annie's visits ended, although Minnie didn't know and couldn't fathom why.

Minnie leafed through the *Brisbane Courier* at breakfast each morning. Since June, news of an industrial dispute affecting tramway workers dominated its pages. She leant to Lizzie across the table. 'The paper is full again with talk of this tram worker's brawl.'

Lizzie looked over her teacup. 'I'm not interested. It doesn't affect us.'

A few days later, Minnie trundled behind her co-workers when a stranger insisted they attend a union meeting. With the machinery dormant, an unusual stillness haunted the factory, although the stale stench of oil-polluted air remained. She paid union dues from her wages but didn't know what unions did.

She followed the stream of fellow workers without questioning the reason for the tearoom meeting. Inside, a ruddy-faced, balding fellow stood behind a table at the front of the room facing the assembly. As Minnie entered, the fellow pumped his fists and boomed, 'In sympathy with our brother tramway workers, all union labour in Brisbane will strike. Effective immediately.'

The staff filed out. Minnie propped herself against the wall outside the room to wait for Lizzie. Groans and expletives rumbled from the line of exiting co-workers. 'It is fine for these union bosses to preach about their high and mighty principles,' said one woman. 'Do they think of our kids? No, they wouldn't give a toss if they starved.'

As Lizzie filed past, Minnie prodded her sister in the back. 'Do we walk out now without returning to our machines?'

Lizzie shrugged her shoulders. 'Yes. I can't say I will miss the racket or Porky, but I'll miss payday.' She slipped her arm through the crook of Minnie's arm, and together, they headed off towards the tram station.

As she listened to the steel tram wheels turn, Minnie considered how she'd fill the days until work resumed. It would take less than a week to read her modest book collection, and she didn't fancy taking up sketching or butterfly collecting. She'd use the time to consider her options for the future.

* * *

Deep in thought, Minnie sat beneath the sprawling jacaranda tree that graced the boarding house's yard. The fragrant scents of blooming garden plants enveloped her senses as the days turned into weeks. Lost, she wrestled with the conflicting thoughts that seemed to tangle and knot within her. The weight of her dilemma threatened to suffocate her like a dense fog clouding her thoughts. Should she flee Brisbane and escape the monotony of her job, or should she stay because of a sense of responsibility and loyalty?

The choice felt impossible, a choice that threatened to tear her apart. While she had never formed a bond with Charlotte, she didn't view her as the wicked stepmother of fairy tales. Charlotte cared for Jeannie and Lizzie as children, stepping in after their father's passing, even through her personal struggles. Charlotte orchestrated their journey to Australia, a decision that, in hindsight, made sense, considering the dire circumstances they faced in Ulster.

The frenzied city life and the monotonous factory job brought no joy to Minnie. Her heart still clung to the dream of crossing the mountains. She could reunite with Jeannie, who now lived beyond the range at Kobble Creek. From Ben's descriptions, Minnie gathered that Kobble Creek was the sort of peaceful rural spot that featured in her dreams.

Her intuition assured her Jeannie would welcome her with open arms, but she couldn't assume anything. She would have to continue her journey alone if there wasn't a place for her under her sister's roof. Finally, she decided. 'Da, now it's my turn. The curse has followed us across the ocean. I will leave on my own and settle in a place further away from it before it brings more death.' *I am brave and can face whatever lies ahead.*

Delighted at her decision but apprehensive about Charlotte's reaction, she jumped up. After taking a deep breath, she ran to find Charlotte. In a voice stronger than she believed herself capable of, she said, 'I plan to leave Brisbane.' Charlotte only gave Minnie a bemused look. Minnie anticipated a strong resistance, but the calm response she received took her aback. Later, Lizzie's face displayed astonishment. 'My, the timid Minnie has grown courageous and determined. She is leaving before me.'

Minnie prepared for her departure, consulting public transport timetables to plan her route to Kobble Creek. She packed her belongings in a worn-out suitcase, placing Bella and *Anne of Green Gables* on top between layers of underwear she tucked the few shillings she had saved from her factory wages

Minnie left on a Saturday. She said her goodbyes when the sun provided enough light to guide her to the tram stop. She kissed Lizzie before they bid each other farewell. Lizzie covered her face with her hands, and when she released them, she whispered, 'Stay safe. Bad things can happen.'

'I'll write,' Minnie replied.

Carrie and Alice showered her with hugs and kisses. 'We'll miss you, but we'll always be friends, won't we?' chorused the girls.

Charlotte clapped her hand on Minnie's slender shoulders. 'To succeed, you need to push like hell. Don't be afraid to fight.' Then she shoved four brown bank notes into Minnie's hands. 'You might need these.'

Minnie, just sixteen, swung her well-worn suitcase as she slammed the lattice door and headed towards Brunswick

Street. She strode along, trembling as she realised she would finally get to cross the elusive mountains, a journey she must make alone. With each step, her confidence increased.

Chapter 28

Minnie, her suitcase heavy in her hand, trudged along the rough, pock-marked track that led to a farmhouse in Kobble Creek. Above her, the sky stretched out in a vast expanse of glass-blue, adorned with a few fluffy clouds that glided effortlessly. In the distance, dogs barking and chickens clucking filled the air, creating a lively symphony of rural life.

As Minnie approached, a figure suddenly appeared on the verandah, causing her heart to skip a beat. Relief washed over her as she recognised Jeannie. A sense of joy bubbled up inside her - she had found Kobble Creek and her sister.

Jeannie hurried down the stairs with her hands resting on her distended belly, her expression one of excitement. Minnie dropped her suitcase and rushed towards her sister. As they embraced, the warmth of Jeannie's touch brought a sense of comfort and belonging. Minnie clung to Jeannie for a long time, savouring the moment of reunion.

Jeannie held Minnie at arm's length, her gaze travelling up from her feet to her eyes, their gazes locking in a heartfelt connection. Concern scrawled on her face, Jeannie remarked on Minnie's appearance. 'I've missed you and the girls. You look so skinny. Have you forgotten to eat?'

Minnie playfully patted Jeannie's swollen stomach, trying to lighten the mood. 'You're far from thin! You mentioned this at Adeline's funeral, but that day is still a blur.'

Jeannie's expression turned sombre. 'Yes, it was such an awful and unexpected loss. Our dear little Adeline.'

'Any preference for a boy or girl?' Minnie asked.

'Not really, neither does Ben.'

Jeannie took Minnie's elbow and ushered her through the rambling house via the cosy sitting room, which opened onto the verandah. A soft breeze sent the lace curtains rippling over the couch near a French door. Minnie's eyes moved past the paintings hanging from the picture rails until they rested at the other end of the room where two cracked black leather armchairs faced the couch separated by occasional tables.

They padded past peeling strips of paint along the maze-like corridor. Jeannie nudged open a once-polished door. Minnie's heart missed a beat as she, oozing with delight, surveyed the spacious bedroom. She discarded her suitcase on the grey blanket that covered a double bed. Her eyes moved to a dressing table and a wardrobe until her vision locked onto the stunning outlook of the distant hills offered through the curtain-fringed sash window. 'Jeannie, the view is superb.'

Jeannie nodded and flashed a cheerful smile. 'Come back to the verandah for a refreshing tea and a chat.'

The pair sipped tea on the shaded verandah as black flies buzzed around them. Jeannie gazed quizzically at her sister. 'How did you get here?'

'I came by public transport. Finding my way here proved an adventure because I'd never left Brisbane before, but I'd studied maps and timetables for days. I didn't know your location in Kobble Creek, but the bus driver on the last leg dropped me at the gate,' said Minnie. 'I've always fantasised about what magic lay beyond these mountains, but I never dreamed of anything like this—the open spaces, colours, and aroma are breathtaking.'

Jeannie's eyes narrowed to a slit. 'Where are you headed?'

Minnie considered the question and resisted blurting out that she wanted to stay forever. It was best to have manners and wait until Ben and Jeannie invited her. Trying to sound and look casual, she replied, 'I'm not sure. Can I stay here while I decide?'

'You're welcome for as long as you wish.'

Minnie scanned the patchwork-like vista. A tall, craggy mountain dominated the horizon and towered over smaller purple hills. On the lower slopes, crops grew in rows hemmed in by split timber fences and herds of cattle. The rolling earth in the foreground hosted the odd farm building and abandoned shack.

Jeannie waved her arm expansively. 'They're our boundaries.'

'So big. Ulster farms are gardens in comparison,' Minnie said.

'Australian farmers need more land because the rain's unreliable.'

Minnie chuckled. 'From one extreme to the other. In Ulster, it rained and rained and rained.'

She trained her gaze closer to the house. Free-range hens and bush turkeys scrambled around. Birds chirped as they glided through the aromatic, eucalyptus-scented air. The rustle of leaves and the trickle of the nearby stream sounded. A creeping plant, which Jeannie identified as a native violet, hugged the ground.

Further away, the creeper gave way to cattle munching Kikuyu grass. Such raw beauty made Minnie's skin tingle. They talked about Jeannie's country life. 'We run a dairy herd and grow bananas and pineapples for extra income.'

'I've seen banana trees in Brisbane, but I don't know what a pineapple tree looks like.'

Jeannie tittered. 'Minnie, pineapples grow on a low plant protruding a foot from the ground.'

Recognition surged through her mind, and she joined Jeannie's giggles. 'Of course, I saw rows of the plants from the train. I still have heaps to learn about this country. Do you farm anything else?'

'We grow vegetables for ourselves and wheat, barley, and corn as food for the cows during dry periods.' Minnie scanned the surroundings. 'It's tranquil here. You must love it.' Her focus jumped from point to point—the distant mountains, the red-coated grazing cattle, and scratching bush turkeys.

Jeannie cast her eyes downwards. 'I enjoy living here, but...'

Minnie dreaded the meaning of the words. 'Please don't say you and Ben are having troubles.'

'Oh, no, we're rock solid. It's just...' Jeannie, brow knitted, inched towards Minnie and stroked her back. 'I'm glad you've come because I grow lonely sometimes.'

'What? In this heavenly place?' asked Minnie, disbelief scrawled across her forehead.

'I give Ben a hand with the morning milking, but later, he tends the crops at a far part of the property. I don't see him again until we milk in the afternoon. In his absence, the house is eerily silent. It's isolated.'

'When is the baby due?'

'Early November.'

Jeannie sprang up and pulled on well-worn galoshes. She shuffled towards the dairy, both hands supporting the small of her back. She called over her shoulder, urgency reflected in her voice, 'I've got to get the milking done. Help yourself to anything you want.'

After patting the two panting dogs curled in a corner, Minnie sprawled in the taut canvas sling of a squatter's chair and stretched her legs on its extended arms as she breathed the muggy air. She opened *Anne of Green Gables,* but Anne and Marilla's antics didn't hold her attention, and her vision strayed to the pristine scenery. This empty country has a unique and breathtaking landscape.

She fought to keep her eyes open but fell into a daze and awoke to a dimming light with *Anne of Green Gables* spread open, face down beside her. Bathed in the golden pre-dusk light, the majestic view took a different perspective. Birds of every colour and size flew in flocks.

She rushed inside, making a mental note to investigate what this view offered at sunset. It would be spectacular.

Ben and Jeannie were in the kitchen. 'Minnie, what a surprise,' said Ben in a haltering voice as he flashed a warm grin. As cooking odours swirled around them, he kissed Minnie's forehead before giving her a welcoming swat on the upper arm.

The trio settled at the table for a steak, onion, peas, carrots, and mashed potato meal. As they munched, Minnie looked towards her sister and asked for salt. Minnie expected the saltshaker to glide across the table in response to her request.

A reply came, but not from Jeannie. Ben asked, 'Who are you speaking to?' with a hint of annoyance. 'There's no Jeannie here.'

Had Minnie heard properly? Her smile wavered as she glanced at her sister, hoping for an explanation. But Jeannie lowered her gaze and arched her eyebrows, leaving Ben to answer. In a monotone, Minnie projected her voice towards Ben and said, 'Ben, whatever do you mean? I don't understand. Jeannie is in front of me.'

'The youngster Jeannie dwells in a doll's house beside a hollow log in the paddock. Jean, a grown woman and expectant mother, lives here.'

Minnie's head spun. Little girls grew up. She'd try to change, but her dear sister would always be Jeannie to her.

Minnie followed her impulse to wash the dishes. As they worked side by side, Minnie cocked her neck towards Jean. 'Enjoy a lie-in each morning. While here, I'll help Ben milk in the mornings.'

After excusing herself, Minnie hurriedly made her way to the verandah. As she stepped outside, a vibrant orange sun descended, sending brilliant flashes of colour across the clouds. Gradually, it disappeared behind the mountains, painting the heavens with a gentle purple hue. Minnie gripped the verandah railing; her eyes fixated on the breathtaking scene. She remained in that position as the moon emerged. Inhaling the balmy night air, she sniffed a subtle hint of eucalyptus as the silvery moonlight illuminated the distant line of rugged mountains.

The verandah boards resonated with the rhythmic thump of boots. Confirming her suspicions, the glowing orange cigarette tip signalled Ben had taken a seat nearby. A familiar voice floated from behind. 'That rocky peak is Mount Samson. The Blackfellas call it *Buran*, which means wind.'

As the light dimmed, a chorus of staccato chirps and croaks

filled the air, causing the skin on Minnie's neck to prickle. Startled, she instinctively stepped back. Crickets, frogs, cicadas, and geckos,' Ben explained. 'They create a racket, but they're harmless creatures.'

Mesmerised, Minnie continued to gaze at the darkening sky, watching as the stars gradually appeared. Wrapping her arms around herself, she felt goosebumps rise on her skin. She raised her eyes towards the star-dotted sky and whispered, 'It is more magic over those mysterious mountains than I imagined. Maybe, just maybe, I've found a place where I can make a life and escape the grip of the curse.

* * *

Minnie woke before sunrise the following morning and noticed the absence of city clamour. Since she couldn't find Ben, she headed towards the dairy. As she stepped outside, a refreshing breeze carrying the scents of turf, soil, and animals greeted her. Overwhelmed by the sweet songs of birds, she paused momentarily and realised that the ground was shaking with moos, swishing tails, plodding hooves, and red-coated cows surrounded her.

The cattle continued their march, and when Minnie reached the dairy, she found more noisy creatures waiting outside the holding yard. They stamped their hooves and pushed the gate with their snouts. The ones who arrived with her crowded in on the early arrivals. Minnie elbowed through the milling beasts and approached the cow standing at the front, looking at her. She gently massaged her wiry coat. 'What's the matter?'

The animal replied with a loud moo and a violent head thrust towards the holding yard entrance. Minnie looked into the cow's deep brown eyes. 'Oh, I see. You want me to open the gate.' She threaded her hand around the fence post and released the twine. The awaiting herd filed in, and Minnie retreated and shooed the stragglers.

Ben arrived at the dairy and saw the cows herded in the holding yard. 'You've done my job. You can be my helper every morning.' A broad smile speaking of surprise and gratitude smothered his face.

Her stomach fluttered at the compliment; she planned to become indispensable. 'It's nothing; it's easy to work out. I shooed them through the gate, but they seemed to head here by instinct.'

'Must have sore udders. They've been giving plenty milk,' Ben said.

'How else can I help?'

'There's not much you can do. I'll need to set time aside to teach ya,' said Ben as he scratched his temples.

'I learned to milk cows in Ulster. It seems the same, although the herd is huge. I bet Jean needed no teaching.'

Ben tilted his head and dissolved into booming laughter. 'You're right.'

Minnie raced to the house when they'd finished milking, jumping fly-ridden cow pads as she went. The tantalising odour of burned sugar and stewed fruit drifted towards her. She found Jean in the kitchen with a multi-coloured apron tied around her bloated belly. 'That's the smell of Ulster.'

'I wanted to treat you to a cake Charlotte taught me to bake in Ulster,' Jean said, flinging open the wood stove door and sliding the tray out. 'I'll leave this on the bench cooling while we bake bread. We'll eat a piece with a cuppa after we've put the bread in the oven.'

The sisters mixed, rolled, and thumped the dough. After replacing the risen cake with the bread mixture, they sipped tea and nibbled it. As a warm, yeasty perfume swirled around them, Jean spoke abruptly, warning Minnie that something was playing on her sister's mind.

Finally, Jean unburdened herself. 'Ben and I talked last night. If you agree, we want you to stay until the baby arrives and settles in, 'she cleared her throat. 'All we can offer is board, lodgings, and some cash.'

Minnie's heart sang, but she suppressed it. 'Why, I'd be happy to. Please enjoy this chance to relax before the birth. 'I'll assist with milking in the mornings and you with washing, ironing and baking after the morning milking. After lunch, I'll help with the crops and later the second milking.' she said. 'And you don't need to give me money. Charlotte gave me enough to survive for a while.'

Jean shot a bemused stare at Minnie. 'Charlotte, what?'

Minnie opened her mouth to explain but shrugged instead.

* * *

Minnie settled into her sister's home. Rising before dawn, she assisted Ben with the milking before helping Jean with household chores.

She took charge of washing and ironing, considering the processes too harsh for a pregnant woman. She ignored Jean's protests. 'Minnie, please allow me to help. I'm fit and healthy.'

'I won't stand by as you haul masses of boiling laundry, scrub clothes on a washboard, and juggle steel irons,' said

Minnie sternly. 'You must allow me to do the heavy chores until the baby's birth.'

When she started as post-lunch crop assistant, Ben suggested Minnie work the grain crops, and he took charge of the pineapple and bananas.

The familiar gritty sensation of soil in her hands and under her fingernails whisked Minnie back to Ulster. As much as she willed her childhood memories to the furthest corner of her mind, she realised that her love for farming would never fade.

Ben waved to her and called, 'Time for milking.' Minnie gathered her tools and dragged her sweaty body after her brother-in-law. Intense-faced, Ben cocked his head to Minnie as they trudged towards the dairy. 'Well, how did ya first day go?'

'I'm familiar with this work, but the conditions are different.'

'What ya mean?'

'I worked in a cooler place before. Here, the sun bore into me, sending sweat dripping from my neck and sides, and giant flies circled me. And the hot, still air tasted of dust.'

After scoffing down the meal of lamb chops, boiled potatoes, beans, and peas cooked by Jean and taking her mandatory view of the sunset, an exhausted Minnie flopped on her bed. As she undressed, she looked down in horror at the reddened skin on every part of her body exposed to the scorching sun. Her muscles ached. She attributed the pain to her long absence from the cropping fields but was sure she'd adjust to the conditions and protect herself from the sun's blanching rays. In a flash, she fell into a blissful, deep sleep.

There was an aspect of Australian farming she couldn't take in her stride. Spiders, lizards, and other pests sent sparks of terror sizzling through her. Her heart hammered whenever one crossed her path. She sprinted and screamed as if she'd encountered a corpse. Invariably, Ben ran to the rescue, but after several repeat performances, he lost patience.

After about a month at Kobble Creek, she felt something slippery slither over her feet. She screeched, and Ben rushed to her side. 'What's all the fuss and screaming 'bout?'

'I think I stepped on a snake. It felt warm and wriggled and—'

Ben looked into her eyes. 'Yeah, but Minnie, did it bite?'

The notion that a slimy creature may have bitten her made her heart hammer in her ears. She shrieked again and sprinted to the safety of a shady tree.

Ben gave chase. When her panting brother-in-law caught up to her, he said, 'Ya gunna have to get used to creepy crawlies. You'll see them plenty in the Australian bush. Screaming and carrying on won't change things.'

Minnie glimpsed him laugh into his hand.

* * *

On her first Saturday at Kobble Creek, Minnie strolled along the corridor towards the sitting room. Her nostrils filled with the fragrance of jasmine, and her ears flooded with the hum of conversation. Her feet barely touched the ground in her haste to discover who was there, although because of the familiar perfume and the voices, she'd guessed.

Reaching the doorway, she peered inside. She blinked and then shrieked in delight. Annie lounged on the sofa while Bill talked to Ben, and they reclined in the black leather chairs.

She hurried over and sat next to Annie. Minnie hugged Annie

tightly and kissed her face. Annie commented it was nice to see her and that Ben had said she would stay. Minnie laughed with joy, and Annie joined in.

Bill chortled from his armchair, and Minnie went to greet him with kisses before returning to the sofa. The reunion made her realise she missed the couple, whose visits had abruptly stopped after Adeline's funeral. Those few months felt endless. She recalled the unwavering support of the pair.

Annie hadn't changed; she was still wearing flouncy clothes, and thick layers of powder masked her face. The scent of jasmine encased her like a bubble. Minnie's relationship with Annie started with anger. Minnie viewed Annie as responsible for her life of servitude in a sweatshop. However, Minnie's attitude slowly softened, and she admired Annie's practicality and determination.

Bill had changed over the years, with lines now furrowing his brow. But Minnie saw the tenderness she had noticed in his eyes when they first met. 'What brings you two here?' Minnie asked.

'We stay at our Samsonvale property, just a few miles away, on the weekends and always call,' Bill replied, waving to the north.

'I knew about your farm and wanted to visit, but my Saturday shifts didn't allow it,' Minnie said regretfully.

Minnie looked forward to their visits, which were the highlight of her week. They followed a predictable pattern: Footsteps sounded on the corridor linoleum, followed by a blast of jasmine. Bill claimed the same leather chair when they reached the sitting room.

Bill passionately followed current affairs. He shared updates on world and local events, shipping arrivals, sports, and parliamentary decisions. Minnie, feeling bored, scanned the room and saw indications of a similar lack of interest. With a tightened expression, Jean flattened her lips. Ben rubbed the back of his neck and tapped his feet. Avoiding eye contact, Minnie thought, Bill, I love you, but I wish you would stop babbling about trivia and tell us things we want to hear. She saw Bill's lengthy news sessions as the price she had to pay for the company of these people who had been by her side since they arrived in Australia. She reminded herself to focus on the positive - they didn't need newspapers.

* * *

There was another regular visitor.

Minnie greeted Albert, Jean's brother-in-law, twice a week. The weather-bronzed Albert, clad in well-worn work clothes, never removed his misshaped coal grey broad-brimmed hat, even indoors. A fulsome grin filled his face, leaving permanent groves at the corner of his mouth, and a cigarette always waggled from his bottom lip.

Minnie caught the odour of tobacco first. She greeted him as he swaggered on his bandy legs towards the kitchen, a brown pint bottle tucked under each arm. 'Good afternoon,' she said, giving a welcoming smile.

He responded by tipping his hat. 'G'day, mate.'

She knew 'mate' was an Australian expression that men used when greeting each other. She peered over her shoulder. There was no man in sight. Did he speak to her?

Chapter 29

31 December 1912

At dusk, the setting sun cast a golden hue as Ben, Jean, and Minnie gathered in their finest clothes. They climbed into the sulky, which creaked slightly as they settled in, ready to attend the district New Year's Eve celebration. The annual happening took place in the hotel's lounge bar. As Ben tapped the horse's back, the rhythmic sound of the oscillating wheels echoed through the quiet evening. Recent rainfall had turned the tracks into muddy paths, causing the horse's hooves to squelch with each step. Towering gum trees lined the route, their branches intertwining above, blocking the starlight from reaching them.

The horse strained against the uphill stretches, its muscles flexing and breaths becoming heavier. Soon, the sights and sounds of the town began to envelop them as they passed familiar landmarks along the way, including the butter factory, railway station, and primary school. They reached the main street, alive with activity, bustling with pedestrians and horse-drawn conveyances. Lively fiddle music wafted through the air as thick as a wool blanket from the local hotel. Minnie, filled with excitement, could feel a tingling sensation running through her entire body as she descended from the sulky. She smoothed her clothes, taking in the vibrant scene around her.

Glancing over to the rig, Minnie noticed Jean remained stationary, though she could see her sister wriggling and struggling. Jean called out to Ben, who unhurriedly made his way from tethering the horse to a nearby hitching post. 'I'm stuck, darling. Can't move.' Jean's voice carried a hint of frustration.

Ben increased his pace when he saw Jean had twisted her skirt around the wheel. Ben freed his wife, and Jean jumped out of the sulky, landing beside Minnie. With her nostrils pinched between thumb and forefinger, Minnie couldn't help but ask, 'What stinks?'

Jean gestured to the trench drain lining the roadway, a stormwater conduit.

A wave of people spilled onto the hotel verandah and flooded the street. The group walked towards the venue, their footsteps mingling with the hum of conversation. Every few steps, they paused to exchange pleasantries with familiar faces.

Upon reaching the entrance, Minnie's eyes widened in awe at the sight before her. An array of colourful balloons and streamers adorned the vast space, equivalent to a football field, creating a whimsical atmosphere. Two long trestle tables displayed freshly baked cakes, biscuits, and sandwiches, filling the air with a sweet scent.

Resolute, Minnie stood her ground amidst the pushing crowd, feeling the pressure of bodies behind her. She resisted, her mouth agape with wonder, until Jean took charge and propelled her forward, urging her inside. Inside, a lively bunch gathered in groups, some leaning against the festively decorated walls, their animated conversations punctuated by laughter. Minnie recognised most of the townsfolk, their familiar faces bringing a sense of warmth and familiarity to the occasion. Yet Jean wound her arm around Minnie's waist and guided her among the partygoers. 'You know Ben's cousin Joe. And have you met Henry, Ben's brother?'

'Is anyone here not related to Ben?'

Jean ushered Minnie to a seat. 'Yes, Mrs Watson, the wife of the butter factory owner. She heads this way.'

Minnie's gaze followed Jean's outstretched arm to a smartly dressed, smiling blonde woman. Jean placed one hand on Minnie's shoulder. 'Mrs Watson, my sister, Minnie.'

Mrs Watson beamed at Minnie and replaced Jean's palm by resting a bejewelled hand on Minnie's shoulder. 'How lovely to meet another Ulsterwoman.'

'You come from Ulster, ma'am?' Minnie felt blood rush to her face. It was apparent, given that she spoke with an Ulster accent.

'Yes, the Shankill Road, the poorest Protestant area of Belfast,' Mrs Watson said. 'My parents moved to Australia, where I seized the opportunities that came my way.'

As Mrs Watson disappeared into the crowd, her bangles tinkled and clashed together. Jean leaned in and whispered to Minnie, 'She's a wonderful woman, down-to-earth, and never loses sight of her beginnings.'

Minnie replied, 'There's not much I wish to remember about Ulster, but I want to stay humble and follow Da's teachings about respecting everyone.'

The master of ceremonies counted the hours, then the minutes, until midnight, when people raised their voices in song and celebration to welcome the New Year. Revellers threw streamers, burst balloons, and whistled before linking hands and hugging. Joy overtook Minnie as she joined the fun and swayed from side to side. They lingered until the end of the function.

On their way home, Minnie wondered how she'd ever settle after such an exciting evening. 'I enjoyed myself. The people are open and accepting,' she said.

'Because many are me kin,' chuckled Ben throwing his head back.

'Ha, ha!' laughed Jean. 'Minnie and I are used to vengeful folk who make blind judgments. Inclusion in this community is a blessing.'

* * *

In February 1913, an out-of-tune chorus of clucking and barking sent Minnie to investigate. She spotted a figure rushing towards the farmhouse and soon realised it was Lizzie.

Minnie sprinted, embracing her sister so close that the ribbed fabric of Lizzie's dress prickled her skin, now several shades darker from labouring in the heat.

Lizzie's smile rivalled the brightness of the sun. The pair clasped hands and skipped in a circle.

'Let's surprise Jeannie,' said Minnie. 'Oh, Jeannie has become Jean. Ben likes it that way. I'm trying to call her Jean, but sometimes my mind drifts back to our Jeannie. You'll need to try, too.'

With their hands joined, they stormed the stairs two at a time. When they set foot on the verandah, Minnie gestured to Lizzie to crawl behind a canvas chair.

Minnie located Jean crouched over the stove, surrounded

by rings of flame and gravy-infused steam. She clapped her hand on her sister's upper arm. 'Come. I have a surprise. And you should get out of the suffocating smell of stale cooking fat.'

Jean untied her apron. 'This isn't a trick?'

When Lizzie pounced from the hiding place, Jean gasped before jumping backwards. Clinging to the table, a smile lit up her face. 'What an unexpected treat!'

'How is the family?' asked Jean as the trio gathered around a wicker table, slurping countless cups of tea while inhaling the spicy fragrance of wattle. They flicked away the annoying flies.

'Charlotte has remarried.'

Jean and Minnie gasped. 'Did she marry Mr Muir?' asked Minnie.

'Yes,' said Lizzie, as she narrowed her eyes and furrowed her brow.

'Does he live at the boarding house?' asked Jean quizzically.

'No, they are about to move to Bulimba, on the river's southern bank, taking Carrie and Alice.'

'An ideal chance to get away without making waves,' said Minnie.

Lizzie tittered. 'Yes, I grabbed the opportunity.'

Minnie interrupted the conversation when she turned to Lizzie. 'You stay here and chat with Jean while I help Ben with the afternoon milking.' She rolled her sleeves and bolted.

She heard the crunch of shoes scurrying and twigs snapping behind, followed by Lizzie's voice. 'I'll help. It'll make for light work.'

At the dairy, Ben raised his head from a cow's flank. He stared at Lizzie as if he saw a ghost. He rubbed his eyes, and the widest grin claimed his face. 'It's you, Lizzie! Thought I was seeing things.'

* * *

When they'd finished the evening meal, Ben excused himself.

'I'll leave you to the girl's talk while I smoke outside,' he said.

The trio talked about the old days in Ulster and aboard the *Rippingham Grange*, shaking as they cackled.

'Minnie, do you still hunt stowaways? I noticed *Anne of Green Gables* in the bedroom. I've never worked out why you love that tale,' said Lizzie.

Minnie sensed heat creep up her face. She shrugged.

'I suspect the appeal of *Anne of Green Gables* is that the story follows an orphan girl who made good even though she faced many obstacles,' said Jean.

Minnie nodded. But while that was true, the book meant more than she cared to share. The tale sparked her budding love of language and storytelling, connecting her to Da, Mr. Underwood, and Frances. It served as a permanent reminder of her friendship with Mr. and Mrs. McLeod and reminded her of reading to Sam and Adeline.

Later, while Minnie introduced Lizzie to the magical sunset, she sensed a presence behind them. When she peered around, Ben, framed by the glow of his cigarette, leant against the door frame.

Minnie whispered to Lizzie, 'Although these sunsets have been with him all his life, he still enjoys them. It's understand-able; they're different each evening.'

* * *

Jean and Minnie were doing laundry with copper sticks in their hands. Their eyes were red from vapour and soap suds. 'Thelma is almost six months old now,' Minnie said.

Jean avoided looking at Minnie, and her body became stiff. 'Doesn't time fly? It seems like yesterday we left the hospital with her, the size of a doll. She has grown so much, already raising her head,' Jean said while swiping at smoke bubbles.

Minnie deduced Jean was pretending not to understand. 'Don't bury your head. You don't need my help anymore. I adore living here and love Thelma, but I don't expect you and Ben to keep me forever,' Minnie said sharply. Minnie's heart hammered as she pondered; I must somehow force Jean to deal with this.

Jean stared at her with a pained frown. 'I'll speak to Ben, but I'm sure you can stay.'

Minnie sought Jean's eyes, and their gazes locked for a long moment. 'You cannot push this onto Ben. Our decision affects you, Ben, Thelma, and me,' said Minnie in a determined voice. Surprised, Minnie sensed her limbs stiffen when she glanced at her sister and saw tears gush down her cheeks. She took Jean's hands. 'We must focus on this together,' said Minnie.

Minnie's words evoked another wave of sobs. Jean burrowed her face in Minnie's chest, and as the tears subsided, muffled speech rose. 'It is hard to find words because of my confusion. I want this to disappear, as I'll miss you. Do you think me a right goose?'

'No. But now you've shared your feelings, we can search for a solution, Minnie said. 'What say I stay, assist with the early milking, and get a job starting afterwards? How does that sound?'

Jean made no response, but a hint of a smile replaced her frown.

'We can't ignore this, especially as Lizzie lives here too,' said Minnie. You and Ben aren't rich, and I can't exploit your generosity.'

Jean scrunched her nose. 'I will ask Ben to enquire about jobs in the butter factory.' Minnie thought she would take that as Jean's acceptance of her idea.

'An improvement on stitching pyjamas.' Images of that sewing sweatshop rotated before Minnie, making her shiver so much she could have sworn the blood in her veins turned to ice.

* * *

A few days later, Jean entered the bedroom shared by Minnie and Lizzie, where Minnie lay sprawled on the bed. 'Ben asked around. The Watsons, who own the butter factory, are looking for a domestic to wash and iron each afternoon while watching their school-aged children. You met Mrs Watson at the New Year celebration. They want someone to start straight away. Are you interested?'

A sense of satisfaction overtook Minnie as she sprang up from the bed. 'Perfect. I can assist with farm work in the mornings. Mrs Watson is kind, and I love children.'

Jean flashed a glowing smile and drew Minnie close to her. 'This way, we get to stay together.'

Chapter 30

Twice a week, Albert appeared, lugging two brown pint bottles.

Minnie was always conscious of allowing Ben and Albert privacy. On one occasion, she peeked around the partially open kitchen door. The brothers conversed and swilled beer.

'Ya have two Jean look-alikes here, mate?' said Albert, eyebrows peaked.

Ben thumped his drained glass on the wooden table. 'They're Jean's sisters, Lizzie and Minnie, so don't get ideas.'

'Is Minnie the mysterious one who wears bright-coloured clothes, goes with bare feet, and is always the first to spot me?'

'She looks pretty, but she's a toughie. You should watch her chop wood and swing a spade, outdoing most men. The three of them are tough. Reckon their hard life as young 'uns seasoned 'em,' said Ben.

Minnie entered the kitchen, and there was a lull in the conversation. She sensed Albert's eyes bore through her. As Minnie checked the cake, she wondered what lurked behind that permanent grin.

Later, she and Jean rested at the verandah wicker table, conversing over tea and a buttered bun. Minnie grasped the opportunity to satisfy her curiosity about Albert without explaining her interest to her sister. 'Judging by the frequent visits, Ben and Albert must be close,' Minnie said, attempting to sound casual.

Jean's face twitched, but no words left her chaffed lips. Minnie's stomach contracted with impatience until Jean said, 'Albert, like Ben, is cheerful, hard-working, and big-hearted, but he has a nasty habit.'

'Not that it's my concern, but whatever is it? He doesn't behave like an axe murderer!'

Jean gave out a one-note laugh. 'Nothing that wicked, but he is an uncontrollable gambler.'

'I've noticed a form guide hanging from his trouser pocket. Horse racing is a fairly harmless pastime that allows people to escape their everyday lives.'

Jean's face blanched as she shook her head and muttered. 'Fairly harmless, indeed. Not on Albert's scale. It's not only horses and cards; he'd bet on anything, even a chicken race.'

Minnie knew little about gambling. She needed time to comprehend what her sister said. Not wanting to hear anymore, Minnie lowered her gaze and devoured the bun.

Eating allowed her to think. The conversation had become uncomfortable, so she would change the subject. When she looked up, she smiled weakly at Jean. 'Why does Albert call everyone *mate?*

Jean chuckled. 'It's a common Australian greeting you must have heard Ben and others use.'

'I often hear Albert using the phrase regardless of the gender and age of the person he speaks to.'

Realisation rippled across Jeannie's brow. 'Now you mention it, he uses the term a lot. It rolls off his tongue.'

Minnie shot her sister a quizzical glance. 'Why do you think that is?'

Eyes sparking, Jean tittered as she gave a mocking smile. 'Mm, maybe it is a guard against forgetting a name.'

Minnie heard male voices and the scrape of boots on the linoleum. It was the perfect opportunity to stop this conversation before it returned to the uncomfortable subject. She exploded from her seat and gathered the drained teacups and the crumb-flecked plates. 'The men have left the kitchen; it's time to wash plates and dice vegetables,' she said to Jean.

* * *

Minnie clasped the verandah railing, feeling dwarfed by the vast open space as sunset colours filled the sky. She sucked in a lungful of the spicy bouquet from the frangipani tree near the front stairs that trembled in the slight breeze.

The odour of beer and tobacco grew closer, and Minnie's heart raced as she peered over her shoulder. Albert approached, face screwed and hands knotted behind his back. She thought him clumsy. He stopped beside her. 'G'day, how are ya goin', mate?'

She trembled. As he fumbled for cigarette papers, Albert turned his head and looked at her expectantly. She tried to open her mouth to return the greeting, but only a rush of breath came. Come on, mouth, open.

Eventually, the words came. 'I am well, thank you.' As she formed the words, she sensed heat burn into her skin.

A satisfied upward arch overlaid his permanent grin. He scraped his hand through his hair and stammered. 'Ya pretty keen on these ahh sunsets.'

'Yes, I look every evening. I love it. The light and the colours are always different.' She smiled demurely.

He didn't meet her gaze and appeared to be in deep thought, and Minnie speculated he searched for words to keep the conversation going. 'Gee, those cockatoos make a racket. Blighters are like a mob of squawking cats.'

'They come every dusk. I enjoy their company. My white feathered friends are not unpredictable like humans; always keep to a schedule.'

Eyes downcast, he stuttered, 'I better make tracks so I git home before it's pitch black. Hope I see ya next time.'

The idea of his next visit made her want to sing from lofty peaks. She pondered why her heart fluttered and tingles tickled her neck and spine.

Chapter 31

Bill's news sessions increasingly focused on European events, and the lines on his forehead deepened with each visit.

At the end of 1913, he strode in with Annie trailing close behind and claimed his armchair. 'Britain is performing massive naval exercises.'

'Why?' asked Ben.

'For decades, there have been ongoing issues in Europe, almost like a territorial dispute. Germany has been steadily strengthening its military capabilities, and the British are showcasing the power of their vast naval fleet.' He gestured with sweeping motions as if trying to emphasise the extent of his knowledge.

Ben's face paled, and his forehead creased in concern. 'Mate, are you saying a war is coming?'

'British politicians claim otherwise, but I think war is unavoidable,' Bill said, eyes filled with worry. He cleared his throat and brushed back what little hair he had left.

Ben exhaled heavily, and barked, 'I'm with Bill. Countries don't gather weapons and parade their fancy navy ships unless they intend to use them.'

Bill's predictions grew more sombre after the assassination of Archduke Franz Ferdinand in 1914. As time progressed, he continued to make dire predictions. 'Politicians in Britain and here may say otherwise, but mark my words, war will break out, and Britain will inevitably become involved.' The room filled with gasps of panic.

Minnie observed Ben's contorted face as his complexion shifted from a soft reddish hue to a fiery red. 'Surely, they can sort this brawl out,' he murmured.

'I doubt it because Germany has set its greedy sights on France and Belgium,' Bill replied. 'We'll see what unfolds, but a war involving every nation on earth is inevitable.'

* * *

In August 1914, Minnie discerned from the gloomy expressions tattooed on Annie and Bill's faces that they brought troubling news. They strode towards the sitting room, permeated with the tantalising aroma of apricot jam wafting from the kitchen. Gripped by a sharp pang in her stomach, Minnie rushed to the sitting room, dragging a smooth vinyl chair and placing it next to Bill's worn leather armchair. Ben and Jean followed. As they entered the sitting room, the colour drained from their faces. With a heavy thump, Bill sank into the armchair. In a shaky voice, he said, 'Britain has declared war on Germany.' The room fell into a stunned silence, only interrupted by the gentle rustle of leaves outside.

Minnie's mind replayed the intense confrontations between Catholics and Protestants after the Orange Day celebrations in Toome. A shiver ran down her spine as she vividly remembered the fear overtaking her, the shattering of glass, the thunderous thump of bones, and the chilling sight of blood staining the cobblestones. Tears began. She pivoted in her chair to conceal them and fixated on what was behind her.

Annie edged over and knelt on the floor beside Minnie's chair. After twisting the girl's shoulders towards her, she folded her arms around Minnie. 'Pet, something troubles you.'

'I just travelled back to Ulster,' said Minnie, eyes glistening. Minnie peered towards Jeannie. 'You remember, don't you? The streets resembled a battlefield.'

'Of course, it will forever be a part of us,' said Jean, recollection shadowing her face. 'But with this trouble, we're lucky we're far away.'

'Don't speak too soon,' Bill said. 'Australia has promised aid. Newspapers predict a rush of volunteers. The politicians expect the war won't last long, but I am unconvinced.'

Minnie sensed a tremble snake through her when Ben, face crimson and nostrils flaring, exploded from his chair. 'I'll not risk me life and me family's future for a country I've never been to. I couldn't find these European joints on a map.'

Minnie returned to her thoughts. The explosion in her head erupted again. This time, images of bloodied soldiers lying dead and dying on a snow-flecked battlefield rotated before her. The grizzly vision caused her to cry out, anger swelling her voice. 'I support Ben. I don't want my brother-in-law killed or maimed fighting in a distant country. And my thoughts extend to Albert.'

Minnie realised she'd made a mistake mentioning Albert when she noticed Jean, Lizzie, and Ben exchange glances.

Annie's knees snapped as she hoisted herself from her kneeling position before strolling across to Ben. She rested her hand on his shoulder. 'Don't panic. They're calling for volunteers, not conscripting men.'

Within minutes of Bill and Annie leaving, Albert swaggered in without the usual brown bottles. With thick tears rolling down her cheeks, Jean rushed and threw her arms around his neck. Albert wriggled from her grasp and held her at arm's length. 'That crying ain't bout this war, I hope.'

Jean let out a tortured wail. 'Bill and Annie just delivered the shattering news.' Albert grinned as usual. 'It's no big deal,' he said. I just came from the Crown. 'The blokes itch to join because they reckon this brawl will end by Christmas. Volunteers get paid six bob a day and git a free trip overseas.'

Ben's eyes narrowed to a slit. 'Steady on, don't listen. The drinkers parrot the politician's line that it'll all be over in months. Bill, a knowledgeable man, believes it will take longer,' said Ben forcefully. 'Mate, I go with Bill over those lying politicians. I won't be volunteering, and you should think carefully before joining.'

With her heart in her mouth, Minnie leaned against the wall and listened to the brothers. After Ben went silent, Albert chewed at his lips, and his eyes became hazy. Minnie felt relief, hoping Albert weighed up the options.

The two sisters left the room, leaving the brothers to their discussion. Minnie hoped Ben would convince Albert to view it as he did.

* * *

Over the coming weeks and months, Bill delivered updates. Within days, he reported that the recruitment office couldn't cope with the flood of volunteers and sent people away. He recounted the support for the war effort expressed by politicians of all persuasions and visited when the first troops sailed in November.

On each visit, he appeared older. Not only did the lines on his brow deepen and new ones emerge, but he also shed weight, and his eyes descended deeper into their sockets.

Minnie's stomach churned every time Bill and Annie arrived as she wondered about the latest instalment. Two months had elapsed since the declaration of war, yet it felt like an eternity for Minnie. She fervently wished for an end to the hostilities.

By the end of 1914, Bill announced, 'Everything is in short supply because of a lack of shipping from the northern hemisphere.'

'No fancy speech required. I can see the shortages meself. It's impossible to git rope, seeds and fertiliser.' In a severe tone, Ben expressed his disbelief in running a farm without those things.

Lizzie cut in. 'I went into town to buy fabric. Because of limited options, I settled for the only available material. Then, I couldn't find buttons and thread to match.' She pouted in disgust.

Minnie looked searchingly into Bill's eyes. 'When is this going to end?'

'The official line is it's a pushover. I disagree; it could be years.'

Minnie's face crumbled. She spotted moisture gleaming at the corner of Bill's eye, and gasps and moans filled the air. When she scanned the room, she saw nothing but tortured expressions of horror.

As he hauled himself from his chair after Annie announced it was time to leave, Bill said, 'This war will change this country.' Since the war broke out, he ended every news session with this prediction.

* * *

Minnie accompanied Jean on a shopping trip. They walked past the hotel. A mist of beer, cigarette smoke, and the clink of glasses drifted out of the casement windows. 'The crowd drinking on the verandah is unusually thin,' said Minnie quizzically as she leaned towards Jean.

Jean giggled. 'Perhaps because a chunk of the male population is overseas fighting a war?' Minnie chastised herself. Of course, the reason was apparent. She giggled with Jean, although she knew she laughed at herself.

They wandered past a butcher's shop, a general store, and a drapery, each identified by stencilled black letters on the display windows. Minnie spread a handkerchief across her mouth and nose to block a foul smell. As she nudged Jean's upper arm, she cast a questioning glare. She followed her sister's eyes to the mosquitoes buzzing around muddy water lying stagnant in the open drain at the side of the thoroughfare. Jean followed suit and wrapped her handkerchief around her face.

They stumbled upon Mrs Crawford, a lady they knew to be the local gossip. 'The three Evans lads have signed up,' she said.

Jean blinked and frowned inquisitively at Mrs Crawford. 'Don't the family have two farms? How will they manage?'

'The grandfather, the women, and young ones.'

'I'm sure they miss their menfolk,' said Minnie, trying to smile. However, a pain pierced her insides at the memories that flooded back of her sisters and her struggle to maintain a farm.

Mrs Crawford toyed with the ribbons decorating the wide-brimmed straw hat mounted on her grey curls. 'Theirs isn't the only district farm left to the women.'

A sad smile swallowed Jean's features. 'Minnie, our sister, and I ran a farm in Ulster by ourselves. We were young, and it also fell to us to nurse dangerously ill family members. It was hard, but we managed. I am sure the Evans family will manage.'

'Dears, those evil Germans have turned our world upside down. The butter factory runs with half-staff because many serve in the army. Elsewhere, a few barmen, the postmaster, and heaps of young local men answered the call. Each person must do their part for the Mother Country.' The woman's face contorted with hatred.

Jean's lips arched downwards into a frown. 'How long can they carry the extra burden?'

'Our boys will return in months because our mighty British Empire will thrash those uncivilised hordes. The Germans deserve everything they get.' Mrs Crawford gritted her teeth and scowled.

Minnie listened intently. Wouldn't it be delightful to see those soldiers she saw set out in khaki uniforms and slouch hats march back? 'I hope you're right because I want this fighting and death over.'

Jean waved her arm in the general direction of their farm. 'Mrs Crawford, we must go, or we'll be late home.'

'Before you go, the town ladies have formed a knitting group to do our duty for king and country and provide our brave lads some comforts. We'll be knitting socks. We're going to meet at four p.m. on Thursdays at the school. You two and your sister are welcome. Bring your needles, but we'll provide the wool. We'll also be sewing clothes and accepting donated garments and preserves.' As an afterthought, Mrs Crawford tittered and said, 'Keep this quiet, but we send white feathers to shirkers.'

Minnie clenched her teeth to contain a giggle and noticed Jean's eyebrows shoot skyward.

* * *

Minnie waited in her usual spot on the verandah. A storm, already delivering claps of thunder, loomed on the horizon, promising the soaking rain constantly on the tongues of local farmers.

A sideways peek showed Albert approaching, the hallmark cigarette stuck to his bottom lip. Anticipation bubbled inside her. Not wanting him to sense her feelings, she spoke casually. 'I didn't realise you were there.'

He slumped on the railing next to her. 'What's a charmin' gal doin' far from your home country—the north of Ireland, isn't it?'

Minnie's body stiffened as she spoke. 'My mother died when I was two. By all accounts, she was lovely, but I have no memory, not even a photograph. My father, my hero, died when I was eleven. My stepmother brought me and my five sisters to Australia in 1910 to escape consumption, which claimed the lives of our parents and other loved ones.' It seemed an eternity to purge herself of her past's details. Minnie took a few rapid breaths of relief when she squeezed the words out.

'Sorry, that's sad. Ben told me about your tough past, but I forgot the details. Where did ya land?'

'Brisbane. I spent two unhappy years there.'

'You've been here a spell. Figuring on stayin'?'

'I suppose I'm looking for a home. There's a comfortable atmosphere among these hospitable folk. I want to stay, but Kobble Creek can only be home while Ben and Jean have me, and I keep a job.'

As they watched the storm move, he stammered, 'There's a shindig, a dance at the Orange Hall, Dayboro, every Saturday. Thought you might come with me?'

Her heart beat faster, and butterflies fluttered in her stomach, but she tried to conceal her delight. 'How far is Dayboro?'

'Five miles. Real hoot; lots of people—band, fiddle and all.'

'Yes, that'd be lovely.'

* * *

Minnie hummed until Saturday, her cheerful mood not going unnoticed.

Lizzie, sporting a broad smile, cornered her, 'You're head over heels.'

Trying to appear casual, Minnie shrugged. But she felt colour creep up her face.

'It's Albert, isn't it?' Lizzie said, her smile broadening into a knowing grin.

'How did you know?' said Minnie.

'Easy. For months, it has been clear from your expression that you're head over heels. Has he proposed?'

'Well, no, but...'

'But what?'

'He's invited me to a dance,' Minnie stammered, wondering what she would wear. She must make a new dress but knew she needed help and was reluctant to ask Lizzie. Her sister could only refuse she thought. She spoke slowly, hesitantly, almost choking on her words. 'I wondered if you and Jean would help me make a dress.'

'Dear sister, with the skills learned in that dismal factory, this master seamstress will tailor a stunning outfit guaranteed to turn heads,' said Lizzie, face claimed by a gloating smirk.

'Ha, ha, you excel at blowing your trumpet, but thank you. We'll ask Jean if she wants to help.'

'I'll ask her, but our obliging sister always does whatever we ask,' said Lizzie.

Relief filtered through Minnie's veins. The sewing team had come together, and now she could choose the fabric.

* * *

The sisters spent every spare minute fussing over their work. Minnie chose a lemon organza for a dress that fell in gathers until it stopped short of the ground. Often, Lizzie and Jean called for a fitting.

'We must ensure it fits like a glove, especially around the hips. Minnie, you'll need to slip it on again,' said Lizzie through a mouthful of pins.

When she wriggled into the dress, Minnie tried to conceal her excitement but failed dismally. She scanned herself approvingly and rubbed the silky fabric between her fingers. Begging for reassurance, she asked her sisters, 'Are you sure it doesn't make me look fat?'

Jean offered a cynical smile. Lizzie's voice bounced across the room. 'No, you're a human sparrow!'

Minnie gazed out the window into the night sky and sensed her eyes grow glassy. She considered everything that could go wrong. What if the dress didn't turn out perfectly? Or worse?

Albert may not like it. Perhaps she would trip and fall on the dance floor. How embarrassing!

'Have you flown to another planet because you're lovesick?' Lizzie asked. 'My fingers ache from sewing your outfit, and all you're doing is staring into the blackness. What's the problem?'

Minnie, vaguely aware of her sister's voice, continued staring and didn't respond.

'What is it?' Lizzie asked.

Minnie moaned. 'I have never been to a dance other than folk dancing at Ulster fairs. Albert is probably an experienced dancer. I'm stressed about making a fool of myself.'

Minnie felt non-plussed when Jean burst out in fits of laughter. Her sister shook so much that Minnie imagined her falling and rolling on the floor. 'Follow him,' said Jean. 'If he's like his brother, he won't recognise the difference between right and left.'

Minnie found no comfort in her sisters' words. The pair teased her, feeding the nervous whirlpool that fed on her insides. The doubts kept orbiting her head.

Chapter 32

The much-awaited evening arrived. Lizzie styled Minnie's hair and helped her slip into the dress.

Lizzie insisted she prance, bend, twist, and turn. At last, Lizzie gave a satisfied sigh. 'You look like a flower floating on water. It's the work of talented seamstresses.'

When Minnie looked at herself in the mirror, she saw a stranger, a grown lady radiant in a light-yellow gown. 'Isn't it a delightful sight?' she muttered as she peered into the looking glass. As she brushed past Lizzie, she kissed her sister's cheek. 'I don't want to give you a swelled head, but the dress is magnificent.'

Trembling, she headed towards the sitting room, where Ben and Jean waited. When she arrived, Ben whistled, sending heat surging to Minnie's face.

The door rattled, and Albert entered wearing dapper clothes and a broad grin. He offered his arm, and they went to the waiting sulky. Minnie flashed a beaming smile, flutters rioting in her belly. Albert guided her by the elbow into the sulky before climbing into his seat and taking the reins.

Few words passed between the pair as the horse drew the buggy along the familiar narrow winding track towards Dayboro. This trip was hair-raising, and Minnie's heart thumped in her ears at each hairpin bend. Convinced that Albert gave the horse too much head and took the corners too sharply, pictures of the sulky leaving the trail and tumbling down the embankment spun around her head. She chastised herself. Albert, a native of these parts, must know every twist and turn.

When they arrived, music drifted from the hall and flooded the town. Albert rested his arm on the small of Minnie's back. Together, they strolled towards the venue through the still night air, rancid with rotting fallen fruit. Groups chatted and laughed on the littered grounds. Tobacco smoke swirled in a funnel shape, leaving its aroma in its wake. Couples sought privacy at the perimeter to kiss.

They pushed through the cheery groups, halting whenever Albert spotted familiar faces. He greeted them with his signature, 'G'day, mate. How ya goin'?' They pumped his hand and swiped his back. Each time they stopped, a conversation began about the dry weather or the war.

They weaved through the crowded entrance. Inside, Minnie lifted her gaze and marvelled at the bevy of women dressed in their finery lining the wooden panelled walls, but there was a sparsity of men. Of course, the war had diluted the male population.

From a stage beneath a framed photo of the king, the band struck up a rendition of popular tunes. Couples surged to the dance floor and began to spin and twist.

Minnie gawked, mesmerised by the fluid movement of whispering feet on the dance floor. Albert excused himself and dashed to the opposite wall, where he exchanged whispered words with a man who looked similar to him.

Albert returned. He led Minnie onto the packed dance

floor, and they danced every number. Despite Minnie's initial concerns about her lack of dancing prowess, she soon realised Albert's movements were stiff and awkward. Nevertheless, she followed him in a shuffle around the floor, chatting with him as they went.

Minnie sensed Albert suffered the same nervousness as her. She should start some conversation to loosen the atmosphere. 'This war brings so much sorrow. I wish it would end,' said Minnie.

'Yeah, that's not wrong. Henry, me brother, who I just spoke to, listed all our schoolmates who volunteered. There are few left around here; they're all in the army.'

Her head spun. Most of the community held views like Mrs. Crawford's, but others thought differently. Bill was an example. She must find a suitable response. 'You must miss your friends, but the King has many loyal supporters around these parts.' She exhaled. That response wouldn't create ripples.

Albert gave her an uncomprehending look, his brows furrowing, and pressed Minnie's shoulder gently, his touch warm and reassuring. She interpreted it as a subtle signal for her to follow him. As they continued their awkward stagger around the dimly lit dance floor, the scent of polished wood and sweat mingled. He accidentally stepped on her delicate feet, causing discomfort and laughter to bubble up within her. She watched other couples effortlessly glide past, their graceful movements starkly contrasting with their clumsy performance, but her partner's ungainly steps did not matter. She relaxed, enjoyed the company, and soaked up the lively music and joyous atmosphere.

After a beautiful evening filled with laughter and lively

music, Albert escorted Minnie to the front door of the old Kobble Creek house. With a gentle peck on her cheek, he bid her farewell, his lips leaving a lingering warmth.

'I'll see you again soon,' he whispered, his voice filled with anticipation. 'And maybe you'll come to the next dance with me?' A tremor of excitement bolted through her, sending a shiver down her spine. The thought of experiencing the joyous moments they had shared once more filled her with pure bliss.

She settled into bed. The moonlight entering through the window illuminated the peeling ribbons of paint on the ceiling. Lizzie's soft snores provided a familiar lullaby, but Minnie's anxiety about Albert's future visits gnawed at her and robbed her of sleep. She yearned to recreate the magic of their time together.

* * *

Albert and Minnie started attending dances and other events regularly. They often met on the verandah, and Albert reduced his drinking time with Ben. Chatting like birds, they shared childhood stories. However, Minnie kept the shocking details of death and suffering in Ulster to herself. For her part, focused on tales of fireside chats, riding on her father's back, and the mountainous bonfire on Orange Day.

One evening, Albert put his arm around Minnie and pulled her close. Goosebumps appeared on her arms, but she enjoyed the touch of his weathered skin. From then on, they grew closer, with sprints to the barn becoming regular. They carefully hid from the stars and moonlight by crouching behind trees and fences as they scurried.

* * *

In July 1915, Annie approached Minnie when the baggy coats no longer hid the barn's secrets. The practical Annie wasted little time organising a wedding despite wartime shortages.

A handful of friends and family gathered in Annie and Bill's Brisbane home to see Minnie and Albert married in a miniature version of the ceremony for Ben and Jean held two years previously.

Framed by a bay window, Minnie leaned over to Albert, wanting to smile or gaze into his eyes. Eyes downcast, he stood as stiff as a statue. As Minnie said, 'Till death do us part,' when prompted by the clergyman, a warm glow rushed through her bones. She and Albert would, as planned, raise a family in a carefree, peaceful environment free from the shadow of consumption, death, and senseless violence. Circumstances, however, forced it upon them sooner than she'd envisaged.

They signed the register, Albert with an illegible scrawl and Minnie in an unsteady hand, reflecting her nervousness. Minnie wondered why Albert remained mute. Surely, he wasn't having second thoughts.

Minnie sensed her muscles slackening when she saw Albert relax as they chatted with guests who mingled in groups among the brown-upholstered couches and lounge chairs. He robustly shook hands, clapped male guests on the back, and brushed kisses to the cheeks of female guests.

Eventually, Albert leaned towards Minnie. 'Love, we'd better git going.'

They were almost at the door when Minnie sensed a nudge on her shoulder. She turned to see a beaming Jean. Her sister folded her arms around Minnie and held her in a vice-like embrace. After Albert tapped his feet several times, Jean released her and held her hands. 'I wish you a lifetime of happiness.'

'Thank you, Jeannie, I mean Jean.'

'Today it's Jeannie. I hope I will always be Jeannie in your heart.' Jean's smile twisted to a frown, and a shadow of concern sauntered across her forehead. 'Please watch his gambling.'

In the yard, Ben, grinning mischievously, slumped against a fence post. He'd hitched the horse to the cart and tied tin cans to the rear.

The guests rushed down the stairs and pelted the newlyweds with rice. Albert slackened his grip on the reins, and, to catcalls and cheers, they trotted off through a sea of rice granules, cans clattering behind them.

Minnie felt warmth snake through her. She was setting off to a new home to compose the next chapter of her life.

* * *

Albert and Minnie travelled by horse and cart to the mountainous land in the Dayboro hinterland, where he lived and grew bananas.

Off the unpaved road, they passed towering gum trees and sparse native vegetation. The incline grew steeper, causing the horse to strain under the weight it pulled. A cloud of dust, kicked up by the horse's hooves, settled on the cart, its passengers, and their clothing. Hazards hindered the journey. Rutted tracks, muddy pools of water, and fallen boulders frequently forced them to stop and clear the path.

In the moments between these enforced breaks, they conversed amidst the rattles and creaks of the wooden wheels on the uneven surface, inhaling the invigorating scent of eucalyptus. After the third stop, Minnie leaned towards Albert. 'This road is rough, it's quite dangerous. Is this the usual route you take?'

'I warned you, love. It's a lonely place, far from civilisation. Only one other farmer and I use it for access. Oh, and a mail cart makes its way up here once a week.'

'I'm not bothered by the isolation. It's far better than fighting in this dreadful war or watching loved ones succumb to consumption like flies.'

'Positive figuring, love.'

Minnie said the right words, but inside, she screamed. Every sound from the bush made her twitch and strain. The relentless heat weighed on her, causing her to wipe the sweat from her forehead. But there were some positives. The remote location provided double protection against the curse; the heat would kill it if it reached this distant place. This place was far removed from the evil war raging for over a year. Earlier in the year, there had been a bloodbath in a place called Gallipoli, where countless Australians lost their lives.

The stunning scenery amazed Minnie as she peered over the edge. The slopes showcased a vast expanse of banana trees. A river snaked through the valley, and the afternoon sun cast shimmering rays of light across its waters. In the distance, a majestic mountain range served as a breathtaking backdrop. As Minnie took in the surrounding beauty, she questioned whether she had been too quick to judge.

Albert tightened the reins, bringing the cart to a halt on a plateau—a flat area of about one acre, which appeared insignificant against the towering background mountain. In the middle of this plateau stood a hut made of split timber and covered with bark, with a roof of thatch.

Several outbuildings stretched across the flattened land. Minnie struggled to escape the cart and hurriedly approached an overgrown garden where weeds choked spindly vegetables. She continued until she reached the chicken coop. The rough lean-to enclosure perched on the edge of the flattened ridge. She peered over the edge and saw the land dropped sharply in vertical rock ribs before reaching the rows of banana trees.

Feeling dizzy, she hurried to join Albert. With a blue-black dog at his side, Albert balanced on his haunches beside the shanty. When Minnie approached, the animal growled, and hackles rose on its back. Minnie jumped back and wrapped her arms around her bosom.

'It's all right,' said Albert. 'Maxi, come here.' The animal raced back and panted as he rubbed against Albert's trouser legs. 'Don't worry, love. He won't attack unless I tell him to.'

The flimsy door, hanging askew from its hinges, complained as Albert nudged it. Two steps inside revealed a single unlined room with a clay floor. Sunlight pierced the web of gash-like gaps, and cobwebs hung from the walls and ceiling. One corner housed a blackened fireplace bordered by a few cooking utensils. A table surrounded by four rickety, mismatched timber chairs stood in front of the fireplace, partially hiding it.

Minnie wandered to the rusty bed frame of the double bed in the opposite corner. The springs groaned beneath her as she leveraged her swollen body onto the lumpy straw mattress. The squalor took her breath away, but she arranged her face into a pleased expression, even though she knew she would forever fear falling from the postage stamp-sized house block.

'I warned you, love. It's no palace.'

Had Albert stepped into her innermost thoughts? 'Yes, but it will do while we save for a farm.'

Chapter 33

Minnie woke before the sunlight penetrated the curtainless windows. Albert slept curled in a ball under a sheet, his presence given away by his protruding shock of hair and the warm cloud of breath emitted after each puff. After about twenty chest rises, he groaned and rolled over.

Struck by the stillness surrounding the hut, Minnie went to investigate. She flung off her nightgown and donned a dress. Without bothering with stockings and leaving her hair flowing over her shoulders, she thrust her boots on, opened the door, and stepped outside.

As she stepped forward, an impenetrable fog enveloped her. The mist pressed in, obscuring visibility to a mere foot ahead. She stumbled upon a fallen tree trunk and settled onto it, feeling its rough, weathered texture beneath her. A sense of unease crept over her as faint sounds reached her ears - indistinct, low-pitched cries and elusive scratching noises, impossible to pinpoint. Perhaps it was the gentle scraping of animals against the underbrush. What if it was something sinister, like a snake? Doubt gnawed at her, urging her to run.

Suddenly, a magnificent spectacle unfolded. Vast waves of mist rose like ethereal curtains from the valley floor towards the heavens. The sun emerged as the last ripples ascended, casting a radiant glow. A whispering wind emerged from its hidden abode among the ridges and hollows, gently rustling through the branches of the trees. At that moment, Minnie's jaw dropped in awe, her senses overwhelmed by the purity of the air. It carried the delightful bouquet of spring growth, which refreshed her lungs with each breath.

As she savoured the intoxicating fragrance, the source of the mysterious scratching sounds became clear. A dozen wallabies surrounded her. Leaning over, she reached out and stroked the soft fur of one creature, which seemed unperturbed by her touch.

'You adorable furry things,' Minnie murmured. 'Have I claimed your viewing spot? Your eyes tell of curiosity about this unexpected visitor.' Memories of encountering kangaroos and wallabies at Ben and Jean's place surfaced, but they had bounded away at the sight of a human.

Minnie stepped back inside as Albert swung his legs from the crumpled sheets.

She cooked porridge. Hands caressed the small of her back as she stirred the mixture. She swivelled and found Albert, now clad in a checked shirt over frayed shark grey trousers, nuzzling into her neck. 'The smell spewin' from that pot makes me belly rumble.' He rubbed one hand in circular motions over his flat stomach.

As Albert plopped into a creaky chair, Minnie placed two servings on the table. After assaulting it with sugar, Albert let out slurps as he shovelled spoons of the bowl's contents into his mouth. Minnie more demurely devoured her portion. As the couple washed down the meal with tea, they discussed their plans for the near future. 'I'll help you with the bananas, but I'll need a few days to transform this shelter into a home for our little family.'

Shamefaced, he gazed at Minnie before rounding his shoulders and fixing his gaze on the earthen floor. Muffled sounds escaped from his hunched form. 'I'm sorry. This place reveals the secrets from me bachelor life.' Then he recoiled and stood upright. 'You shouldn't help with the bananas. The path to the banana trees is steep and slippery, and creepy crawlies lurk between the trees. It's not safe in your condition.' He spoke with a sternness that surprised Minnie.

Minnie tilted her head, laughed heartily, and flashed an appreciative smile. 'I worked each day, in similar conditions, at Ben and Jeannie's farm until a few days before our wedding. Thanks for your concern, but give me a few days to scrub and clean, and I'll work with you each morning and return here in the afternoon.'

With a slow nod, Albert signalled his reluctant agreement.

'We must organise a few things before the baby joins us.'

'Such as?' asked Albert, looking inquisitive.

'We must build an extension and get a crib,' said Minnie, her voice lowered.

'Of course, the little fella will need somewhere to sleep,' said Albert. He scratched his temples, and a pinkish glow moved across his forehead. 'But I can't figure out why you want to extend this joint.'

Minnie mused. He doesn't comprehend the necessity for the extension. 'There's hardly enough space for two. Three will stretch it beyond its limits. The baby will need space to learn to crawl, walk and run.'

His face reddened, and his body quaked as he repeatedly shook his head. Minnie realised she hadn't convinced him. 'What you want won't be cheap. As a leased holding, any hut changes remain after we depart,' Albert snorted.

They held each other's gaze in the thick silence. It was a competition, with the winner being the first to speak. I'm not giving in, Minnie thought and remained silent. Eventually, Albert pierced the silence. 'Alright, I'll find someone at the Crown to build onto the hut and to cobble a crib.' Minnie drew her eyebrows together, reducing her eyes to narrow slits. 'Whatever are you speaking about … finding a worker in a pub?'

'In these parts, people conduct business at the pub—anything that can be bought, sold, or traded.' He gave her an incredulous glare as if he had just stated the obvious.

'You talk about going to the Crown Hotel in Dayboro. I assume I'll get off this mountain to visit Jean. Otherwise, I'll miss her.'

'Of course, we'll need to shop for tucker every week. We can combine that with a visit to Ben and Jeannie.' The enormous grin reclaimed its place on his face.

Minnie sighed under her breath. Seeing the hallmark grin return brought relief, but the morning's events forewarned her she must carefully handle any suggestion involving spending money. She flashed a bright smile. 'Could we make the journeys to town to coincide with Bill's news sessions? They're interesting and will allow us to follow war news.'

'Na, that is usually Saturday, race day, but we'll get ya a newspaper, and ya sister will pass on Bill's wise words.'

Minnie found it challenging to control her emotions. She choked back a lump in her throat. Albert was always going to consider horseracing his priority. She detected a hint of sarcasm about Bill in his voice. Jean had warned her about his passion for racehorses so she would not create an argument about it.

To conceal her hurt, Minnie changed the subject by describing her early morning encounter with the rising mist and the wallabies.

'I'm glad you're so taken; sounds like something from a painting. I've never noticed it.'

She wondered how anyone living here was unaware of this unforgettable spectacle. There was no point in trying to convince him of its merits, but she would enjoy the magic every morning. My furry friends may join me. What a treat! Before heading out for work, I will watch the sunrise and the mist roll.'

Minnie transcended into deep thought. Although her new life had just begun, they had nutted out many details of their daily lives. She'd learned a lot about her new husband, some good and some bad.

* * *

In her first days on the mountain, Minnie cleaned and scoured every surface, ridding the space of rot and mould. Before commencing the day, she darted outside to watch the day break. The wallabies hopped along and arranged themselves into their viewing formation. The animals brushed against her, which she took as a welcome to the sunrise audience.

At dusk, Albert trudged in, clothes sweat-stained and face blackened by dust. He collapsed into the chair nearest the ashtray, where he sucked a cigarette. 'This joint stinks of bleach.'

'I've finished the cleaning, so the smell will soon disappear. In the morning, I'll work alongside you.'

When the first bird called the next morning, Minnie freed

herself from the bedclothes before Albert and rushed, with a spring in her step, to join her bouncing friends for the majestic sunrise. To guard against the morning chill, as she waited, she wrapped her arms around her rounded breasts. She spoke to a wallaby who balanced on his hind legs beside her. 'I'll never tire of this.'

After devouring their breakfast, Albert and Minnie departed from their modest home on the first day of work. They carried spades and rakes on their shoulders as they followed Maxi down a path carved into the rugged mountainside. The trail vanished before them, causing Minnie's heart to race as she peered over the edge of the steep descent. Her feet trembled as she cautiously descended, occasionally taking sideways steps to maintain her balance. She couldn't help but imagine herself stumbling and tumbling down the slope, ending up bruised and battered in the valley.

They reached a level expanse of land, where vast stretches of banana trees stood in perfect rows, resembling a regiment of soldiers standing at attention. Minnie realised she had much to learn about banana cultivation. While Ben had grown a small crop of bananas, it was nothing compared to this sea of trees.

Pressing onward, Minnie stepped back when Albert dropped his tools with a thump. 'This is where we'll be working today,' he declared. A narrow, barely two-foot-wide corridor-like space separated two rows of trees, their branches intertwining to form an archway. Minnie squinted as she peered down the tunnel-like passage.

She took a few tentative steps into the dark tunnel. On her first step, she slid on sludgy soil rancid with decaying leaves but steadied herself using the rake she carried. Low tree branches slapped her as she edged down the tunnel.

At about midday, she called to Albert. 'I'll leave you here and climb back to the hut.'

'Step carefully. That track is steep, and there's loose soil,' said Albert. 'At home, put ya feet up.'

She gave out a one-syllable chuckle. 'I won't be resting because there are loads of washing, and I must bake some bread.'

When she reached the top, she busied herself washing, avoiding the sparks flying from the fiery copper behind the hut, and baking over the indoor fire. At sundown, an exhausted Albert shuffled in.

After the evening meal, under the dim lamplight, Minnie plunged a needle into fabric destined to become baby clothes. Today, she set a routine that would dictate the rhythm of each day ahead. Would their routine change with the baby's arrival? She turned towards Albert. 'Will it be different when the baby arrives?'

'Nothing will change. The sun will rise, rain will come, and the bananas will grow. Only difference is we'll be Mum and Dad.' His words sent tingles pulsating down her arms.

It wasn't long before they collapsed into the bed. Albert snored as soon as his head touched the pillow. Minnie reflected on her new life as she tethered her gaze to the stars, winking through the scar-like crevice in the thatched roof. The drone of insects, punctuated by nocturnal animal calls, serenaded her to sleep.

* * *

'Childbirth is not for the faint-hearted. Hurts like hell.'

'Last time, my labour lasted twenty-four hours. Thought I'd die.'

'This is my tenth time. The baby died the last time.'

These comments and similar remarks ping-ponged across the corridor between the narrow iron beds in a ward staffed by nurses cloaked in starched white uniforms with stiff cardboard-like caps.

Minnie took a deep breath of air tainted with floor polish and disinfectant as cold shivers attacked her spine. Why did she allow those girls to frighten her? Her mind flittered back to the backstreets of Fortitude Valley, the dingy clothing factory, and the constant racket of machinery. She recalled an assembly line staffed by mindless, trained monkeys who gossiped endlessly and brutally bullied a young Minnie. Choking a giggle, she likened the talkative patients to the factory girls.

She felt a gush of relief when the woman with a mane of brunette curls tucked into the neighbouring bed flashed a broad, friendly smile, revealing pearly white teeth. 'My name's Marjorie. Don't listen to those silly girls. They're trying to frighten you.'

'They've succeeded. But I should've known to close my ears.'

Marjorie spoke across the space separating their beds. 'Motherhood is wonderful. You forget the pain when you hold your adorable newborn.'

'I can hardly wait to hold the baby and find out if it's a boy or girl,' said Minnie, as joyful anticipation washed her.

'I'm sure your mother prepared you, but ask me anything. I'm an old hand; I've had four children.'

Minnie dabbed her cheeks with the handkerchief she re-trieved from under her pillow. 'My mother died when I was two, so I've plodded through this pregnancy without support.'

Marjorie's smile faded, and her brow folded. 'I'm sorry. You seem young. I suspect I'm almost old enough to be your mum.'

Lately, Minnie has missed the mother she'd never known, and she envisaged freely discussing the baby's movements and the onset of labour with a woman she trusts. To some extent, Jean and Annie have filled the void.

She gave Marjorie an appreciative smile. Although she could not meet her need for the support of an experienced fellow female, it warmed her to know she could count on this stranger's protection during her hospital stay.

* * *

When Minnie left for the labour ward the next day, Marjorie blew kisses and mouthed encouraging words.

Before long, a sharp cry echoed.

The midwife handed Minnie the screaming, blood-smeared infant. 'A lovely boy with a patch of straight brown hair and a healthy set of lungs.'

'Is he all right? He looks blue.'

'You're mum to a strapping lad,' said the midwife. 'What are you going to call him?'

'Harold.'

Back in the ward, she sensed droplets of moisture sliding down her cheeks. She heaved, and the trickle became a torrent cascading down into the bedclothes. Some other mothers rallied from their beds to comfort her. Minnie felt a rush of gratefulness when Marjorie waved them off. 'Let the girl cry. She is young, and this is her firstborn. They are tears of joy that she needs to release.'

A nurse padded to her bed holding the infant, now washed and smelling of soap. Although she yawned from exhaustion, Minnie drew the wrapped bundle close, and tiny fists flew when she loosened the wrap. She stared at the scrunched apple-shaped face, pouted pink lips, and closed eyes. The small but strong heartbeat and the delicate baby breath made her nerve endings tingle, resulting in a flow of protective love.

Nothing had prepared her for this unbridled joy. 'Hello, little man,' she said, giving an adoring sigh. 'I'm your mummy, aged just eighteen. We'll grow up together because I grew up in the shadow of a curse. As your mummy, I aim to give you a carefree childhood. '

Harold cried a bleating sound that escalated to a screech, and a nurse took him away.

Chapter 34

Within days of returning home with the newborn baby, Minnie followed Albert and the tail-wagging Maxi along the rugged trail to the banana plants. She tucked baby Harold into a Moses basket. As they walked to the tune of bird chirps, the warm sunlight filtered through the swaying leaves, casting dappled shadows on the ground.

Minnie's heart skipped a beat when she felt a firm grasp on the basket handles. Panic surged as she imagined a stranger trying to snatch the precious bundle. As she turned, her anguish dissolved into laughter as she saw Albert's face, his wide grin expanding to that of a clown. He chuckled uncontrollably, his laughter echoing through the quiet surroundings.

When they reached the bottom of the slope, Albert pointed his nicotine-stained finger towards a row of trees, showing where they would be working for the day. Minnie's gaze followed his gesture, the rough bark of the trees contrasting against the backdrop of the clear blue sky. A sense of familiarity and purpose surged through her.

She took the basket from Albert, its weight reminding her of the treasured cargo inside. Finding a patch of shade beneath a clump of wispy grass, she placed the basket down. Fatigue washed over her, and she sank to the ground, the coolness of the earth seeping through her clothes. With her legs tucked beneath her, she scooped up the now-crying baby Harold, his cries piercing the tranquillity. Minnie felt a pair of eyes fixed on her. She turned and noticed Maxi, his tongue hanging out, watching her every move with an unwavering focus.

As she returned the baby to his makeshift crib, Maxi followed closely behind, peeking over the basket's side and inspecting the tiny occupant from head to toe. The dog buried his snout deeper, sniffing the basket and the infant. Then he licked the newborn. Minnie felt satisfied that Maxi offered his friendship by licking every inch of the tiny body. Maxi gave a protective woof to solidify their bond, standing rigidly as if guarding the basket.

Before beginning her work, Minnie bent down and patted Maxi's steely blueish coat. 'Maxi, you're such a good boy,' she said, 'please look after my baby.' With those words, Minnie went about her day, working alongside Albert. She swung a hoe and skilfully wielded a banana knife with all her strength. Whenever the baby whimpered, Maxi wagged his tail and bounded down the dark corridors until he reached Minnie. He tugged her skirt with his teeth and nudged her towards the basket.

Minnie turned around when Maxi's fierce bark echoed. She playfully poked Albert in the ribs and giggled, gesturing towards Maxi, who growled and bared his teeth at a lizard dangerously close to the basket.

Albert and Minnie toiled until the afternoon shadows closed in. As they lumbered up the track, balancing their tools and the basket, Minnie sensed sweat stream down her spine. She likened the heat to a raging bushfire. After almost six years, the Australian climate still tested her!

* * *

Each day after that mirrored the first workday for the family of three. With no fanfare, 1915 melded into 1916. Guarded by the ever-vigilant Maxi, Harold passed his early months, except for shopping trips, in the Moses basket set among the banana trees. He later graduated to a larger pillow-cushioned box. Before long, the arrangement ended abruptly.

When Harold turned eight months old, Minnie stopped labouring among the bananas when she felt a series of jabs to her waist. She turned around and noticed Albert, whose throat rippled as if he were trying not to laugh. She followed his gaze. 'That kid will be a circus performer because he seems to figure out how to climb anywhere.'

Aghast, Minnie saw Harold had climbed over the side of the makeshift crib and doggedly crawled towards the sunshine creeping through the ragged leaves at the entrance to the corridor. Maxi, barking and frothing at the snout, did a backward shuffle as he faced the crawling baby. Albert pressed a splayed hand to his mouth. Minnie gazed at Albert, 'Too late, Dad, I know you find this a joke. Well, I don't think it funny,' she said. 'We cannot have our son crawling in leaf mulch on the stinking sludge and clay between the trees.

Minnie bit her lips to ensure no further words tumbled out. She exhaled, grabbed Harold, hitched him onto her hip, and hurried up the track, muddied by recent rain.

That night, Albert pushed the door open less aggressively than usual. He offered a slow, almost apologetic smile. She threw him a weak smile in return. 'I won't be working in the bananas anymore. I will be staying here and caring for our son.'

Albert stared at her. He seemed stunned, but she interpreted this as reluctant acceptance.

Each morning from the following day, she leaned against the doorway, balancing Harold on her hip. Juggling his tools and the tail-wagging Maxi bounding beside him, Albert disappeared over the mountain edge.

* * *

A few months into 1916, lost in the scent of cut grass, Minnie wandered the Kobble Creek Township with Jean during a shopping trip. Minnie luxuriated in being alone with her sister, freed from the demands of babies and young children.

Ben and Jean had welcomed another daughter, and Ben and Albert's mother stayed with them. They enthusiastically accepted the older woman's offer to care for the little ones, as neither Ben nor Albert had ever changed a nappy.

The town still carried the ghostly, deserted feeling inflicted on it since the war robbed it of a sizeable slice of the male population. However, one thing varied from the Kobble Creek of August 1914. Each rusty lamp post featured recruitment posters bearing slogans like: *Don't stand looking at this—GO and HELP, Man—you are wanted*, and *Australia arise, save her from this shame.*

As the sisters strolled further along the abandoned streets, similar posters smothered every visible space—tree trunks, fences, shop fronts, and hitching posts. The poster exhibition prompted Minnie to ponder. Just over a year ago, they were chasing volunteers away, but now, they can't get enough.

Someone called to them, and Minnie spotted Mrs Crawford's signature straw hat bobbing in the muggy breeze. When Mrs

Crawford caught up with them, Minnie noticed frown lines marred her face. She spoke in a raspy voice that carried more than a hint of agitation. 'This war has been raging for years. Too many of our soldiers have died or returned home injured or disfigured. When will it end?' She drew her hands to her face and covered her eyes.

'Yes, Australian casualties in Gallipoli were boggling, and reports of dead and injured soldiers pour in from battlefields in places I have never heard of,' said Minnie.

'This country has paid a high price. It's unfair to keep pushing lads into fighting in distant countries. Loads of district boys have laid down their lives for king and empire, many leaving children without dads,' said Mrs Crawford.

'Yes, it's awful. They must wonder what it was for,' said Jean.

Later, at Jean and Ben's house, the two sisters and two brothers, with Albert's mother, a short, plump, stern woman, gathered around the lunch table. In a husky voice, Minnie detailed the chance meeting and conversation with Mrs Crawford. 'And posters calling for volunteers plaster every empty space.'

Ben arched backwards and grunted. 'Them posters been there since news of Gallipoli reached 'ere. Bill calls them a fancy big-word, propaganda, I think.'

Albert cut in. He sprayed minuscule undigested parts of a ham sandwich into the air as he spoke. 'Ha, ha. Blokes now realise that being shot at is not the six-bob-a-day brief adventure they expected. Posters are not gunna convince a sane person to put their hand up be cannon fodder.'

'There is more to it. The prime minister, Billie Hughes, is so keen to supply more soldiers he wants conscription,' said

Ben.

'Hang on, mate. Does this conscription business mean they can make you go in the army, whether or not you like it?' barked Albert.

Ben's face looked bitter as he nodded. 'Bill reckons Hughes can't rally the support he needs in parliament, and there'll be a referendum. That's when everyone gets to vote on it.'

As Ben spoke, Minnie couldn't take her eyes off her husband sitting opposite. His body resembled a volcano bubbling before exploding. His eyes widened by the minute, and his face glowed pink, a soft red, a fiery red, and finally crimson bordering on purple. She wondered what was next. Would steam curl from his ears? The veins on his neck protruded, and his nostrils flared. He jerked as he rose, sending the chair to the floor. He crashed his fist to the table with so much force the plates and cutlery jumped.

'Tis a free country, and no politician can force me to go to another country and risk losing me life or limb. Hughes will need to find his way up the mountain if he wants me. I can't guarantee that I won't be hiding up a tree armed with a banana knife,' said Albert, staring at Ben.

'Don't panic yet,' Ben replied, offering a rallying smile. Many people are against this idea. Bill doesn't believe the referendum will pass, and many women's groups protest.'

A rasping cackle rose from the far end of the table. All eyes focused on Albert's mother, usually a quiet lady. Her lips tightened into a frown. 'The women's stance is understandable. I struggled to raise my five sons, not expecting them to be soldiers and die on a distant battlefield.'

As Albert and Minnie rode home in their creaky cart, Minnie broke the uncomfortable silence. 'You should be thankful to Bill and Ben. They convinced you not to enlist when this began,' she said.

Albert turned to her, looking indignant. 'I never even considered enlisting. I always thought it would be foolish.'

Minnie recalled Albert accepted the advice of his drinking buddies. However, Ben persuaded him that the conflict could continue longer and was dangerous. She knew that arguing about past events was pointless and that Albert's current position was correct. She verbalised her thoughts by saying, 'Dad. I've lost too many loved ones, and I don't want to lose you to a war someone else started.'

* * *

As time passed, Minnie's life became increasingly monotonous. She grew impatient with what seemed an endless war, spending her days tending to household chores and the vegetable garden. In July 1917, she gave birth to a daughter, Hazel.

With only children and wallabies for company, she often found herself lost in thought or feeling sorry for herself because of her loneliness. She longed for companionship, but Albert worked long hours and spent all day Saturday at the racecourse. Her thoughts often led her to imagine worst-case scenarios, such as one of her children falling off the cliff or a poisonous snake entering the house.

On a Sunday, late in 1917, Albert and Minnie spent some rare time alone. Minnie thought I've got to raise this with him. She held her breath for a long minute before holding his gaze. 'We must buy a less remote farm,' said Minnie in a timid, almost pleading voice. 'It's unsafe for me and the children in this remote place. There could be an accident, and I can't call for help.'

'We need to keep working hard and put more money aside. Anyway, it's best to wait until this war is done. Billy Hughes doesn't want to take the "no" answer he got last year. Blokes at the Crown reckon he will have another go 'fore Christmas. This war makes everything unsure.'

Minnie's face creased into a frown. 'Will this war ever finish?' she asked.

He offered a half-hearted smile and shrugged his shoulder. 'Every brawl ends.'

He jumped up and hurried to the door, leaving Minnie to ponder the circumstances. *How did she make her dream of their farm become a reality? Standing still for a war that showed no sign of finishing lacked sense.*

* * *

At dusk on 11 November 1918, Minnie looked down lovingly at the feeding Baby Annie, the couple's third child named after Charlotte's sister, Annie, born the month before. The other two children played at her feet. The flimsy door shuddered as Albert charged in, bringing the last slivers of dappled daylight. An enormous grin smothered his flushed face, and he jigged and threw his hat in the air.

'Haven't seen you so happy in ages. What is it?' asked Minnie.

'I've come from Dayboro. Folks are dancing, throwing rice, kicking up a real shindig. The church bells ring, and the Crown is handing out free beer,' said Albert. 'Some are so drunk, weaving and falling in the street. Young fellas are throwing water and even stripping down to their jocks.'

Minnie's neck tingled, and a desire to know more washed her mind. 'Why the celebration?'

'Them Germans gave in, and, at last, the war is over.'

'Dad, are you sure? This is a joke. It cannot be.'

'No mistake and no joke.' More fun and shouting fill the packed streets than New Year's Eve and the King's Birthday.' Albert jumped on the spot several times as if to emphasise his point.

Minnie thought this war, now in its fifth year, would never end. She smacked her head several times, hoping this action would assist her brain in processing this news. Then she raced to Albert, hugging him until he coughed. 'Such a wasteful loss of life. But it's terrific.'

'Stop squeezing so hard, woman. You're crushing me.' He yanked her away and looked into her eyes. 'And you're right about the waste. Some are not cheering but wailing 'bout those who won't be comin' back.'

Shivers coursed through Minnie. 'Many will return minus arms and legs. Life-altering effects await many wives and children.'

Albert's smile temporarily gave way to a frown. 'You right 'bout the waste, Love. It's over, although the stupid brawl got no-one nowhere.' The exaggerated grin reclaimed its position on his face. 'Why don't we join the fun?'

How she wished she could! 'It's not practical. Baby Annie will go down as soon as she finishes feeding, and the others won't be far behind.'

'No worries, I heard fellas talkin' about organising a peace parade this Sunday with fireworks, a band, and donkey rides for kids. Tonight, we'll have some tucker and a private shindig.'

Later that evening, with the children fed and in bed, Albert brought out two brown bottles. He motioned towards the bottles. As she mused, wondering if he knew the answer, she shook her head.

After he gulped a few glasses of beer with his usual awkwardness, Albert swung a laughing Minnie around the floor. Eventually, she collapsed into his arms, gasping for breath.

Later, Minnie sank into bed next to Albert, who already snored. Minnie drifted into deep thought. No longer would uncertainty and the ever-present threat of conscription shadow them. Today, a new world order began. Undoubtedly, the countless deaths and injuries would make everyone see the fruitlessness of war. Such a catastrophic loss of life! It would have to signal the end of all wars, giving their children the promise of a peaceful existence.

With the long war and the uncertainty it brought behind them, they could now buy their farm!

Chapter 35

In November 1919, Minnie crouched on the fallen tree trunk. Surrounded by her wallaby friends, she scanned the horizon for the flash of pink light to emerge from behind the twirling mist. Leaves rustled behind her. She glanced over her shoulder. A bolt of panic shot through her when she set eyes on Harold, standing silently with his shoulders hunched as he kicked the earth with his bare feet.

She spun. 'Darling, whatever is wrong? It's unusual for you to be so quiet and look sad.'

'Hazel won't get out of bed. I shook her, but she just groaned, and heat pumped out of her.' A look of panic overtook his sunburned features as he wrung his four-year-old hands.

Minnie, nausea churning in her stomach, rushed inside and bent over her daughter's bed. She fumbled with the girl's wrist and expelled a lungful of air when she found a pulse. She touched her daughter's forehead. It was blazing hot.

'Mummy,' Hazel panted, 'I'm so cold.' The girl's body began to wrack with shivers.

At least she's alive, thought Minnie, as she expelled more air.

Minnie spent the day feeding the feverish Hazel sips of water and morsels of bread, but the girl vomited them straight back up. Harold stayed close to her. He looked up at his mother through narrowed eyes from beneath his fringe. 'Mum, you and I will make Sis better.'

When Hazel heaved and retched as if in sympathy, Harold placed his trembling fingers over his open mouth.

As the light faded, a dishevelled, weary-looking Albert lumbered in. Minnie glanced over her shoulder but did not greet him. Next, she felt a stream of warm breath on her neck. She spun around and spied a blanched-faced Albert with thumb and finger clamping his nostrils. 'A stink of sickness knocked me over when I opened the door.' He pushed past Minnie and stood by the bed's edge, muttering, 'Poor Slim Jim.'

Albert and Minnie stayed there well into the night, wiping sweat from their daughter's forehead and fanning air across her body. The fever grew as midnight approached. Harold yawned, and Albert rubbed his eyes.

Minnie turned to Albert. 'Someone needs to sit with her all night. I'll do that. Dad, you go to bed. You have some shut-eye, so you can work tomorrow because we can't afford ripe fruit falling and rotting on the ground.' As he stumbled towards the bed, Minnie called, 'Please put Harold in bed.'

A squark, 'No, no, no,' rose from where Harold sat cross-legged on the floor. His little blanched face dripped with fear. 'Mum, I want to be with you and Hazel.' She could see he struggled to keep his eyes open, but she could also see determination etched across his brow.

Despite his protests, soon Harold slumped to the floor in a deep slumber. Suddenly, a groan rising into a piercing shriek of agony erupted from Baby Annie's crib. Filled with an adrenaline rush, Minnie hurried to her baby's cot. The escalating heat emanating from the cot took her aback. The little one had kicked off the covers and sprawled on a damp, sweat-stacked mattress. Even more distressing, she had pushed aside Bella, whom she clutched tightly every night. Oh, how Minnie wished Bella could speak! The doll had seen countless events and comforted many. Such an unwavering friend! Minnie darted back and forth between the two feverish beds, gently massaging her daughter's foreheads, which both glistened with sweat, and stroking their damp hair.

Minnie stirred Albert from his sleep as the first rays of dawn light peeked through the flimsy walls. 'Baby Annie fell ill after you went to bed, and now she burns with the same scorching fever as Hazel,' Minnie gasped, her breathing unsteady.

Albert knelt between Annie and Hazel's beds. 'Their heartbeats are far from steady,' he observed grimly. 'We must git them to a hospital.'

The mere suggestion that she couldn't adequately care for their daughters rendered Minnie speechless. Her legs turned to jelly, and she took a few steps before leaning against the wall for support, fearing its fragile structure would crumble under her weight. Amidst the bitter taste of bile rising in her throat, she said, 'What they need is the tender care of their mother.'

'The heat pours off them, their hearts beat unevenly, and they can't keep anything down. Both look terrified. They train nurses and doctors to deal with these illnesses,' said Albert as he raised one eyebrow and clenched his teeth.

'The difference is they don't love them as I do. I cannot abandon them in a hospital because if anything happened, I'd blame myself.'

Albert did not attempt to conceal his impatience. His focus

moved between the beds of the sweating girls. Then, face overtaken by a scowl, he paced. He stopped inches from Minnie's face and spoke with a note of urgency. 'Mum, we can't take risks. Plenty are dying from that illness brought back by the soldiers, The Spanish Flu.'

The talk about risks and her husband's tone stiffened Minnie, but she remained unsure, believing her children were better off in her care. 'If there's no improvement by tomorrow, we'll take them to a hospital',' she said.

Albert sighed but didn't push her any further.

'I'll take you to a hospital near Bill and Annie's place in the morning. You can take the girls to the hospital, and you and Harold can stay with Bill and Annie. You might be in Brisbane for a few days, so take a few changes of clothes.'

Minnie's voice cracked in a ragged sob, 'But, Dad, I assumed you would come with me. I can't do this alone.'

Albert looped his arms around his wife's shoulders. 'Let's look at this from every angle. We want our kids well, but we need to feed 'em. I'd love to be there, but I can't walk off leaving the bananas.'

Minnie shot him an incredulous stare. 'For the sake of our sick babies, surely you can tear yourself from this place?'

Albert's shoulders slumped. Before he dipped his eyes towards the floor, Minnie caught sight of his quivering chin. 'Bananas aren't like other crops where there's one harvest. They ripen all year round,' he said. 'I work my fingers to the bone for you and them kids. Please do not make me feel guilty.'

* * *

Minnie spent another sleepless night watching over her sick

children, feeling her heart was being dragged down her chest into her stomach. Nothing improved. The listless girls lay on sweat-soaked sheets. Minnie hoped this battle wouldn't end like her fruitless fight to save dear Sam, George Junior, and Adeline. It seemed her only alternative was to succumb to Albert's wishes.

After sunrise, Albert took them by horse and cart to Brisbane.

Albert helped Minnie from the rig and set the perambulator down on the compacted earth. He pointed with his nicotine-stained finger. 'The hospital is a hundred yards away.'

Four-year-old Harold bolted ahead at a speed that rivalled a champion athlete, wheeling Hazel in the pram. Dress billowing in the wind, carrying Baby Annie and Bella wrapped in a shawl, Minnie followed Harold as he pushed the pram. She rushed and panted but couldn't keep pace, so she called for him to slow down.

Minnie trembled as she mounted the stairs. She elbowed through a crowd of people milling around the reception desk. When she reached the top of the queue, she answered the questions fired at her by an officious balding man. He scribbled down some details before asking her to wait beyond the polished swing doors he motioned to with his chin.

With Harold wheeling Hazel a few paces before, she stumbled, cradling Baby Annie, as they approached the doors. A stranger held the door open for her, and she cast an appreciative smile. She found herself in a dim, shadowy area, full to overflowing with bewildered parents with wailing children and bereft older people who wheezed and moaned.

Minnie lowered herself into a wooden bench seat that offered little comfort. Holding Baby Annie close to her, she beckoned to Harold by tapping the space beside her to sit. People kept pouring into the area. Minnie's heart sank when she looked at the sunken eyes and pallid faces of those seeking treatment.

Minnie waited for what seemed forever, almost choked by the smell of antiseptic, cleaning fluids, and body odour among the unmusical chorus of laboured breathing, coughing, and cries of pain. Stretchers carried by men in ambulance uniforms and doctors in white coats whizzed past.

A tall, thin, veiled figure clad from head to toe in starched white strode down the corridor. Holding some papers, she peered at the girls before turning to Minnie. 'So, this is Hazel and Annie.' She consulted the papers. 'Both have fevers, vomiting and diarrhoea.' Bending over, the nurse placed her palm on Annie's forehead, only to wince and hastily retract her hand. 'The poor darling sizzles.' Then she knelt beside the pram and slid her hand inside. She emerged saying, 'This little one boils too.'

'They're both so bad, I'll decide to admit them personally,' she said. 'I'll place them in freshly made cots and request an urgent examination from the doctor.' A sudden chill followed by a wave of dizziness seized Minnie. A tortured yelp escaped her throat. Stroking Minnie's shoulder, the nurse spoke in comforting tones. 'Now, you need to go home and let us help them. Try to sleep and not to worry. They're in the right place as we provide excellent care.'

Minnie nuzzled into the hot crook of Baby Annie's neck and felt a shudder charge through her. Tears tracked down her cheeks as she handed her precious baby to the nurse. She took a few steps sideways and knelt before the pram. Her hands went clammy as she cupped Hazel's sizzling face. Through a sniffle, she muttered, 'I love you.' Then she thrust Bella towards the nurse. 'Baby Annie cuddles this rag doll for comfort. She'll scream without it.'

As she walked back down the corridor, Minnie's heart shattered when the girls gave tortured cries. Biting her bottom lip, she willed herself not to turn back, but Harold wriggled his hand, trying to free himself from her grip. 'They're crying. I must help.'

Minnie fought to drag the dead weight of her reluctant son to the entrance and down the stone stairs. She stopped about halfway and released Harold. To shield herself from the glare of the midday sun, she placed her splayed hands above her eyes as she searched for the tram stop.

When she looked down, Harold, arms crossed and fixed to his chest, sat on the step. She gestured to him to rise. He didn't move or respond but stared with a look of defiance. It took all her self-control to say, 'Wouldn't you like to ride on the tram to see Auntie Annie and Uncle Bill?'

'Yes, but I want my sisters to ride too.'

'Darling, your sisters must stay here for the doctors and nurses to make them well.'

'Mummy, I can't leave my sisters here. This place looks and smells horrible.'

Harold remained as if glued to his perch. He wailed and released a flood of tears. Frustration tempered with empathy pulsated through Minnie's veins. The boy's reaction reflected the feelings she wanted to release. To coax the lad to move, she completed her flight down the stairs and strode toward the tram stop. Before long, scurrying tiny feet echoed, and a clammy child's hand wiggled into her hand.

An unsteady sensation overcame her, and she tripped over

her feet. She'd never been drunk, but the way she staggered matched the descriptions she'd heard and read. A persistent voice inside yelled at an ever-increasing volume: *This is a mistake!*

* * *

The next day, after a night fraught with worry, Minnie returned to the hospital. A sister wearing a stiff veil met her. 'I'm Sister Thompson. Hazel slept through the night. The doctor thinks she'll recover.' Although the woman wore a kind but impersonal smile, her expression was earnest, cheeks flushed, and sorrow lurked behind her eyes.

Minnie, feeling numb, could tell from the sister's expression that something was wrong with Baby Annie. Finally, Minnie blurted, 'Is she dead? Is my baby dead?'

Sister Thompson nodded sadly, her smile fading. 'Last night, she lost a lot of fluid and had a high temperature. Then, she started having spasms. We did everything we could, but...'

Minnie's limbs tingled with a painful sensation as she recalled the horror of Adeline's last hours. 'Can I see her?'

'Of course. I'll find a nurse to watch your son.' She turned, and the soft squeak of rubber soles on the linoleum faded down the passageway.

Harold rubbed his temples. 'Mummy, won't Baby Annie be with us anymore?'

'No, darling. Poor sick Baby Annie has gone to heaven where she'll be an angel,' said Minnie between snivels.

Harold looked down. 'Mummy, don't cry. We'll all miss Bubby.' The boy's gentle manner and reassuring words sent Minnie into a wave of tears.

Two pairs of rubber soles glided down the corridor. The sister rested her hand on Minnie's shoulder and turned to Harold. 'I'll bring Mummy back soon. While we're away, be well-behaved for Nurse Taylor.' She motioned to her companion.

Sister Thompson led Minnie to a room. She twisted the brass doorknob of a door leading to a small space, its walls and ceiling painted sterile white. Dull ribbons of light penetrated the room through high, unopened windows. 'I'll allow you privacy,' said the sister as she softly pulled the door behind her.

Minnie stepped gingerly towards the metal-framed cot in the middle of the room. There lay her treasured daughter, locks of hair spilling onto her cheeks, clad in a pure white nightie trimmed with seashell lace around the neckline and cuffs. Despite the dullness of Baby Annie's skin, she looked peaceful, as if in a sound sleep.

A sour taste gorged Minnie's throat. 'My baby, my little girl, why did you leave me? You're too young and have a whole life ahead of you. I have suffered so many losses, but nothing compares with this!'

Taking small steps, she approached a pile of Baby Annie's belongings, which someone had placed on a table. After rummaging through them, she picked up Bella and held the doll six inches from her face. She pressed the button nose, now hanging by a single thread. 'You've been such a faithful friend. You stood in for me as my baby took her final breath. I'll leave you with her to watch over her forever.'

Minnie returned to the cot, where she tucked Bella into the crook of Baby Annie's neck. She gazed down at the peaceful form. 'Darling, it's unfair you had just over one year, but you'll live in my heart forever. I'm sorry I wasn't there to hold you. However, my oldest and dearest friend took my place. Because the souls of those I have loved and lost live inside Bella, I want her to be forever with you.'

After a tap, Sister Thompson poked her head around the door. Minnie leaned over the cot and pressed a lingering kiss to Baby Annie's cheek before trailing her out of the room.

Minnie's chest constricted, overwhelmed by conflicting emotions, as Sister Thompson guided her towards Harold. A sinking sensation gnawed at her stomach, intensifying her turmoil. Hoping for solace, she turned her face towards Sister Thompson, her eyes pleading. 'Can you help me with these troubling feelings?'

The sister's compassionate smile offered reassurance. 'Of course, anything at all.'

Emboldened by her response, Minnie tried to speak, but her words became lost in her tears. As her sobs subsided, she found her voice. 'We live in the mountains outside Dayboro, and I desperately need to tell my husband about the heartbreaking loss of our baby. But I also long to be with my daughter, Hazel, to hold her hand and caress her cheeks.'

Sister Thompson rubbed Minnie's right shoulder, her touch comforting. 'I can't imagine your pain, but perhaps this will help. Hazel is peacefully asleep. It's against the rules, but I'll allow you to see her. It might bring you comfort, and you can travel home and return during visiting hours tomorrow.'

Leading Minnie to a ward lined with steel-frame cots, the sister gestured towards Hazel's cot. As Minnie crouched over her daughter, a wave of relief washed over her at the sight of Hazel deep in sleep, her face regaining its colour with each measured breath. Minnie's palm grazed Hazel's forehead, feeling the coolness of subsiding fever. 'Darling, rest well. We'll come back to see you tomorrow.'

Tears streamed down Minnie's cheeks, a mixture of sorrow and gratitude. At least one of her daughters was on the path to recovery.

* * *

Leaving the hospital, Minnie grasped Harold's hand as she focused on getting the distressing news to Albert. She set about finding the way home. Their belongings would have to remain at Bill and Annie's.

She boarded a bus for the first leg of their journey and claimed a seat. Harold nuzzled into her side. He gazed at his mother, his eyes large and a tortuous look on his face.

Her thoughts turned to Hazel. Her girl had turned the corner, but faceless nurses would watch her recovery. Every bone in her body ached to hold her darling and rock her better. She averted her gaze to the heavens. *Thank you for sparing one. Losing another child would shatter me into a thousand pieces.* A wave of nausea attacked her when her thoughts took her to the loss of Sam and George Junior. She understood how Charlotte must have felt when she'd lost the boys within six days of each other.

When she reached Dayboro, she accepted the mail cart driver's offer to ferry her part of the way home. After jostling along the rugged mountain track, gripping Harold's tiny hand tightly, she trudged the remaining distance on foot.

Outside the hut, Albert balanced on his haunches, the spicy scent of tobacco lingering in the air as he clamped a cigarette between his lips. As Minnie approached, her steps heavy with sorrow, Albert inquired, 'Which one, Hazel or Baby Annie?'

Salty tears traced down her cheeks. 'Baby Annie,' she whispered.

Albert's eyes glistened. 'An empty feeling overcame me when I saw ya climbing the hill, the empty baby shawl draped over ya arm.'

Their gazes locked, and their emotions palpable. 'I should have been with you,' he lamented. 'I was only thinking of feeding our little team.'

Minnie retreated into the hut to deal with her emotions, leaving Albert to grapple with his.

She guided Harold inside, his innocent eyes mirroring her grief. Collapsing onto the nearest chair, Minnie cradled Harold in her lap. He curled up like a frightened cat, his head buried in her chest, seeking solace in her warmth. She sensed moisture bleed through her blouse as she combed her fingers through his cropped hair.

As she stoked her son's head, blows of guilt struck like clockwork, hurting more each time. She could see herself slipping into a murky, black pool of despair, but one glance at her son told her she couldn't allow grief and self-pity to swamp her. He needed her. Hazel also needed her mother's love. Her precious daughter lay in a sterile hospital, fighting for life. She must weather this challenge.

After displacing Harold, she walked purposefully to Baby Annie's crib. A shiver ran down her spine at the sight of Harold, who perched on the crib railing. 'No, bubby,' he said. He tiptoed over to Hazel's bed and looked across it. 'No sissy.' His words triggered a waterfall of tears.

The shadows crept in, plunging the interior of the hut into darkness. Minnie didn't bother to light the lamps. The sound of boots crunching on gravel echoed around the hut as the door moaned open. Albert plopped himself down onto a kitchen chair. His face was several shades lighter, with deep furrows in his brow and folded skin around his eyes. The permanent grin had disappeared. He didn't look at his wife, instead staring without blinking at a slit in the earthen floor.

He rose from the chair and shuffled around, igniting the lamps. When he returned to the rickety chair, Minnie stared into his eyes, forcing him to meet her gaze. She knew he had trouble discussing his emotions, but this was the most significant trial they'd faced together.

He snorted and cleared his throat but didn't speak. Minnie broke the heavy silence. 'Please take me to Brisbane tomorrow so I can stay close to Hazel,' she said.

'Yes, we'll visit Hazel, and then I'll leave you and Harold with Bill and Annie.'

* * *

Minnie sprinted down the hospital corridor to find Hazel's bed, hearing the echo of Albert's measured strides behind her. She saw Harold sliding several yards along the waxy floor, but she didn't stop him. Nothing could detract her from her goal of seeing and cuddling Hazel.

She entered the room first, and when Albert approached, Minnie spun around and inclined her chin towards Hazel's bed.

Hazel gazed up at them. Although her eyes were blinking and weary, a spark of light burned behind them. 'Mummy, Daddy.'

Harold, looking dejected, burst out, 'Don't forget me. I'm

here too.'

Minnie placed her hand on her daughter's forehead and felt that the fever had subsided. She extended her finger, and Hazel weakly took hold of it. Pure ecstasy flowed through Minnie's veins.

Chapter 36

At Bill and Annie's house, Annie stood at the door, her face tear-stained and puffy, as she welcomed them. Annie cradled Minnie in her arms. Minnie buried her face in Annie's embrace, finding comfort in the warm, jasmine-scented touch.

Minnie tried to speak, but sobs choked her words. 'She's dead,' she finally whispered.

Annie's face contorted with sadness. 'Darling, I know my dear little namesake had left us because Bill went to the hospital when you didn't reappear,' Annie muttered. 'For one so young, you've been through many ordeals.'

'But why did you take off and find your way home?' Annie questioned, her brow creased. 'I'm sure Ben and Jean would have told you about our new automobile. Bill would have driven you home and back to Brisbane.'

Minnie sighed, her voice quivering. 'There's one bright spot,' she said, her voice filled with hope peppered with sadness. 'We have visited Hazel, who improves by leaps and bounds.'

Annie threaded a comforting arm around Minnie's waist. She turned to Albert, who hovered in the background. 'Are you staying?' she asked.

Albert shook his head, his face filled with regret. 'I'd like to stay and watch them and see Slim Jim get better,' he replied, taking a deep breath. 'But if I don't look after 'em bananas, we starve.'

Bill's voice drifted from behind. 'We'll take care of Minnie and Harold,' he said, offering support. 'Annie and I will accompany them to the hospital to visit and bring young Hazel home when they discharge her.' The promise of togetherness and support filled the room with relief.' Minnie won't be coming home by bus and mail cart because we won't let her out of our sight.'

'Bill, Ben told me about your flashy, shiny, blue automobile. Since the war ended, I've seen plenty on the roads but never been in one. Would you show me the machine as I head home?' The two men headed towards the door.

Minnie stood at the bay window and watched Albert attach the horse to the cart and rumble off. When the cart became a speck on the horizon, an exhausted Minnie flopped into the window seat and lowered her head. Her heart flooded with grief for her lost baby, but elation tugged at the sadness. Hazel would recover.

* * *

'Don't you like riding in the car, mate?' asked Bill as he glanced over his shoulder from the driver's seat to Harold, who lounged in the back passenger seat beside his mother. Annie occupied the seat next to her husband as the foursome made the trip for the fifth time for the daily hospital visiting hour.

'Yes, it's such fun when you whizz past the horses dragging those carts full of boxes, and you push on that button that makes toot, toot sounds.' Pointing with his index finger at the space beside him. 'Sis will sit here when we go home. We'll vroom, vroom, past horses, carts, trams, and people.'

Harold sprinted ahead when they reached the hospital, leaving the rest of the party behind. As Harold lunged on it, Minnie, flanked by Bill and Annie, arrived at Hazel's bed. Oblivious to the other visitors, brother and sister stared adoringly at each other, and Harold clasped his sister's hand. The pair bantered in a language known only to them, a covert means of communication between the two.

'I talked to the nurse as I came in. She gave me some good news,' said Minnie, smiling for the first time since Hazel and Baby Annie had taken sick. With eyes wide and mouths drooping, brother and sister shot questioning gazes.

'Although Hazel is still sick and weak, she's improved enough for us to take her home tomorrow, but she must sleep and rest.'

Hazel's face shone as if Christmas had arrived early.

Harold's smile was so wide it seemed to swallow his face. Eyes tethered to his sister, he clapped as he said, 'Yippee. I know she must rest, but I must hold her hand to guard against anyone taking her away. We can play inside. I'll put a gigantic pile of pillows behind her, and she can watch me do cartwheels and handstands.'

With one hand hooked behind his braces, Bill tousled Harold's hair with the other. 'You've got it all mapped out, young man. We'll collect Hazel and take her home in the shiny car tomorrow.'

'Yes, yes. Vroom, vroom.'

A bell tingled from the nurse's desk.

Minnie glanced down at Harold. 'That bell says we must go.'

She breathed a lungful of air as she reflected on the dramatic days just past. One sick child had battled through. Not so, baby Annie. She would live in her mother's heart and soul forever.

Chapter 37

In early 1920, Minnie's heart sang as she watched Harold and Hazel hold their stomachs as they laughed, rolled around the grass, and called to each other in their secret language.

In the short months since Hazel had returned from her hospital stay, she made a miraculous recovery, something Minnie attributed to Harold's undivided attention. She could swear he hadn't taken his eyes off her for a second.

Minnie pictured Baby Annie joining the game. Her poor, sweet baby was not here because she had made the heart-wrenching decision to abandon her to the care of strangers. If only she had cared for her precious darling herself, Baby Annie would play the game alongside her brother and sister.

An intense fire burned in Minnie's belly as Hazel stumbled towards the embankment's edge. Terror filled her lungs as she took a deep breath, and her heart soared when Harold gave chase, tackling his sister and yelling, 'No, sis!'

Minnie joined her loyal wallaby friends for the sunrise show the following day. The breathtaking display never failed to captivate her senses. However, the once-alluring isolation had lost its charm. Minnie now endured long stretches alone with her young children, exposed to the worry of accidents, the creaking of ancient bark, the blistering heat of the sun, and the occasional visits from slithering reptiles.

Albert, his tousled hair hanging in greasy clumps across his sun-kissed forehead, wiped his weary eyes as he wandered outside and settled himself at Minnie's side. Her voice trembled with concern as she pleaded, 'We need to move, Dad. My heart is in my mouth all day. I can't help but see and dream of one of our children tumbling down the treacherous rocky slope or falling prey to a venomous snake's bite. How would I cope? How would we even get them to the hospital in time? We've toiled and sacrificed for years, carefully saving every penny. Couldn't we secure a small bank loan and purchase a less remote farm?'

Albert pivoted to face her, his chin raised defiantly, yet he avoided meeting her gaze. 'There you go again, fretting over the kids. They need the freedom to learn and grow, not you fussing and watching over them. We're not in Ulster. No thug is gunnna leap from the shadows and throw rocks.'

Minnie felt her face flush with anger and frustration, but she held another card to play. 'Soon, my love, we won't have to gaze longingly at that empty crib.'

He shot her a puzzled frown and scrunched his nose. When Minnie stroked her belly, realisation rippled across his face, and his lips arched upwards into a huge grin. 'Chuffed about that, Mum.'

Minnie seized the opportunity. 'We must consider our growing family. Harold and Hazel now run so fast that I can't catch them. We will overcrowd this place with two boisterous toddlers and a newborn. And this place reminds me of Baby Annie.'

Albert nodded and snorted but made no other response.

Minnie could see from the set of his jaw that she had lost the battle, so she rose. 'You win, Dad. I'd better stoke the stove.' As she retreated inside, she whispered to herself. 'Arguing with that man never works. *But he is mistaken if he thinks I will passively follow his every whim.*

'I'm going to get a farm. I'll try to make him think it's his idea. That should work.'

* * *

Later in the year, Harold and Hazel briefly stayed with Ben and Jean while Minnie gave birth to another baby girl.

Harold and Hazel arrived home a few hours after the new-born and their parents. Harold clasped his sister's hand as they made timid progress to the crib. Albert and Minnie hovered in the background and watched the children take an inquisitive peep at the baby. Hazel whispered a few words to her brother, dashed to her mother, wrapped her arms around her mother's legs, and buried her face in her skirt folds.

Minnie's legs jerked at the tight grasp. She grabbed Harold's shoulder and rotated him towards her. 'Why is your sister upset?'

The boy looked straight into his mother's eyes but didn't answer. She placed her thumb under her son's chin. 'Darling, please tell me so Mummy can help.'

Words erupted from the lad's mouth. 'Sis thinks it is Baby Annie, and that scares her.'

'Daddy and I explained to you that a new baby would soon join our family,' Minnie said in her gentlest voice. Her mind raced. *Seeing Hazel's actions, we did a terrible job explaining.*

He pursed his lips while tugging at an ear. 'Because I'm big, I know Baby Annie will always be an angel. But you didn't say the bubby would sleep in Baby Annie's bed and wear her clothes.'

Minnie realised she needed to explain the situation differently. 'There's nothing for you and your sister to worry about. As a family, we share everything. You and Hazel used the same crib before Baby Annie. Although Baby Annie is no longer with us, Daddy and Mummy know that she would have wanted your new sister, Edna, to have her crib, clothes, and toys.'

Harold gave a half-hearted smile, which suggested to Minnie she failed to convince him. Albert walked over, tickled Harold's cheek, and coaxed Hazel to let go of Minnie. He picked up Hazel and walked over to the crib. Leaning over the railing, he pointed at the sleeping baby. 'Look, Slim Jim, this is your new baby sister, Billie. She looks comfortable in Baby Annie's bed and wearing her clothes. Mum is counting on you to help wash and feed the new baby. She's asleep now, but you can give her kisses and cuddles when she wakes up.'

Hazel's eyes sparkled, and her bright smile lit up the room. However, Harold pouted and said, 'Mum said the baby's name is Edna, but you called her Billie.'

'Your dad thinks Billie suits her better. What do you think?' said Albert.

The children clapped in agreement. 'Yes, Billie!'

Minnie shrugged. He even wins about the name! But at least the nickname caused the children to settle down. Hopefully, they'll soon love Edna as much as they loved Baby Annie.

* * *

'Quick, Harold, grab Hazel's hand and come inside,' said Minnie as a lightning flash filled the sky. What had begun as a shower quickly became a violent storm. The children played outside since Albert's brother, Henry, grinning with pride, had collected Albert for their weekly Saturday race meeting trip in his shiny new red car.

Minnie shivered as she pressed her weight against the crude door, and the stinging rain wet her to the bone. Sheets of water driven by a blistering gale lashed the flimsy external walls.

Her temples throbbed, and her muscles stiffened as she propped herself against the open door, watching Harold, hunched against the beating rain, shepherd his wailing sister across the grass. Harold called to Hazel, but the relentless howl of the wind smothered his words. Minnie supposed they spoke their gibberish, and she wouldn't understand.

When they reached her, she drew the drenched children to her, shouted at them to shelter inside, and spun around, intending to close the door. But when she released her weight, the wind swept the door, pulling a vacuum of air.

Claps of thunder came in waves, shaking the entire structure, and water gushed through the roof thatch. A weeping Hazel tugged her mother's skirt. The thin external walls gave way in several places, allowing water to pour in. Gusts of wind sent containers and their contents crashing. Tea, flour, and sugar littered the sludgy mud floor. Terror rose within Minnie, who heard her heartbeat thrash in her ears, but she cautioned herself to be strong for the sake of her little ones.

The filthy hem of her skirt clung to her legs, making each step a struggle. She sensed a soft but persistent rub on her thigh. Competing against the pounding rain and the roar of the wind, Harold yelled, using his cupped hands as a megaphone, 'Billie is crying and screaming in her crib.'

Minnie froze like a statue and couldn't move as bolts of

fear whisked through her. 'We must cross the room to Billie. Harold, be careful and go first. I'll rest one hand on your shoulder to steady you. Hazel, you crawl up on my hip and balance, and I'll grip you with my other hand. We'll sit on the bed near the crib when we reach the other side.'

They slipped and slid across the quagmire of mud that had been the floor. Harold and Hazel collapsed onto the bed at the end of their scramble. Like a crab, Minnie dragged her drenched skirt with her and took sideward steps to the crib, where Billie, her face tear-stained, clutched the railing. A light twinkled behind the toddler's eyes when her mother reached her. 'My poor darling, when there's a break in that naughty wind, Mummy will lift you out, and you can cuddle your brother and sister,' soothed Minnie.

After rescuing Billie, Minnie shuffled to another bed and grabbed a few blankets. She shook them open, and mother and children huddled under the blankets. Water spouted from the roof and walls, and tins and containers flew like missiles. Minnie prayed silently, asking for protection and courage.

Rage boiled inside her. Anxiety was a constant factor in her life, and this storm topped it all. No longer would she allow herself to spend hours alone in this isolated place with three young children, soon to be four. She would canvass buying a farm with Albert but expected the same excuses.

We'll get a farm. I'll do anything to make it happen!

***

Relief swept over Minnie when the furious flapping and lashing ceased. It seemed an eternity that she'd cuddled her children beneath the blanket, but only an hour had passed.

Hazel peered out from beneath the blanket tent. 'Mummy, has that angry wind and rain stopped?'

Harold leapt out from their hideaway, grabbed a metal bowl dumped on the muddy floor by the wind, and shoved it over his head until it reached his eyebrows. He pranced in circles. 'I'm a big, brave soldier.'

Minnie giggled. 'It'd be helpful if that soldier could help clear the floors.'

Zig-zagging the items flung on the floor, Minnie cautiously stepped towards the door and opened it just a little. A shaft of light broke through the opening, and specks of dust danced in the light as the gap widened.

She wandered outside, gulping the soothing balm of refreshing air. The ground, trees, rocks, and distant mountains sparkled as if scrubbed clean. Glistening raindrops weighed down and dripped from every leaf and blade. Water rushed across the land and down the cliff face.

She returned inside and, with Harold, scrubbed and scoured to restore order to the storm-damaged hut.

When Minnie ventured outside again, the sun had descended over the mountains, and pink and hazy purple ribbons cascaded. She spotted two glaring lights bob along the winding entrance track, followed by the rumble of an engine. As the lights grew closer, they blinded her. A red car halted outside, and Albert's wiry form slid from the passenger door.

'We sheltered at Henry's place in Dayboro,' said Albert. 'Henry is gunna turn and go home. He fusses about that Ford like it's a baby.'

Albert and Minnie watched the vehicle negotiate the hairpin bends until it became a speck in the distance. With stars shining in his eyes, Albert said in a dreamy voice, 'Beaut machine.'

After the children went to bed, Albert and Minnie slouched in the upright chairs. Albert studied his boots and then shifted his gaze to the sludgy floor. But Minnie knew the signs—something consumed him. He twisted his hands after letting out a throaty cough.

Then he said, 'Ran into Jack Williams.'

'Yes, he owns that dairy farm about three miles out of Dayboro on the Brisbane Road,' said Minnie.

'He has this Ford truck he wants to sell. A truck, not a sedan like Henry's,' said Albert. 'Hardly used and cheap.'

He's desperate for the truck. Minnie had gambled on this moment arriving. She flung herself out of the chair, raced to Albert, and kissed his forehead. 'You're the best husband and father.'

Albert searched her face, a confused expression smothering him.

'I heard about Jack Williams leaving the district and selling his farm. I knew as soon as I heard that you'd buy it for us. And now you get both the farm and the truck. We'll need the truck if we have the farm.'

Albert's eyebrows pulled down. 'How did ya know Jack had headed out?'

'Mrs Crawford told me when I bumped into her at Kobble Creek.' Minnie cocked her neck towards Albert. 'You've made my dreams come true. Tomorrow will drag because you won't be able to visit the bank until Monday.'

She waited for him to contradict her, to say it was a dream or it would have to wait. Instead, Albert lifted his shoulders, grunted, and strode towards the bed.

Does this mean I've finally won? Minnie could only hope.

* * *

'We've got wonderful news,' said Minnie as she struggled down from the cart while Albert tethered the horse to a crumbling fence post.

Ben, canvas water bottle in hand, bolted down the stairs of his Kobble Creek home, taking two treads at a time. 'I hoped you'd come to help chip bananas. Whatever it is, it better be worthwhile.'

To Minnie, it was. 'It's the best news, and we wanted you and Jean to be the first to hear.'

Expressionless, Albert nodded his agreement.

'Sounds interesting. You better git inside to spill it.' After beckoning Albert and Minnie to follow, Ben vaulted back upstairs.

At the top of the stairs, Jean, reeking of yeast, emerged from the kitchen. Expression perplexed, she wiped her hands on her flour-smudged navy apron. 'Whatever brings you so early?' She looked Minnie up and down. 'I can tell from your face that it's something fabulous.'

'I'll take me brother and ya sister into the sitting room. Jean, could you fix tea? I'll settle them so we can be together when they break their news.'

Albert and Minnie took seats, and within minutes, Jean entered the room carrying a flower-embossed tea set on a tray.

After she'd poured piping hot tea, Ben looked at his brother. 'Well, you've got us guessing. Now spit it out.'

Albert, a grin tugging at his lips, shot a teasing smirk. 'I'll leave it to Mum to tell ya.'

Minnie rushed the announcement. 'At last, we've bought a

farm. It is a gorgeous dairy farm three miles from Dayboro on the Brisbane Road.'

Ben grinned and turned to Albert. 'An ideal choice. Rush Creek winds through that land, so there's plenty of water and fertile land. The property carries a herd of Illawarra Shorthorns'.

'Sixty of the blighters. I'll be joining the four a.m. starters,' said Albert.

'It has a quota—a contract to supply city milk. Hang on to that quota. They're scarce,' said Ben.

'The place comes with a Ford truck,' said Albert, the first hint of excitement rising in his voice.

Minnie threw her head back and gave an amused laugh. 'He's chuffed with that truck. He's more excited about it than the farm.'

'Typical man,' Jean shot back.

On a serious note, congratulations. 'You've both worked hard', said Jean, her cheekbones prominent from smiling. 'Minnie, it's your dream come true. You've never lost sight of your goal, and your efforts have finally paid off.'

Minnie smiled so broadly that she felt the skin on the bridge of her nose wrinkle. She jolted from her chair, ran to Jean, and embraced her. 'Only a sister could know how long and hard I've craved this,' she said.

Chapter 38

At last!

Minnie sprawled on a bed of coarse Kikuyu grass beneath the massive Moreton Bay fig tree that guarded the Oaklands farmhouse. A dense evergreen canopy of fluttering leaves shielded her from the blazing sun. Hugging her pregnant belly, she looked at the fresh roots dripping like candle wax from the upper branches and descending to the ground by twisting around an existing trunk to form a fresh one.

One of the free-range hens scratching and making cosy nests in the folds at the foot of the tree clucked as it lunged towards her, shedding feathers and glaring at her. She stared head-on at the bird. 'Cluck. Cluck! I've just scattered a feast of grain and food scraps for your family. Please let me share your home for a few minutes. I won't bite.'

Hazel forced the birds to share when she spent hours playing at the same spot. At the dinner table, she entertained the family with tales of her visits to the boomerang-waving fairies who lived in the crevices and caves formed by the roots.

The tree was hundreds of years old. It had survived drought, wind, fire, rain, and even the settler's axe. *Its twisted trunk must hold more history than any textbook*, mused Minnie.

As Minnie gazed at the view of distant mountains, similar

to the Kobble Creek outlook, she took gulps of air smelling of native plants and chicken food. Her eyes darted across lush paddocks in the foreground, full of fat grazing cows, towards the farmhouse—a humble three-bedroom cottage but a mansion compared to their last home. The once cream house, hemmed by a sturdy fence of branches tied together with heavy wire, crouched under a shimmering corrugated roof that sloped like a slippery slide.

Yesterday, she walked along the well-worn banks of Rush Creek, the life-giving water source for their farm. A persistent horde of buzzing insects followed her every step, their incessant hum filling the air. She tried to swat them away, but they remained steadfast in their pursuit. The creek flowed into the farm at its farthest boundary, meandering through rows of pineapple plants. As she gazed towards the farm buildings, only a few scattered trees were visible, aside from the ones lining the creek. However, she-oak trees, with their greyish bark and teeth-like leaves, hugged the watercourse. Ben had pointed out the species at Kobble Creek. They flourished in greater abundance here than on Ben's farm.

Gullies created by the land's contours created gullies, turning the waterway into calm pools and marshes. The creek gradually flowed over rocks, becoming a magnificent stream that continuously widened. The sound of rushing water drowned out all other noises as the creek snaked its way past the dairy, a building that bustled with activity during the twice-daily milking of the herd. Continuing its journey, the watercourse flowed past the barn, which served a dual purpose as a garage, before billowing into a serene swimming hole.

With hands shielding her eyes from the sun's glare, Minnie's stomach fluttered. Life here would be simple and good.

Her children could roam in the wondrous natural playground that stretched seemingly without end.

Music played in her heart. She lay under a shady tree on the farm that mirrored the farm she'd sketched in her mind's eye as the *Rippingham Grange* had steamed up the Brisbane River. It had taken over a decade, a war, hardship, tireless toil, and determination, but she'd made it.

She averted her gaze to the clear sky. 'Da, this is home. No more running.'

* * *

Minnie penned a list for provisions on the morning of Albert's first trip into Dayboro.

'I'd like to come,' she said. 'It's a chance to inspect the town. I didn't take notice when we came to the Orange Hall dances and on shopping trips.'

'Great. I'll start the truck, and you git yourself, Hazel and Billie ready.' Albert headed to the door, and before long, the vehicle was rumbling and spitting as it idled.

Minnie joined her husband, abandoning her housedress and apron for a powder blue maternity dress and matching hat. Billie clutched her hand, taking unsteady toddler steps, and Hazel skipped a few paces behind.

They bounced along the windy track to Dayboro, a long plume of dust rising in the air behind before flattening and settling.

After passing farm trucks and some horse-drawn carts, they rumbled into town, a web of rough, narrow tracks blanketed by stillness. Retail stores and public buildings lined the main street, McKenzie Street. Behind an overgrown hedge, with the lock-up bars visible, nestled a red brick building signposted *Police*. The lettering on the cracked sign affixed to the adjoining timber building said, *Ambulance*.

They passed the primary school—a tidy timber building of about four rooms resting on wooden stumps on enormous grounds with swings and a flag post. They drove past two churches—simple timber structures, unlike Ulster's ancient stone places of worship. A cross and statutes adorned one building, hallmark signs of Catholicism.

Rainwater flowed through narrow trenches on both sides of the roads. Some pooled and had become brown, transmitting a foul stink towards the vehicle and drowning the wattle and gum tree scent. Withered men with knotted joints slumbered on footpath seats. Mangey dogs dribbled as they sprawled under the shade cast by shop awnings.

'The town's sleepy,' said Minnie. As they veered left, about fifty men clad in ragged trousers and dark singlets rocketed out of a windowless building. 'This flurry puts an end to my description of sleepy. What's happening?' said Minnie.

'It's the butter factory lunch break. Me mates who didn't go onto the land work there.'

As sludgy water from a puddle sprayed the vehicle, Minnie followed her husband's finger to a steep-roofed building. He grinned. 'I hope you remember that joint.' Instantly, she recognised Orange Hall. She slumped deeper into the passenger seat and chuckled at the memories.

'Well, Mum, the local boy has given you a tour of all the town offers. Now let's explore on foot.'

Albert claimed a vertical parking spot shaded by overhanging trees. Minnie leveraged herself over the running board as she held Billie against her enlarged belly. She gave Albert a thankful smile when he scooped the little girl from her. Hazel seemed content to trail them.

Minnie shuffled behind her husband, who, with Billie in his arms, headed off, tipping his hat and pausing every few yards to chat with locals.

Albert led Minnie to a shop, displaying *General Store* in cursive letters stencilled on the window. He thrust the solid double doors open, activating a bell. They stepped into air tinged with a medley of smells and rows of shelves bursting with foodstuffs, hammers, axes, tobacco, slates, cotton reels, and preserves.

An assistant stood behind the dark timber counter wearing a starched white apron and a pencil resting behind his ear. As he peered over metal-framed glasses, he gave Albert a benign smile. 'May I help you?'

Albert coughed and spluttered before thrusting the list over the counter. The assistant counted and weighed each item before wrapping it in brown paper and tying it with string.

Albert volleyed the *Brisbane Courier* newspaper at Minnie when they left the store. 'Here, Mum. When you've finished reading this, save the horse racing section. Don't worry about the rest; you know where I git news.' The couple exchanged knowing glances. Bill was still a more reliable source than any newspaper.

Minnie shadowed her husband, who continued striding along, the sleeping Billie nuzzled into the crook of his shoulder. He stopped outside a weatherboard building with barred windows displaying *Bank* in faded, once-black letters on a weathered signpost. He turned to Minnie. 'Wait here, Mum. I won't be long.' Still holding Billie, he sprinted inside.

After Albert had exited the Bank, he laced his arms around

Minnie's neck and kissed her cheek. *What a surprise. What does he want?* He pulled her to him and whispered, 'I'm tonguing for a glass of amber liquid.'

Minnie pretended to smile, but under her breath, she said, 'That explains the smooching!'

Albert grinned and dashed towards the Crown. On arrival, he passed Billie to her mother and guided Hazel towards her, his hand resting on her curls. He waved towards a group of women and nudged Minnie in their direction.

Thrust together by laws forbidding their presence in public bars, the women gathered on the verandah in the shade of the overhanging roof.

* * *

Minnie watched her husband sprint towards the public bar door. With Billie on her knee, she parked herself at the edge of the ten women sheltered under the overhanging roof of the hotel's verandah. The women waved headwear, palms, and handkerchiefs at the circling fly swarm. They spoke of local happenings and their children to the background click-clack of knitting needles.

Panic climbed from the pit of her stomach. How could he abandon her to this gathering when he knew of her lack of experience interacting with groups of strangers? She'd forged a friendship with Leena at school in Ulster and Harriet and Peter aboard the *Rippingham Grange*. Since leaving Brisbane, however, she'd lived in isolated places where socialising opportunities were non-existent. The invitation to join Mrs Crawford's knitting circle didn't count.

She released Billie, who joined other toddlers, including

Hazel, who played with a motley collection of playthings at the far end of the verandah. Imagining curious eyes bore into her, Minnie smoothed her clothing and fidgeted with her hair. She gave her companions a half smile that faded quickly. Then she rummaged in her handbag for her latest novel before burying her face as a shield against unwanted attention.

However, she'd only read a little. When she felt a palm tap her shoulder, she looked up at a stranger's dimpled, plump face wearing a narrow-brimmed hat plonked on top of an unruly mop of fuzzy brown hair. 'I'm Betty. You're new to the district. Where do you live?'

'I'm Minnie. My family and I have just moved to Oaklands, a farm about three miles from town, on the Brisbane Road,' stuttered Minnie as her chest tightened.

When Minnie's eyes darted past Betty, a sea of smiling faces greeted her. One after another, the women rattled off their names and welcoming messages. They spoke so rapidly that Minnie found remembering the names difficult, although she mused about her luck finding herself among this agreeable bunch.

A matronly woman with her white hair pulled back in a coil beneath a battered black velvet hat patted the empty place beside her. 'Can you move here? That way, we can all hear you.' Minnie obliged and trembled as she wormed closer.

The woman patted Minnie's shoulder. 'It would be difficult to remember all the names spruiked to you. I'm Gladys. Minnie, I hear you're from the new Oaklands family. Welcome to the district. We are the town's sisterhood. You're one of us and can rely on us for support.'

Minnie sensed the tension inside her evaporate, and warmth gurgled in her insides. Wow! She'd made many new friends, and her inexperience didn't matter. She chatted and laughed with them, sharing secrets about child-rearing and knitting patterns.

At one stage, the barman slid the window open, releasing the odours of beer and cigarette smoke. He thrust his head through the open window. 'Which one of you ladies is Albert's missus?' He slid a frosted glass towards her. 'Shandy, one part beer and nine parts lemonade. Albert says it's your favourite.'

As Minnie settled into the camaraderie of the kindred spirits, she heard Albert call, 'Quick, Mum. Them red-coated cows are waiting, and the milk truck will be there soon.'

Chapter 39

December, 1921

On a boiling afternoon, dogs barked as the Ford, steam spewing from behind, crawled up the bumpy track leading to the Oaklands farmhouse. It stopped inside the wire fence barricading the house.

Minnie peered from the passenger seat. Albert, a cigarette hanging from his bottom lip, hunched over the steering wheel. Minnie glanced at the sleeping baby in her arms. Little Eunice was the latest family addition. Not stirring, the baby snuggled in the shawl held close to her mother's chest.

Her attention shifted towards the verandah, where three barefoot children were playing. Harold, Hazel, and Billie were energised, excitedly shrieking and waving their arms. They scaled the railing, their tiny bodies just visible behind the thick wooden posts. Harold effortlessly climbed while Hazel struggled slightly, gripping the top horizontal timber. The youngest Billie tried to mimic her siblings' movements but stumbled each time, falling to her spindly knees. Despite her falls, she remained undeterred, determined to reach the top using her steam. Her smile was infectious, and her fair cheeks

"

dimpled as she giggled.

Minnie noticed Harold. Scratches covered the skinny legs protruding from beneath his shorts, and his straw-coloured hair was full of tangles. She hoped he had brushed his teeth that morning and wondered why Albert hadn't supervised him more closely. In contrast, Hazel, clad in a navy blue pinafore, had better-cared-for almond curls cascading over her shoulders.

She missed the children during her brief absence. She took a deep breath of the crisp air, which carried the familiar smells of Oaklands—grass, gum, wattle trees, and animal excrement. Minnie couldn't help but contrast the fresh air to the second-hand air that ventilated the city hospital where she'd been.

Albert alighted, sporting his trademark broad grin. Harold, grasping Billie's hand, followed Hazel down the rickety stairs. The three children gathered at the bottom of the stairs before dashing to their dad. Hazel lifted her porcelain face towards her father and fluttered her ample eyelashes. 'When do we get to see our new sister, Daddy?'

'Daddy,' said Billie in adoring tones as she lifted her pudgy arms towards Albert. He obliged and hoisted his daughter up to his chest.

He tickled his son's mud-smothered cheek. 'How've things been today, mate?'

'I climbed a giant tree and swung on a high branch. Because Hazel kept yelling, I crawled down. Hazel is a crybaby.'

Minnie chuckled as the three eager, bantering youngsters jumped on the spot close to the passenger exit of the truck. She thought I couldn't shoo them, so I'll try to miss them. After checking the delicate bundle, Minnie swung her legs from the passenger door and leapt over the running board. A whimper escaped the shawl when she hit the ground, and the waiting youngsters pounced like a pack of yapping dogs. They jumped and snapped at the hem of their mother's coarse, light pink, linen calf-length dress.

Hazel begged her mother to let them see the baby.

'We know you've got baby Eunice in the shawl because we heard her squark,' said Harold with a smirk of self-satisfaction at his powers of deduction.

Albert, his face twisted in anger, glanced at the children. 'Stop the racket, kids. Get out of your mother's way, or she'll trip her.'

'Do as Dad says, darlings. When I get inside, I'll lay Eunice on the bed so you can say hello.'

With a smile tugging at her lips, Minnie fought the milling children as she inched towards the door. Despite their mother's assurances of time with Eunice, the children tried to glimpse the baby by jumping and clutching the mother's dress as she walked down the hall. *I need not have concerned myself about jealousy.*

* * *

In the main bedroom, Minnie gazed lovingly at their newborn daughter as she lowered her onto the quilt, sniffing the unmistakable scent of a new baby. The baby wore a pastel cotton dress and matching booties, which the other girls wore as newborns. An image of her darling Baby Annie dressed in the outfit flashed before Minnie's eyes.

She laughed when the children pouted and showed no interest as she kissed them, their eyes glued to the gurgling Eunice. They squabbled over who got to cuddle the baby first.

Harold mounted the bed and, bedsprings groaning beneath him, squirmed on his bottom towards his new sister. Minnie grinned. 'The ball of energy wins again.'

With a cheeky smirk, he tested the baby's limbs. Eunice whimpered as he bent elbows, knees, and each chubby finger. Minnie pulled him off her as he poised to grasp a clump of the baby's fine hair. 'You know not to be rough with babies,' said Minnie, recalling the endless times she had lectured him about this topic. Because Eunice is small, you need to be gentle, or you might hurt her.' Minnie stroked Eunice's soft skin. 'Don't worry, darling,' she said to her newborn. 'You'll get used to him. He's harmless, really.'

Hot on her brother's heel, Hazel struggled up the bed, curls tumbling around her face. When she neared Harold, the pair chatted in their secret language. Hazel pushed Harold away and kissed the baby's blotched, rosy cheeks. Eunice gurgled, and when Hazel offered an index finger, the baby curled her hand around it.

Minnie flinched when her ears filled with a thump, shrill screaming, feet stamping and crying. Billie had landed on her backside on the floor after attempting to scale the sheets. Minnie scooped her up and put the toddler on the bed. 'Here she is, darling. You can see her now.'

'Bubby, dolly,' Billie said, mouth drawn in an amazed circle. She crawled to the baby and smothered her with kisses.

Bored with the baby, Harold started doing somersaults. He craned his neck towards Hazel. 'Look at me! Because I'm a big, strong boy, I can do these clever things!' he said as he bounced off the bed.

Hazel ignored him and scattered more kisses on her baby sister.

Once the children met their sister, Minnie laid Eunice in the crib beside their bed. After feeding the family, a weary Minnie slumped into a seat on the verandah. Not even the sweet baby could prevent her from watching the magical meeting of daylight and night. While awaiting dusk, her mind replayed the children's enthusiastic welcome of their new sister.

After the glow slipped over the mountain range, stars provided the only light. Stillness reigned except for trembling leaves, scurrying animals, and the distant croak of frogs.

The sunset cast a mantle to allow the earth to slumber. Yet, for Minnie, sleep wasn't a choice. She must prepare for Christmas day, two days away. She gave herself a stern lecture as she gazed at the darkening sky. *While there's a pile of work, panic won't help. As always, it'll happen.*

* * *

They busied themselves with preparations for Christmas Day over the next two days. The children's laughter flooded the farmhouse. Minnie hoped the swelling ranks would keep the usual cheerful family celebrations the same.

Albert felled a she-oak sapling and delivered it to the sitting room, where Harold and Hazel took control. Minnie, propped against the doorframe of the hallway entrance to the room, watched as the giggling pair placed the tree against the tongue-and-groove wall. They secured it in a bucket crammed with rocks before decorating the prickly branches with homemade streamers and ornaments. The pair argued about placing decorations. Harold won each time because he used furniture to climb, getting to the higher parts before Hazel.

Although the decorations were lopsided, Minnie praised her

children. 'Why, that's beautiful, darlings.'

Harold swung from where he dangled from the picture rail and landed on the floor with a thud. 'Now I've got to help Dad break the neck of the chicken for Christmas dinner and pull its innards and feathers out.' He raced out the door. Minnie wondered how she had raised such a bloodthirsty son.

Christmas day dawned as another sweltering summer day, and by ten a.m., it boiled. The burning timber stove transformed the farmhouse into a steam bath, and buzzing flies orbited, but nothing quelled the children's zeal.

After milking, everyone gathered near the Christmas tree to open presents. Minnie looped her arm around Albert's waist as they watched the children rip through the wrapping to see their gifts while baby Eunice dozed in the crib.

Minnie placed the stuffed hen and farm-grown vegetables into the mammoth wood stove in the kitchen's corner. Soon, mouth-watering smells wafted through the multi-coloured fly deterrent strips that hung from the ceiling, separating the sitting room and kitchen. Minnie lifted her apron and wiped the beads of sweat from her forehead. She went around the half-wall into the dining area, her shoes padding softly on the bare floor, and removed most of the china from the dresser.

Attracted by tempting aromas, the family filed in and took their places on the chairs arranged around the pine table. Hazel, monitored by her mother, set the table. Albert carved the chicken, and Hazel filled everyone's plates with generous helpings of meat while Minnie followed, heaping vegetables on each plate. Everyone helped themselves to the gravy before attacking their portion with salt.

Cooked by Minnie months in advance and suspended, wrapped in a cheesecloth to mature, the plum pudding bubbled as it warmed. Minnie had used her family's unwritten recipe. As the children ate their portions, Minnie and Albert exchanged knowing looks. The youngsters looked for the coins hidden inside.

Harold dangled a silver coin. 'Ha, ha, I found one.'

Hazel held a shiny coin to the shaft of midday glare piercing the window. 'Smarty, I have one too.'

'But I found mine first. That means I am cleverer than you,' said a gloating Harold.

Albert winked at Minnie as he placed a coin he'd found in his portion into Billie's bowl.

Minnie gazed at Billie, who squatted in a highchair beside her. 'Mummy can see one in your bowl. Do you see it?' The child's eyes sparkled as she trailed her mother's eyes to the glint in her pudding.

Once each child had a healthy collection of three pence pieces, they noisily vacated the table. After lunch, the children played indoor games while gulping sweets. The children grumbled and complained when afternoon miking time arrived, but they trekked to the dairy.

Dusk ushered out Eunice's first Christmas celebration. At sunset, as Minnie sunk into her verandah chair with her little girl in her arms, she realised the baby had slept through most of the day, but everything had still been beautiful.

* * *

On Boxing Day, Minnie said, 'There's a surprise.'

The children stopped scurrying about the kitchen and stared. Hazel, eyes expanded to the size of saucers, spoke over her siblings, 'Well, what is it, Mum?'

'If I tell, it won't be a surprise.'

As Minnie cleared the table of plates, the children looked up, begging her with their eyes. Minnie grabbed her broom and swept the floor of the dusty imprints of tiny feet. Finally, seeing the children squirming from the suspense, she turned to them. 'Aunty Jean and Aunty Carrie will be here soon with their families to meet your baby sister.'

As Minnie anticipated, cheers rose all around. Harold performed one of his gymnastics displays. 'Great, we can play with our cousins, and I will win every game.'

When the visitors arrived, everyone scrutinised the baby like a museum piece—cuddling her, making cooing noises, and tickling her stomach. Eyes tinged with eagerness, Jean's older two children watched as the adults cradled the tiny bundle. Before long, they tugged their mother's clothing. 'Mum, can we please hold Eunice? We promise to be careful.'

Jean glanced at Minnie. 'Is it all right for them to hold Eunice if I supervise?'

Jean's oldest daughter, Thelma, waited stiffly on a tapestry-covered chair, arms upturned on her lap. Jean lowered the wrapped bundle into her daughter's waiting arms. 'Sweetie, be gentle and support the baby's head.'

As she hugged her, Thelma concentrated on Eunice. Then her gaze jumped to Hazel. 'Your little sister is cute and has that lovely baby smell.' She looked at her mother. 'Can we get one?'

Ben and Jean chuckled and squirmed, holding each other's gaze. Jean changed the subject. 'Minnie, your baby's angelic, and no one can keep their hands away from her.'

Minnie saw Carrie studying the framed photograph of the tiny Baby Annie, who, with haunted eyes, peered down at them.

Carrie turned to Jean and whispered, 'A close resemblance.'

'Yes, poor Baby Annie. Billie looks like her too,' said Jean.

Minnie grimaced, and her chest tightened. Why had they said that? Couldn't they see how much it hurt? Although two-and-a-half years had passed, she continued to mourn her lost daughter and disliked reminders of the tragic loss.

The children raced outside, and the babies and toddlers remained inside with the adults. Carrie made several trips from the kitchen carrying cups and a teapot covered by a green knitted tea cosy. Minnie followed, balancing a plate of buttered scones heaped with lashings of jam and cream. The women indulged in endless cups of tea while the men downed beer.

Ben looked at Minnie. 'Did you bake the scones? They're so tasty, I could woof the lot.'

'The shape and taste are familiar,' said Carrie.

Jean's face lit up in delight. 'They're the scones Aunty Sarah made in Clonkeen, as did all the district women.'

Minnie nodded. 'The recipe travelled across the sea in my head.'

She sensed tears pricking the back of her eyes. This conversation stirred up those memories she couldn't bear to recall, and relief rushed through her veins when Albert changed the subject. 'This year has flown,' he said.

Ben caught his brother's eye. 'How're things goin'?'

'Heaps of work, but Minnie and the young-uns chip in, and the cows produce plenty of milk.'

Children's giggles and shrieks floated in from outside. Minnie giggled as she leaned towards Jean. 'They're having a ball, but Carrie's Bert is supervising, so they're safe,'

The men moved away with their beers, leaving the women

to talk.

'Harold is at school now, and Hazel is starting next year,' said Minnie.

'Does he attend Dayboro Primary?' asked Carrie.

'No, Forbes Creek, a one-teacher school with twenty pupils.'

The women drained their teacups before Jean disappeared, teapot in hand. On her return, Minnie said, 'Molly's returning once school starts.'

'Who's Molly?' asked Carrie, a look of curiosity shadowing her.

'Miss Gormley, the Forbes Creek teacher, our boarder.'

'Why are you taking boarders? There's no sign of poverty,' said Carrie, eyes darting around the house.

'With bush schools, the government places the teacher if the parents organise the accommodation. When Miss Gormley arrived, we figured we should do our bit,' said Minnie. Minnie's mind wandered back to Molly's arrival in August and how she felt drawn to the tall, thin, bespectacled woman. Within days, she and Molly enjoyed evening chats, becoming trusted confidants.

Albert's voice boomed from where he chatted to Ben. 'The few shillings board doesn't cover her tucker.'

'Doesn't it feel odd to have a stranger under your roof?' asked Carrie.

'She's a cheerful soul with a distinctive laugh. Molly is a family member now, and she and I often chatter until late.' Minnie thought. Surely, she couldn't think of any more questions. But when Carrie leaned forward towards Minnie, dragging her chair with her, Minnie registered there were more questions.

'How do the children cope with sharing their home with a

teacher?'

Minnie thought her sister's questions were tiresome but arranged her face into a weak smile. 'They love her like a second mother. Harold easily separates school and home. If Miss Gormley corrects his grammar, he protests, 'You might be boss at school but not here.'

The group burst out laughing.

Carrie's eyes scanned the space, pausing at each doorway. 'Hardly roomy. Where do you all sleep?'

Not another pointed question! 'One bedroom is Molly's. Hazel and Billie share a bedroom. The crib is in our room, and Harold sleeps on the closed-in verandah. Cosy but not the tight fit of our Ulster cottage.'

The sun sauntered towards the horizon. 'Them shadows say it's time for milking.' Albert wandered to the verandah where, one hand on his hip, the other on the rail, he bellowed to the revellers, 'Kids, the cows need us.'

The children, smelling of grass and greenery, drifted in with twigs hanging in their tangled hair and minor scrapes and scratches covering their limbs.

'Harold climbed a tree and pelted us with leaves and sticks,' said Thelma.

Ben smiled at his daughter and then looked at Jean. 'We must get going to our cows, but miking may soon be history because we're thinkin' of moving to the city for our children to attend high school. We don't want 'em at boarding school.'

After the visitors had said goodbye, Albert, Minnie, and their tribe trudged towards the dairy.

Chapter 40

The seasons and the twice-daily milk truck visits dictated every aspect of farm life.

But a day in March 1922 brought a rare change. The change started the night before.

Albert raced to the door and let it slam behind him as soon as he'd cleaned his plate. Minnie knew he headed to the nightly poker tournament at the hotel. After settling the children, she darned socks in the sitting room with Molly, who stitched complex embroidery. Molly said goodnight at about ten.

Minnie stayed alone after Molly wandered towards her bed-room, squinting each time she speared the woolly fabric with the threaded needle until she realised milking was starting in a few hours. Albert's appetite for the Crown Hotel and gambling wasn't a secret, but he never missed milking. She took herself off to bed.

Later, the skid of wheels sounded, and harsh lights glared through the window. Boots thumped up the stairs before the door creaked open. The house shook as footsteps staggered down the hall.

When Albert entered the bedroom, Minnie pretended to be asleep.

Minnie woke before the sun and struggled to rise from the

bed. Albert slept on, his chest rising and falling with each breath. Each exhalation reeked of stale alcohol, confirming her suspicions that he had engaged in more than cards.

Minnie crept through the house, the swaddled Eunice resting on her shoulder. Everything was silent except for the rasping of sleep. She lit the stove before stirring the children, and the drowsy youngsters plodded into the kitchen.

'Where's Dad? He usually beats us,' Harold said.

Minnie retreated to the bedroom and poked Albert's ribs, but he groaned and rolled over. They'd have to milk the herd without him.

Minnie went back out to the children. 'Daddy is sick, so we'll need to pitch in and milk the cows ourselves.'

Hazel nestled into her mother's side. 'Mummy, we'll help.'

'You must follow instructions, as milking is a grown-up's job.'

'Your big boy knows the ropes 'cause Daddy taught me,' said Harold.

Minnie untied her apron and lobbed it onto the dresser. She tucked a napping Eunice into a basket. As a dishevelled Albert emerged, she headed out with the other children in tow. 'Mum, organise the kids, and I'll meet youse at the dairy.'

When Minnie and her gaggle arrived, the clatter of buckets spilled out, and she surmised Albert was preparing inside the building. 'Did you grow wings and fly?' she yelled to Albert.

A razor-sharp rasp drifted from the dairy. 'That milk truck ain't gunna wait at my farm.'

She settled the children in the holding yard and selected a spot next to the fence, hidden by a clump of ragged weeds, for the baby's basket. Cows gathered, sticking their wet snouts into the basket as they examined the miniature person through huge, deep brown eyes. Unaware of her audience, Eunice slumbered beneath a sheet.

Minnie rushed to join her husband after saying, 'Harold, be a good boy and watch your sisters.'

Once in the dairy, she peeped into the holding yard, where Billie and Hazel tittered as they attempted to grasp a cow's tail. Whenever their tiny hands came close, the animal flicked its tail. Minnie chuckled at her daughter's antics.

The chuckle grew louder, and warmth radiated through her veins when she spotted Harold preparing a twin-wheeled billy cart with a fruit box as a seat. He laid hay, ensuring a smooth distribution before guiding Hazel and Billie into their carriage.

After warning the pair to hold tight, the lad, straining every muscle, sped around the holding yard, bumping over potholes, loose soil, and stinking cow pads. Hair blowing in the wind, the girls giggled as the speed increased with each circuit. 'Come on, Harold, faster, faster!' Minnie had introduced the billy cart when Oaklands became home. She smiled inwardly as she contemplated how it continued to entertain the children.

After milking, the house echoed with juvenile voices and clambering footsteps crisscrossed the floor. Minnie cut sandwiches for Harold and Hazel to take to school. Hazel had begun school that year. As she waved to her eldest children, Minnie's chest expanded with pride that they independently tackled the two-mile hike.

Her unmistakable laugh preceded her as Molly clip-clopped towards the kitchen. After laughing and chattering with Minnie, she grabbed her cut lunch and hurried off on the same path as the children. Albert's boots scraped across the floorboards. He swigged some greedy gulps from his canvas water bottle before scooping it up again in his work-worn hands and darting toward the back entrance.

'I thought you might rest, Dad.'

He grunted, his breath ripe with remnants of last night's alcohol. 'Work needs doing like every day. A few beers too many ain't gunna stop me.' Minnie noted her husband's jaw's rigid set and penetrating stare. She knew not to labour the point.

She rested her hip on the door frame and watched him disappear into the distance, carrying an axe, rifle, and a can of poison. The tail-wagging Maxi trailed him, yelping and jumping. Minnie had already toiled for five hours, but an ocean of jobs lay ahead, which she must do with only pre-schoolers and black flies for company.

It was Monday—washing day, which was always a challenge. She lowered Eunice into the crib and slid a fabric pacifier soaked in milk and honey into her mouth. Then she swept the linoleum to rid it of the dusty imprints of tiny feet and dead and alive pests. Next, she erected a playpen of timber, dowels, and hessian and popped Billie inside. The toddler sat cross-legged, swaying her petite form, a sign for Minnie to scatter her playthings inside the barrier. With a determined sparkle in her eyes, the child glided on her bottom towards a teddy bear.

Minnie scowled, anticipating the hot, gruelling task ahead, as she descended the five steps from the kitchen to the bare-earthed annex. After boiling the water, she lit the fire beneath the copper and added soap and clothes. Surrounded by a soapy scent, she stirred the heated mixture and fished out the steamy contents. The ground became sodden, and Minnie felt droplets of sweat tracking down her spine and legs and into the creases behind her knees.

Before hanging the garments on the line, Minnie rubbed each item on a washing board's unbending, wavy surface. When finished, she winced as she gazed at her hands, left scaly and scarred with several broken fingernails.

Minnie felt wrung out and longed to flop down and doze, but many other tasks remained: bread baking, butter churning, and ironing.

Before long, Harold and Hazel hurtled up the rickety staircase. Minnie wiped the sweat from her brow and neck with the back of her apron. 'I've had a trying day, children, and still haven't finished my work.'

'Harold and I'll help, Mummy,' said Hazel.

The girl swept the floor and collected, sorted, and folded laundry. Minnie, shoulders squared and chin held high, spied the youngster unpegging clothing on tiptoes from a stool under the rope line.

Then, mother and daughter shelled, peeled, and chopped the vegetables for the evening meal. Hazel peered through eyes set deep in her earnest six-year-old face to meet her mother's gaze. Minnie interpreted the expression as a request to cook alone and inclined her head. The giggling girl clasped her hands to her chest. Then, with only limited supervision and instruction, Hazel mixed, cut, minced, and sliced. 'A pinch of salt, a tablespoon of flour,' said Minnie. Hazel nodded as she flung an adoring smile to her mother.

Metal wheels screeched on gravel. Harold, so dirty that the whites of his eyes and front teeth glowed from his black form, tore in, pushing a cart crammed with kindling. He unloaded the cargo at the same breakneck speed and then hurtled off. He returned in a flash, propelling the same cart filled with a fresh batch. Then he removed the spent coals and copper from the stove, replenishing the firewood piles again before heading towards the front door.

While his perpetual motion tired her, Minnie also found it infectious. His appearance was comical. Perhaps boys all behave that way. She didn't know, as her other children were all girls.

The food for the evening sizzled and bubbled. With the help of the two eldest children, Minnie achieved her goal and completed all her tasks.

She was so thankful for her children's help. Each one possessed a unique personality, from the cheeky eldest to the angelic baby. None of them were lazy.

* * *

As the day faded, birds chirped, hens clucked, and cows lowed like an unconducted orchestra. Minnie peered up from the range, watching the blood drain from the browning steaks. Albert lumbered up the track towards the house, his boots grinding through the gravel, with Maxi, his tongue hanging out, close at heel. After recovering his breath, Albert used his sleeve to wipe beads of sweat from his brow.

Crouched on a bowed step leading to the kitchen, he sifted through his pockets for tobacco and papers before rolling a smoke. The step creaked under the strain of his weight as a concocted smell of dry sweat, the tangy bouquet of pineapples, bananas, tobacco, and soil drifted inside. Minnie studied him. 'You look about to drop. You've got dark bags under your eyes, probably because of last night.'

She chastised herself. Jean had warned of Albert's love of

gambling. From their wedding day, she'd treated his visits to racecourses and hotels with passive acceptance. Despite his passion for gambling and alcohol, he worked long and hard.

Albert scanned the horizon with spread hands, protecting his eyes. 'There are no clouds, so there will be no rain tomorrow.'

'I know we need rain, Dad, but staring at the sky won't make raindrops fall.'

'You're wrong, Mum. Them clouds are like a weather book.'

She threw her head back and laughed with disbelief, but she knew he had an uncanny ability to read the seasons. *Not that I would tell him. It would just make him stick his chest out.*

The mouth-watering aromas of steak and onions wafted from the kitchen to the step. 'That smell is making my stomach grumble,' said Albert, flicking the remains of his cigarette under the stairs. After ordering Maxi onto the hessian bag bed beside the stairs, he entered the dwelling.

Chapter 41

In early 1923, Minnie told Albert she expected again. 'Might be a boy, as we've produced four girls in a row.'

'Ah, no matter, Mum. Them's all lads.'

He was probably right, given how they ran around and how hard they worked. 'I thought the masculine nicknames you give our girls were hiding a lurking desire for another boy.'

In June, at the hospital, the nurses announced that she'd had a healthy baby boy, and tears of joy burned Minnie's pain-etched cheeks.

The next afternoon, Minnie woke to find Carrie, perfumed with a sweet, tangy substance—magnolia perhaps—slumped in the chair beside her hospital bed.

'Another boy, at last. Have you settled on a name?' enquired Carrie.

'Not really. I'll leave it for Dad to decide. Finally, he gets to choose a boy's name for a real boy.' She sighed. 'What counts is not the gender, but that the baby is in excellent health.' Minnie's mind retraced a pregnancy fraught with problems of morning sickness, swollen feet, lethargy, and a racing pulse. She constantly harboured the concern that her ailments would affect the child she carried.

'A difficult delivery and long labour, the nurse told me,' said

Carrie.

'I battled through, and because of the pregnancy complications, the nursing staff insisted on a doctor assisting.'

'Did he make suggestions?'

'Oh, he visited this morning.'

Impatience rose in Carrie's voice. 'What did he say? Did he offer advice?'

'He suggested I abandon farm work and advised against expanding our family as he hastily departed.' Minnie felt a flush of warmth spreading across her cheeks as she spoke. Anticipating her face turning a fiery red, Minnie averted her gaze to the fluttering clothesline outside the window.

She'd miss seeing cows swishing their tails, the melodic sound of milk hitting the metal bucket, and even the humming buzz of black flies hovering above the pungent cow dung. Farming had become an integral part of her very being, starting from her captivated stares across the lush fields of Antrim to the image of her father's mighty scythe slicing through the air.

Bert received a warm welcome to Oaklands, equalling Eunice's hearty reception less than two years prior. When the newcomer arrived home, Eunice gave up the position in her parents' bedroom and moved in with her sisters, who shared a double bed.

Minnie's farmhand career ended. She no longer took a place on the milking assembly line, instead confining herself to the cottage and its surrounds.

Deep inside, she knew the scent of the farmyard would stay with her.

* * *

In late 1925, Minnie sensed herself shrink into the chair. In a diminished voice, she broke some unexpected news to Albert. 'Early next year, there'll be another baby.'

Albert arched one eyebrow in surprise and returned to studying the form guide.

'Billie and Eunice start school next year. I was looking forward to spending time alone, away from the constant babble of whining children and grubby hands tugging on my hem,' Minnie said, attempting to spark some conversation.

After a long second, he raised his shoulders and offered in a monotone, 'Oh, Mum, these things don't go as planned.'

* * *

In March 1926, Albert chauffeured Minnie home. She cradled her newborn daughter, Peggy, close to her chest.

Minnie laid the infant down and loosened the shawl. The three girls cooed before planting sloppy kisses on their tiny new sister's cheeks.

Billie's eyes bulged. 'A little princess. Her pearly skin smells of soap.'

'No, Billie,' said Eunice, 'She is our doll, and we can help Mummy with her.'

Eleven-year-old Harold entered and crawled onto the mattress after tripping over every object in his path. Supporting the side of his face on his elbow, he bent and lifted the baby's every body part, although he obeyed his mother's plea to be gentle. He held up a tiny leg and chuckled. 'It beats me how this scrawny leg will support a person, so we'll need to make her our mascot.'

Minnie's eyes panned the room. 'Have you seen your father?

He disappeared the minute we arrived.'

'He's on the back step with Maxi beside him, staring at the sky and clouds,' said Hazel. 'I knelt beside him for a while because he looked unhappy, but he wouldn't say what worried him.'

Minnie wondered what troubled her husband, but she had enough to keep her busy with another baby. Her husband's problems would have to wait.

Chapter 42

In 1926, Mother Nature showered the earth with not even a splash of moisture. Each day replicated the last: dry, hot, and still.

At dusk every day, Albert crouched on the back stairs, relaying a commentary to Minnie as he monitored the sky for signs of rain. Sometimes, he reported that the fuller, darker clouds looked promising, but they didn't deliver. 'Crown talk is always about the weather. Fellas reckon it'll rain soon, and the water will bucket down.'

'I hope they are right. If they're not, many people, including us, will face disaster,' said Minnie.

The children talked a lot about the weather at dinner.

'Huge drops of sweat were plopping from my face onto the slate at school. The air outside is full of dust,' said Billie, between filling her mouth with food.

'My bottom sticks to the seat,' said Eunice, as she raised her glass to her lips.

'Kids tell stories about their cows dying, which makes their dads and mums mad.' Hazel's eyebrows pulled together, and her brow wrinkled. Minnie mused that the girl's words mirrored the intense expression that occupied Albert's face.

Not wanting to panic the children, Minnie whispered to

Albert. 'The *Brisbane Courier* predicts the dryness will continue into 1927.'

His eyes held more hope than she'd expected. 'I hope the paper is wrong, but we'll cope. I've survived droughts that lasted years.'

As the papers foreshadowed, pre-Christmas 1926 didn't bring seasonal storms, but the temperatures rose to oppressive levels. Post-Christmas rain didn't arrive either. When Minnie flicked through the newspaper, she saw no predicted break in the dry conditions. The steamy, arid conditions continued.

A heavy atmosphere, devoid of the slightest breeze, engulfed Oaklands. The surrounding hills had lost their vibrant colours, appearing drained and lifeless. Minnie no longer gazed at a magical view but a desolate dust pool.

Death hung in the air as beasts perished, their stinking, rotting remains becoming a feast for circling crows. The surviving cattle, their rib cages exposed, moved listlessly in search of food and water. Above them, a few thin dust-stained clouds floated, but the sky itself was a blinding glare, cruelly mocking any hope for rain.

Whenever Minnie reluctantly visited Rush Creek, once the soul of life for Minnie's family and their animals, her stomach knotted with disbelief. The creek had dried up into a slimy, stagnant pool infested with swarms of mosquitoes that buzzed constantly. Vegetation that once thrived on its banks now lay withered and lifeless. Wildlife had abandoned their once vibrant habitat, driven by the search for sustenance elsewhere.

Their income took a drastic hit because of a decline in milk production and stock losses. One morning, after completing the morning milking, Albert sat down to enjoy a cup of tea.

However, before he finished, he left the kitchen and headed towards the back stairs with a slightly hunched posture. Minnie observed him scanning the sky again for signs of rain.

Under her breath, she muttered to herself, 'He's always so optimistic.'

When Albert returned to his unfinished cup of tea, Minnie leaned over and said, 'Dad, we can't endure much more of this. Even the crops we rely on for fodder have failed. Maybe you should approach the Bank for a loan?'

Albert growled, rising from his seat before leaving for the barn, slamming the door with a thud.

Minnie blew out a breath. Experience had taught her of her husband's stubborn streak, and she knew never to labour a point with him. She would back off and allow the planted seed to take root. Hopefully, it will grow.

* * *

Towards the end of 1926, Albert scraped his chair from the table after lunch. 'That tucker filled an empty spot in my innards, Mum,' he said as he traced his tongue around his lips.

'Are you going into Dayboro? Do you have the shopping list I wrote?' asked Minnie. 'Actually, I'll tag along.'

'Don't come, Mum. We're gunna have to lump the young fella and the baby. Getting them organised will take ages.'

Minnie's chest tightened. She glared at Albert. 'I need an outing after spending each day at home among babies and dying animals in this never-ending heat.'

Albert held her gaze but didn't speak.

Minnie wasn't giving up. She needed a break from the farm.

'I miss my friends. I could chat with them on the verandah while you quench your thirst at the Crown after shopping.'

Albert gave a curt nod and made a beeline for the barn. Rumbles and splatters shook the house as he started and idled the truck.

After preparing herself and the family's babies, Minnie, cradling Peggy and Bert tottering behind her stockinged legs, joined her husband. Albert leaned over from the driver's seat. 'Put the kids on the seat before hurdling the running board.'

They chugged towards Dayboro, their old truck rattling and groaning, through a desolate landscape of parched, sun-baked paddocks. A barren expanse dotted with brittle gum trees replaced the once-lush grass, now a distant memory. The air was heavy with the smell of dust and dried earth, a reminder of the relentless drought. A heartbreaking sight, a stark contrast to the previous lively fields.

Amidst this desolation, the occasional person tended to their paddocks. They waved at the passing truck. With a smile, Minnie waved back, feeling a sense of kinship with these determined individuals. She admired their ability to maintain a positive, friendly attitude despite the harsh conditions.

As soon as they reached town, Minnie noticed how different it was. A haunted stillness shrouded the streets. Not far into their stroll towards the shops, she noticed a marked decline in pedestrian and vehicular traffic. Those vehicles that entered the town churned up the dirt tracks, adding to the veneer of powdery dust.

A stench drifted from the clogged drainage channels that had become slime puddles. Chains and padlocks secured closed shops on both sides of McKenzie Street. The prolonged dry spell had spread its wicked tentacles into the entire district.

With the shopping completed, Albert broke into a trot as he hurried to the Crown. With the sleeping Peggy in her arms and gripping Bert's hand, Minnie limped after him, but Albert ran at a punishing pace. Puffing, she arrived at the Crown and saw him disappear through the door.

A subdued air blanketed the hotel. The customary merriment and the whiff of alcohol didn't pour out. Her heart sang when she spied Gladys's steely grey hair on the verandah in the company of about five women, not as many as usual.

With little ones under each arm, Minnie stumbled towards the rhythmic click-clack of knitting needles and the joyous sound of laughter. She recognised each woman, and memories flooded back about their histories. The atmosphere was warm and welcoming. Gladys gestured towards the empty bench space between herself and Beatrice from the local drapery shop. Other women leaned over to peek at Peggy and tickle Bert under his chin.

She sat across from Joan, a thin woman with silver-blonde hair tied back with a broad yellow ribbon, the wife of a local schoolteacher. 'My husband is on edge about the children's misbehaviour,' she said, over the clacking of her knitting needles. 'Because the absenteeism rate is so high, he thinks the coming generation will end up illiterate.'

Gladys tutted. 'My dear, there are things you don't understand about the farmer's plight. As a farmer's wife, I have first-hand experience of several droughts. We had no choice but to keep our children home to help on the farm to avoid the cost of labour hire. The children's home life may cause unacceptable behaviour. They live with parents stressed by stock losses caused by lack of food and water and ever-growing debt.'

To Minnie's horror, Beatrice burst into tears when Gladys had barely finished speaking. She peered into her friend's brown eyes as tears cascaded down her cheeks. Her meaty shoulders and ample chest heaved.

She threw her arms around Beatrice and whispered soothing words as she massaged the woman's shoulders. Gladys's eyes were full of concern. 'Beatrice, my dear, talk to us. How can we help?'

Over Beatrice's head, Minnie whispered, 'Let her sob. When she is ready, she'll tell us.'

After a few long minutes, Beatrice raised her head. 'I'm so sorry.' She wiped her face with her handkerchief.

'There's nothing to apologise for. We're friends and provide shoulders to cry on,' said Gladys. 'Would you like to share?'

Beatrice shook so violently that Minnie imagined her friend was about to have a stroke. She placed one hand over her mouth, and when she released it, she spoke in a crackling voice. 'Last week, we closed the doors of the drapery shop run by my husband's family for three generations.'

An audible gasp orbited the group of women. Minnie felt her eyes fill with tears.

Beatrice released more tortured sobs. 'We had no choice. The custom had dropped to nothing, and the bills from suppliers piled up. 'Bordering up the display windows brought me to tears.' Her head shook as words emerged from her mouth and became faster with each syllable.

Albert charged out the public bar door as Beatrice finished her tale. His expression said *hurry*. Minnie gathered the children and followed Albert as swiftly as she could.

On the return trip, Minnie said, 'Beatrice from the drapery shop shared that her family had closed their shop because of reduced trade and growing debt. Dad, it makes me feel low; merely retelling the story makes me want to scream with grief. What sort of future awaits them?'

'Tis sad, but there's nothing you can do. We must watch out for our problems, like ensuring the milk cheques keep coming. I'll put me foot down so we get home in time for that milk truck.'

They passed the rest of the homeward journey in silence. Minnie reflected on the outing, a rare event since Peggy's birth, her friend's stories, and Albert's words.

Warmth flooded her insides at reuniting her friends, but an icy feeling replaced it when she thought of what the drought had done to them all. It was ravaging the entire community.

* * *

The year 1927 crept in, but it brought no rain. Albert's exaggerated grin transformed into a worried frown, carving deeper lines on his weathered forehead, but he stubbornly resisted going to the Bank.

Ten-year-old Hazel gazed intently into her mother's eyes. 'Why don't you smile, Mummy? Why do your eyes look sad?'

To avoid the uncomfortable questions, Minnie averted her gaze to the floor and didn't answer. She and Albert tried to keep their conversations about the persistent lack of rain and their mounting debt out of their children's hearing, but they couldn't conceal the effects of the dry weather. The dusty smell and the squark of crows hovering above dead or dying cattle spoke for themselves.

After the children left for school, Albert and Minnie perched on the creaky kitchen chairs, gazing through the window at the parched earth. Minnie tried to ignore the mounds of papers cluttering the table. Her hands shuddered as she organised three piles: bank statements, paper scraps with scribbled notes of the daily tally of silver milk tins supplied, and invoices payable. A stone-faced Albert looked on.

The milk yield had slid below the levels of earlier years. Many of the invoices were already past their due date.

Albert pushed the bills away. 'I know things are tough, and I don't need fancy papers to tell me.'

Minnie knew the Bank was their only hope. How did she persuade Albert to agree? 'For the children's sake, we must get a loan or face ruin.'

Albert's nostrils flared in a lobster-red face. 'Them city newspaper fellas got no idea of the problems facing the farmer.'

Minnie edged her chair closer to her husband and rested her hand on his leathery hand. 'Calm down, Dad, you'll give yourself a heart attack. Every business carries a risk.'

'You're right, but on top of what city folk endure, farmers battle the weather. Our whole family can work our fingers to the bone, but we can't make rain.' He slumped back in his chair.

'Bellyaching will not help. We must get through this,' said Minnie.

'Well, we'll have to take money-saving measures and stick this out. Crawling to that self-opinionated, plummy-voiced bank manager isn't an option—not now, never. Anyway, me mates at the hotel are studying the skyline. They reckon rain will come soon. It always rains after these dry spells do their damage.'

Within days, Albert, shoulders slumped and face desolate,

faced Minnie. 'I'm gunna see that stuck-up bank bloke 'bout a loan to tide us over.'

Minnie flopped into a chair, overcome by relief.

That afternoon, lips pressed into an angry straight line, Albert grabbed his hat and donned his ancient coat. Minnie watched as the clay-baked Ford spluttered and let out grey gases stinking of petrol as Albert turned it over and steered it towards Dayboro and the Bank.

* * *

'Quick, quick, hurry!' It was Albert's voice, ringing down the hallway with the momentum of a machine gun.

Distracted from pummelling and rolling a lump of dough, Minnie headed for the kitchen door. Something serious was amiss.

The floorboards shook. 'Two cows stuck in the muck. I need help!' Further down the corridor, he issued orders. 'Quick, hurry, I need youse all, except baby Peggy.'

The children rocketed from the house. Minnie grabbed Peggy, who was playing with a scruffy teddy bear on the kitchen floor. 'Don't worry, darling. Mummy wouldn't leave you.' After she'd gathered Peggy in her arms, she followed Albert as he rushed towards the sludge puddle that had been Rush Creek.

A foul odour overwhelmed them as they arrived, causing them to stop at the sight of the sludge. Countless flies buzzed above the swampy creek, creating the illusion of a blackened sky. Two lifeless cows were visible, sticking out from the mud pool, hitting Minnie with the overpowering stench of death and decaying flesh.

After catching his breath, Albert spoke through heavy breaths. 'The cows got stuck while searching for water. They couldn't free themselves.' Minnie crossed her arms over her chest, imagining the animals meeting a slow and painful demise.

Harold frowned as he rubbed the skin on his neck while dried tears stained Billie's cheeks. Hazel held Eunice against her chest as her sister let out a wail.

Minnie lifted her skirt, tying it loosely at her thigh, and followed Albert and Harold into the slimy mess, their backs covered in black flies. Harold had grown taller and more robust, which was much needed. As Minnie pushed through the long, dry grass at the edge, the sharp blades cut into her arms and legs, and the ground beneath her squished as mud oozed between her toes.

They pushed, shoved, and used wooden poles as levers to remove the beasts from their muddy graves. Minnie winced as her foot struck something hard, possibly a rock, but she ignored the pain and continued wading and heaving. Sweat poured down her back as she glanced over at Albert and Harold, noticing the glistening beads of moisture on their brows. However, the carcasses remained firmly anchored in the swamp.

'Git out,' Albert called. 'This ain't working.' He squatted on the rough ground in the scorching heat, removing his misshapen hat. 'I need to think of another way.' He ran his fingers through his hair, signalling not to disturb him while he thought. Then, after about fifteen minutes, he jumped up and looked at Hazel. 'Slim Jim, run and fetch some sturdy rope from the barn.'

Hazel tore off as Albert barked further orders at Harold.

'Hurry, son, grab a horse.'

When they returned with horse and rope, Albert whispered to Harold before the lad waded through the boggy soil. He tied the rope to the lifeless form of one beast and secured the other end to the horse. While Harold, knee-deep in slime, planted himself near the dead bodies, Albert took control of the horse.

Terror vibrated down Minnie's limbs and into her torso as she spun to Albert. 'This won't work, Dad. We'll end up with the cows—dead in the mud.'

Disregarding Minnie's words, Albert instructed the children to grip the rope between himself and Harold. Minnie vowed to take more than her share of the load. *There is no stopping that man when he sets his mind to it.*

When Albert signalled, the horse trundled off as those in line heaved in unison. Minnie's muscles ached from the strain but resolved to do more than her share burned within. Young Bert found the pressure of yanking too much. He plummeted, skinning both knees, but avoided sinking into the oozy ground.

The team, straining every muscle, repeated the heaving exercise several times. The muddy swamp gurgled, and the sludge crumbled. Then, with a mighty wrench, the horse, assisted by the army of helpers, dragged the foul-smelling, rotting remains of one beast to stable ground.

Minnie took several deep breaths. They'd done it and emerged unscathed, except for Bert's injury and some rope burns. Her hands stung and throbbed. She looked down, and her head spun at the blood seeping from open welts carved into her chaffed hands by the coarse, stringy twine. She glanced sideways at Albert, who seemed to have come through unscathed, but sweat sketched crevices on his grime-encrusted face.

One cow remained in the mud, so they needed to do it again, bloodied hands and all. They dragged the second carcass out by some miracle and a great deal of huffing, puffing, and straining muscles.

Later, they sat on the grass, exhausted, looking into each muddy face, all drawn with an equal measure of caked dirt and despair. Minnie raised her eyes to the skies. *When would this nightmare end? How many cattle would they lose before the drought broke?*

* * *

When 1927 neared its end, two years had passed since rain had fallen.

The family gathered at the dinner table. Like other evening meals, Albert recounted tragic tales he heard while visiting the town. District farmers left their farms en masse. 'Some snooty bank fellow tossed the Lane family off their land,' Albert said. 'And the Jackson clan left their farm and headed to the city.'

'Did the Bank sell the Jacksons up?' asked Minnie.

'Nah, they were tired of their debt piling up while they waited for the drought to break.'

Minnie tried to feel something like hope, but every day, she looked for rain, and every day, she saw nothing. 'You realise, Dad, we could be next if it doesn't rain soon?'

Albert attempted a smile. 'Don't worry, Mum, I've spent me forty-odd years on farms in these parts. Rain comes, even if it takes years. Winners are always the folk who don't git desperate. We'll keep working hard, counting the pennies and sticking it out. Mark me words, it's gotta piss down soon.'

Hazel looked up from her plate of mince pie, her face alert. 'I hear raindrops.'

Could it be...? Minnie strained her ears. Was her daughter right? She had been too busy to search the sky since the early morning.

Soon, persistent drops pounded on the roof. Albert broke out into a genuine grin. 'That sure ain't possums.' One by one, each family member burst into the broadest smile. Warmth radiated through Minnie.

Albert got up from the table. 'Kids, we wanna git a close gander at this. There has been no rain for ages, so it's a rare sight.'

Everyone dashed to the verandah, Minnie cradling Peggy and Bert perched on Hazel's hip. A tremendous rolling clap of thunder greeted them. The night sky lit up with multi-coloured flashes of lightning and then opened as if broken into two pieces. Nature bombarded the countryside with diagonal sheets of water.

As they laughed, cheered, and whistled, the family bounced down the stairs, letting the downpour fall on their clothes. With their faces uplifted, they massaged the raindrops into their skin. They laughed as they flicked rainwater at each other.

Albert rushed inside to get his mouth organ. Billie retreated inside, too, and re-emerged with various pots and cooking utensils.

'We need music and dancing,' said Albert.

With hands linked, the family danced a reel to a tune from Albert's mouth organ, the children beating a rhythm by thumping cutlery against pots.

'We're saved! We're saved!' Harold yelled at the sky.

When the merrymaking calmed, Albert, the broad grin having reclaimed its rightful place, dragged Minnie from the circling dancers and embraced her. 'We've been together for ages and weathered some tough times. Isn't it time you trusted me? I told ya it'd rain. And now it's raining, the sadness has gone from your smile.'

Minnie could taste salty tears on her cheeks. The misery of her childhood has been a frequent reminder for her lately. It had felt like the curse had caught up with her, but perhaps it wasn't to be. Maybe, finally, she'd outrun it for good. 'My life has been full of disasters,' she said, 'and other trials lay ahead, but hopefully, this one is over.'

Minnie knew and sensed that Albert knew too, that one storm wouldn't end the drought.

Chapter 43

On 31 October 1929, nothing stood out as unusual—thin clouds propelled by a gentle, warm breeze danced across an azure blue sky. The steamy, hot weather hadn't yet begun.

Minnie lounged on the Dayboro bus, one arm draped over the back of the seat. Her fellow passengers—a crowd of commuters—hid behind newspapers. Others chain-smoked, flinging the spent butts from the window. Minnie felt smothered by the body odour that competed with the flowery scent of women's perfume and the acrid cigarette smoke.

With her head resting on her mother's shoulder, Peggy napped, undisturbed by the coach's ear-splitting clanks and shudders of the coach.

Minnie travelled to the premier shopping area of Fortitude Valley, which she enjoyed visiting, although visits had been rare in recent years. She planned to buy towelling and clothing supplies. The family's constant use wore out the existing ones so quickly, and she'd been unable to replace them because of the money problems caused by the drought.

As the bus neared the city, Minnie peered out the dust-streaked window at the purple blooms of the jacaranda trees. She shifted her gaze to her sleeping daughter, passing her fingers through her baby's translucent locks.

Her thoughts flitted to the years ahead. They promised to lessen her responsibility and allow time for resting, reading, and visiting. Harold worked on the farm daily, and Hazel would join him next year. Peggy began school in January.

The bus driver assisted Minnie and Peggy as they descended the steep steps upon reaching the terminus. Grateful, Minnie expressed her thanks with a warm smile. With a tap of his helmet-like cap, the driver said farewell as she confidently strode towards the bustling main street. The precinct, a sea of department stores and hotels intersected by a gravel road, resonated with the clatter of trams. As Minnie envisioned a lavish assortment of elegant underwear, plush towels, and delightful tea towels, her pace quickened, fuelled by anticipation.

'You go too fast, Mummy. I can't keep up,' complained Peggy.

Minnie slowed, but it didn't stop the grumbles. 'Mummy, my feet hurt because the shoes pinch my toes. Why do you make me wear them?'

Would anything dampen the girl's criticisms, thought Minnie.

* * *

The complaints ended when they entered a department store boasting marble walls, bright lights, and pressed metal ceilings. Although Minnie tugged on her hand, Peggy stood as if rooted to the spot. When Minnie looked down, she noticed the girl's mouth hanging open and her enlarged eyes jumping between the features of the rich interiors. 'Come on, darling, keep moving.'

Peggy, busy eyeing a crystal chandelier shining over an

entrance display of scented soap and embroidered handkerchiefs, made no response. Seconds later, she snapped out of the trance and gave Minnie a baffled look. 'Is this a castle, Mummy? Do fairies live here?'

'No, darling. It's a shop where we can buy special things.' She coaxed Peggy to move.

They edged into the shop, giving the toddler more wondrous sights to feast on. Assistants wearing black outfits staffed carved counters crafted of reddish polished timber. Displays arranged in the aisles featured many products, from makeup, socks, and underwear to dresses and swimsuits.

Minnie inspected the goods, rubbing her hands over the ridged surfaces of tea towels and stretching underwear seams. Each time she selected an item, she handed notes to an assistant who wrapped the purchases in brown paper tied with hessian string.

As the pair left the shop, Minnie hummed a tune to herself as she swung a wicker shopping basket crammed with the wrapped treasures. *The hard times are behind us. The relentless work and frugality were worthwhile.*

Minnie spied a paper vendor. 'Extra! Read All About It!' he yelled from the intricately patterned tiled entry to the adjoining hotel. She rummaged around the shopping basket and dredged some penny coins, which she handed to the paper boy. With the *Telegraph* tucked under her right arm, she climbed onto a passing tram to take the brief ride to Jean's.

* * *

They rode the tram to Commercial Road, New Farm—home to Ben and Jean since they'd sold their Kobble Creek farm.

Their house stood among a cluster of factories, warehouses, and homes. Twirling odours almost knocked Minnie over as her feet touched the roadway after jumping from the tram, juggling Peggy, the basket, and the newspaper. Molasses mist curled from the sugar refinery, and the sickly sweet pineapple aroma rose from the fruit cannery.

Jean, dressed in a flouncy floral dress, answered the doorbell. She embraced the pair, produced a jar of boiled lollies, and extended the bottle to Peggy. 'Take a few, darling.'

At the tempting offer of sweets, Peggy popped out from the ruffles of her mother's skirt. Jean waved towards the sitting room with one arm resting on Minnie's back. Minnie and Peggy settled in the sun-streaked room among the tantalising aroma of brewing tea drifting from the adjoining kitchen.

After about five minutes, Jean returned, bringing a plate of egg sandwiches, which mother and daughter devoured in a heartbeat. Minnie savoured the tea her sister offered while they ate their fill, and Peggy guzzled cold milk.

'To what do I owe the pleasure?' asked Jean.

'I shopped in the Valley and thought I'd call before starting home. Soon, with Harold and Hazel helping and the other children in school, I should be able to visit more often.'

'Excellent. It'll be like old times,' Minnie mused, the expression moving across her sister's forehead, replicating the excitement fluttering in her stomach.

The thump of footsteps scaling the stairs stilled the conversation. Jean's four children burst in. The younger three said a fleeting hello before making a beeline for the backyard. After kissing Minnie, Thelma hoisted Peggy onto her hip and hurried towards the laughter and shrieking rising from the backyard.

Jean brought a pot of tea into the room and poured two fresh cups. Alone, the sisters chatted. Minnie described her shopping trip to Jean. 'The simple act of purchasing new towels consumed me because, at last, we have the money to replace the old, ragged ones.'

Jean picked up the *Telegraph* Minnie had bought and leafed through the pages before thrusting it onto an occasional table. 'I won't read a word because the newspaper has been full of this business with the American stock exchange.'

'What has happened? They starve us of news out our way.' Minnie grabbed the paper and studied articles describing the Wall Street crash as 'An Orgy of Speculation' and 'Frenzied Sales'.

'It surprises me that the news hasn't reached you. It's the topic of conversation in the street and the shops,' said Jean.

'I've flicked through the pages, and they seem to predict far-reaching effects,' said Minnie.

Jean gave a faint smile. 'I don't understand the talk of volatility, bulls, and bears. How could an event in America affect distant Australia?'

Minnie wasn't so sure. Although the Great War was in faraway Europe, it affected Australians. 'I hope you're right.'

The afternoon shadows closed in, signalling it was time to go. 'I must hurry to the bus terminus for the afternoon Dayboro service.'

Jean hugged her at the door while waiting for Thelma to bring Peggy. 'Keep in touch. Hopefully, you'll be back soon. By then, the news might predict improved times.'

* * *

Minnie considered the day's events during the bus ride home. She hoped Jean was right about Australia being safe, but her intuition warned against optimism.

Back at Oaklands, Minnie told Albert about the American stock exchange crash. He shrugged. 'I was in Dayboro but heard nothing about it. I think ya sister's right—trouble doesn't swim seas.'

'The Great War did,' Minnie said, cynicism rising in her voice.

It didn't change his expression. 'This isn't a war. It's a problem with some companies in America. It won't affect us. Did ya git those fancy sheets an' towels you wanted?'

Later, with Albert in bed, Minnie retrieved the newspaper from the shopping basket. Under the lamplight, she scrutinised every page before opening the stove door and flinging it in. *I hope Jean and Albert are right. Hopefully, tragedy has stopped pursuing me.*

A few days later, Albert returned from Dayboro, lobbed the *Brisbane Courier* onto the dresser, and flopped into a chair. He planted his elbows on the table and rested his hands on them.

'What's wrong?' Minnie asked, ridding her hands of breadcrumbs.

'Blokes at the Crown are full of this American share business. The whole thing collapsed on 29 October, and some who lost truckloads of cash jumped from buildings. The American money problems arrived in Australia like wildfire, and farmers out west have had problems selling wool and mutton. It looks like there are tough times ahead.'

As Albert clomped out, Minnie scanned the newspaper abandoned on the dresser. Everything her husband had reported rang true. *Surely not! Is this foreign money disaster going to rob me of the relaxed years I'd hoped for?*

To prepare for possible difficulties, she added more stock to their vegetable patch—potatoes, peas, beans, and tomatoes—and increased the number of hens. She'd faced challenges before, and the financial crisis wouldn't beat her.

Chapter 44

The economic woes grew. Unemployment rates grew each month, with youth unemployment topping the numbers. The paper told of office workers who traded pen and ink for shovels as part of a relief work scheme implemented by the Queensland Government.

Albert arrived home from each trip to Dayboro carrying the *Brisbane Courier*. At first, the newspaper reported the loss of wool and wheat markets. Later, it covered massive job losses and slashed wages and eventually became a narrative of poverty.

The children reported signs of the Depression at school. 'Everyone wears patched clothes,' said Eunice.

'The Ramsey share-farming family kids came without lunch, so I shared,' said Billie.

'We're lucky,' said Minnie. 'Times are tough, and people don't have money for food and clothes, but we still have money from the milk, a roof to shield us, fresh vegetables, and eggs.'

Albert returned home, panting and smelling of sweat. 'To-day, half of the butter factory workers got retrenched. Those who escaped the chop are already on reduced wages. This news filled the Crown, where I went after wandering streets crammed with closed businesses. Fellas reckon things are worse in Brisbane.'

It was a tale Minnie didn't want to hear. 'Talk of gloom doesn't help, Dad. You should be grateful. We are faring better than most.'

Albert scowled. 'Why make that stupid remark, Mum?'

'Dad, folk need milk. The wholesalers have dropped their price, but the milk lorry and the reduced milk cheques keep coming.'

Albert's face was still severe. 'What about the kids' future?'

She was worried about that, too. Harold and Hazel worked on the farm, but there was insufficient work for the rest of their large family. 'At least none of them are standing in the unemployment queues.'

Albert's face turned a fiery red, and his nostrils flared. 'We'll starve before this American thing ends.'

Minnie continued preparing dinner, determined to paint things as brightly as possible. 'Things don't always follow our plans. We've weathered choppy storms before. We'll do it again.'

Albert snorted. 'This isn't like the weather. I can't see an end to the drought in the sky. We must hope for better times before we go broke.'

Chapter 45

Minnie descended the front stairs and joined Billie, Bert, Peggy, and Eunice near the rear of the Ford. Today, they were travelling to Lutwyche, an outer Brisbane retail precinct, on their family's monthly trip to buy supplies not sold locally.

Over the years, the preschool children accompanied their parents, but with Peggy at school, the numbers joining the trek had dwindled to Albert and Minnie. However, as it was the mid-year school holidays of 1932, four children were going.

Albert puffed a cigarette, one bent leg resting on the truck's running board. He sucked on the smoke one last time, wetted the tip with saliva, and slid the remains into his pocket. He strolled to the rear, released the tailgate, and urged the four children to climb in the truck. 'Hurry, time to go.'

Minnie stood with her legs apart beside Albert as she helped the children climb aboard the truck. Hay bales filled the truck's tray, and the children lounged among the itchy parcels. Then Albert and Minnie climbed into the cabin.

The truck, leaving a trail of dust in its wake, lumbered out of the gate and wound over rutted bush tracks. They passed cattle grazing beyond rows of crops. Grasses tall enough to hide the odd milepost grew near the roadway, while abandoned sheds and shacks freckled the landscape.

From the front cabin, Minnie listened to the children hum and sway in time with the rocking vehicle. Eunice's laughing voice drifted from behind, 'The view hasn't changed since I was tiny.' Minnie's stomach gurgled. Today's excursion turned the clock back to when they journeyed with a truck full of children. She leaned back in the seat and closed her eyes as she sensed the familiar children's laughter and banter chase all tension from her body.

A few miles on, they entered the main road. The surface became smoother, and Albert increased the tension on the accelerator. Bert's voice wafted into the cabin. 'Phew! The gas pumping from the exhaust pipe stinks like rotten eggs.'

As the Ford rounded the first corner, some pitiful sights sent a bolt of shock pulsating through Minnie, abruptly ending her carefree mood. Mattresses of newspapers and cardboard lay in the gullies and ditches, shouldering the road.

A makeshift village of shelters of discarded sheets of rusty iron, scrap pieces of timber, and other junk bordered a murky, brown watercourse. Women washed clothes in the water. A foul smell of stagnant water mixed with rotting garbage poured into the vehicle. Children with swollen stomachs wearing faded, dirty rags wandered between the shacks. To protect herself from the signs of abject poverty, with her hands jammed over her nostrils and mouth, Minnie cemented her gaze to the road.

She'd seen the outlook from this roadway decay over the last several years. Her stomach sank. Their children hadn't seen these sights. She should have prepared them. If these devastating scenes gave them nightmares for years to come, the blame lay at her feet.

Their journey took them past more mind-boggling sights.

Against a backdrop of unused factories, a party of relief workers trudged in single file. The skeletal men wore the standard working attire of thick grey flannel singlets, stained and patched, and carried picks and shovels.

A sore feeling attacked Minnie's throat. She cocked her head towards Albert. 'We should have warned the children of what to expect.'

He took his hands off the steering wheel and raised one hand, his characteristic grin twisting into a frown. 'They seen plenty signs of the times around Dayboro and the school, but not this bad.' Minnie interpreted this as a sign of agreement.

Minnie's mind locked into thought. *These tough times now spanned years. Would they ever improve, or was this the dim future their children faced?'*

* * *

At Lutwyche, Albert parked the vehicle in the shade of a tree. When Minnie and Albert jumped over the running board, the overpowering stench of sweat, rotting garbage, dust, and stale urine met them. Minnie shuddered and feared the stench would choke her.

The once vibrant centre was now unrecognisable. Albert drew his lips into a solid line and called to the children to gather. 'There are plenty of ugly sights in the streets. I'll go first. Youse kids follow closely, and Mum will bring up the rear. Stay together, hold hands, move fast, and make eye contact with no one.' Head bent, Minnie, in a whisper, reinforced the instructions.

Albert took the lead, taking long strides. The older children jogged, and the young ones panted. Minnie hastened at the rear. Hard on the heels of one pitiful sight came another.

Empty shops that had once housed thriving enterprises freckled the streetscape. Bert dashed from the procession several times to investigate the padlocks on boarded-up shop fronts. Minnie dragged him back, kicking and screaming. Minnie knew Bert constantly pulled items to pieces, but there was a better time for curiosity.

When Minnie hauled him into line, Bert collided with a rusty pram—propelled by a family of four. The gadget, one wheel missing, overflowed with bedding and clothing. Eunice broke ranks and sidled up to her mother. Her eyes swam with tears. 'Is that their bed they're wheeling in that old cart?'

Sadness consumed Minnie as she nodded. She leaned down and ran her hands through Eunice's hair. 'Times are hard, and many people have no job, money, or house. We're lucky we have a house and a farm and earn money from milk.'

Eunice threw her arms around her mother and buried her face in her bosom. Sobs rose from the girl's convulsing body until Minnie peeled her daughter from her.

Next, they came upon an endless snaking queue of shrunken bodies at the entry of a red brick building displaying the *Labour Exchange* sign. After inching through the mass, they saw another row of ravaged bodies. This line weaved along the footpath until it reached a charity stand where volunteers ladled soup into tin bowls.

'Why the lines?' chorused the children. Minnie opened her mouth but couldn't find the right words, so she jammed it closed again.

When they finished grocery shopping, Albert rushed his family to the Ford. Before taking her place in the passenger cabin, Minnie propped her hip against the tailgate to help the children, but she needn't have bothered. The youngsters piled in with unusual speed.

As she climbed into the vehicle, teardrops rippling down her face, Eunice turned to Minnie. 'I never want to leave our farm again.'

Chapter 46

As the press predicted, the jobless rate peaked in 1932, when almost one-third of the workforce struggled to find employment. While the jobless figures decreased after that, the hardship didn't end, but Minnie clung to the hope shown by the slow improvement.

The Christmas festivities in 1932 followed the usual pattern, but the children took charge. Hazel cooked a mouth-watering meal, and everyone polished off the delicious food before praising the chef.

Minnie still made the classic boiled plum pudding but heard Eunice whisper to Billie, 'Mum doesn't trust anybody else.' Minnie imagined she had become royalty as she lounged back and watched Billie and Eunice lay the crockery while Peggy and Bert added decorative touches to the table setting. When they opened presents earlier, Harold acted as Santa Claus.

Droning flies tried to snatch their share, but the diners batted them away.

Harold and Hazel, conversing in a secret language, although more sophisticated, sat to Minnie's right, and Billie and Eunice were to her left. As she chewed on a chicken bone, Minnie leant forward, laced her hands behind her head and strained to listen to a conversation between Billie and Eunice.

However, the words got lost in the laughter. From the phrases she could decipher and the smiles the two shared, she knew the girls spoke of an exciting, shared future living, studying, and working in Brisbane. A warm feeling of pleasure spread across her chest.

As daylight faded, they all chipped in and helped with the second milking, leaving Minnie alone in the farmhouse. City folk expected milk deliveries even on Christmas Day.

When Minnie heard the distant rumble of the milk truck, she ventured onto the verandah. She listened to her children's gleeful laughter as they approached the farmhouse.

Through eyes that had witnessed many births and deaths, she gazed at them, arms joined, as they bounced across the paddock, green from the recent downpour. She was so proud of them. They were all so different but healthy, cheerful, and hardworking. She angled her head towards the heavens. 'Da, you never met your wonderful grandchildren.'

Later, Minnie lingered longer than usual as she watched the sunset. Under the starlight, she released her hair and brushed it vigorously. She rocked back in her chair, watching the full moon replace the orange sun.

How far she had travelled since her stepmother had shepherded her onto a boat, fleeing a country that was every conceivable shade of green. Most of the secrets of her sorrowful childhood lay secured in her heart. Having lived in Australia for over twenty years, she was used to the reversed seasons and differences between the countries. Despite some hardships, it seemed the curse hadn't continued to plague her.

An image rotated before her of a timid young girl gripping her little sister as she gingerly stepped off the gangway of a migrant ship onto a pier in a fledgling, humid city twelve thousand miles away from all she'd ever known.

The following image depicted the same girl about two years later. Her skinny arm swung a battered suitcase as she raced up a pock-marked country track. Toughened by two years as a factory worker, she's stepped out alone.

Her life in Australia hadn't begun until she'd taken off alone. She'd found Jean and met Albert. While their union had difficulties, and the weather was sometimes unkind, it satisfied her. Despite enduring a world war and a crippling Depression, she emerged better than most.

Tears dribbled down her face. She wasn't yet thirty-six but lived on her farm with her husband and their six wonderful children.

About the author

This is the debut novel of the author, a retired lawyer. Over 20 years ago, Wendy's life was turned upside down by a rare neurological disease that left her with speech articulation dysfunction and impaired mobility.

Acknowledgements

This book has been six years in the making. I began this project to keep my mind active after my mobility slowed. The long gestation period was due in equal part to my one-finger typing skills being slowed even further by my neurological limitations and learning a writing style entirely different to legal drafting.

I thank my cousins and the descendants of Jean, Lizzie, and Carrie for the information and photographs they supplied. I also benefited from the insights of Minnie's last surviving children, the late Eunice Poulsen and the late Peggy Bradley.

I am deeply grateful to my sister, Marie, for reading many drafts of chapters, including my early clumsy attempts. Her assistance did not end there. She accompanied me on a fact-finding trip to Northern Ireland.

Thanks to Alistair Craig, who graciously allowed us access to the property where Minnie was born, and to Marty McAuley, who gave us a most informative tour of the Ballymena/Toome district.

Lynne Stringer edited this book. She went far beyond the traditional role of an editor and guided me by both my right hand and my left hand. I am so grateful to her for her patience.

My niece Naomi proofread several drafts, commissioned the

cover design, and formatted the final product. She generously gave her time, and I want to thank her sincerely.

Last but not least, I thank my friends Rosa, Joe, Maria, and Anna, my nephew Tony, and my nieces Claire and Ainslie for their unwavering support and patience with my obsession with this project.

Wendy Hart.

www.ingramcontent.com/pod-product-compliance
Lightning Source LLC
Chambersburg PA
CBHW070421170726
48291CB00002B/304